THE WORMTON LAMB

BY

BOB BLACKMAN

AN ANARCHADIAN NOVEL

HOW A GROWTH HORMONE EXPERIMENT WENT
HORRIBLY WRONG AND HOW AN ISOLATED RURAL
COMMUNITY DEALT WITH THE MONSTER THAT AROSE.

INTRODUCING THE MOTORSCOPE —
A NEW MEANS OF TELLING THE FUTURE.

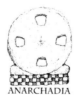

ANARCHADIA

www.anarchadia.co.uk

First published in Great Britain in March 2009 by

Anarchadia Publishing

Copyright © Bob Blackman 2009

A CIP catalogue record for this book is available from the British Library.

Maps and quotations from *Wrainwright's Guide to the Wold* are
reproduced by kind permission of Transwold Publishing.

ISBN   978 0 9555927 1 3

Anarchadia Publishing
PO Box 119
Liskeard
Cornwall
PL14 9AN

For H.M.G.

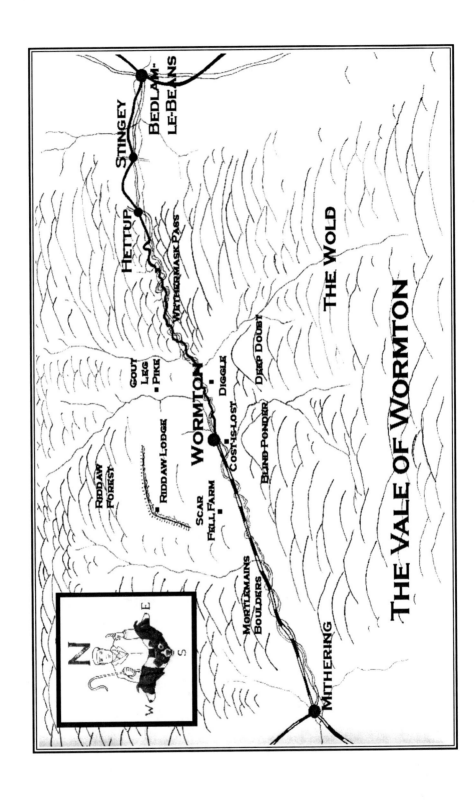

The Vale of Wormton

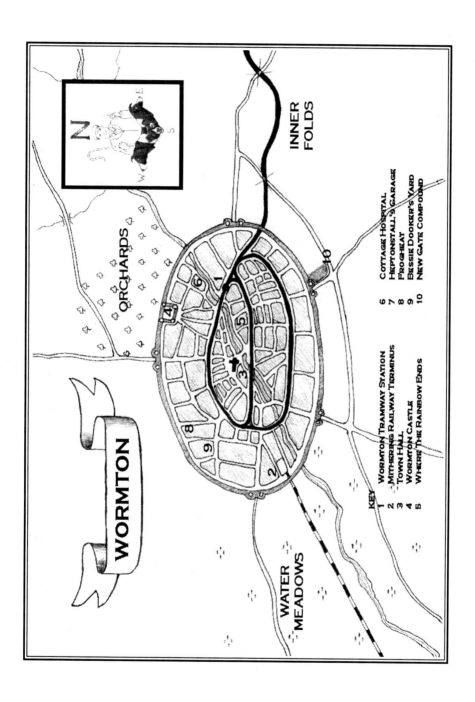

WORMTON

INNER FOLDS

ORCHARDS

WATER MEADOWS

N

KEY
1 WORMTON TRAMWAY STATION
2 MITHERING RAILWAY TERMINUS
3 TOWN HALL
4 WORMTON CASTLE
5 WHERE THE RAINBOW ENDS
6 COTTAGE HOSPITAL
7 HEPTONSTALL'S GARAGE
8 FROG-HEAT
9 BESSIE DOOKER'S YARD
10 NEW GATE COMPOUND

ADDITIONAL WEB RESOURCES

You might read this book and find that afterwards you have
more questions than answers.

In that case, I cordially invite you to explore the Anarchadia website.

Its additional multi-media features include blogs, links, news, interviews,
glossaries, readers' questions and additional artwork.

It may reassure you, confirm a funny feeling, help you recollect a distant
memory, make new connections or allow something that has piqued your
interest to metaphorically emerge from the shadows of obscurity.

It may also serve as a warning to the curious.

www.anarchadia.co.uk

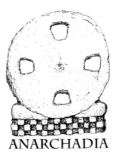

ANARCHADIA

BOOKS WITH GO FASTER STRIPES

CHAPTER 1

The man who was about to sell his soul pulled off the road, got out of his Hillman Imp and trod in something disgusting. It was always the same. Wherever he stopped, something nasty was waiting for him. The Wold was spattered with foul-smelling fallout from the local experiments in animal husbandry, and production organisms, instead of being managed efficiently in a pen somewhere, were free to roam around.

He squelched over to the roadside, selected the cleanest section of dry stone walling he could find and leant on it to scrape his feet in the long grass. Billy Brockhouse found potential fertiliser easily, but since it seemed to be everywhere this was not such an achievement.

"God, I hate this place!" he said aloud.

Angrily, he smeared his shoe on the uneven verge, lost his balance and steadied himself by treading in the mess he'd just scraped off.

"Oh, hell!"

Now he had two dirty shoes.

"God, damn this country!"

The dry stone walling hadn't been as dry as he'd hoped. The sleeve of his purple velvet jacket was damp and smeared with green.

Billy usually used stronger language but lately he'd noticed that it had lost its potency, probably through overuse. Feeling cursed by being allotted the Wold as his sales territory, he found himself resorting to good old-fashioned blasphemy, delivered as forcefully as he could manage, and it felt strangely gratifying.

He began to scrape his feet more vigorously. The ground was soft, and as if by capillary action mud worked its way up his inside trouser legs.

"God damn the whole wide Wold to kingdom come!"

It was then that he noticed the big black motorcycle.

He'd been sure that the lay-by had been empty when he'd pulled up.

Billy didn't like motorbikes.

This one was an engine on wheels, long and low and not very wide. It was either black or chrome or polished aluminium. The petrol tank had an oily spectrum of colours to it, like the feathers of a raven, and *Nosferatu* was written in Gothic script on the tank.

Billy turned his back on it and applied himself to cleaning his shoes.

Nosferatu ticked as it cooled.

"God! I hate it here!" he declared. "I'd give anything to get out of this place!"

"Anything?"

Billy span around.

A stranger stood by *Nosferatu* as if he'd just popped out of the ground. His black leather jacket was badly scuffed and his jeans were faded. He wore a plaid shirt and a black open-faced helmet with a peak. His eyes were covered by a wrap-around visor that swirled in the same way that *Nosferatu's* tank might swirl when reflecting the clouds passing overhead.

"Anything," replied Billy, although, even as he said it, he had the uncomfortable feeling that it might not be wise to say such things in the presence of some people.

"Why?"

"Everything's ... covered in crap!" exclaimed Billy, wiping his shoes in the grass, like a dog marking its territory.

"You travel in fertiliser."

Billy stopped wiping his shoes. "You taking the piss?"

"You seek to cleanse your sole."

"What?"

"You seek to cleanse your sole, your foot sole. Of crap." The next moment, the stranger stood beside him. "You're Billy Brockhouse, aren't you?"

"How do you know my name?"

"I know many things. Your bosses have given you the Wold as your sales territory."

"Who *are* you?"

The stranger reached inside his leather jacket. "My card."

Billy stared at the business card. "There's no name on this," he said.

"Modesty forbids it," replied the other.

Billy turned the card over.

"And no address, either!"

The stranger smiled and shrugged. "I'm never at home."

And then something made Billy turn the card over again and, on what had been blank, there were now words. " 'Nicholas Eldritch Hob'," he read out. " 'Soul Trader and Holder of Soul Rites.' What odd spelling. 'Horsepower Whispering a speciality.' What sort of business is that?"

"I ... facilitate self-fulfilment."

"Really?"

"I can grant you your heart's desire."

"My heart's desire?"

"Yes."

Hob leant on the dry stone wall beside Billy and stared out over the valley below.

Although the cloud base was low and visibility not good, a mixture of open moorland and apparently random enclosures stretched out before them. Here and there, the vivid green hills were punctuated by small earthbound clouds of wool.

Billy felt much more comfortable out of Hob's line of sight.

"I can grant you your heart's desire and sate the hunger in your soul," said Hob, as they gazed at the Wold. "Shall I tell you what your heart's desire is?"

"Go on then."

"You want to be BiggaBeast's number one salesman." Hob turned to look at Billy again. "Don't you?"

"How the hell did you know that?"

"Call it intuition. Or telepathy. Or a good guess."

There was a pregnant silence.

Billy could see his chubby features reflected in Hob's visor. Beneath this reflection, the fathomless swirling continued.

"So … do you know how to break into the Wold market for growth hormones? If there is one here in this godforsaken place?"

"Oh, there's always a market." Hob laughed. "I should know that."

"But if you do know, and you tell me, you want something in return. Right?"

"Correct."

"Like what?"

Hob paused.

"Your soul."

"My soul?"

"Mm-hm."

Billy laughed.

"Do I have a soul?"

"At the moment, yes. Not a bad little soul, actually. It just needs to … live a little, have a couple of good breaks, learn how to enjoy itself, as it were. Then it could be quite something."

"I've got potential, then?"

"Your soul has. I can't say much for the rest of you."

"Hmm. So. What's the deal? I give you my soul and you let me into the secret of how to break into the Wold market for growth hormones. Is that it?"

"That's right."

"That's some exchange."

"I'm feeling generous," said the Soul Trader, although that wasn't quite what Billy had meant.

"What would you do with my soul if you had it?"

"I would treasure it."

"Is that all?"

Hob nodded. "Or I might swap it for another one."

"You're mad!"

"Possibly. But you are intrigued. And what do you have to lose?"

"My soul, it would seem!"

"You didn't even know you had one until I told you."

"Why did you tell me, then? Why didn't you just take it?"

"Souls that are exchanged by their own volition are worth much more than those that are simply taken. The transaction does things to them."

"How would you make me BiggaBeast's greatest salesman, then?"

"You don't get to be a Soul Trader without knowing how to sell." Hob picked a piece of grass and chewed it thoughtfully. "Or how to buy," he added quietly.

He jiggled his eyebrows at Billy, which is quite a trick whilst wearing a crash helmet and dark glasses.

"The choice is yours," said Hob, in a way that made Billy think that the choice was anything but his.

Just then, the sun almost came out. It was suddenly warmer and brighter, and Billy's eyes smarted from the unexpected glare.

"If I agree, what exactly do I get?" he asked, squinting.

"The power to persuade."

"I might have that already."

Hob gave him a penetrating stare. "How much have you sold since arriving in the Wold?"

Billy winced. "Okay. Keep talking."

"That is all I have to say," replied Hob. "I can make you the greatest salesman there ever was and ever will be. But I wouldn't want your soul straight away. I'd let you keep it for a while. You see, Billy, when a soul is finally granted that which it craves the most, interesting things happen to it. Over time, and with guidance, it develops and becomes far more precious."

"So how long would I have my soul to keep?"

"That depends. No two souls are alike. They develop at different rates."

The depths of the purple-black visor tugged at part of Billy.

"And you'd look after my soul?"

"Believe me. I would. Some might even say that it would be in better hands."

Billy glanced at Hob's hands. They were grubby and covered in oily sticking plasters. "I'm not sure I believe you," he said.

Hob sighed. "I can understand that. It's not every day you're faced with realising your heart's desire. What have you got to lose? Only your soul. Will you ever have the opportunity again? Probably not. My sanity may be seriously in question or I really am a Soul Trader. Either you become a great salesman or you don't. Either you take me up on my offer or you walk away."

"There might not be a Wold market for growth hormones."

"You," said Hob, pointing at him with one of his grubby fingers, "might be just the fellow to create one. Consider it! A market nobody thought existed before, all to yourself. Think of the potential there is here!" He gestured to the moors around them. "Plenty of space for growth!"

"I'd be starting from a long way back."

"Just as ye sow, ye shall reap. I know what you're thinking. I'm not of this Wold – but then, neither are you. I like you, Billy, so I'm going to make a proposition to you, okay? I'll give you what you want, the success you desire, on a trial basis."

"A trial? A free trial?"

"That's right, and with no obligation. If after 30 years you're not totally satisfied with your newly acquired, irresistible sales skills, you can return them and owe me nothing."

"Er, sorry, Mr ... er ... Hob, but did you say 30 years?"

"I did."

"So I get to try them out for the rest of my working life?"

"Only if you really want to keep working that long. I would have thought that you'd be able to retire in a few years. Unless, of course, BiggaBeast make you their chief executive."

"It's very tempting."

"It is, isn't it?"

"Okay," said Billy, and after Hob spat on his palm they shook on the deal. "So what's the secret?"

"Let me see your samples."

Billy led Hob to his car and from it produced a small but beautifully made suitcase. He undid the combination locks and opened it. Inside were hundreds of little glass phials.

Hob reached out to touch the phials with his oily fingers and tapped out a little tune upon them.

"Science," he said. "You believe in science?"

"Of course."

"You don't need to understand it to believe it," Hob told him. "Now we have science, whereas once we had only magic. You must learn to use them both together."

"Magic? You mean tricks?"

Hob made a glass phial vanish. Then he produced it from behind Billy's ear. He turned another into a rather surprised crow that flew away.

"Hey, those are my samples!"

Hob took another phial from behind Billy's other ear and gave it back to him. "Tricks, *legerdemain*, sleight of hand. Call them what you will. Nothing in life is really what it seems. And there are tricks to every trade."

"Tell me. I want to know."

The crow had perched on the dry stone wall and was watching them quizzically.

"Mix magic and science," Hob told Billy. He shook his box of phials. "Make magience. With your next customer, daemonstrate."

"Demonstrate?"

"No. Daemonstrate." Hob emphasised the daemon in daemonstrate. "Show them. Show them these in action. Don't just tell them. Convince them! Sell them!"

Billy and the crow exchanged glances.

"Is that it?"

"It's all you need," said Hob, and he turned and strode back to *Nosferatu*.

"Hey! Wait a minute! There must be more to it than that!"

"No, it really is that simple. Try it and you'll see. I must go. Just think on what I've said and put it into practice. And if it doesn't work, then you'll never hear from me again. Trouble's going!"

He kicked his bike into life.

The bark of *Nosferatu*'s engine nearly bowled Billy over and echoed off the valley sides, sending the crow vertically into the air.

"Goodbye, Billy! Until the next time! Trouble's gone!" and with that and a roar from his engine and a scream from his supercharger he was gone.

CHAPTER 2

Mrs Osmotherly burst into the study of her cottage.

"A supercharged Vincent!" she announced to her cat.

Rain lashed against the windows. The heavy curtains shrank away from her in the draught from the hall.

She grabbed a dog-eared copy of *The Observer's Book of Motorcycles* and thumbed through it.

"In an Egli frame and with disc brakes!"

Her old grey tomcat lay asleep in an armchair by the fire. He made no response. None had realistically been expected.

Candles and an oil lamp provided light, but the ticking coals on the fire gave the room a red glow. Even the clock sounded comfortably tired.

Mrs Osmotherly pulled one arm out of her waxed cotton cape and grabbed a small black box with a winding-handle and an aerial. She breezed back out of the room and the curtains set sail after her, brushing the old grey cat who flicked an ear. In the hall, she shucked off her boots, flung her sou'wester over a hat stand, wriggled her cape onto a coat rack and re-entered the study in another sweep of curtains as she closed the door behind her, still brandishing *The Observer's Book of Motorcycles*. She wound up her clockwork two-way radiophone and dialled a number on it before stoking up the fire and warming herself in front of it.

"Another busy day for you as well, Greymalkin?"

Mrs Osmotherly thought Greymalkin was a good name for her cat. He was old and enigmatic and his grey fur might once have been black.

But he did not recognise Greymalkin as his name. He only answered to Indoors or Food although Mrs Osmotherly never seemed to notice. And, on a night like this, he was definitely Indoors.

He opened an eye and then closed it again. Mrs Osmotherly was standing in the way of the warmth but she wouldn't be still for long.

Just as he was working himself up for another bout of unconsciousness, Mrs Osmotherly suddenly said, "Dorinda!"

"Who's that?" muttered a sleepy voice on the other end of the phone.

"It's me, Hepsibah Osmotherly. I'm sorry to call you so late …"

"It's so late it's early," grunted Dorinda Prevoyance.

"I'm sorry, but this can't wait. I've just come off the moors and I've made a significant observation in the traffic movements."

"On the moors? At this time of night?"

Mrs Osmotherly began to pace. Indoors Food fitted his tail more snugly around his feet and nose.

"It was on the other side of Wormton towards Mithering. I've only just got back. I tried to track him for as long as I could, but I couldn't keep up with a motorbike."

"What's so significant about that?"

"First of all, I must tell you about my earlier observations. This morning, there was a Hillman Imp in Bedlam-le-Beans."

Indoors Food opened his eyes.

"A Hillman Imp?"

"Yes. You know what an imp is! It's a child of the devil!"

Over the years, Mrs Osmotherly's cat had absorbed a great deal from the wisest woman in the Vale of Wormton. He knew all about Hillman Imps. They were rear-engined so their boots were warmer than their bonnets to sit on and he preferred their flatter contours to those of Volkswagen Beetles. Beetles had just an awkwardly shaped shelf over their rear number plate, which was totally inadequate for a cat of his torpidity.

He also knew that in certain road conjunctions at certain times, certain cars could be bad news.

"And look at this!" continued Mrs Osmotherly, forgetting Dorinda wasn't there and stabbing a finger at the latest edition of *The Piston Wheel*. "A Dodge Demon is for sale in Mithering!"

Indoors knew all about Dodge Demons, too. They had nice, big, V8 engines in the proper place at the front under a comfortable expanse of bonnet.

"So you are flanked by an Imp and a Demon," Dorinda summarised.

Indoors had met Dorinda Prevoyance. She was editor of the well-known wise woman's magazine, *Wise Woman's Own*, and visited occasionally to interview Mrs Osmotherly about her pioneering work on a new system of fortune telling.

"And," went on Mrs Osmotherly, "the motorbike I saw today, travelling along the Mithering road as if it were possessed, was a supercharged Vincent."

"Ooooh," said Dorinda Prevoyance, now wide awake, "I don't like the sound of that!"

"Some strange agency is abroad, tonight," said Mrs Osmotherly. "I can feel … something." She picked up her *Bumper Book of American Automobiles* and leafed through it. "Of course, I could be wrong."

"Frankly, I doubt it," said Dorinda, "not with your reputation."

"It might not have been an Imp at all. It might have been a distant

Chevrolet Corvair. Or the vendors of the Demon could be mistaken. It might be a Plymouth Duster. They both use the same body shell."

"Hah!" snorted Dorinda. "A pox on thee, Logo, deceitful god of badge engineering! How are we to divine the future with such a masquerade?"

"A big, bad, blown Vincent," muttered Mrs Osmotherly. The cogs in the fruit machine of her memory were turning. They just needed a little nudge to help them.

Unsure of what she was remembering, she went over to her bound collection of magazine back issues.

"What are you doing?" asked Dorinda.

"There was something about a blown Vincent a few years ago. I don't think it was in *Wise Woman's Own*. Maybe *Wise Woman's Realm*? Or *Cognopolitan*?"

"Oh no, surely not!" cried Dorinda.

Mrs Osmotherly rummaged away feverishly.

The smell of pages that had lain close together since nearly new wafted across the room and provoked a strange dream for the slumbering Indoors.

"Aha! Here it is! *Harbinger's & Queen*."

Mrs Osmotherly went back to her desk and sat down. Dorinda waited patiently. There was a pause in the storm outside, as if it, too, was desperate to know what a big, bad, blown Vincent with an Egli frame and disc brakes really meant.

"Of course!" said Mrs Osmotherly. "That's it! It's him. It has to be him. The Horsepower Whisperer rides in the Wold tonight!"

The wind gasped and hailstones rattled on the tiles and windowpanes as if the storm had dropped them in horror.

"The Soul Trader?" queried Dorinda.

"Yes! Old Weird Wheels himself. The Metal Guru, the Repossession Man, the Crypto-Engineer, His Malign Weirdness, the Grand Whizz-Herd and Master of The Engine Henge, the Lord High Prince of Rock'n'Roll, the Horsepower Whisperer and Soul Trader! None other than that infamous libertine and free radical, Nicholas Eldritch Hob!"

Some rain found its way down the chimney and fell into the fire, creating a great fizzing and hissing.

Indoors woke up. To him, it sounded like a cat swearing. He looked around to see an old woman dancing with glee at solving the conundrum of the motorscope but then she stopped in mid-hop.

"But this is terrible!" Dorinda was saying. "What in the Wold does he want?"

Mrs Osmotherly swallowed hard. "And from whom?" She shook her head. "Answers only make more questions."

She walked slowly over to the wall and pulled off what looked like a calendar. It was, in fact, *Old Maureen's Almanac*. She studied Old Maureen and grunted. "Of course, he would come now during Dark Time. The Horsepower Whisperer always picks his moments well!"

"Whose soul could he possibly be after?" wondered Dorinda, fearing for her friend and contributor.

But Mrs Osmotherly was thinking hard again. Back to the fire she went.

Indoors pretended to be asleep. He was so good at pretending to be asleep, sometimes he found himself waking up.

Mrs Osmotherly had overlooked a notebook that had fallen to the floor. She snatched it up and examined it closely. Slowly, she began to understand.

"A wolf? No! It's a cub! A wolf cub! A giant wolf cub!"

She snorted in disbelief.

"Can this really be true?" she asked Indoors as much as Dorinda. "A giant wolf cub?"

Indoors opened his eyes and winked at her with a sort of half smile.

"Unless," said Mrs Osmotherly, "I've missed something."

CHAPTER 3

"Mr Heckmondwike!"

A thickset, craggy individual looked up. As he did so, the food on his fork fell into the gravy and splashed the napkin tucked into his collar.

"Slake?"

Slake grinned back. He was a gawky youth with long, dark hair who looked as if he'd been grown in a cupboard without any sunlight. He wore a leather jacket and jeans that started off as very tight at the hips but at the knees they spread out into flares so big they were still entering the snug of *The Golden Fleece* as he stood there. He wore a tee shirt under his leather jacket that bore the legend *Too fast to live, too young to die.*

"Ah thought tha were int Petropolis," said Mr Heckmondwike.

"Not any more," replied Slake.

"Ah can see that."

"I came back."

"Appen?"

"Sfunny," mused Slake. "After a while, all I could think of was coming home."

"Ah thought tha hated it here," said Mr Heckmondwike, and he trapped and ate the elusive piece of shepherd's pie.

"I did," admitted Slake, "but I began to miss Wormton all the same."

Mr Heckmondwike, who never spoke with his mouth full, nodded sagely and, as he chewed, pointed with his knife to his empty glass of Old Sawe's Irascible Anorak.

"Thanks," said Slake, misinterpreting the gesture on purpose. "I'll have a pint of The Usual, please Betty, if it's still on."

"It's still on," said Betty. "Would you be wanting a bacon and potato fritter, too?"

"Ooh, yes, please!" Slake turned to Mr Heckmondwike. "Can I have mushy peas, as well?"

"If he's treating you, you can have the lot," said Betty.

Slake grinned at his unwitting benefactor and began to study the blackboard with the menu on it.

Betty smiled as well. This was good sport.

Mr Heckmondwike became a little restless. It wasn't that Woldspeople were stingy. They were just sensitive – sensitive about legal tender.

"No, better not be greedy," Slake replied, turning back to Betty. "Just bacon, potato and mushy peas."

"In a fritter. Be with you in two shakes of a lamb's tail."

"That's what I like about being at home!" Slake said, gleefully. "I'm known here!"

"Knawn to t'authorities," pointed out Mr Heckmondwike.

"Ah. Yes. The anonymity of the crowd can be useful, sometimes."

"Tha's not anonymous here, lad."

Slake laughed. "True but I can still do my speed testing out there in the Woldernesse."

"Speed testing," said Mr Heckmondwike. He tried to add a dismissive snort, but his happiness at seeing Slake again with his infectious enthusiasm, got the better of him and it sounded as if he wanted to go speed testing, too.

"Don't worry," said Slake, "I'll keep clear of Wormton. Well clear."

"And Diggle Cottage, lad. Mrs Osmotherly needs 'er peace and quiet to do 'er reckonin'."

"That's a point. I've got to speak to her about the next phases of Dark Time. I don't want to find myself in a DT like the last one." He sat down next to Mr Heckmondwike. "How's the flock, by the way?"

"Nobbut graidly, tha knaws. Lambing's nearly ower and we've just come out of Dark Time. Could be a lot wuss."

"How's the Mudlark going?"

"Heck as owt! Tha did a grand job there, lad, and nay mistake. It must be t'fastest Mudlark this side of Bedlam."

"My dear fellow, you are too kind!"

"But tha can stop that Petropolitan talk now you're back in Wormton. Right away."

"It's going to be expected of me. How many horsepower whispering Woldsmen do you know?"

"Well there's Loncaster."

"Yeah …"

"Mickleness. And Dobson."

"Obviously."

"And our very own Mr Macklefract. Point is, Slake, ah can think of a few."

"The point is there's not so many."

"Ah've given thee four already, lad, and ah'm just getting' warmed up to t'task."

"Okay, but if I admit you're right and I'm wrong it doesn't mean to say I haven't lost the argument, okay?"

"Now that's a Woldsman talking."

"Yeah and don't you forget it."

"And don't thee forget it, nayther. Anyroad, ah suppose tha'll be looking for summat like Riddaw Lodge to live in."

"Not for me. I need to be near my customers, inside the town's walls. Riddaw's fine for you because you can commune with your flock. I'll find some nice big old sheds here in Wormton. There's plenty of 'em around."

"Ah heard tell tha rode int Wild Hunt," said Mr Heckmondwike, in a lowered voice.

Slake leaned forward. "What if I did?" he whispered.

"Is tha gonna ride in it again?"

"Of course. It'll come to Wormton before too long."

"That was a lifetime ago."

"My lifetime, certainly," replied Slake.

"It came through here before tha were even a twinkle," said Mr Heckmondwike, "a twinkle in t'milkman's eye."

"The Wild Hunt's long overdue here," Slake told him. "Once I've sold my engines to the young farmers and the miners, we'll soon have our own one."

"What? Mudlarks included?"

"Of course! Yours, Mr Heckmondwike, could be the leader of the pack!"

"Aye, it's a good un and nay mistake."

"Thank you."

"Ah would've thought that it would make better sense to have stayed int Petropolis if tha was serious about engine tuning."

"I enjoyed it to begin with," Slake admitted. "The pace of life, the freedom and the opportunities it offered were all brilliant. But it took too long to get known. You can't approach city people to ask them if they'll help you bleed your brakes. Nobody starts a chat. They don't get to know you well enough to commission some exquisite piece of engineering from you. You'd never get the service from someone like Betty here, either."

"So did tha feel a bit of a small ram in a big flock?"

"Yeah but not so tired. In The Petropolis there were simply too many people to get known by. And then the novelty of the big city wore off after a bit."

"What novelty?"

Slake looked at him hard. "I didn't suppose you'd understand," he said.

Mr Heckmondwike took another mouthful, munched it, swallowed it, and said, "Lonely places, cities," just to show that he did understand, although he had no personal experience of them himself.

Slake was so surprised by this, he was speechless until Betty came over with two pints and his fritter, and then he had to deal with the serious business of eating it. Just before he began, he asked, "So. What's new?"

Mr Heckmondwike supped from his fresh pint of Old Sawe's Irascible Anorak. "Tha'd be surprised," he said, at length.

"I would?"

"See? Ah told thee tha'd be surprised."

"Nothing's new. That's the surprise, right?"

"Wrong."

"Go on, then. Astound me."

"Well, ah've got a new tractor."

"A Wolseley?"

"Aye! Of course!"

"Wow!"

"Ah'll show it thee, later."

"You do that and I'll take you for a run in my trike!"

Mr Heckmondwike dropped his knife and Slake laughed out loud. It bounced onto the bare flagstones and the sound echoed around the snug, making the other customers look around. Mr Heckmondwike cursed under his breath and reached down with a groan to retrieve his knife from under the settle where they sat.

"It's not still going is it?" he muttered.

"Of course!" replied Slake.

"Is that a promise or a threat?"

"For you, it'll be a treat. A taste of life in the fast lane."

"Oh, aye?"

"I'd charge anyone else for the privilege. Just think of all those beers they'll stand you down at *The Young Farmers* as you regale them with your astonishing account of how you cheated death on the highway as passenger in my trike!"

"Ah'm not convinced that all experience is valuable. And just by way of an experiment, ah'm prepared to forego t'adventure to explore ma theory."

"I'm sure you'll reconsider. It's a once-in-a-lifetime experience."

"Sounds more like t'end-of-a-lifetime experience from where ah'm sittin'. So, Slake. What's thine plan, lad? Eh?"

Slake looked suddenly serious. "I'm not sure. 'The Wold is my hamster.'"

"Aye. Well. Don't let it get out of its cage and run it ower wi' settee tryin' to find it agin."

"I thought I might get a spannering job somewhere. You know, a bit of servicing, some accident repair, neutralize a few gremlins, that sort of thing."

Mr Heckmondwike looked at him very hard.

Slake began to fidget.

"Nay, tha doesn't," said Mr Heckmondwike. "Tha doesn't want to do that. Tha wants to open up thine own engine tuning shop. That's what tha wants to do."

Slake was a little red in the face.

"Okay. So I want to open up my own engine tuning shop. What's wrong with a bit of ambition?"

"Nowt's wrong with it, lad. If tha doesn't have a dream, how's tha gonna have a dream come true?"

"Exactly!"

"Just don't expect it to come true in Wormton, that's all."

"That," said Slake, with some feeling, "was just why I left in the first instance."

"Meaning, tha could leave int next?"

"Mebbe," mused Slake. "I don't know. For the moment, it's good to be back."

"And now ah suppose everyone with a doorstop for an engine will beat a path to thine door?"

"Something like that. A door with *Slakespeed Engine Emporium* over it in red neon letters."

Mr Heckmondwike chuckled as Slake munched his fritter.

"What?" Slake wanted to know. "What is it?"

"Red neon letters? The parish council would never approve that!"

"Oh, oh. Look who's just come in."

"Ow canna? Ah'm not a bloody owl!"

"It's ..."

"Slake!" boomed a foghorn voice.

Slake stood up. "Mr Grandlythorpe!"

Slake and Mr Grandlythorpe went back a long, long way, beyond the genesis of Slake's infamous trike, beyond when time trials were spontaneously held on the ring road within the town walls – right back, in fact, to that first and rather ill-advised attempt to supercharge an electric milk float, which saw the whole of Wormton being plunged into darkness for a week.

Since Slake had been in The Petropolis, Mr Grandlythorpe's life had been almost tranquil. Mr Heckmondwike couldn't help but feel as if the Town Clerk was being loud on purpose, as if he were warning the whole of Wormton that Slake was back in town.

"Ow ta fettlin, lad?"

"I'm fettling very well, thank you, Mr Grandlythorpe. And you?"

"Heck as owt!"

They shook, or rather pressed palms, their arms rigid, knuckles white, squeezing each other's hand from the shoulder in a typical Woldsman's greeting. They let go of each other and Mr Grandlythorpe surreptitiously clenched and unclenched his knuckles. Slake had come of age.

"Ow do, Mr Grandlythorpe," said Mr Heckmondwike, standing up and quickly pressing his own vice-like grip on the Town Clerk.

"Mr Heckmondwike. Fettlin' well thysen?"

"Aye, nobbut graidly, tha knaws."

"Appen? Those hoggs o'thine look reet fair to middlin' these days."

"Aye. Heck as likely as happen as mebbe tha's reet. Not too scabby e'en tho it's me that says so as shouldn't."

"If tha will excuse me, Mr Heckmondwike, ah just wanted to have a word wi' young Slake here. It won't take long."

Slake was pulling a face behind Mr Grandlythorpe's back. Mr Heckmondwike pretended not to notice.

Mr Grandlythorpe frowned slightly and turned to a suddenly attentive Slake. "Y'see, Slake, the parish council 'ave a problem wi' some of our vehicles."

"Oh, yes?" said Slake.

Mr Heckmondwike grunted. A true Woldsman would have said "Oh, aye?" That was what life in The Petropolis did to you.

Mr Grandlythorpe pulled up a chair. It grated loudly across the flagstones. They all sat down together and formed a conspiratorial huddle.

"As a young engineer, fresh from T'Petropolis, ah was wonderin' if tha could see thine way to looking at our fire engine and t'ambulances over at t'cottage hospital."

"I'm sure I could, at the very least, have a look."

"By t'powers invested in me as Town Clerk, ah am empowered to appoint, on behalf and for t'benefit of t'people of Wormton, in furtherance of our municipal services, a professional engineer – a professional engineer that knaws his stuff, mind – to enhance t'performance of our emergency vehicles. We'll pay professional rates, 'n all, mark me and mark me well. We need summan who knaws what they're about."

"But tha heard Slake was in town," put in Mr Heckmondwike, "and thought tha'd have a talk wi' him fust."

"Aye, ah did at that."

"So what exactly is wrong with them, Mr Grandlythorpe?"

"Well, it's like this, lad. They're just not bloody fast enough."

"I see." Slake winked at Mr Heckmondwike.

"We can't 'ave leisurely ambulances or dawdlin' fire engines."

"Of course not," agreed Slake.

"Wormton Parish Council would be t'laughing stock of t'whole Vale. It's said that Mithering District Council have some ambulances that can do nowt to sixty in under fifteen seconds!"

"That's not fast!"

"That's just what ah was hoping tha'd say, lad!" and Mr Grandlythorpe slapped Slake on the back so enthusiastically he nearly pitched the young engine-tuner into his fritter.

"Y'see, Mr Grandlythorpe," said Slake, who'd had to brace himself with his hands on the table, "speed is simply a function of how much money you are prepared to spend."

Mr Heckmondwike thought Slake had blown it there and then, but Mr Grandlythorpe replied, "Ah shall report back to t'parish council that, with thine expertise, Wormton'll be able to show them Mitherers a thing or two."

"It's a matter of civic pride, isn't it?"

"Aye. The honour of Wormton is at stake here, lad. Ah want thee to turn our fire engine and ambulances into t'eppytummy of alacrity."

Out of Mr Grandlythorpe's line of sight, Mr Heckmondwike shook his head.

Mr Grandlythorpe continued. "We'll pay thee good rates."

"Really?" replied Slake, hoping he didn't sound too surprised. It wasn't like Mr Grandlythorpe to say such things.

"Almost as good as they'd pay summan to do a proper job," put in Mr Heckmondwike, but the others ignored him.

"What make are they?" asked Slake.

"Wolseleys, all of 'em."

"Naturally. I'll have a look at them," he told Mr Grandlythorpe, "and let you know what can be done. Once we have negotiated my rates."

Mr Heckmondwike pursed his lips in a soundless whistle.

"Aye," said Mr Grandlythorpe, with barely a twitch of an eyelid. "And we can establish thine terms o' contract. For let's be clear abowt summat before we begin. Ah don't want thee getting carried away."

"How d'you mean?"

"They've got to be reliable. If they keep breakin' down, that'd be wuss than having bloody doorstops for motors! And none of this Horsepower Wars nonsense, nayther."

So far, Wormton had remained largely untouched by the Horsepower Wars. The Wild Hunt had roared through the Vale of Wormton only once. The force that powered the economy of the rest of Anarchadia had yet to make an impact on the town. Mr Grandlythorpe was determined to see that the Wild Hunt never again got any closer than Bedlam-le-Beans.

That he had, so far, largely succeeded had been the main reason why Slake had left.

"I promise I'll be very careful," Slake assured him.

"Aye, tha'd better be. They're not thine to race. And ah don't want to see thee racin' that trike o' thine ont parish roads, ayther."

"Who have I got to race against here in Wormton?" Slake asked him, all innocence.

Mr Grandlythorpe couldn't help eyeing him with suspicion. "Ah dunnaw. Reckon tha could allus find summan daft enough. Besides. Ah reckon a lad like thee has demons of his own to chase."

"As you will, Mr Grandlythorpe, as you will. But I give you my word. I will have to test your vehicles extensively, though, as part of the development process. I hope you understand."

Mr Grandlythorpe narrowed his already small eyes even further, but Slake kept on smiling and said that subject to the conclusion of mutually agreeable terms he could probably be around the fire station the day after tomorrow. "I've already got a couple of jobs lined up with Heptonstall's Garage," he explained.

"Now then, that's graidly. Ah'll meet thee at t'fire station at nine if that's convenient." Mr Grandlythorpe rose from his seat and the others mirrored his actions, either knees or chairs creaking. "Ah'll sithee, then. Slake. Mr Heckmondwike. "

"Did ah just hear thee promising the unpromissable?" Mr Heckmondwike asked Slake as they sat down again and resumed their meals.

"Not quite. I started by assuring him that I would be very careful."

"Aye. Careful tha won't get caught."

"He then went on to say that he didn't want to see me racing my trike on his roads, and I simply promised that he wouldn't." Slake swigged some Usual and gave Mr Heckmondwike a sideways glance. "Wouldn't see me."

Mr Heckmondwike grinned.

"Mr Grandlythorpe knows me. We have an understanding. I think."

"Reckon tha'll get away with it, lad?"

Slake nodded. "So long as I don't rub his face in it. The odd little burnup is as nothing compared to the hideous excesses that I've seen in The Petropolis or the Horsepower Wars. And, even if I had promised him not to do it on the parish roads – which I do not believe I did – then it would still be worth doing it for all the good business I shall get from souping up these ambulances and that old fire engine."

"He seems to have forgiven thee since the last time tha set fire to t'road."

"That was his own fault for authorising the use of an asphalt with too low a flash point," retorted Slake.

"Oh aye? Anyway. Summat of a challenge, int it?"

"They'll need a service for a start, then I'll probably junk the air filters, improve the carbs and exhaust and flow the heads. Once I've checked the bottom ends, of course."

"Eck as like?" said Mr Heckmondwike but Slake's eyes had glazed over.

"This could be the first step towards those neon letters over my own workshop."

"Neon letters!" Mr Heckmondwike toasted him with his pint of Old Sawe's Irascible Anorak. "Welcome back, lad," he said. "Welcome back!"

CHAPTER 4

It was as they left the pleasant gloom of *The Golden Fleece*, still deep in conversation, that Mr Heckmondwike and Slake were confronted by a green Citroën 2CV tearing up the wide expanse of Sheep Street. Its wheels bobbled over the cobbles as if disconnected from the rest of the car, which sailed along, independent of the road beneath it. It pulled up beside them with a familiar figure behind the wheel.

"Mrs Osmotherly!" exclaimed Slake.

An unconscious grey cat was curled up on the seat beside her.

"Hallo Mr Heckmondwike," said Mrs Osmotherly. "Slake! This is a pleasant surprise! What are you doing back here?"

"I've come home!"

"For good?"

"Yep! Well, I think so."

"Oh, that is good news! I had an idea you would."

"Really?"

"Yes. But I suppose you still can't leave things with engines and wheels alone, can you?"

"Nope!"

"Hmm." Mrs Osmotherly was suddenly serious. "Look here. If you see a black rider on a supercharged Vincent special, don't talk to him."

"Why? We don't get many of those around here!"

"We don't want any of them round here, thank you very much. He rides at a very difficult time."

"And it's blown?"

"Apparently." She frowned. "Look, Slake, I don't actually know anything about motorbikes or engines. I just know what they mean. Something is awheel."

Slake and Mr Heckmondwike exchanged glances.

"I see," Slake lied. "So what does this big, bad, blown Vincent mean?"

"It's bad, very bad."

"On a scale of one to ten?"

"It is infinitely bad."

"Right off the scale?"

"It would break the scales, Slake. The rider is dangerous."

The two men knew better than to laugh at anything Mrs Osmotherly said. She knew about things, like when the next Dark Time would come.

"Dangerous?"

"More dangerous than you could ever imagine. And that goes for you, too, Mr Heckmondwike."

"Me? What's to do?"

"Something. I don't know what yet, but I mean to find out. Keep an eye on your flock. Be particularly vigilant. Slake? Keep your eyes peeled for Hillman Imps and Dodge Demons."

"Okay. Fine."

"If you see one, tell me."

"Are they dangerous, too?"

"Not in themselves."

"I was thinking more whether they'd be dangerous to me."

Mrs Osmotherly smiled a tired, motherly smile at him. "No. Not in any way that you could understand."

"Anything else?"

"Possibly a Guy Wolf. Maybe a Leyland Cub."

"I think Mr Floridspleen used to have a Guy Wolf out at Gout Leg Pike. I don't think it works any more, though."

"I hope not. Something special happens when an engine springs to life. What's involved is beyond me, but the effects are plain to see."

"They are?"

"To me they are. Usually."

"Such as?"

"It's better you don't know, Slake. Believe me."

"Please yourself," he said, glancing at Mr Heckmondwike. "How's the car going, anyway?"

"Oh, extremely well, thank you. It absolutely flies since you last looked at it. Anyway, I must be off. I've got cars to spot and fortunes to tell. Nice to see you again, Slake. And you, Mr Heckmondwike."

"Mrs Osmotherly."

"Remember what I said. No talking to any strangers riding a super-charged Vincent. Okay?"

"Okay."

"Promise?"

"All right. I promise."

"You, too, Mr Heckmondwike. Next Dark Time is a week yesterday, Erratics or Occasionals are not forecast in the interim."

"Graidly," replied Mr Heckmondwike. Although Dark Time was to be dreaded, a prolonged interval between each one was to be welcomed.

"Fare well, both of you," she said and she fired up her 2CV with a roar and zoomed off.

"Goes well," said Mr Heckmondwike, as they watched her disappear round a corner at a potentially cat-disturbing angle.

"Not too shabby," agreed Slake.

The sound of her exhaust echoed off the thickset limestone buildings of Wormton.

"Didn't used to go that well," mused Mr Heckmondwike.

"Really?" replied Slake, innocently.

"Or sound like that. It couldn't pull t'skin off a Mithering pudding! Slake? Tha didn't service it, did tha? Tha souped it up!"

"Well, I might've made it a little bit more efficient here and there."

"What did tha do to it? It goes like a ferret up a drainpipe!"

"All I did was put a Citroën GS engine in it."

"A what? And tha didn't tell 'er?"

"Course not! She's not interested in engines. Just what … cars and … things mean when they're on the road."

"She'll find out int end."

"I doubt it. I did it for her the last time I was home and she hasn't spotted it yet. You wouldn't believe how awkward it was, squeezing it under the bonnet once I'd welded up the flywheel and then re-drilling it. The engine bolted straight onto the gearbox all right but I had to relieve the bellhousing. I also had to modify the gear change and move the umbrella handbrake but she never noticed. And then to fit the exhausts …"

"But why, lad? What did tha do it for?"

"Because, Mr Heckmondwike, I could. And I did. I just charged her for a major service and now she's delighted with the way it goes."

"Ah bet she is," said Mr Heckmondwike. "That car's a bit of a wolf in sheep's clothing and nay mither."

CHAPTER 5

The Vale of Wormton was Wold-renowned for its rainfall. Even inside his new car, Billy felt surprised that he didn't drown. A fine mist was falling and even the air in between each droplet seemed to be a clearer form of moisture.

His new Dodge Demon was going better than ever but he had pulled over to consult his copy of *Wrainwright's Guide to the Wold*. How could something as insubstantial and lightweight as the atmosphere hold such a density of water? His search for an explanation was in vain. Even the most woldly-wise couldn't understand it.

"One might be forgiven," Wrainwright had written, "for expecting that Woldspeople have separate words to describe each different type of rainfall. If they do, they were never disposed to share them with me, despite my gaining their confidence on other matters, as if they were acutely aware that this kind of behaviour was expected of them and, somehow, it reflected badly upon their characters, perhaps suggesting a certain narrowness of outlook. At last, I drew the conclusion that Woldspeople did, indeed, have many different names for the abundant varieties of precipitation they could expect and – I am now ashamed to say – I took recourse to stealth in an effort to discover the variety of their alleged nomenclature. However, it was all to no avail. I caught the odd snatch of 'stair rods', 'kittens and puppies', 'cats and dogs' and 'tiddley-push'. I never discovered precisely what constituted the difference between these terms, for, as soon as my presence was noted, I was met by a determined, 'Turned out nice again, int it?' despite irrefutable evidence to the contrary."

Billy glanced up from his book and through the steamed up windows of his Dodge noticed about twenty people, dressed in colourful waterproofs. They were looking at him with great curiosity and one of them had begun to approach his car. Billy wound down his window.

"Greetings, my son," said the wiry ascetic. "You're Billy Brock-house, aren't you?"

Billy fidgeted. Complete strangers knowing his name made him nervous.

"Yes," he replied, "who are you? Do you have a business card?"

"No."

"That's good," said Billy, who these days neither swore nor blasphemed. "I had a feeling a pattern was emerging."

"We are the redeemers of souls."

"Redeemers? What? Like old lemonade bottles?"

"This is no laughing matter, Billy. We save souls from fulfilment."

"Not like lemonade bottles, then."

"No. We take our work very seriously."

"How d'you know my name?"

"You are a growth-hormone salesman who is enjoying tremendous success at the moment, and we take a particular interest in these things. You realise that your good fortune cannot continue."

"Do I? It sounds as if you disapprove."

"I'm merely warning you of the inevitable."

"Who are you exactly?"

"We are Mithering Brethren. I am Brother Guy."

"What a large family you have, Guy."

Brother Guy smiled. "It is the Brotherhood of Man."

"Really?" exclaimed Billy. He quickly looked around them. "*The Brotherhood of Man*? I prefer *The New Seekers* myself."

A nearby outfit of canary yellow oilskins pulled back its hood to reveal the face of a pretty girl with a wide mouth and very full lips. She was smiling. "He pretends to mistake us for a popular beat combo," she told Brother Guy.

"Ah, thank you, Sister Elspeth. We are Mithering Brethren, Billy, and we save souls rather than encourage impure thought through music."

"I would never have described *The New Seekers* as encouraging the impure," said Billy.

"We care about our fellow men," said Brother Guy.

"And women," put in Sister Elspeth.

"And women," admitted Brother Guy. "We care about them so much we work for their salvation."

"Uh-huh," said Billy.

"We work to protect them from themselves to ensure an uninterrupted passage into righteousness."

"Are you a Wild Hunter?" Sister Elspeth asked Billy. Her eyes shone with a light that had a source of its own.

Billy glanced at his new car. Since the last time anyone had guessed his name correctly, his fortunes had improved dramatically. Although it was difficult to completely daemonstrate growth hormones in such a short period of time, he could still daemonstrate zeal and the people he met had obviously felt it, too, for they had become his customers.

He'd suddenly made a lot of sales and, when his commission cheque had arrived, a lot of money. He'd been in Mithering at the time and the yellow Dodge Demon 340 had become a must-have.

Quite how this change in fortune had come about was something he preferred not to dwell upon.

"No," he told Sister Elspeth. "I've seen the Wild Hunt once or twice, but I've never taken part in it. I just like the cars. This one is thirsty and I have to be careful not to run out of fuel."

"Some people make their own fuel around here," said Sister Elspeth. "They don't want to pay the high rates of tax."

"Who does?"

"It is our responsibility to each other to pay our taxes!" insisted Brother Guy.

" 'And it came to pass in those days,' " said Sister Elspeth, " 'that there went out a decree from Caesar Augustus, that all the Wold should be taxed.' "

"As Mithering Brethren …"

"And Sistren!"

"We take an especial interest in those that plan to achieve fulfilment. We save people from themselves. Tell me something, Billy. Do you need saving?"

"Maybe."

"My brothers …"

"And sisters!"

"My brothers and sisters watch over you."

"That's really very nice of you," Billy told them earnestly.

"Billy," said Brother Guy. "I think you are in great danger."

"Really? What from?"

"Fulfilment."

"That's bad, is it?"

"I have the strangest feeling about your soul, Billy. I have met many in peril over the years and for yours there seems hardly any hope."

"Hang on a minute. Can I ask you a question, a moment? Do you save souls *from* fulfilment or *through* fulfilment?"

"*From* fulfilment," Sister Elspeth assured him.

"And none of you ride motorbikes?"

"We go everywhere by foot," said Brother Guy. "Billy, this is an important day for you. We can help you."

"Of course, you can," replied Billy. "But you want something in return, first. Right?"

Brother Guy smiled sadly at Billy. He beckoned to Sister Elspeth and there was an animated exchange of whispers. Billy tried to follow what they were saying but failed. When they stopped, both of them were glowing with delight.

"A little to the west of here," said Brother Guy, "is a farm called Scar Fell Farm, and what we would like you to do is to apply your products to the flock there. The owner is called Mr Gaffathwaite and his shepherd is called

Mr Heckmondwike. They are Woldsmen, so hard to deal with, but do not be disheartened. The more you try, the more you will succeed. And they are in sore need of help, although, in truth, their flock looks the best for many leagues around here."

"Okay. So what you want me to do is go to Scar Fell Farm and sell some of my stuff to them."

"Sell it to them if you can, but make sure it is applied to the sheep in their flock."

"I get it," said Billy. "You want me to daemonstrate to them."

A cloud passed over the usually confident features of the Mithering Brethren.

"Okay," said Billy. He checked the map in *Wrainwright*. "Scar Fell Farm you say?"

"Yes."

"Right. Well. I'd better be on my way, then."

"Goodbye, Billy. Fare well."

"Okay. Same to you." He fired up the engine. "Er, thanks again," and off he went.

CHAPTER 6

High up on the fell side, dwarfed by the vastness of the Wold around them, two figures were leaning on a gate, each chewing on a long piece of grass. Both were around the same age. One wore a flat cap, a collarless shirt, a tweed jacket and heavy corduroy trousers. The other was dressed the same apart from sporting a collar and tie and a pork pie hat. Before them, sheep grazed within the dry stone walls of the sheepfold while they chose which animals to keep for breeding and which ones to "send for to market".

Mr Gaffathwaite had inherited Mr Heckmondwike from his father, along with the rest of Scar Fell Farm. As far as Mr Gaffathwaite was concerned, Mr Heckmondwike's purpose in life was to promote sheepkind in every and any way possible and Mr Gaffathwaite generously allowed him to practise on the fabulously fecund flock of Cornucopian Tablebacks for which Scar Fell Farm was justifiably famous. If, in the process, he made Mr Gaffathwaite one of the richest men in the Wold, then Mr Gaffathwaite was intent on seeing to it that Mr Heckmondwike was not obstructed in any way.

When Mr Heckmondwike looked at a sheep, he could place it perfectly in the context of its bloodline and recall the minutest personality trait it had displayed since birth. His estimating skills at assessing the weight and value of a fleece, or a carcass, were Wold-famous and he had an uncanny empathy with his charges that, in any other society, would have brought him scorn, ridicule or fear. Here, however, in the district around the market town of Wormton, it earned him awe and admiration and a healthy income for his indulgent employer.

They were so engrossed in their flock-taking that they didn't notice the rumble of an exhaust until it was almost on top of them. A Dodge Demon bumped and crashed its way up the pot-holed track towards them.

"Eh up," said Mr Heckmondwike.

"What's to do?" answered Mr Gaffathwaite.

"Trouble, ah'll warrant."

"Looks like another rep," remarked Mr Gaffathwaite.

"Is tha gonna buy?"

Mr Gaffathwaite glanced at Mr Heckmondwike with mock contempt. "Am ah heck!"

The car stopped. A smartly dressed chubby young man, in a purple velvet suit, alighted from behind the wheel and, after treading right in the middle of a cow pat, greeted them pleasantly and vigorously.

"Hi! My name is Brockhouse, Billy Brockhouse, and I represent Bigga-Beast, the Wold's largest supplier of agrochemicals and animal husbandry products."

"Ow do," said Mr Gaffathwaite

"Ow ta fettlin?" enquired Mr Heckmondwike.

"Heck as owt," replied Billy, "graidly, graidly, you know."

First one and then the other, Mr Gaffathwaite and Mr Heckmondwike put their calloused hands into Billy's clean and soft one. They let him shake their arms and resisted the temptation to crush his knuckles in a typical Woldsman's clench. Then they stared at him in silence, waiting for his performance to begin. His progress across the Wold was already the talk of *The Young Farmer's Club*, where they were plotting the course of his exploits on the walls.

"Now then, gentlemen," went on Billy, "may I ask if you use any BiggaBeast products on this splendid farm of yours?"

Mr Gaffathwaite looked at Mr Heckmondwike. Mr Heckmondwike chewed on his grass stalk and nodded.

"Tha can ask," said Mr Gaffathwaite.

Billy's smile faded but a little. "Well? Do you?"

"Nay," said Mr Heckmondwike.

"Have you ever tried any BiggaBeast products, I wonder?"

"Nay," said Mr Heckmondwike.

"Have you ever used any of our competitor's products, perhaps?"

Mr Heckmondwike pretended to think about this for a moment and then said, "Nay."

"Well, may I say that you really have done a most remarkable job here using only organic farming methods!"

Mr Heckmondwike looked at Mr Gaffathwaite.

"Tha may," said Mr Gaffathwaite.

"Well, you really have," said Billy, earnestly. "I mean that. No, really. I mean, just look around us. This place would be nowhere near as successful, as it is today, without your hard work and long hours."

"It would, tha knaws," corrected Mr Heckmondwike.

"Er, would it?"

"Aye. Ma father kept sheep here," said Mr Gaffathwaite

"And thine father before him," pointed out Mr Heckmondwike. "And thine father's father before that!"

"Aye. Reet back to t'stone men. They knew what they were about."

"I see," said Billy. "So generation after generation has farmed this valley and bequeathed it to those who follow."

"Dunno bowt that," said Mr Gaffathwaite.

"What would you say was the last innovation that was adopted on this farm?"

Mr Gaffathwaite and Mr Heckmondwike looked skywards and then turned around slowly. Billy followed their gaze.

Parked in a field on the other side of the lane was Mr Heckmondwike's brand new Wolseley tractor. Despite the leaden sky above, its gloss black paint gleamed and its chrome radiator grille dazzled.

In the valley below, lay Scar Fell Farm. There was a sizeable manor house, built in the provincial Georgian style from the mellow local stone. A Wolseley road tanker, full of Mrs Osmotherly's herbal sheep dip, was reversing up to one of the equally impressive farm buildings.

Just audible across the valley was the sound of the milking flock coming in. They were being funnelled into the milking parlour to climb, one by one, onto the carousel of the milking machine.

Next to the milking parlour was the dairy where the cream and cheeses were made and next to this was the lorry park where the Scar Fell Farm distribution fleet of Wolseley lorries would have stood had they not all been out on the road.

And all around the moated boundary of the homestead and farmyards were little orchards and spinneys and copses where once-revolutionary farm implements lay discarded, something better having come along.

"Young man," said Mr Gaffathwaite. "If innovation were good enough for ma grandfather, then it's good enough for me."

"Aha," said Billy. "I get it. You may follow the same furrow as the stone men but now you can plough more than just the one. Change is the only constant. Am I right?"

They had to think about this before they agreed with him.

"What would you say to me," Billy went on, warming to his subject, "if I told you that I could show you how to increase your yield by a factor of four by using the products of BiggaBeast?"

"Ah'd say tha were lyin'," Mr Heckmondwike told him.

"Yes, I suppose you would!" laughed Billy. "Direct. I like that! Yes, very direct. I understand your disbelief but wouldn't you like to increase your yield by four times at only a third more cost on average?"

"That would depend."

"By purchasing just a basic package of BiggaBeast's products, you could…"

"Young man," interrupted Mr Heckmondwike, "ah don't want to waste any more of thine valuable time just t'same as tha doesn't want to waste any o'mine."

Billy quickly produced a pamphlet. "One small syringe for each lamb, one giant leap for lambkind."

"Ah don't need thee to tell me how to run ma fecund flock. Ower t'years, if ah had a fecund ewe for every person like thee trying to persuade me that ah should be using this wonderful concoction, or that splendid implement, then ah would have to have me own pack of ravening wolves just to keep t'sheep numbers down. If ah reckons ah needs summat, ah goes out and ah gets it mesen. Ah'll never buy owt from the likes o'thee! Ah'll tell thee that for nowt!"

"But …" said Billy.

"Oh, they may work all right to start with," conceded Mr Heckmondwike, "but they allus work out for the wuss in the end. Tha can't get summat for nowt. It's a fact of life."

"'Ang abowt," murmured Mr Gaffathwaite, "let's just hear what the lad has to say."

"Eh? What?" Mr Heckmondwike looked quickly at his employer. Mr Gaffathwaite's eyes were becoming glassy.

"He might have summat for us after all," said Mr Gaffathwaite. "Nowt ventured, nowt gained, tha knaws."

Mr Heckmondwike grabbed Mr Gaffathwaite. "Don't give me any o' that claptrap!" he said.

He shook Mr Gaffathwaite until the clouds in his eyes parted and the real Mr Gaffathwaite looked out at him again.

"Aye," said Mr Gaffathwaite slowly. "Aye!" he added more forcibly. "Tha's reet! Tha can't have owt for nowt! That's a fact of life and fecundity!"

"And the way of t'Wold," put in Mr Heckmondwike.

"There's allus summat thee beggars don't tell us," went on Mr Gaffathwaite, turning to Billy, "and when things do go wrong, and they allus do, it turns out we're developing thine product for thee."

"We must work wi' nature, not agin it," explained Mr Heckmondwike. "The stone men knew that and we're followin' their example. If tha thinks we're gonna give up evolving, then tha can start revolving on tha … "

"What Mr Heckmondwike is saying," Mr Gaffathwaite enlarged "is that we're not going to jeopardise our flock, which has tekken generations to build up, to fund thee leading a playboy's lifestyle." The disapproval of Billy's velvet suit was writ large on his granite-hewn features. "So save thine time and save thine breath and go home."

Dejectedly, Billy bowed his head and walked back to his car.

Mr Gaffathwaite and Mr Heckmondwike watched him as he left. Any remorse they might have felt was more than compensated for by the knowledge that their flock of Cornucopian Tablebacks was still safe and sound and unadulterated.

"Knaw what? Ah don't like to admit it, Mr Heckmondwike, but ah could feel mesen weakening back there."

"Aye. Me n'all. Ah've nivver knawn the like bayfore."

"But tha didn't fail. Tha were resolute and led me back to t'course o' righteousness."

"That's all part of the shepherding service. And see this?" Mr Heck-mondwike showed Mr Gaffathwaite a small medallion around his neck. "Ah were wearin' ma St. Punter. Ah usually wear it to protect me from hornswog-glers on market days but ah've tekken heed o' Mrs Osmotherly's latest warnin' and just now it's reet buzzin'. Feel it. It's almost hot."

"Heck as owt! Good thing tha was wearin' it!"

They turned back to their flock and the pale light of early spring slowly warmed their old bones, which were still tired after the lambing season. A gentle breeze sprang up, scented with lush pasture and early meadow flowers.

"That fecund ewe's had it," Mr Gaffathwaite ventured. They watched an elderly sheep, once an efficient lamb-producing organism, kneel down arthritically on her forelegs to graze more comfortably. "Arthritis, foot rot and teeth goin', too. We ought to fetch her for to market."

"Allus produced twins," Mr Heckmondwike reminded him. "Ere! What the … ?"

A figure in a purple velvet suit had just leapt over the dry stone wall and landed in the mud. It sprinted over the meadow and grabbed one of the decrepit ewe's twins.

"I'll show you!" cried Billy Brockhouse, as he brandished an enormous syringe. "I'll give you a daemonstration, a free daemonstration! Soon you'll believe! Soon you'll understand what BiggaBeast can do for you!"

Billy knelt in the mud and held the little lamb. He plunged the syringe into the short wool of its fleece and squeezed it. The lamb bleated, in surprise as much as anything, and then struggled out of his grip.

Billy watched it re-join the flock. "It's only small now but you watch it grow!" he called out.

But Mr Heckmondwike and Mr Gaffathwaite were no longer staring in open-mouthed amazement at Billy. Something else behind him held their attention, something approaching Billy fast.

Billy was about to turn and see for himself what it was when a solid object cannoned into his back and sent him sliding across the wet grass.

When he looked up, standing at the other end of his skid marks was a large and aggressive ewe, the same ewe that Mr Gaffathwaite had just been mentally earmarking for the great sheep pen in the sky. Two lambs, one of which had been Billy's victim, scampered up to her and began to suckle. The old ewe, suddenly a fine specimen of a Cornucopian Tableback, shook her horns at him and double-stamped her forefoot. She had unknowingly just earned herself a reprieve.

"Where are t'dogs?" demanded Mr Gaffathwaite.

Mr Heckmondwike couldn't say. They were around somewhere. "Let's get 'im!" he growled, but Mr Gaffathwaite, in his agitation, fumbled at unlatching the gate. Cursing, Mr Heckmondwike did that most unwoldsmanlike thing and began to climb over it. Mr Gaffathwaite followed his example but, as they swung their legs over the top bar of the gate, they accidentally kicked each other in the groin, lost their balance and fell into the muddy field as an enraged heap.

Billy Brockhouse quickly clambered back out of the field and made good his escape behind the wheel of his Demon.

CHAPTER 7

The Mithering Brethren had been watching developments through their gloating glasses and had seen the agitation breaking out in the fields above Scar Fell Farm. Then Billy's Dodge had stormed off in the direction of Wormton and they had folded up their telescopes and binoculars before embracing each other, saying "Rejoice!"

"I never thought it would work as well as that!" Sister Elspeth declared to Brother Guy.

"The Lord is with us, Sister Elspeth. We could not fail. Billy was frustrated, we have succeeded and his soul is saved! Mr Gaffathwaite and Mr Heckmondwike failed to protect their flock from adulteration and their salvation has been assured, as well!"

"It's taken us months to find a way to get at them."

"We were equal to the challenge, Sister. Their souls are saved. Rejoice!"

"Billy's car has stopped not far away," said one of the other Brethren.

"Let us go to him," said Brother Guy, "and look upon him with satisfaction."

They squelched through the fields to the east until they came to the summit of a small but steep hill. Below them, through some leafless trees, they could see Billy's car parked on the road to Wormton. And as they approached they could see someone getting changed inside it.

Billy emerged, backwards from the driver's seat, dressed in tee shirt and jeans. In his arms he carried a bundle of muddy purple.

"Hallo, Billy," said Brother Guy. "You did well. Rejoice, rejoice!"

"No!"

"Everything has worked out beautifully."

"Has it? Have you seen the state of my clothes?" Billy strode to the back of his car and threw them into the boot.

"Ah. That's a shame," said Brother Guy, but he couldn't hide his additional pleasure at frustrating Billy's aspirations towards sartorial elegance although some might say the shop that had sold Billy the suit had beaten him to it. "And you were thwarted in your efforts to make a sale! Been a while since that's happened, hasn't it, Billy? But rejoice! Rejoice!"

"Rejoice!" chorused the other Mithering Brethren and Sistren.

"Your soul has been saved!"

"You wanted me to fail!"

"Rejoice! Your soul is saved!" went on the Mithering Brethren.

"I may have been thwarted, but my soul has not been saved!"

"What do you mean, Billy?"

Billy approached Brother Guy slowly. "Before I met you bunch of religious nutters, I met another chap who was also concerned about my soul. That was before I started getting good at making sales."

Brother Guy's smile froze.

"We came to an arrangement."

"Who was this man, Billy?"

"He enabled me to achieve self-fulfilment."

"No!" cried Brother Guy. "Stop this blasphemy!"

The other Mithering Brethren began to chant some litany of frustration.

"Thanks to him, I am a success!"

"What was the arrangement?"

"I sold him my soul."

The chanting stopped.

"No!"

"It's true!"

"Billy! Listen to me! I must know about your God-given soul. Wait! I can't believe what you're telling me!"

Billy got back in his car. "Believe it," he said, firing it up.

"But your soul!"

"I told you! The Horsepower Whisperer offered me the deal of deals and I took it. The ability to sell is a bargain at any price!"

The Dodge squirmed under full throttle and powered up the road and around the corner, leaving the Mithering Brethren shrouded in tyre smoke.

Silence remained for a while, apart from an occasional quiet coughing.

"A Soul Trader thwarted us today," said Brother Guy grimly.

"But all is not lost," Sister Elspeth told him softly. "Today we saved the shepherd and the farmer. They failed to protect their flock against our agent. Think how long we have wanted to achieve that aim. We have worked so hard to get at their flock and now, thanks to Billy, we have."

"I know," said Brother Guy, "but Billy's soul is lost! I was so sure we could frustrate him, too!"

"We did frustrate him. We really frustrated him very well."

"But his poor soul! Do you think he was telling the truth? Could he have been just saying it to spite us? Do you think he really has made a deal for his soul?"

Sister Elspeth took some time to answer. "I fear that he has."

"It could have been – should have been – so perfect!"

"There's no such thing as perfection in this Wold," she reminded him. "It is an affront to the Creator. We are personally responsible for many imperfections. We have heightened His glory and contributed to the salvation of many souls. Besides, the Scar Fell Farm flock is at last adulterated, and that means we have finally thwarted the souls of two of the most successful men in the Vale of Wormton. Rejoice, Brother Guy!"

"Rejoice!" echoed the other Mithering Brethren, a little uncertainly.

"Yes, you're right," sighed Brother Guy. "Rejoice."

"We still frustrated Billy," she went on. "We didn't save his soul but we must have improved it a bit."

"Not if a Soul Trader's got it!"

Sister Elspeth looked around them. "Quickly, we must leave the road. You, you and you. Cause a tree to fall across it. Do it on a blind bend. You, lead the others to the top of the hill. I'll follow with Brother Guy."

"Quickly!" Brother Guy called after them. "Tonight we sleep in a safe house instead of out on the moors."

Sister Elspeth smiled. Brother Guy could usually be counted upon to bounce back.

CHAPTER 8

Mr Gaffathwaite and Mr Heckmondwike took some time to pick themselves out of the mud. Their dogs turned up eventually and, seeing something was wrong, tried to make amends by jumping on the men and each other.

"Nobbut a word to anyone about this," muttered Mr Gaffathwaite.

Mr Heckmondwike did not answer immediately. He grabbed his St Punter and threw it into the mud where it spat and sizzled.

"Nay mither," he sighed as he wiped burnt fingers in the wet grass. "He made us climb a gate! Sorry ah kicked thee int groins."

"And ah'm sorry ah kicked thee int groins, n'all."

"Nay mither."

"By 'eck, ah think ah broke me toe! What does tha reckon we ought to do wi' lamb?"

"Keep it apart from t'others, at all costs."

"Best do that now, then."

Mr Heckmondwike helped Mr Gaffathwaite up. "It must've looked bloody funny," he said.

"Mebbe," conceded Mr Gaffathwaite, "but not from where ah'm doubled up."

"Widdershins!" called Mr Heckmondwike.

Widdershins was his three-headed collie. The Greeks may have conceived the idea of a three-headed dog but the Wormtonians had given the concept practical reality through very selective breeding. They had endowed every Three-headed Wormton Sheepdog with, as well as three heads, three tails and twelve legs.

The master stroke, however, was to give each Three-headed Wormton Sheep Dog three bodies. These bodies were completely independent of each other and came complete with a tail and a matched set of legs. The result was a sheep dog that could be in three places at the same time.

Consequently, it was a simple task for Wid, Der and Shins to round up the unfortunate lamb and bring it, bleating and confused, to Mr Heckmond-wike.

He picked up the lamb and examined it while its concerned mother looked on.

"Ah reckon ah'll have to keep an eye on this young rascal mesen, now," he said.

"What does tha suppose he put into it?" asked Mr Gaffathwaite

"Haven't a bloody clue. Ah'll keep this family group together," he said, "but separate from t'rest of t'flock. We can check any changes against its twin." Mr Heckmondwike stared into the eyes of the injected lamb. "What did he do to thee?" he asked it. "Eh? What did he do to thee? And when shall we knaw?"

CHAPTER 9

Mrs Osmotherly's forecast for the next Dark Time was characteristically accurate. Magnetic fluctuations disrupted all electrical equipment. Across the Wold, nothing moved. Even the fires of the Wormton tram's steam engines burned sulkily. People stayed indoors, rather than watch the spectacular aurorae in the darkened sky, and some nursed headaches or even had nosebleeds.

The only person who was active at this time was Mrs Osmotherly. She watched the aurorae unfold from the south and marvelled at the pink flashes given off by the standing stones on the moor but, on the whole, it was not a particularly noteworthy Dark Time.

The following day, everyone felt much better.

"The best thing about Dark Time," Wrainwright said in his book, "is when it stops."

However, that very morning, which seemed brighter than normal, Mr Floridspleen of Gout Leg Pike discovered a sick sheep. It was infected with scab, caused by a mite that feeds off the skin.

An emergency session of Wormton Privy Council was immediately held to address the problem.

Privy had nothing to do with outside lavatories. It was an old word meaning private, but news that the Privy Council was sitting was always imparted with something of a smile.

Mrs Osmotherly had an unelected and non-executive seat on the Privy Council. She didn't contribute much to the debates, but as Wormton's wise woman her role was to warn all ratepayers about the next Dark Time, Erratics and Occasionals allowing. Most wise women found Erratics and Occasionals extremely difficult to predict, but they were no problem for Mrs Osmotherly. What was often beyond her, however, was the sudden change in personality people underwent once within the privy chamber.

Mr Floridspleen and Mr Gaffathwaite were both privy councillors and had plenty to say about the outbreak of scab. Outside the privy council, they were great rivals in the flock market and once inside the privy chamber became the worst sorts of pedants and agenda benders. Mrs Osmotherly initially detected some degree of *schadenfreude* over Mr Floridspleen's misfortune, but this soon evaporated when Mr Gaffathwaite calculated the time, effort and, worst of all, the cost needed to safeguard his own valuable fleeces.

That morning there were all sorts of recriminations, and his indulgence the mayor struggled to direct the debate. Mrs Osmotherly knew that Mayor Naseby wanted to be remembered for his firm handling of the Mithering Brethren, and was constantly vigilant against their dead hand in the smooth running of the WPC. Disaffected WPC commentators, who made up most of the adult population of Wormton, said that the mayor wanted to be remembered for *dealing* with the Mithering Brethren but without actually *doing* anything about them. Mrs Osmotherly felt this was unfair, because it was the schemes and schisms within the privy council that caused his apparent ineffectiveness.

Mr Floridspleen and Mr Gaffathwaite were in agreement about the need to dip the flocks around Wormton as soon as was reasonably possible but it was the question of what was reasonable that sparked an intense debate, and Mayor Naseby became increasingly frustrated, particularly as he undoubtedly blamed the Brethren for the outbreak of scab.

Mayor Naseby was not a charismatic leader. He wore his chain of office over the brown coat that he wore every day behind the counter of his ironmongery shop. "Ah am a man of t'people," he had declared to Mrs Osmotherly on his appointment. "Ah will not hide behind pomp and ceremony," but Mayor Naseby got really cross if anyone referred to him as Mayo. Instead of the tricorne hat mayors normally wore, he chose a flat cap for health reasons.

"Anything else gives me an 'eadache," he said.

He still had to sit in the mayor's chair, however. This stood between rows of elaborately carved pews, so that in a lively debate the privy councillors had him in a crossfire. It was exposed on a raised platform at the head of a large table so well polished he could see his reflection in it. Unfortunately, this depicted a tradesman masquerading as the mayor, which did nothing for his confidence.

There is a saying that behind every great man there is a great woman, and there was an enormous one behind Mayor Naseby. Wormton's first lady sat in the public gallery, looking over his shoulder. From there she would glare at his opponents from under the brim of her hat, the female equivalent of a flat cap but with more fruit. She would also have her knitting with her, and the sound of this was subtly moderated according to who was speaking at the time and how she felt disposed towards them. Obviously, any sort of presence in the public gallery went against the principles of a privy council, but any objections soon withered when exposed to her scrutiny.

This morning she felt it necessary to put down her knitting and rise to her feet, whilst glaring alternately at Mr Floridspleen and Mr Gaffathwaite. She did this without a word, and her air of authority was such that Mr Floridspleen and Mr Gaffathwaite had fallen silent.

Mayor Naseby suggested that 'reasonable' meant by the end of the week, and in the face of no dissent the discussion was ended and his wife sat down again.

"Ah would just like to propose a vote of thanks to Mrs Osmotherly," said Mr Gaffathwaite, "for inventing her safer herbal alternative to conventional sheep dip."

Mrs Naseby's knitting ticked with approval.

"Ah would like to second that," agreed Mr Floridspleen. "Ah think that we would all agree that everyone involved int flock market has enjoyed greatly improved health ever since t'introduction of oregano phosphates."

"Hear, hear," said the rest of Wormton Privy Council.

Mrs Naseby nearly smiled. Rarely did her knitting needles exude such approbation.

Mrs Osmotherly tried to look gracious and not bored.

"Could you record that in the minutes, please, Mrs Blenk?" Mayor Naseby asked the WPC stenographer.

Mrs Blenk nodded and Mayor Naseby clapped his hands as they came to the standing item on the WPC agenda.

"So, what news do we have of t'Mithering Brethren?"

Constable Arkthwaite stood up. "Ower t'last week there has been evidence of Mithering Brethren activity among t'north western farms of t'Outlands," he told them, while Mrs Blenk, the stenographer, rattled the keys of her machine. "Nubuddy has seen owt, o' course, but there have been sheep let out, machinery tampered with and walls pulled down."

Mayor Naseby shuddered.

Mrs Osmotherly knew that the head that wears a crown may lie uneasy but those girdled by the chain of office for Wormton often woke up shouting.

"Does Wormton remain secure?" demanded the mayor.

"Nothing is entirely secure," replied Constable Arkthwaite.

"Aye, ah knaw that, but are t'walls and gatehouses as secure as we can make 'em?"

"Aye, Thine Indulgence. They should protect us from t'deliberate mischief-making of t'Brethren."

"Graidly."

"Some people regard three-metre-thick walls wi' gatehouses as acronicronisms," said Constable Arkthwaite sternly, "but for keeping out destructive religious fundamentalists they're most efficacious."

"Ah'm sure nubuddy here regards t'town's walls as anachronisms," ventured Mrs Hammerhulme of the Knitter's Guild. "Far from it – many of us regard t'town walls as a tourist attraction. Wrainwright certainly did."

"Ah, Wrainwright!" sighed Mr Grandlythorpe, the town clerk. "What would he make of t'Mithering Brethren if he were here today, eh?"

"Mincemeat," said Mayor Naseby, with feeling.

His wife's knitting needles clicked angrily.

"Er, t'walls are rather expensive to maintain," pointed out Mr Whimsleypleat, the town treasurer, but nobody paid him any attention.

"Is the compound secure?" the mayor asked Constable Arkthwaite.

An ugly, wire-fenced compound had been erected next to the New Gate, in which any vehicles too big to enter Wormton could be left.

"Volunteer constables still patrol it at night," Constable Arkthwaite explained, "but compared to t'town walls t' compound is vulnerable to attack. As t'councillors may be aware, since t'erection of t'fence some vehicles 'ave been interfered with. Some of t'Transwold luxury coaches had sugar tipped into their fuel tanks and an articulated pantechnicon ended up wi' sand in its engine."

"Aye, ah remember."

"Mithering Brethren were also seen lurking around Scar Fell Farm again at one point last week, but, ah'm 'appy to say, nay harm appears to have befallen the flock or the estate. Is that still t'case, Mr Gaffathwaite?"

"Aye, 'appen tha's reet," answered Mr Gaffathwaite, a little hesitantly.

"A tree was deliberately felled across t'main road to Mithering," Constable Arkthwaite told them, "but it were discovered by Mr Heptonstall driving his breakdown truck and he heaved it out of t'way and took it home for firewood."

This met with a small ripple of approval from the WPC.

"That's t'way to fight 'em!" said Mrs Hammerhulme. "Turn their wickedness into goodness!"

"Any more evidence of t'safe house you suspect they have?" asked Mayor Naseby.

"None," answered Constable Arkthwaite.

Mrs Naseby's knitting needles, which had positively purred at the news of Mr Heptonstall's firewood, tut-tutted loudly.

"It remains just a theory at t'moment," continued Constable Arkthwaite, "but it is inconceivable that without some sort of shelter close by they could still operate. They have nay form of transport, save Shanks's pony, and little or no camping equipment. And no visible protection against t'privations of t'elements or Dark Time, either."

"Summan's gotta to be givin' 'em shelter," said Mayor Naseby.

"Aye, Thine Indulgence."

"Who then?"

"Ah accuse no-one yet ah accuse everyone."

They all looked a little perplexed. Even Mrs Blenk glanced up from her stenograph.

Constable Arkthwaite sighed. "T'Mithering Brethren should not be able to continue to operate."

"And yet we are still plagued by 'em!" muttered Mr Grandlythorpe, through gritted teeth.

"Somebody, somewhere, is helpin' 'em," insisted Constable Arkthwaite.

"Thank you, Constable," said Mayor Naseby. "We understand thine point. But we are still nay further in identifying t'source of this evident … nay, apparent, aid?"

"Correct, Thine Indulgence."

"How does my learned friend consider t'position of anyone aidin' and abettin' t'Mithering Brethren?"

Justice Jaglinlath, the beakiest of all beaks, puffed out his pale jowls.

"The precedents are clear enough," he began. "In 1734, for offering succour and shelter to an old woman subsequently convicted of witchcraft, one Obadiah Heckmondwike was …"

"Enow of t'historical precedent!" interrupted Mr Floridspleen. "What would we be able to do to 'em today?"

Justice Jaglinlath collected his thoughts. "Without giving you as fully briefed an answer as I believe you deserve, your indulgence, as enemies of the community, the Mithering Brethren could be heavily fined and their property seized, as well as that of those who aid and abet them."

"Ah still fail to understand what they seek to achieve," muttered Mayor Naseby.

"They aim to save the souls of those they thwart," Reverend Chunderclough told them. "I should point out that frustration is not a state they relish themselves. From my research, I have concluded that the Mithering Brethren are motivated by the belief that man was born to sin, that true salvation can only be achieved by being frustrated utterly, and that they can redeem souls by preventing them from doing anything. In the eyes of the Mithering Brethren, anything that we do to improve our earthly lot is a sin, and they are determined to save our souls by seeing to it that we do not succeed in improving our lives."

"But we *do* succeed," put in Mr Grandlythorpe.

"Our success merely makes them more determined," said Reverend Chunderclough. "They genuinely do believe they are holier than thou. Or any of us, come to that. Particularly me."

"Do we think they're growin' in numbers?" asked Mayor Naseby.

"T'range of their activity is consistent with a steady level of membership," Constable Arkthwaite told them.

Now Miss Reeth, the school headmistress, spoke up. "Certainly, members of my teaching staff have kept an eye on any impressionable youngsters within the school, and I am sure that the Mithering Brethren have not recruited anyone recently from my pupils."

"Good," said the mayor. "But ah still worry about t'children growin' up beyond t'walls of Wormton."

"If I may," said Mrs Osmotherly, "I would suggest that because the outlying farms are in the front line, as it were, and experience much greater interference from the Mithering Brethren, their sons and daughters would be completely against the Brethren from a very early age."

This brought conspicuously positive clacks from the public gallery.

"Ah think tha's reet," said Mr Gaffathwaite. "Ah reckon ah speak for all t'Outlanders ..."

"Tha'll nivver speak for me," interrupted Mr Floridspleen.

"... when ah say that reducing or eradicating t'menace is more important than ivver."

"What's this ah hear about a giant lamb at Scar Fell Farm?" asked Mr Floridspleen.

"We have bred a large lamb," Mr Gaffathwaite said simply.

Mr Floridspleen was looking for another argument. Consequently, Mr Gaffathwaite was determined he wouldn't get one. Mrs Osmotherly knew there was a little bit of Mithering Brethren in everyone.

Mrs Blenk looked around them and, seeing there was nothing to be said for a moment, took the opportunity to crack her knuckles.

Everyone winced.

Mrs Osmotherly found herself wondering if they all kept talking to stop her doing this.

"And Mr Quirkmaglen," said the mayor. "Ah think everyone has spoken on this subject to some extent except thee. What is thine opinion?"

Mr Quirkmaglen stroked his chin languidly. He was directly descended from the ancient lords of the Wold and still lived in the apartments of the old castle that occupied the least sunny corner of Wormton's protective walls. Even if he didn't enjoy a guaranteed seat on the WPC, he would probably still be elected onto it by the people who lived, on a grace and favour basis, in what remained of the castle's accommodation.

"The Mithering Brethren continue to be a nuisance," he said after due consideration. "We can only do what we can. However." Mr Quirkmaglen turned towards Mr Gaffathwaite. "A giant lamb, you say. How intriguing."

When it was clear that that was all they were going to get from him, Mayor Naseby said, "Well, ah think that just about sums it up. We follow t'same path as before but wi' renewed vigour!"

CHAPTER 10

"Aye," said Mr Gaffathwaite. "It's big, int it?"

He was in his customary pose, leaning over a gate and chewing a stalk of grass. Next to him was Mr Heckmondwike. They were psyching themselves up for the task of dipping the whole flock in the next few days but were looking at what appeared to be a medium sized but very woolly pony.

"How old would tha say that hogg was?" Mr Gaffathwaite asked Mr Heckmondwike.

Mr Heckmondwike said he knew exactly how old it was because he knew precisely when it was born. However, it was by far the biggest in the Scar Fell Farm flock, although obviously an immature animal.

The lamb lifted its wild and woolly head and gambolled grotesquely towards its contemporaries in the next field. The other lambs panicked and scattered in all directions, leaving the leviathan peering over the wall at them. Even from a distance, the other lambs feared the giant's potentially lethal cloven hooves.

"It misses t'flock," said Mr Gaffathwaite.

"It'll go on missing it then," replied Mr Heckmondwike.

"Does tha think it's stopped growin'?"

"Nay. Ah do not."

"How big does tha think it'll get?"

"Ow should ah knaw? Ah've not come across t'like bayfore."

"Tha can still guess."

Mr Heckmondwike pursed his lips, puffed out his cheeks, blew a small raspberry and took a fresh blade of grass to suck. "At this rate, mebbe three times the size."

"It can't be far off mebbe three times normal size as it is," remarked Mr Gaffathwaite.

"Awreet, then. Four or five times bigger."

"Thing is," went on Mr Gaffathwaite, "is that a good or a bad thing?"

"Bad," said Mr Heckmondwike, straight away.

"Not necessarily. Ah was just wonderin' what it would be like if we were to have a whole flock of t'things."

"How's tha gonna get a whole flock together?" asked Mr Heckmondwike, incredulously.

"We could breed 'em!" Mr Gaffathwaite had gone all glassy-eyed.

"Breed 'em?"

"Aye! It's a female, int it? We could mate it with t'biggest ram we could find!"

"Be no good!" snorted Mr Heckmondwike.

"Why? Why not?"

Mr Heckmondwike pointed at the lamb with the end of his shepherd's crook. "Because that there lamb is not a freak o' nature that we can use in a selective breeding programme. It's an artificial freak caused by that little beggar wi' syringe. Any offspring it might produce will be normal sized."

"Ah ha! Ah see! We'd have to treat the whole flock int same way! Give 'em t'same kinda dose! Whatever that were."

"Aye. Cost a bloody fortune!"

"It didn't look as if he gave it much."

"We dunnaw what he gave it."

"We could find out."

"Still cost a bloody fortune."

"But just think of all that wool! And all that lamb! And then all that mutton!"

"If tha uses thine option on 'all that lamb' tha won't have any mutton," Mr Heckmondwike pointed out to him. "It's like eating thine cake and havin' it."

"And t'lamb chops!" went on Mr Gaffathwaite, dreamily.

"We'd need bigger walls to t'fields. And a new sort of sheepdog. Cattle grids won't work nay more, ayther. Hoggs that size'd just step across 'em in a single stride."

"All that wool though!"

"How would tha shear summat that big?" Mr Heckmondwike demanded. "Breed a bigger New Zealander?"

"Ah wonder if she'll be a good milker?" The pupils of Mr Gaffathwaite's glassy eyes had become pound signs.

"Ah'm sure she'll be an excellent milker," answered Mr Heckmondwike. "She is from thine suckler flock after all. It's just that we'd never be able to get her int byre."

"Think of t'quantity she could produce!"

"Think of t'amount of good pasture needed, n'all! Best part of t'moor ah'll warrant! Even if tha could afford to create a whole flock of those things, tha couldn't afford to keep it! Nay! Not even thee."

At the thought of his all wealth being insufficient, Mr Gaffathwaite seemed to surface from his reverie. He gazed at the lamb as it wandered about by itself. It looked around forlornly and gave a pitiful bleat that was an octave below what one might expect from a lamb that age.

"There will only ever be the one," Mr Heckmondwike assured him. "Come on. Let's send these hoggs for to market."

Mr Gaffathwaite nodded sadly. Then his eyes glazed over and his pupils began to form pound signs again.

"Still, nay harm in trying. Eh?"

CHAPTER 11

Mr Gaffathwaite's blindness to the fey nature of the lamb bothered Mr Heckmondwike. Technically, Mr Gaffathwaite was his master, but Mr Heckmondwike had made the Scar Fell Farm flock what it was today and so it was as much his as Mr Gaffathwaite's. Besides, it was his duty as a shepherd to protect his flock, even if that meant protecting it from the greed of his employer.

As he bounded home that night behind the wheel of his splendid new Wolseley tractor, he felt that it was not just his employer's greed that he had to contend with. The lamb was undoubtedly a freak, but he was not convinced it was entirely a freak of nature. Nor, for that matter, was he convinced it was completely a freak of science.

Some other agency was at work.

His route took him by the field in which the lamb had been nobbled by Billy Brockhouse. He pulled up for a moment and, from his vantage point, looked over the wall at the tall patches of grass that grew there. They were now starting to grow, as well, in the field where the lamb was enfolded and kept isolated.

There was another oddity about the grass. Not far from the gate was a patch of scorched earth, and in the middle of it was something bright. Mr Heckmondwike climbed down from his tractor and entered the field carefully to have a closer look. What had caused the dead grass he didn't like to wonder about, but there was his St Punter. Gingerly, he touched it. It was cool now and he picked it up.

He closely examined the tall grasses. Then he turned on his heel, strode back through the gate and climbed into his tractor.

"Herb don't grow that well without good reason," he told Widdershins in the link box behind him, and he set off for home at Riddaw Lodge.

CHAPTER 12

"I have an idea about Billy's soul," Brother Guy announced to Sister Elspeth, later that same evening.

They were in their safe house, lying low with blankets draped over the windows to deter prying eyes. Sister Elspeth had a small room of her own with bare plaster walls and a crucifix above the bed, where she sat cross-legged. The only other furniture in the room was a table made out of an old cable drum. Both this and the bed overflowed with learned texts.

"What can you possibly mean?" replied Sister Elspeth.

Brother Guy hovered in the doorway. "It concerns the Soul Trader," he began.

Sister Elspeth cleared a space on the bed beside her and patted it.

Brother Guy sat on it with great dignity.

"Billy happened to mention that it was to the Horsepower Whisperer that he'd promised his soul."

"That's right."

"We can redeem Billy's soul from the Horsepower Whisperer by thwarting his soul trading activities."

Sister Elspeth's eyes grew wider and wider.

"Our ultimate aim," went on Brother Guy, "should be to save the Horsepower Whisperer from himself."

"But how do we thwart a Soul Trader?" whispered Sister Elspeth, shocked at the magnitude of his idea.

"We offer one of us as bait. We'll need a volunteer and some evidence of susceptibility to horsepower."

"Like a big fast car."

"Exactly!"

She moved closer. "But what happens if the Horsepower Whisperer successfully corrupts our volunteer with his power?"

"Then we learn from that mistake and try again."

"We could lose many souls that way."

He smiled at her. "Only temporarily. First of all, we pick someone who is not tempted by the lure of horsepower. If the Horsepower Whisperer still gets their soul, then we try with others. It's risky and it's likely that many volunteers will part with their souls before we succeed."

"They will be martyrs!" breathed Sister Elspeth, and her skin glowed with the force of her passion.

"Exactly! Gradually we will learn every cunning stratagem he can muster. So we keep tempting him until he runs out of temptations! As soon as he is thwarted his soul is saved. Once he sees the error of his ways, he will rescind his claim on the souls of the martyrs."

"And all those he has traded for in the past!"

"Including Billy's!"

"Brother Guy – that's brilliant!"

"Thank you," he said.

"Nobody's redeemed the soul of a Soul Trader before!"

"I learnt an important lesson from our dealings with Billy," he told her. "Sometimes we get too used to ensuring failure for others. It is difficult for the thwarter to become the thwartee."

"Do you think horsepower played a part in Hob's bargain for Billy's soul?"

Brother Guy nodded. "You saw the car he drove. But what I still don't understand is why Billy's guardian angel didn't save him."

"They are misguided and capricious creatures," said Sister Elspeth with some feeling. "I don't believe I ever had one. And sometimes they spoil *our* plans! Who can say why Billy's spiritward didn't intervene?"

"A Soul Trader could tell us."

"Once we've saved him from himself," said Sister Elspeth, breathing deeply.

"My idea does have a certain spiritual elegance," Brother Guy was prepared to admit.

"Spiritwards oppose us so much!" exclaimed Sister Elspeth. "A Soul Trader's secrets would aid our work immeasurably!"

A thoughtful silence spread out between them like spilt treacle.

"We are so misunderstood," said Brother Guy at length, in a weary voice.

She put an arm around his shoulders.

"We thwart in the wilderness," she told him, "but He sees us and He understands what we are doing."

They leaned on each other for support and closed their eyes.

"Rejoice," he murmured.

"Rejoice," she whispered.

There was an electric moment full of potential.

Slowly, they opened their eyes again and laboriously disentangled themselves. Brother Guy rose carefully, with his hands in his pockets. He stood in front of her, a little more round-shouldered than usual, searching for something to focus his thoughts on, and at last his eyes came to rest not on the chain of her crucifix, which was hidden in the curve of her bosom, but on the crucifix on the wall behind her.

"We must be steadfast," he told her. "Frustration in our ends is sometimes too hard to bear."

"I am incredibly unfulfilled, Brother Guy."

"I know," he breathed. "It is not good for those who save souls to be thwarted."

"Then perhaps we should indulge ourselves," suggested Sister Elspeth.

Brother Guy's face brightened. "Yes," he said eagerly. Then he frowned. "It's getting late, Sister Elspeth."

"Perhaps we should go to bed."

"No!"

"Whyever not? I was just about to when you came."

"Ah. Right. Well so will I, then. Here I go. Goodnight, Sister."

"Goodnight, Brother."

After he'd gone, Sister Elspeth reached under the cable-drum table, produced a bar of chocolate and began to eat it, deliciously.

CHAPTER 13

Mr Floridspleen declared himself ready for anything the Mithering Brethren could throw at him while he was dipping his flock but, come the day, they were nowhere in sight. The loudly expressed view in *The Golden Fleece* and *The Tin Cur* that same evening was that the Mithering Brethren had been frightened away. A more considered opinion, voiced later in *The Young Farmers* and *The Agricultural Mechanics' Institute*, was that the Mithering Brethren hadn't actually planned anything and could never be realistically expected to attack such a high profile operation.

Once the flock of Gout Leg Pike had been dipped, it was the turn of Scar Fell Farm, and the method would be just the same. The sheep would be rounded up and brought to a complicated network of dry stone walls and enclosures known as Cost-is-lost.

Cost-is-lost lay to the south west of Wormton and some scholars of old stones argued that it may have been the original settlement built by the stone men and much older than the present walled town. Its name indicated that it was either worthless or beyond value. Nobody owned it and it was deserted for much of the year, but at certain times the whole of the Vale of Wormton would descend upon it so that flocks could be sorted, split up or augmented by means of strategically placed gates or collies along its passages.

Wrainwright had gone into raptures over Cost-is-lost and had even flown over it in a dirigible especially transported for the occasion from Bedlam-le-Beans. His balloon arrived on a trailer drawn by a Rolls-Royce Silver Ghost belonging to the Honourable C. S. Bilston-Thingme. Getting the balloon to Cost-is-lost had caused them countless punctures on the stony hill passes, and the aeronauts had joked that they had better not have any more air leaks since they had run out of India rubber glue. On the day, however, the sun had shone and they had enjoyed a faultless flight over the whole Vale, one that had moved Wrainwright to even more intense passages of purple prose. His editor, however, wisely cut these paragraphs and let the aerial photographs speak for themselves.

These showed what had excited Wrainwright so much. From above, the stone passages and enclosures of Cost-is-lost took on the signs of the zodiac. You had to look very closely to see it, for all the characters were in the form of sheep, even Leo and Taurus. Gemini was a push-me-pull-you, Sagittarius a kind of fleecy centaur and Scorpio an aggressive, armoured, multi-jointed sheep with a woolly exoskeleton. Pisces was even weirder with its snorkel and flippers, but once their images had been worked out they leapt off the page at you.

Since Wrainwright's day, Cost-is-lost had grown a number of sheep dips along its southern extremity, and from here freshly dipped sheep went into another series of large fields where they would be observed for a while to check for any post-dipping lameness. This could sometimes occur in warm weather if the dip had become contaminated with a bacterium that could cripple or kill.

All being well, the sheep were then released and driven back to their heafs, unfenced pastures on the edge of the moors in which the sheep habitually grazed. As the high fells are unfenced, it was important to have heafed flocks that would not stray from their own land.

There were just about enough people, and just few enough sheep, to manage dipping the whole Scar Fell Farm flock in a day, but it would be a very long day.

Even Slake had been roped in for dipping duties. Since his return from The Petropolis, he had been very busy helping Mr Heptonstall, who owned the principal garage in Wormton. They had been mortified to discover that the engines in the latest batch of Wolseley Walrus trucks had been poorly assembled, and it was a case of all hands to the machine tools to protect the good name of Wolseley. Slake was confident, however, that he would turn up in time to help with the back shift.

But despite Mr Floridspleen's success at avoiding the attentions of the Mithering Brethren, Mr Heckmondwike and Mr Gaffathwaite still expected trouble.

During the night before the Scar Fell Farm sheep drive, two of Mr Gaffathwaite's most trusted men, Mr Ransomes and Mr Totteridge, took turns to guard Cost-is-lost.

George Ransomes was a bodger, a hedgerow carpenter, who could make a perfectly serviceable chair out of twigs and other naturally shaped pieces of timber. While on duty he bodged up some new gates.

Ted Totteridge, known for packing the strength of two normal men into his nondescript frame, prowled the perimeter of Cost-is-lost.

Soon after sunrise, Mr Gaffathwaite pulled up in one of the Scar Fell Farm Mudlarks.

"Ow ta fettlin', Ted," he said.

"Graidly, graidly, Mr Gaffathwaite."

"And thee, Ted? What sort of night has tha had?"

"Now then, Mr Gaffathwaite. Nowt to get mithered about."

Ted was the human antithesis of a Three-headed Wormton Sheepdog.

His personality wasn't split; it was simply that he should have been born as at least two separate people, and neither of them liked to be ignored.

Shouts and whistles from across the valley heralded the arrival of a mass of Cornucopian Tablebacks.

"Here come our pilgrims," said George Ransomes, taking off his jacket and rolling up his sleeves despite the early morning chill. "Behold their gradual progress as they present themselves for baptism."

A Wolseley tanker pulled up, brimful with Mrs Osmotherly's oregano phosphate, and they quickly emptied it into the dipping troughs.

On the fells above them, figures on foot followed the sheep or rode on lightweight Wolseley motorcycles. Four-wheel-drive Wolsleley Mudlarks took up their positions at strategic points and sheepdogs were everywhere.

The first sheep, a well chosen bellwether, came scurrying down the stone passages and found itself at the foot of a trough of sheep dip. Behind it came others in a relentless but controlled stream.

The bellwether baulked at the sheep dip, nostrils flaring but Mr Gaffathwaite unceremoniously shoved it into the milky liquid. After that, the others followed easily.

George Ransomes gently dunked the head of the sheep under the foaming liquid with a sponge on a pole.

"I baptise thee Aaron," he said.

"It's a female," hissed one of the Teds, still on the prowl for Mithering Brethren.

"All right, then," said George. "I re-baptise thee Aaronetta." He dunked her head under the surface again and then beamed at her. "What a pretty name!"

CHAPTER 14

It was that same day when Mrs Osmotherly finally realised that it was not going to be a giant wolf cub that would shortly threaten the security of Wormton.

She lived a few miles out of Wormton at Diggle, a small, fortified farmstead that stood in a small, fortified farmyard on the north-western slopes of a hill called Deep Doubt. Deep Doubt was a very old name that had probably meant something else in a different tongue many years before, but Mrs Osmotherly liked the idea of a wise woman living in the shadow of Deep Doubt.

Diggle was also undoubtedly very old. It had low doorways so that, if necessary, a single-handed but determined Woldswoman could keep any attackers at bay armed only with her bucket and mop. The need rarely occurred these days, but it was still a comforting thought for someone living on her own.

This morning she felt tired after preparing all the herbal sheep dip for the dipping operations. It was to her own recipe and demand had recently been intense.

As she saw to the goats and her hens and her cow, she pondered on the workings of the motorscope. She wondered about the influence and meaning of Wolseleys, Armstrong-Siddeleys and Jowetts. She worried about the presence of the Soul Trader and she fretted about Demons and Imps. A small part of her was puzzling about the Giant Lamb, an oddity that should have been apparent from some sort of portent in the motorscope. The more she thought about it, the more certain she was that she'd missed something, and the more perplexed she became as to what it might be.

She had business in Wormton that morning, so she drove her car out of its little garage, stopped and got out to shut the doors behind it. When she returned to the driver's seat, there was Indoors Food sitting on the wing of her car staring at the bonnet. He looked at her, looked at the bonnet and looked back at her again.

"Greymalkin?"

The naming of cats is a difficult matter. As far as Mrs Osmotherly's efforts were concerned, it was a case of the right cat and the right colour but the wrong name.

"What are you doing there?" she asked him. "Are you trying to tell me something, Old Grey?"

Indeed he was. He knew all about the modifications that Slake had made to her car even if she didn't. He crouched down, raised his tail into a question mark and rubbed his top lip along the edge of a headlamp.

Mrs Osmotherly looked thoughtful.

"The car. It's something to do with the car, isn't it?"

Indoors slowly closed both eyes and opened them again, giving her an encouraging double wink.

"What is it about the car?"

Indoors willed her on like a teacher with a slow learner.

"I know! You want to come for a ride!"

Indoors looked up at the sky, deeply disappointed. Sometimes it was difficult to believe she was a wise woman at all.

"That is it, isn't it?" She opened the door for him and he thought about it. "Come along, Grey! Puss, puss, puss!"

He stood up, gave her a look just to see if she wasn't having him on and jumped down. He picked his way fastidiously through the mud of the yard, put his front paws on the sill and inspected the interior. He sniffed deeply, his faded grey sides puffing in and out. Then, with an agility that belied his age, he jumped in, curled up on the back seat and stapled himself to the upholstery.

Mrs Osmotherly closed the door, climbed in and turned around to stroke him but Indoors had positioned himself very carefully, and by lifting up his head he put himself just out of reach.

"Contrary old cat," she said and smiled at him.

Indoors was determined not to let her stroke him until she'd worked out the truth about the engine in her car.

They bumped down the rutted track but by the time they joined the main road he was fast asleep. The Citroën suspension system was very much to his taste.

Mrs Osmotherly turned towards Wormton and put her foot down. Sometimes the answers she sought came to her while she was driving, but not today. She drove on automatic pilot until she reached the twisty section where the valley narrowed. The road dipped and rose around the clear running waters of the Wilber Mere and crossed and re-crossed the tracks of the railway line connecting Wormton to Bedlam. The stream played innocently around great boulders, spotted with lichen, and ancient stunted oaks stood like sentinels on the valley sides above, camouflaged in suits of moss.

Mrs Osmotherly saw a couple of motor coaches ahead of her, and she slowed as they wound their way through the gnarled trees and the haze of the bluebells. She soon caught up with a particularly smart example of a sight-seeing coach belonging to Bawdrip's of Beckenckle. It had extra glass panels in its roof and was towing a trailer piled high with rucksacks. She smiled.

This was the first coach load of ramblers that spring and definitely a good portent in anybody's motorscope. She tucked in behind it and soon Mr Grandlythorpe's familiar Wolseley 6/110 appeared in her rearview mirror.

The road might just as well have been a collie chasing a bouncing rubber ball through the valley. It leapt from bank to bank on hump-backed bridges and even skipped across the rather dour permanent way of the Wormton Tramway in crossings that were not so much unguarded as positively reckless.

As soon as the road opened out again, her little car scampered past the coaches, and Mrs Osmotherly sensed surprise at the ease with which it shot by the slower traffic. She checked her rearview mirror to see if either coach was a Guy Wolf or a Leyland Cub but they were both Bedford OBs. Mr Grandlythorpe, in his much bigger car, hadn't enough speed to copy her manoeuvre before the next bend, so he had to tuck in behind the leading coach. Mrs Osmotherly zoomed off leaving them all behind.

Just below Gout Leg Pike, Wilber Mere discharged its contents into the River Mither and the road became straighter towards Wormton. After a quick dash across the downs, Mrs Osmotherly was soon at the East Gate.

The great oak gates were open and the portcullis was up. On either side were stout stone towers that featured arrow slits and cunningly angled gutters and gargoyles for pouring boiling oil, Greek fire, stones, dead animals, soil or sewage onto anyone below with a battering ram.

Nowadays there was also the big sign that read, *Wormton does not welcome careless drivers.*

She pulled up to pass the time of day with the part-time Special Constables on duty.

"Morning, Mrs Osmotherly," said one volunteer. "How ta fettlin'?"

"Good morning to you, Constable Braithclough. I am very well, thank you. And you and yours?"

"Awreet, mind ah'd like a word with thee about our Jenny. She's a bit sickified."

"Oh dear. Perhaps we might talk about it when I've finished shopping."

"Aye. Graidly."

"Good morning, Constable Blenk," Mrs Osmotherly called out to his companion but Constable Blenk was looking behind her at a car that was approaching rapidly from the east, followed at a distance by two overloaded coaches.

"Ay up," he said, "there's Mr Grandlythorpe and ee's in a heck of a hurry!"

The black Wolseley came charging forward, still at great speed. The two constables made way for it to sweep in through the gates but it braked heavily and slewed to a halt alongside Mrs Osmotherly's Deux Chevaux.

"Mrs Osmotherly!" exclaimed Mr Grandlythorpe.

Everyone coughed in the tyre smoke and dust.

"That's a remarkable little car tha hast there!" said the town clerk.

"Thank you, Mr Grandlythorpe."

"Aye! It took off like a bird back there by Wilber Mere. Did tha not see me?"

"I did notice you in my rearview mirror."

The constables grinned.

"Well said, that woman!" laughed Mr Grandlythorpe. "What sort o' punch does that little car carry?"

"Well, I don't know about any punch," demurred Mrs Osmotherly. "I just had young Slake give it a major service a while ago and it's been going well ever since."

"Oh, aye?"

She smiled. "Yes. Almost too well, in fact."

"That's grand, that is. Ah've asked 'im to look at t'cottage hospital ambulances as well as t'Wormton fire engine to see if he can make 'em go quicker. Stuff a bigger motor in 'em or summat!"

"Oh, really?"

"Aye. Mind thee, if he can reap those sort of changes wi' just a service, then a decoke could make 'em supersonic!"

"Well, I suppose if anyone can, Slake can."

"Aye. Tha's not wrong there! That's a real wolf in sheep's clothing tha hast there and nay mistake."

"I beg your pardon?"

"Ah said, 'That's a real wolf in sheep's clothing tha hast there.'"

CHAPTER 15

Everyone had settled into an easy rhythm when, over the sound of the bleating, the sheep dippers heard the sound of an engine. Something familiar was
approaching them at great speed.

Two winters before, a gale had blown through Wormton and a big tree
had come down on Old Mr Irthlingcock's nearly new Wolseley. It had
squashed the middle of his car completely and left the front end staring in
apoplexy at the sky. When Slake had come home from the Petropolis for the
Easter holidays, Old Mr Irthlingcock had received a new Wolseley 18/85
from the insurance company, and his old banana-shaped car was surplus to
requirements. Slake immediately adopted it and incorporated its vital organs
into a trike. One of his arty friends at the Polytechnic christened it *Simurg*,
meaning some sort of weird creature. Slake proceeded to terrify Old Mr Irthlingcock with it, clearly regarding a ride in *Simurg* as a rare treat for the old
gentleman. Much later on, Old Mr Irthlingcock, who was of advancing years
and failing faculties, claimed that he'd thoroughly enjoyed the experience.

Simurg came barrelling up the track to Cost-is-lost so fast Slake
couldn't have had a filling left in his head. It slithered to a halt in the mud,
and Slake disembarked even before the trike was stationary.

"Ow ta fettlin', Mr Heckmondwike? Mr Gaffathwaite?"

"Graidly," said Mr Heckmondwike. "And thysen?"

"Top of the Wold. Mr Heptonstall and I are making good progress with
the Walrus engines, and I've just fired up the first of the cottage hospital
ambulances and it sounds like ripping calico."

"Oh, aye? Is that good then?"

"Indubitably. Things seem to be going my way at the moment."

"Well, praps tha can persuade t'hoggs to do likewise."

"I could watch and tell you where you're going wrong, if you like."

"Tha'll do nay such thing. Make thysen useful by opening and closing
a gate or summat."

Around the newcomer, everyone settled into a slightly different routine.

Slake grinned at the outflanking techniques of the sheep dogs. "It's like
some game of animal chess," he said.

"Aye," grunted Mr Heckmondwike, "white outnumbers black but it is allus black's move."

"Good thing you don't have any black sheep."

Some way off, George Ransomes was saying, "I baptise ewe, Desdemona."

By now the sheep were even making a token effort to dip their own heads beneath the surface but, although the instinct to follow one's bellwether runs as deep as sheep dip, it was obvious that their hearts weren't really in it. So George helped them with his sponge on a pole. Then they would scramble out of the trough and skip through the gate to the lush grass of the water meadows beyond, under the watchful eye of Mr Heckmondwike and one or other of the Teds.

At midday, when the uncharacteristically good weather began to make them really sweat, Mrs Gaffathwaite and some of the women from the dairy brought over a great feast for them in one of the refrigerated vans, and everyone sprawled with sudden indolence in the sun, wherever they could get out of the wind.

CHAPTER 16

Ted had, typically, achieved the work of nearly two men that morning. Many years before, it had occurred to Mr Gaffathwaite that he could pay one man for twice the work but George Ransomes had objected. George knew that, if left to their own devices, Ted and Ted would wear out the body they shared. As physical fatigue set in, Ted would accuse himself of loafing and an argument would break out. George soon learnt to intervene by saying, "Okay, you lot, time to change jobs," and Ted would pause and re-start a little more slowly, doing things slightly differently before carrying on faster than ever.

Consequently, Ted got time and a half although his collective output was prodigious. Any other, more single-minded, employees at Scar Fell Farm who complained about this arrangement were invited to try and keep pace with him.

Mr Gaffathwaite wandered over to Mr Heckmondwike who sat in the lee of his great Wolseley tractor. "Still nay sign o' Mithering Brethren," he said.

"Nay," said Mr Heckmondwike.

"Ah'll keep George and Ted wi' me, just in case. We're making good progress."

"Aye," agreed Mr Heckmondwike. "Ah'll get Mr Kindlysides to replace me. While ah'm patrolling, ah'll fetch t'big lamb."

The hours passed and so did the sheep. Mr Gaffathwaite began to flag. George was moving a little less freely as well, as if he was worried that the aged elastic that held him together was perishing. In his baptisms, he'd got as far as Marionette.

Mr Gaffathwaite looked up and saw Mr Heckmondwike prowling about forbiddingly. Then he lost sight of him and reasoned that he had gone to fetch the injected lamb.

"Hang about!" shouted Mrs Gaffathwaite. She had joined the dipping operations now, and was overseeing the assembly of any stragglers.

Mr Gaffathwaite was grateful for the pause. He stood up and stretched. It was sunny but windy. Occasionally, the wind caught fragments of conversations and flung them to him over surprising distances.

Far away, Slake glanced carelessly over the wall to the sheepfold.

"This one next, Barry?" Mr Gaffathwaite heard him ask Mr Kindlysides.

Mr Kindlysides, a New Zealand sheep shearer who had stayed for a year, looked at the Giant Lamb thoughtfully. Most people looked at it that way. "Naow's as gude a time as inny, mite," he replied.

"Okay. It is pretty big."

"Nah, it ain't. It's bleedin' inormous."

"How are you gonna shear that then?"

"I'll find a way. No worries."

"Is it gonna fit in the trough?"

"Stop iskin' stupid quistions and git on with it."

A very dubious looking Widdershins ushered the Giant Lamb up to the entrance to Cost-is-lost. When it gambolled, the ground shook.

"Oh, boy," said Slake, as it cast a shadow over him. "What a big, er, girl. Nice sheepsy. What a pretty baa lamb. No, don't look at me like that. Come on, through the gate now, there's a good freak."

The Giant Lamb peered down the passageway and sniffed the stones. Then Widdershins did something subtle, like change one of its expressions or lick some of its lips, and the Giant Lamb stepped forward into the network of stone walls. It walked carefully, placing its feet delicately within the narrow confines of the passage. The sides of its fleece were well above the top stones of the walls.

Strange ripples appeared in the surface of the oregano-phosphates with each approaching footstep, although the trough was empty of struggling sheep. From somewhere within Cost-is-lost came the clatter of falling stones. Mr Gaffathwaite prodded a hesitant backside into the trough and felt himself being engulfed by the chill of a shadow. He turned and looked up into the eyes of the Giant Lamb as it loomed over him. He hadn't realised it had grown as big as this. For the first time, it occurred to him that getting it into the sheep dip might prove to be a little awkward.

"Well, is tha goin' in or not?" he asked the Giant Lamb.

The Giant Lamb turned its head to see him better with its monocular vision. It was so tall, Mr Gaffathwaite suspected it could see the horoscope in Cost-is-lost's walls.

"Now then," he said. "Remember me?"

One enormous eye considered him. He wondered what it was thinking. He wondered if it thought. He wondered if any sheep had thoughts. Were they thoughts, but not as we thought of them?

It was not a truly ovine eye. It couldn't just be a question of scale. There was something else about it, something new.

On the extremes of his vision, Mr Gaffathwaite could see two figures approaching. One was his wife. The other was Mr Heckmondwike. Sweat prickled on his brow as he realised that everyone who worked for him was watching.

"Is tha awreet, Mr Gaffathwaite?" asked a voice behind him. It was George.

"Aye, ah'm awreet," he replied gently. "If thee and Ted could just move behind it ont ayther side...."

He sensed their movement, then saw them lurking behind the Giant Lamb. The Giant Lamb watched the two men take up their positions with a mild lack of interest. Its path of least resistance now lay ahead of it, through the trough and out into the pasture beyond. All it had to do now was walk forward and step down into the sheep dip.

"Awreet, then! Let's be havin' ewe," quipped Mr Gaffathwaite, and he brandished his pole, with the sponge on the end of it.

The Giant Lamb put its woolly head down and shook it.

"Ay up, Mr Gaffathwaite, careful as tha goes!" warned George, passing his sponge pole from hand to hand. He gazed at the Giant Lamb for some time. "I baptise ewe – let me see – Mephistophelena!"

"We're reet behind it!" the Teds called out.

The Giant Lamb looked over at the other members of its flock, now drying out in the sun and grazing in the Water Meadows.

Mr Heckmondwike was poised with Widdershins to ensure that it didn't mingle with them

It raised its head and gave out something like a bleat, albeit deeper and more decisive.

The empty liquid in the trough boiled and rippled at the sound as if a drowning sheep was floundering in it. Somewhere, stones clattered as they fell, and George, the Teds and Mr Gaffathwaite held their heads.

Mr Gaffathwaite recovered quickly and hopped over to the other side of the sheep dip, moving around his quarry like a lion tamer behind a chair.

"Careful!" warned Ted.

"Don't tell me, tell him!" he added.

"We've got this end blocked off!" George called out.

The Giant Lamb took a step forwards.

It was time for Mr Gaffathwaite to do or die. He brandished his sponge pole at the Giant Lamb, but to no effect. The Lamb looked at him in a mixture of surprise, disappointment and anger. And he had never seen a sheep look so – there was no other word for it – haughty.

He prodded its flank and it delicately raised a front hoof. It looked at him hard and gave another hideous bleat that gave ample warning of its nature, whatever that might be. It held its head sideways just like one of the farm cats did before a fight. Behind it, George and the Teds were prodding it quite vigorously but to no effect. Mr Gaffathwaite lunged at it again.

This time the Giant Lamb was too quick for him. It grabbed his pole between its teeth and began to nod its head like a frisky colt. Up and down and up and down went the pole, until at last it was shaken out of Mr Gaffathwaite's hands. Expertly, the Giant Lamb flicked its head and let go of the sponge pole, sending it cartwheeling into the sky, and, before anyone could do anything else, it lowered its head and thrust it forward at Mr Gaffathwaite. It scooped him up on its broad nose and jerked him upwards just like the sponge pole. Mr Gaffathwaite spread out his arms and legs in a last desperate attempt to hold onto anything and span, star-shaped, up into the sky.

As he rotated above the Wold, he watched the Giant Lamb step contemptuously over the dry stone walls of Cost-is-lost and run away. Then the sun blinded him. He stopped rising and there was a sickening point of weightlessness before he fell back to earth.

But he couldn't even get that right.

He scattered the upturned faces of his earthbound employees but missed the ground and fell straight into the sheep dip.

CHAPTER 17

Quickly, they hauled Mr Gaffathwaite out of the trough.

"Is he all right?" asked Slake.

Mr Gaffathwaite groaned and coughed up some sheep-dip.

There was a strong smell of oregano.

"Reckon he'll live," said Mr Heckmondwike. He peered into the distance. Slake followed his eyes and saw the Giant Lamb was already on the far side of the Water Meadows, still moving fast.

"How are we gonna catch it now?" asked Slake, thinking out loud.

The Giant Lamb reached a small wood beyond the Water Meadows. Over the distance, there came the sound of groaning and crashing trees. Then the Giant Lamb reappeared, accelerating rapidly out of the Vale of Wormton.

"Ah dunnaw lad," answered Mr Heckmondwike. "We'll worry about that once we've got Mr Gaffathwaite looking a better colour."

"Yes, he does look rather pale."

"Well, wouldn't you after being dipped in sheep dip!" Ted pointed out. "And being butted," he added.

They became vaguely aware of a car drawing up nearby. As the Giant Lamb disappeared over the horizon, the driver got out and began to accost them.

"Listen to me!" she said. "You're all in terrible danger!"

"What?" said George. "Again?"

They turned around and saw a very agitated Mrs Osmotherly.

"And you, Slake, are in deep trouble."

"Why?" he asked.

"The Wold is going to be visited by a terrible giant lamb!"

"What?" said George. "Another one?"

"Yes. I don't know when, but soo ..." She frowned "What do you mean, another one?"

"Well, there was one here just now," replied Ted. "Aye," he pondered. "A bloody great beggar!"

Mrs Osmotherly sagged profoundly. She sat down on a low wall and put her head in her hands. They began to wonder if she was crying.

"Too late," she moaned. "I'm too late!"

"It butted Mr Gaffathwaite," George told her.

"Too late," she repeated.

Mr Gaffathwaite groaned.

"Shouldn't we irrigate his eyes or something?" asked Slake.

There was an uneasy silence apart from the sound of the wind buffeting them. Even the sheep were quiet now.

Mrs Osmotherly looked up. "If it hadn't been for you, Slake, none of this would've happened!"

"Me?"

"Yes! You!"

"What? How d'you work that out?"

She stood up. "If it hadn't been for you, I would have foreseen all this."

"Oh yeah? Like how?"

"I would have charted the future properly."

"Come again?"

"I would have interpreted the motorscope correctly."

"What the hell are you talking about?"

"You souped up my 2CV, didn't you?"

"Yes! All right! So I souped it up. But you didn't notice! You said how well it was going! You liked it!"

"How many times do I have to tell you, Slake? I don't know anything about cars! I just know what they mean!"

"I was doing you a favour!"

"No, Slake, that's one thing you were *not* doing. I didn't want a quicker car! If I did, I would've gone out and bought one!"

"But I made you a special!"

"I didn't want a special! You were supposed to just service it, not soup it up and make a kind of freak out of it. You made a freak out of it and I didn't realise!"

"So what?" demanded Slake.

The other men were drawing away from him. It was not a good idea to argue with a wise woman, but there he was, doing it.

"There were signs in the motorscope ..."

"Signs? Road signs, I suppose!"

"Yes! All manner of road signs! I warned you about them, remember?"

"What? All that nonsense about Hillman Imps, Dodge Demons and blown Vincents?"

"I gave you specific instructions!"

"Yeah and I followed them. Look. Just what, exactly, am I supposed to've done wrong, Mrs Osmotherly?"

Mr Heckmondwike and the others looked at her in silence. They wanted to know as well.

She took a few steps forward.

"I knew that there was evil abroad in the Wold as soon as I saw the blown Vincent," she told them. "It portended the Soul Trader. Slake? Does the name Nick Hob mean anything to you?"

"Yeah! He's the Horsepower Whisperer!"

"So you've heard of him?"

"Of course! Everyone in The Petropolis has! He rides in the Wild Hunt with the *Terminal Murrain*!"

"And you know what you would sell to him if your paths crossed?"

"He wouldn't have my soul!"

Mrs Osmotherly shook her head sadly. "The Master of the Engine Henge would have it if he wanted it!"

"No. No way. Not me. Not mine!"

"As soon as I knew he was in the Outlands, I looked for other signs. I searched and I found clues, but there was nothing conclusive. I had no proof. The final part of the jigsaw was missing."

"But tha has it now, though, hasn't tha, lass?" said Mr Heckmondwike.

"Yes. It was Mr Grandlythorpe who made me realise what I'd over-looked."

Again, she paused. She stared at Slake, fixing him with a terrible glare. He didn't want to ask her, but she was willing him on. "Which was?"

"A wolf in sheep's clothing."

"Ah," sneered Slake. "You mean your car!"

"Yes! Do you know what this means?"

"You were driving around in the clue you were looking for!"

"Yes!"

"All this time you were driving around looking for clues in your own car. And that was the clue you were lookin' for!"

"Exactly. Thank you for spelling it out for me! And I never even knew! And do you know what else I found out? The motorscope is interactive! My journeys with my wolf in sheep's clothing produced the Giant Lamb!"

"Oh, no! I'm not having this!" declared Slake. "You're mad, completely off your rocker! You can't blame me for that sheep freak … thing!" He glanced back towards where they had last seen the Giant Lamb. There was no sign of it now. "That lamb was created by that bloke from BiggaBeast, the growth hormone pusher, nobody else!"

"But Slake! If only you hadn't souped up my car without telling me! I would have discovered all this so much earlier!"

"This is just nonsense," replied Slake. "I don't believe any of this. You couldn't foresee anything! And if you could've foreseen it, you couldn't have done anything about it!"

"That's not true, Slake. The motorscope's interactive!"

"Fine sort of wise woman you are! You're trying to cover up your own shortcomings, your own shortcomings as a seer! And I'm not sticking around to be insulted! I might just do something that you'll regret! Trouble's goin'!"

In one continuous movement, Slake leapt into *Simurg*, fired it up and floored the throttle. *Simurg* squatted and two great rooster tails of stones and soil shot out from its front wheels as he shouted "Trouble's gone!" over the engine noise and turned it around for Wormton. When the fallout of his anger began to rain down over everyone else, his tyres bit the stones of the track and he shot off down the valley.

"Oh, what a mess," groaned Mrs Osmotherly.

"Ah think tha should take a look at Mr Gaffathwaite," said Mr Heck-mondwike. He touched her arm ever so lightly. "He doesn't look too clever."

CHAPTER 18

Mr Gaffathwaite was rapidly yet comfortably taken home by souped-up 2CV and put to bed. It was not altogether clear whether he was conscious or not. Mrs Osmotherly had examined him by the side of the sheep dip and assumed that he was in a deep state of shock. The only thing to do was to get him dry, and put him to bed in a well-ventilated room where Mrs Gaffathwaite could keep a close eye on him.

Mr Heckmondwike put Ted and George in charge of dipping operations and went off to follow the tracks of the Giant Lamb. Without the disturbing presence of the Giant Lamb, every living thing felt a lot more comfortable, and the dogs, sheep and men finished their business in double-quick time. When at last George said, "I baptise ewe Zucchini and I baptise ewe Zymotia," the light was waning.

The workers had been drifting away for some time before that, and it didn't take long to clear everything up as Zucchini and Zymotia were escorted back to their heafed pastures.

The Teds suggested they popped back to Scar Fell Farm to check on Mr Gaffathwaite, and George offered to accompany them.

"Ah suppose, Mr Heckmondwike won't rest until t'Giant Lamb's enfolded again," mused Ted, as he climbed aboard a Mudlark.

"Reckon as as like 'appen as maybe tha's reet," replied George.

He thumbed the starter of the Mudlark and they burbled their way over to the farmhouse.

Daisymaid was standing on the kitchen table when they entered. She was coaxing a kitten down from behind the dinner plates on the topmost shelf of the big dresser.

"Ee, the rascal!" Ted said. "How did ee get up there?"

"Well, Daze, 'appen tha's got thine work cut out there and nay mistake," agreed George.

"Well, don't just stand there gawping, ya daft morpeths! Why don't you give me a hand?"

The spontaneous burst of applause they gave her was not at all what she had in mind.

"You're going to make me cross in a minute!" she told them but, try as she might, she couldn't help smiling.

So the two or three old men stopped admiring her ankles and clambered up onto the kitchen table beside her, and the three or four of them managed to corner the tabby kitten who, by now, had got bored with the game anyway. But instead of thanking them, Daisy scolded them for the mess on the table.

"Look at all that mud! Didn't your wives ever teach you anything?"

"One day, Daze," George told her, "tha'll make a happy man very clean. Anyroadup, where is everyone?"

"Upstairs. They've been up there ever since they came back."

"How's Mr Gaffathwaite?" asked Ted.

"What do you mean, how is he?" Daisy vigorously scrubbed the tabletop.

"He were sent back unconscious," George said dreamily as he watched her.

Daisy stopped scrubbing "Really?"

"Aye," he went on. "The sheep butted him."

"The sheep?"

"Aye. T'Giant Lamb, tha knaws."

"Nobody told me. I've been slaving away down here all the time."

"In between playing wi' this little chap, eh?" Ted remarked. "Ah, tha little sod! Keep tha pins in, will tha!"

"It's not serious is it?" Daisy asked them.

"Nobbut a scratch," Ted said, checking his calloused hands.

Daisy rolled her eyes and put her hands on her hips.

They loved it when she did that.

"Not you! Mr Gaffathwaite!"

"Ah dunnaw. We were hopin' tha could tell us."

Without another word, they set off upstairs. Behind its ordered façade, the farmhouse had evolved organically. Generations of Gaffathwaites had played hide and seek in its peculiar corners. Daisy, as a farmhand's daughter, had been a participant in these games, just as Ted had been in his youth. Daisy, being young and lissom, was still in demand for games of sardines when the Gaffathwaite's grown-up brood came home. Ted only had a dim recollection of the layout of the old house. He was always in two minds at every turning, and his limbs were stiffening up.

George had never been inside Scar Fell Farm before, apart from the kitchen and Mr Gaffathwaite's office. He followed Daisy up the stairs and took the opportunity of admiring her ankles as they skipped about in front of his eyes.

She paused outside the master bedroom and listened at the door before knocking. Ted and George just caught up with her as she entered and, with their caps respectfully in their hands before them, they shuffled in behind her.

They were a little surprised by their employer's bedroom. Many years ago, the Gaffathwaites had holidayed in Lanson and visited the Quintessent Dwelling Exhibition. This had had a profound effect upon Mrs Gaffathwaite who had re-decorated their home as soon as they had returned.

Mrs Gaffathwaite and Mrs Osmotherly were sitting on opposite sides of the bed, with Mr Gaffathwaite between them. He was still unconscious under a huge flouncy bedspread that threatened to engulf everyone in the room, never mind the sleeper beneath it.

"Begging your pardon, mum, but Mr Totteridge and Mr Ransomes here told me that Mr Gaffathwaite had been took bad."

"He's tough as old boots," said Mrs Gaffathwaite. "He'll probably be as right as rain tomorrow."

"I wouldn't be at all surprised," said Mrs Osmotherly. "I just hope he hasn't swallowed much of the sheep dip."

"Oh, he's absorbed enough oregano-phosphate over the years to kill twenty ordinary men. You mark my words, he'll be fine."

Mrs Osmotherly smiled at her good sense.

"But did tha see t'bruises on his shoulders? I meant to ask when we were puttin' him in his pyjamas."

"That must be from when the lamb butted him," said Ted. "He did fly up in the air a bit," he added.

Mrs Osmotherly examined Mr Gaffathwaite's shoulder closely. "Hmm. That's odd. There's bruising, which is only to be expected, but also the hair over the area of trauma has been turned white. Have you ever noticed that before?"

Mrs Gaffathwaite had a look and pulled a face. "Nay, Mrs Osmotherly. Ah don't really like hairy backs. Ah'm sure ee nivver had owt like that bayfore. And whenivver did ee start growing those mutton-chop whiskers?"

"It's probably nothing," said Mrs Osmotherly, in the unfortunate tone that suggests that, actually, this is really important. "The main thing for him is to have rest. He's had a terrific shock. Sleep is a great healer."

"Shall I call the doctor?" asked Daisy.

All present considered the suggestion.

Daisy sighed. "I know. Stupid question," she admitted.

"Reckon Daisy just wanted to do t'best for him, Mrs Osmotherly," said Mrs Gaffathwaite.

"Then we should not involve Dr Worstedwright," replied Wormton's wise woman.

"Fair enough," said Daisy. "Is there anything else I can do to help?"

"Aye that goes for us n'all," said Ted.

Mrs Osmotherly smiled. "Thank you, no. At least, not for the time being. If you can be of any assistance we'll let you know."

"Aye, just so long as tha does," said George.

"I'll make some tea for us all then," said Daisy. "I expect you're all very hungry."

Their faces said that they were but hadn't given it a thought.

"Right, well, I'll go and sort that out then."

CHAPTER 19

Once she had left Mr Gaffathwaite in the capable hands of his wife, Mrs Osmotherly drove back to Wormton without sparing the horses, straight to Bessie Dooker's. Bessie Dooker ran Wormton's principal scrapyard. There were one or two smaller ones, but Bessie Dooker's was the biggest, and occupied one of the first areas to become de-populated as the old town had gone into decline.

Mrs Osmotherly pulled up outside the solid-tyred bus that served as an office. Although it was well past Bessie's normal opening hours, she knew Bessie Dooker lived on site. Bessie's moon face appeared at the back of the bus, and Mrs Osmotherly told her that she was to ensure that her car was scrapped immediately.

"Don't sell off any bits of it, to anybody," Mrs Osmotherly insisted.

"There's not much call for Citroën parts in Wormton," Bessie Dooker replied. "Thine is t'only one."

"So much the better, then. Nothing must be left remaining of this car. Do you understand? Nothing. Here's thirty pounds. Make sure that it is totally destroyed."

"Hang on a minute …" Getting a car and money as well was beyond Bessie's experience.

Mrs Osmotherly brought out her purse again. "Here's another ten pounds if you carry out my instructions to the letter. All right?"

"Awreet."

"Totally destroyed," insisted Mrs Osmotherly.

"Totally destroyed," Bessie echoed.

"Nothing of it is to remain."

"Nowt of it is to remain."

"And no parts are to be sold on."

"'N nay parts are to be sold on."

"To anyone."

"To anyone. 'Sept to Slake."

"Especially not Slake!" bellowed Mrs Osmotherly.

Bessie Dooker stared at her in terror.

Mrs Osmotherly turned on her heel and strode out of the yard.

Bessie Dooker breathed out again. Mrs Osmotherly was usually more composed. Bessie began to wonder what was so dangerous about a small, green 2CV. She approached it cautiously and peered through its windows.

"Excuse me," said somebody, through clenched teeth.

Bessie Dooker shrank back.

Mrs Osmotherly had returned.

Without another word, she opened one of the rear doors and unhooked an elderly grey cat from the back seat. He was quite well fixed there, and she paused half way through detaching him to see if rigor mortis hadn't set in. But, as she lifted him from the car, the old cat opened a bleary pair of yellow eyes in a vaguely curious manner, as if to say, "Couldn't you keep it down a bit, please?" Mrs Osmotherly hoisted Indoors Food over her shoulder and walked out of the scrapyard with Bessie still holding the money in front of her.

Mrs Osmotherly walked purposefully towards the centre of town, leaving the overgrown, deserted back lots behind her.

Indoors looked torpidly at the receding view over her shoulder. These days he couldn't sustain any level of interest for very long, so he licked Mrs Osmotherly behind her ear, which he found strangely soothing, and then settled down to sleep again.

Mrs Osmotherly made straight for Mr Heptonstall's garage. He was just shutting up shop when she hove into view. She marched right up to him and insisted that she buy a car from him, immediately.

Hiding his surprise, he asked her if she had anything in mind.

"Something small and economical," she replied.

"A Wolseley Mini, perhaps?"

"Yes. That would do fine. Thank you, Mr Heptonstall," she added, relaxing a little, but beginning to feel the weight of her cat. "I'll have that one," and she pointed at a car in the showroom.

"Certainly, Mrs Osmotherly. Does tha want a test drive?"

"No thank you."

"When would tha like it delivered?"

"Delivered? I must have it now."

"Er, now?"

"Yes. Why? Is there a problem, Mr Heptonstall? I've got to get home."

"Nay, nay, Mrs Osmotherly. Nay problem, tha knaws, it's just that it just seems so precipitous like, so out of character, if ah may. Tha's taken me quite aback. And there was thee, only this forenoon, in that little green car o' thine, without a care int Wold."

"So I was. But that was then. This is now. I'm afraid I need another car."

They entered the showroom, which was more room than show. A pair of Wolseley Minis and a new Wolseley 6 looked a little lost. On the back wall was a large yellowing poster depicting two smiling men in old fashioned clothes. Underneath was a caption – *Enjoying the new Wolseley, gentlemen?*

Advertising had never really been necessary to sell Wolseleys to the upwardly mobile of Wormton, but Mr Heptonstall still had a go. Besides, the posters brightened the place up. He wanted to live in a world where they really did ask gentlemen if they were enjoying the new Wolseley.

"Does tha have a part exchange?"

"No, I don't."

"Nay?" To Mr Heptonstall, not pursuing this line of enquiry suddenly seemed very sensible. "Aye, well then. That's grand then."

"How much is a new Wolseley Mini?"

"It depends on the specification, tha knaws. Tha can have one with a boot or without a boot. There are two engine sizes, a litre and a thirteen hundred."

"How much is this one?"

Mr Heptonstall gently guided her attention to the windscreen sticker. It consisted of the slogan *Buy wisely; buy Wolseley* and an optimistic asking price that usually served as the opening gambit for long-drawn-out negotiations.

Mrs Osmotherly produced her chequebook and wrote out a cheque for the asking price. "Here you are."

"Er, thank you, Mrs Osmotherly. Thank you very much."

Obviously there was money in being a wise woman.

Mr Heptonstall actually bowed to her. He'd met tough customers before, but never such an awe-inspiring purchaser

Mrs Osmotherly opened the door of the Wolseley Mini and poured Indoors over the back seat. From the tips of his extended forepaws to the end of his tail he stretched from one side of the car to the other.

"Is there any fuel in it?" she asked Mr Heptonstall.

"Aye, a little. But allow me, Mrs Osmotherly. Ah'll top it up wi' some premium quality brew to help thee on tha way."

"Thank you, Mr Heptonstall. You are, indeed, most kind."

Still she did not smile.

Mr Heptonstall began to push the showroom door open. "Please be sure to read t'runnin'-in instructions and familiarise thysen wi' controls."

She opened the glove box, flicked through the owner's handbook and found the gremlin-containment psalm at the back, written in Mr Heptonstall's best copperplate handwriting.

"May ah ask what happened to thine little green Citroën?" he asked, once she was safely outside.

"It's been scrapped."

"Oh aye?"

"Yes. Now, if you'll excuse me, I need to cover a great deal of miles in a short space of time using a Wolseley. The development of the motorscope

and all our futures depend upon it."
  "Oh aye? Ah'd best fill it up then."

CHAPTER 20

Slake arrived home in a thoroughly bad mood and threw himself into his workshop. He cut and hammered and welded for nearly four hours, and if he'd had any neighbours they would have emigrated. Gradually he began to tire and at last succumbed to a cup of tea.

It was as he was mulling over the preposterous charges levelled at him by Mrs Osmotherly that he heard a knock at the door. When he opened it, he was surprised to find that darkness had fallen, and a cowled figure stood just beyond the arc of his outside light.

"Can I help you?" asked Slake.

"Dark Time is upon us," said the newcomer, without any introduction. The voice was dramatically hoarse and rasping with a crude disguise.

Slake looked up the sky. He'd been so self-absorbed that Dark Time had crept up on him.

"Looks like a bad one tonight," he said. "The quiet ones are always the worst." He turned back to his visitor. "What can I do for you?"

"Are you the engine tuner?"

"I may be. Who wants to know?"

"An enthusiast."

"Then come forward and be recognised," said Slake, folding his arms over his chest.

"I regret I cannot. However I can make you an attractive offer." The figure produced a small box and waved it. It rattled richly.

"What's your name?"

"I am Brother ... Mr Brother."

"And what do you want from me?"

"I want a car souping up. I want one that can run with the best in the Wild Hunt."

"Any particular class?"

"No. Er, Open Class, I think."

"You don't actually know what you want, do you?"

"Not really, no," admitted the cowled figure. "I just want something worthy of the Wild Hunt, something to humble onlookers and to make skir-rows offer up their souls for it."

"You don't look or sound like a skirrow, but you speak the right language, my friend."

"I have money," said the figure. It made a flourish and seemed to peel back the night, but it was really a black sheet covering a black car in the dim light.

Slake peered at it in disbelief. "That's a 24/80 Blue Streak, isn't it?"

The cowled figure said nothing but seemed to swell with the barest hint of pride.

Slake walked over to it and Mr Brother withdrew into the shadows as he approached.

"It's not in bad nick," he said, after a close look, "but did you push it here under cover of Dark Time?"

"It's got cop brakes, cop suspension and a cop transmission," went on Slake's potential client.

"Really?" Slake opened the bonnet.

"Well, that's what the last owner told me. He said it had a pursuit motor as well."

"It probably was a pursuit motor," said Slake, looking at the oil on the dipstick and a mayonnaise-like deposit on the inside of the oil-filler cap. "It's a bit tired now. Whaddya want me to do with it?"

"Soup it up please."

"Was this the one advertised in *The Piston Wheel* last week?" Slake had a good memory for prospective bargains. He'd read the spec on the ad and decided it was expensive for what it was.

"It might have been," said the other.

"Do you want to keep the silhouette?"

This was an important question. The answer would determine whether it was pitted against other Blue Streaks or even more competitive specials.

"Er. Yes."

Slake wasn't sure as if his question had been understood. "Okay," he said. "It'll need a de Dion rear end. I mean you can forget about the cop rear end if you wanna be really competitive."

"That sounds perfect."

"I can do it in a couple of weeks."

"Really? Couldn't you make it one?"

"I could, but it'll cost you."

"Very well." The cowled figure produced another rattly pencil box.

"How many more of those have you got tucked in there?"

The cowled figure said nothing, but placed the rattly pencil boxes on the bootlid.

"Hah!" said Slake. "Just wait until I tell Mr Heptonstall!"

"Er, no. I must have complete secrecy."

Slake looked around for the cowled figure. It had melted into the shadows completely.

"You don't have to worry about Mr Heptonstall," Slake said.

"Nevertheless," said the now unseen figure, "I really must insist that you tell no-one about your commission. Otherwise, I withdraw the offer."

"Not much incentive if I can't crow about it."

"I have left my money on the boot lid."

Slake picked up a pencil box, slid the lid back and gasped. Although it was Dark Time, his face lit up with a golden reflection. A breeze rustled the thickets around Frogheat.

"Half now, and the rest on completion. Do we have a deal?"

Slake composed himself and said thickly, "We do." He turned around with arm outstretched to shake on the deal in the time-honoured fashion, but nobody came forward. And after a few minutes of waiting it became obvious he was alone.

CHAPTER 21

The following Sunday, Mr Heckmondwike drove into Wormton as usual, but everyone in *The Tin Cur* or *The Golden Fleece* and especially *The Young Farmers* wanted to talk of nothing else but the extraordinary lamb still at large on the moor. From perpetually answering the same questions, Mr Heckmondwike soon felt like a cracked gramophone, and by late afternoon he craved the company of someone with a different obsession.

So he decided to visit young Slake, who, it was said, now occupied an old forge in Park Bottom, a particularly run-down part of town.

The streets in Park Bottom had once been wide enough to take a flock of sheep, but now they were narrowed to a single track with occasional passing places of crushed vegetation. Grass grew up the middle of the road as if it were a country lane and, occasionally, the outline of once impressive buildings could be made out. Here and there, against the darkening sky, the chimney of a hapless traction engine could be seen poking up out of the brambles. Elsewhere, the raised arm of a hay turner, entwined with bindweed and honeysuckle, made a silent and unanswered summons for assistance as it was dragged down under the greenery, perhaps with a tractor still attached at the other end.

It was clear something much larger than a Mudlark had recently burst through the undergrowth. Here and there, trees had been chainsawed. Great broken vines dripped sap onto the road. Mr Heckmondwike's Mudlark groped its way along with its headlamps. Even in its warm cab, he could smell recently disturbed earth.

A light flickered between the trees and he came into a clearing. Here were the remains of a proper tarmacadam surface, and somebody had uncovered an iron water hydrant by the kerbside. Ivy-covered buildings stretched back into the darkness, but one of them, proudly bearing an outside lantern, was recognisable as a house. Another clue stood under a tin roof on stilts – *Simurg*, Slake's trike.

Every town has dundyards and idlings. Already renowned for its mossy roofs, ivy-clad walls and bushes growing on chimney stacks, Wormton had many sheds and yards harbouring disused machinery, more than was good for any old town. Slake had investigated each one before settling on Frogheat.

There were other vehicles littered around the yard, but Mr Heckmond-wike did not think Slake had company. He parked his Mudlark by the water hydrant and encouraged Widdershins to get out, but it didn't like this wild wood, even if it was within the great walls of Wormton. Widdershins looked nervously at the trees around it and licked its various noses to clean away unfamiliar smells.

Over the sound of the light rain on the tin roof, Mr Heckmondwike could hear someone singing along to a gramophone record, a song about all the young dudes. He went up to the back door and knocked. Abruptly, the singing stopped but the music didn't, and shortly afterwards the door opened.

"Mr Heckmondwike!" exclaimed Slake enthusiastically. He resembled a bleary-eyed, oil-stained dormouse. "You found the place all right, then?"

"Aye."

"Whaddya reck?"

"Reckon it suits thee down t'ground," said Mr Heckmondwike, looking at all the boxes stacked up in the rooms on either side. "No mother to mither thee here, lad."

"No. I can make as much mess as I like."

"And ah can see tha has, lad. Well done."

"Fancy that spin in my trike?" Slake was reaching for his crash helmet.

"Nay," Mr Heckmondwike said, hastily. "Ah ate just before ah came out."

"Fair enough," said Slake. "I'd show you around except it's dark."

"Not necessarily a bad thing," replied Mr Heckmondwike.

Instead of ushering him into the house, Slake ushered him out of it. "D'you like my new Wolseley? Mrs Amplepance gave it to me!"

"Gave it to thee?"

"Yeah. She's given up driving and has owned it from new. She thought I would like a car with a roof."

"That, lad, is an element of *Simurg* that is decidedly lacking."

"I must admit that I had not allowed for the annual plashfall in Worm-ton when I designed it."

"Design? Who's tha trying to fool?"

"It's really no good, Mr Heckmondwike," said Slake in a mockingly patronising tone. "Your jealousy is quite transparent to me."

"Ah would say that tha's blinded to t'inadequacies of t'freak tha's created. It's only got three wheels."

"It's minimalist."

"It may be minimalist, but if tha thinks ah'd willingly sit beside thee with our guardian angels pleading with us as we hurtle towards certain doom, then tha's not all there. Just like thine trike."

The grin Slake had been trying to suppress suddenly broke surface, but he managed to turn it into an expression of mock outrage. "Just what are you trying to say, Mr Heckmondwike, hmm? Come along. Out with it!"

"Ah do not consider mysen to be a coward, tha knaws, but t'underwear to contain my emotions provoked by a ride in that thing has yet to be invented."

"Well, if it's just a question of heavy duty underwear that's stopping you ..."

"The answer is still nay."

Slake nodded.

Mr Heckmondwike continued to hold him with his gaze to emphasise his point.

Slake nodded again and glanced at the floor, thoughtfully. "Of course," he said, looking up again, "if ever you change your mind ..."

"Nay, no, nivver. Nay, no, nivver no way! Ah decline, ah refuse, ah reject, ah repulse and ah rebuff thine offer to appear int next life down there before ma time up 'ere is fully ower."

"Spreading such disappointment amongst your closest friends won't help."

"Ah'm not goin' in it and that's final."

"I could drug and kidnap you."

"Thine soul would turn black!"

"Would it? I'd better not do it, then, had I?"

"Nay, lad."

"I still reckon I'll get you in it one day."

"Nivver."

"And you'll thank me afterwards."

"Ah am convinced that there would be no afterwards in which t'opportunity could arise."

"Poor deluded shepherd! Let's agree to differ on the whole question. Then I can invite you in as if you're an entirely rational being."

"And ah can hide any sharp objects with which tha may use to pursue this death wish o' thine."

Mr Heckmondwike paused to peer at the gleaming black Wolseley 8 that stood next to *Simurg*. "Hey, lad. Is that mileage reet?"

"Yep. That envelope on the back seat contains its service history and provenance. Everything since 1947. And," he added, dropping his voice, conspiratorially, "its original invocation to the gremlins is still intact."

"Aye. Ah don't doubt it. It looks like new. Tha knaws this little car's wasted on thee."

"Yeah. It has a certain charm, but it's not really me. Don't worry though. I won't soup it up. Mrs Amplepance was quite clear about that."

"Would she ever find out, though? Look at Mrs Osmotherly."

"That's true."

Slake ushered the shepherd and his dogs inside and down a passage.

Along t'way, Slake threw open doors left and right, and showed Mr Heckmondwike a variety of lathes and milling machines
    "I had all this gear shipped up from my old place in The Petropolis last
week," he explained. "There's more to come. Here I will be able to make all
sorts of engine modifications."
    "Starting with a cottage hospital ambulance?"
    Something vaguely medical lurked in the gathering gloom outside.
    "That's right."
    Mr Heckmondwike grunted. He couldn't really see the point. Surely if
an engine needed modifying, you took it back and got one that didn't.
    "And look over here!" Slake said reverentially, approaching a complic-
ated apparatus. "With this rig I can even gas-flow my own cylinder heads!"
    "Appen?" said Mr Heckmondwike, hoping this was the correct response.
Slake beamed at him.
    "What ever will tha think of next?" added Mr Heckmondwike, but nothing
could touch the nascent horsepower whisperer in his little bubble of euphoria.
    "And this is the drawing-board room," he announced.
    The walls were either covered in bookshelves full of manuals or wall-
papered in design-engineering drawings. In the middle of the room, underneath a clerestory roof and a magnificent oil lamp, was a massive drawing
board. The room had originally been conceived for entertaining, but evidence
of a creative flux was everywhere. Notebooks and tools were scattered on
every horizontal surface as if they'd just been dropped as another idea had
occurred to whoever had been holding them. Manuals lay everywhere and on
the mantelpiece was the usual skirrow reading matter – Thrupp's *Wild Hunt
Chronicles*, popularly known as *The Vrooms Day Book*, the famous guide on
horsepower whisperers and engine tuners called *Whose Watts?* and a selection
of heroic epics and verse including *Motion in Poetry, Lyrical Torque* and *The
Song of The Machine*. In some corners there were engine components in cardboard boxes. Everything had the mark of slightly oily hands about it.
    Despite this, the drawing-board room was surprisingly comfortable. It
certainly had Slake's relaxed and easy style all over it. Despite his recent
impact upon the place, the windows were already being reclaimed by con-
volvulus, and several small tendrils had even crept inside. If it smelt a little
damp, it was a damp being driven off by a fire sizzling away in the grate. An
impressively modern-looking gramophone stood on a low table, and a gas
ring was heating up some organic matter in a frying pan.
    "Banana fritter?" Slake asked Mr Heckmondwike, as he replaced his
Mott the Hoople album in its sleeve.
    Mr Heckmondwike scrutinised the contents of Slake's frying pan from
a safe distance, and wondered how long Slake was likely to survive on a diet
like that. Then he wondered how long he himself would be likely to survive
on a diet like that. So he politely but firmly declined, repeating that he had

already eaten that evening. When Slake offered him a beer he did admit to being a little thirsty, however.

"Take a seat," said Slake and he gestured Mr Heckmondwike to a moth-eaten brown armchair next to the fire before going to close the door but, as he did so, Mr Heckmondwike's Three-headed Wormton sheepdog slunk in. Widdershins gave its surroundings several cursory glances and then lay down in a doggy pile on top of Mr Heckmondwike's feet.

"How's tha diddlin', lad?"

"All right. I suppose." Slake sat down in a similar armchair, kicked off his boots and put his feet up on an old tea chest. "I'm doing a lot for Mr Heptonstall. The latest Wolseley Walruses are full of disaffected gremlins."

"What's to do?"

"They keep blowing head gaskets. We pulled 'em apart and found the cylinder liners are all at odd heights."

"Doesn't sound like Wolseley quality, lad."

"That's because it isn't. The Nuffield Organisation has been taken over again."

"Appen? Who by?"

"Your guess is as good as anyone's. The other day it was BMC. Best guess now is British Leyland."

"Mrs Osmotherly won't like that. It messes up her motorscope."

"Mebbe that's why she didn't see the lamb coming."

They both wondered about this for a few seconds.

Then Slake said, "I had a very odd commission last night."

"Oh aye?"

"Yeah." Slake stoked up the fire rather unnecessarily. "I had a stranger on the doorstep with a 24/80 Blue Streak. You know the sort. Looks like a Wolseley 16/60 but has a two and half litre straight six. They make 'em down under but they crop up throughout Anarchadia on account of the Horsepower Wars. Mr Kindlysides's got one."

Mr Heckmondwike nodded.

"Well, not only did this fellow have a 24/80 and wanted me to make it go faster but he kept his face away from the light. He said his name was Mr Brother. You don't know anyone called that around here, do you?"

Mr Heckmondwike slowly shook his head.

"The other odd thing was that he didn't really know what sort of tune he was after. What would anyone like that be doing with such a car? And around here, n'all?"

"Was he a miner? Maybe he came from Hettup or Stingey."

"Yeah. You're probably right."

"Tha could ask t'constables ont gates if they'd ivver seen owt like it."

"That's a good idea."

"Or," said Mr Heckmondwike, "Mrs Osmotherly."

"Huh!" grunted Slake with an ironic smile.

"There's some bad business goin' on, Slake. Ah had a strange dream last night."

"Really? I just thought you counted sheep and the next thing you knew you were waking up."

"Ah nivver fall asleep counting sheep, lad, tha should knaw that. Last night I dreamt of the Great Shepherd."

Slake gaped. The Great Shepherd was so highly revered by Wolds-people they hardly ever mentioned Him. "You'll be seeing the Big Grey Man next!" he exclaimed.

"Nowt out of the way if ah do," replied Mr Heckmondwike, a little stiffly. Some people believed they were one and the same. "Anyway, in ma dream, ah were dippin' a huge flock o' fine lookin' hoggs when ah seen some fey sheepdogs. There were Woolverteens, too, like little centaurs wi' bodies o' sheep. Ah looked up and there was this tall shepherd looking at me. He said, 'Dark Time is coming Mr Heckmondwike, Dark Time is coming.' 'Aye,' ah said and pulled out *Old Maureen's Almanac* wi' Mrs Osmotherly's notation on it, but He said, 'A darker time is upon us and tha shall be sorely put to it.' 'Appen?' ah said. 'Aye,' He said. 'Bit of a beggar, all round, in fact.' So then ah asked Him, 'Willus pull through?' and then ah woke up."

"Bloody hell, that's like me dreaming of the Great Smith himself!"

"Aye."

"And He spoke like a proper Woldsman!"

"Aye, nay mither."

Slake frowned. "Mind you, I had an odd dream the other day."

"Oh aye?"

"Yeah."

"Well? What were it about?"

"It seems silly now."

"Come on, lad! Ah told thee about mine!"

"Okay, okay." Slake leant forward and said, in a hushed voice, "I dreamt that my big toes were on the outsides of my feet."

Mr Heckmondwike considered his own feet and suddenly became quite rigid.

Slake nodded at the shepherd's feet and then crossed and uncrossed his own by way of an explanation.

Mr Heckmondwike sighed with relief and uncrossed his boots so that his big toes were on the insides again.

"Not quite in the same league as your dream," admitted Slake, "but I woke up thinking I'd have to swap my shoes around. Have you told Mrs Osmotherly about your chat with the Great Shepherd?"

"Not yet. She's very busy at t'moment, it seems. Summat's still awheel, tha knaws."

"Huh. I can imagine. Anyway, how's your new tractor?"

Mr Heckmondwike began to swell with pride and his eyes sparkled, but all he said was, "It'll serve."

Slake grinned. "As good as that, eh?"

"Aye." And that was all Mr Heckmondwike would say on the matter, so Slake must have known he was pleased with it. He munched hungrily on a portion of banana fritter and passed Mr Heckmondwike another stone jar of Old Sawe's Irascible Anorak.

"I've got some cans if you'd prefer."

"Tha's doin' just fine lad, just fine." Mr Heckmondwike sighed, contentedly. "T'Mithering Brethren have been keeping a low profile, and Mrs Osmotherly's given us a regular Dark Time forecast wi' every indication of little or no Erratics or Occasionals."

"Yeah. That's good isn't it? Means a lot to everyone."

"Aye."

"So life is pretty good for you at the moment?"

"Oh, pretty fair. Pretty fair. So long as nubuddy's trying to steal it from me prematurely by talking me into ride in summat wi' an unnatural number o' wheels. This is t'time of year when everything quietens down a bit for t'hill farmer."

"That's a very fine crop of hills you've got, too."

"Ha, bloody ha."

"Must be a sod getting them to market."

"The only blot ont landscape is that lamb."

"Ah, yes. The Giant Lamb. Everyone's talking about it."

"Ah knaw."

"What's Mr Gaffathwaite reckon to it?"

"Mr Gaffathwaite was talking, only t'other day, if we could breed from it."

"Well, could you?"

"Nay lad. Not unless we had a ram t'size of a shire hoss."

"A shire horse? How big is it now?"

"In feet or hands?"

Slake shrugged.

"Ee, ah dunnaw. It's getting bigger by t'minute, lad."

"Effective stuff these hormones, then."

"Mebbe. Ah'm wonderin', though, what effect all this rapid growth is having upon it. It could shorten its life span dramatically."

"Poor little lamb!"

"Tha wouldn't say that if tha saw t'bugger now!"

"And Mr Gaffathwaite wants more!" Slake grinned and swigged some beer.

Mr Heckmondwike gave him a slightly sideways glance that said, "Ah'm not abowt to hint to thee that sometimes ma employer doesn't seem to 'ave a pair of brain cells to rub together, but ... "

"I can kind of understand why Mr Gaffathwaite would want to breed from it," mused Slake.

"Aye. So can ah. In a way."

"An animal like that could be worth an awful lot of money."

"Aye. But tha saw for thysen we couldn't dip t'bloody thing! Between thee and me, ah don't reckon it'll take notice of sheepdogs for much longer. He forgets all t'practicalities of sheep rearing."

"Commercial considerations," sighed Slake.

"Greed, ah call it."

"You don't share his enthusiasm."

"No, ah do not. And neither does the rest of the flock. Now, thanks to our friend in the purple pantsuit, we have a lone sheep out there somewhere."

"That bothers you, doesn't it?"

"Aye, it does. It's still one of ma flock."

"We'll probably sense it lurking in the fog one day, like the Big Grey Man."

Mr Heckmondwike shuddered. He'd seen enough strange things in the fog as it was.

"Has Mr Gaffathwaite recovered from his dunking in the sheep dip?"

"He's still unconscious. Ah dare say ee'll be as reet as rain before long."

"Funny expression that," mused Slake, "as right as rain. I can imagine a desert dweller feeling that way but not a Woldsman."

"In the desert, rain's a blessing," said Mr Heckmondwike, glancing at water splashing down the window from a broken drain. Wet ivy leaves nodded in agreement.

"Here, sunshine's a blessing."

"Anyway, Mrs Gaffathwaite is lookin' after him with Mrs Osmotherly's help. They seem to think he'll be awreet. Meanwhile, muggins 'ere is gonna have to think of a way to catch t'Giant Lamb."

Slake banked up the fire with rather green timbers and fell back into his chair. "Any ideas?"

"One or two."

"Is it a hazard yet?"

"All sheep are hazards, lad, usually just to 'emselves. Every single one is born with a death wish."

"That's because they've got chaps like you to look after them. If you left 'em alone they'd have to look after 'emselves."

Mr Heckmondwike shook his head. "It just doesn't work like that," he said.

"Bit of an oversight, wasn't it? Breeding out what precious little survival instinct they had in the first place?"

"Hindsight's a wonderful thing, lad."

"Maybe the Giant Lamb will kill itself."

"Ah'm not so sure."

"What do you suppose we'll be saying in the future about this Lamb?"

"Probably ' ow much we wished we'd had some foresight."

"Yeah," said Slake, "which just goes to prove that anyone who is good at hindsight has simply got their head up their arse."

CHAPTER 22

A bad-tempered little train rattled into Wormton's second-best station, stopped, sagged and sighed. The passengers alighted slowly, too tired to complain about the delay, and began to unload their luggage. They knew better than to take issue with the servants of the Wormton Tramway Company. It wasn't their fault. It wasn't anyone's fault. It was all down to Providence and when they caught up with her she wouldn't sit down for a week.

The Wormton Tram's public address system crackled into life but all it produced were squawks and crackles. The station staff shuffled into action. Their shoulders were hunched and they kept their heads down.

Mr Charabangwrath, the stationmaster, went up to the cab of the engine and greeted its crew grimly. "Tha's late," he said. "What's to do?"

Pa Coppitt took a deep breath before answering him. "Same as bloody always, Mr Charabangwrath. It's the bloody track."

"Aye. Well then," was the stationmaster's response.

Slake drummed his fingers absent-mindedly on the side of the water tower. Mr Charabangwrath came over to him. "The goods is reet behind this train, Slake, ah promise thee that," he said, earnestly.

Slake gave him a philosophical smile. "No problem, Mr Charabang-wrath."

Mr Charabangwrath gave Slake a tight little nod. Slake didn't like dealing with the general public, so he always treated those who did very gently.

"It's the last of my shacons from The Petropolis." He waved a thick volume of yellow pages at the stationmaster. "I've got my copy of *The Piston Wheel* and my clockwork two-way so I'm quite happy for the time being."

"Is that t'latest edition, lad?"

"It is, and you can have a look in it later, if you like."

Slake knew the Wormton tram was always looking for more motive power. Most of it looked like it had come from one of *The Piston Wheel's* Bargain Boxes. It had started as a horse-drawn tramway, using what looked suspiciously like converted secondhand stage coaches. Probably because some good secondhand axles had come up at the right price, it had been built to the standard railway gauge. When Railwaymania reached Bedlam-le-Beans it seemed easy to join Wormton up to the network especially as Steam Sorcerers looking for Perfect Coal noticed two smudges on a geologist's map of the Wold that lay under a couple of desolate farmsteads between Wormton and Bedlam.

While the Wormton, Hettup and Stingey Tramway crept out from Wormton to negotiate the difficult terrain towards Hettup, the Bedlam, Stingey and Hettup Railway forged across the moors from the east. After the the railways had met, just to the east of Hettup, through working of trains from Bedlam to Wormton should have been possible but wasn't. The Wormton section avoided any sort of embankment or cutting by following the lie of the land. This used up a lot of rails so they used the cheapest available and the track was too lightly and tightly laid for anything but the smallest of trains. Only the most anaemic of locomotives with a very short wheelbase could negotiate the track above Hettup, and on the longer section to Stingey they just ran out of steam. So Wormton remained connected to the vast network of rails that girdled the Wold, but the link was a weak one.

Later a narrow-gauge line approached Wormton from the west. This was a branch line of the 3' 6" gauge Mithering Railway and it proved much cheaper to build as it made a smaller hole in the scenery. Money saved on civil engineering was spent on spectacular locomotives and rolling stock. These were built to quite a generous loading gauge and dwarfed anything the Wormton Tramway had, if not quite in width then certainly in length. For a long time, unkind souls wanting some cheap sport would bait the staff of the Wormton tram in *The Tin Cur* and *The Golden Fleece* about the branch line that was bigger than their homespun tramway. Things became so bad the landlords had to put up signs banning the discussion of religion, politics, sheepdog trials and gauge disputes.

If you wanted to travel efficiently and comfortably by rail, the Mithering Railway was the only choice. However, Wrainwright always championed the tram, citing it as the best way to approach Wormton.

" 'It enables one to adopt a Wormton state of mind. The walls of the old town are glimpsed from time to time, on different sides of the coach, as the tram winds its way up into the highest reaches of the Wold. The Mithering Railway, on the other hand, is too direct and offers little chance for contemplation. It skulks under topographical features in tunnels, instead of coiling lovingly around them.' "

Over the years, countless numbers of young Wormtonians had left their hometown via the Mithering Railway, draining the vitality out of Wormton. As that rarity in Wormton, a returned exile, Slake inevitably supported the tram. He'd already made good progress on the first cottage hospital ambulance, but one or two special tools would shorten the process even quicker and that was what it was all about.

Speed.

In which case, it was rather a shame that the Wormton tram was delivering the last of his shacons.

These were an early form of standardised container and Slake's were the old Imperial ones that hardly anyone used any more. Because they rattled and quivered as they were carried, they were called shaking containers or shacons, although there were also alleged to be derivations from the French word *chacun*. One possibility was *chacun son tour* or each in turn, often corrupted into "shacons on tour." Then there was *chacun de son côté* meaning each went their separate ways or *chacun a son gout*, literally every man to his taste or each to his own, sometimes interpreted in many goods yards as "Shacons to go!"

And now whenever Woldspeople were in a hurry they said, "We'd better get a shake on!" as if they were sagging iron containers rattling on a wagon.

Slake sat down by the window of the waiting room.

In anticipation of a train bearing shacons, some of the tramway staff were firing up the steam crane. This was an impressive device that occupied its own platform on the far side of the goods yard. It was only supposed to lift three tons, but the tram staff would habitually load it up until its chain and cables were humming and the big dressed stones around its base were rubbing their shoulders nervously as flakes of rust the size of a man's palm pinged off the ironwork of the crane's jib.

To pass the time, Slake flicked through his latest copy of *The Piston Wheel*. However, most items were too far off, so his clockwork two-way remained on his belt. Eventually, he saw an old Wolseley Hornet for fifty quid in Bedlam-le-Beans. He wound up his two-way, punched in the number and gazed out of the window as he waited for an answer.

The earlier passenger train was still standing in the station. One of the elderly porters was somnambulating to the open end of one of the passenger saloons when one of the most beautiful girls Slake had ever seen appeared from inside. She was tall and fair and talked blithely to the old man who immediately gained several springs in his loosely loping gait.

She wore a dark coat that even Slake, who knew nothing of clothes, could tell was of the highest quality. As she boarded the train, Slake noticed her shapely calves and was immediately reminded of the lively young things at the tennis club in The Petropolis.

He watched her climb onto the open ended carriage and follow the spritely porter inside the saloon. Slake saw their darkened outlines moving about and then they slowed down, obviously moving something heavy between them. They emerged again, the porter leading and walking backwards. Slake could see they carried an enormous trunk. At the sight of it his heart skipped a beat. This surprised him but then he realised that his heart had worked out before the rest of him that the girl must intend to stay in Wormton. Down the steps she came, obviously straining with the weight but smiling all the time. Once on the ground, they adjusted their grips and grins and began to walk by. As she passed his window, she glanced up and their eyes met. She smiled brilliantly at Slake and he realised that she was simply returning his own smile. So he broadened his even more and never thought about rushing out to help her, which might have been a better idea.

"Hallo? Hallo?" said a voice in his ear.

With an effort Slake pulled himself out of his reverie. "Er, I'm ringing about the car in *The Piston Wheel*."

"Oh, aye."

"Is it still for sale?"

"Aye, it is that."

"Okay. I'll have it."

There was a slightly non-plussed pause. "Appen? Says he'll have it, mother. Awreet, then." There was a muffled muttering on the other end of the line, something about not asking enough for the old Wolseley.

"Whereabouts are thee?"

"I'm in Wormton. My name is Slake."

"Oh aye. Ah've heard of thee."

Quickly, Slake found out where his new car was and promised to pick it up the following day. He hung up and dashed outside, but of the girl there was no sign.

CHAPTER 23

The young woman who had made such an impression on Slake had not gone out into the street. She had superintended the loading of her travelling trunk onto one of the Wormton Tramway's urban services, on the other side of the station.

These never ventured beyond the walls of Wormton and squeezed between the houses and shops to describe an irregular circle. Small, low saloon cars were propelled singly by cautious little locomotives panelled in to look like other passenger saloons, although a real passenger would not have been fooled for a moment. The external similarity was heightened by covers over the wheels to prevent very slow victims being run over.

At the insistence of Mr Quirkmaglen, each saloon car on the town service had to be named. And according to some ancient documents that he had produced in front of the WPC, he was the only person, legally entitled by hereditary right, to name them. Consequently, the streetcar that she now boarded was named *Covetousness*. It had replaced *Craving*, which was worn out and under repair.

Like many local transport services, there was not much provision for the transport of heavy luggage, but the porters were occasionally called upon to squeeze cases as large as hers onto the local trams and had also just managed to do the same to an immense rucksack, the owner of which she recognised from her earlier journey.

"Professor Cluttercrap, I presume." She sat down beside him on the thinly upholstered seat that ran the length of the saloon.

"Hallo again, Miss Gubbergill," he replied.

"Call me Gloria," she said.

"Then you must call me Jeremy."

Professor Cluttercrap was a slightly built man, of any age between twenty and fifty. His beard and hair had joined forces to form a great black mane, but the expression behind his thick spectacles was one of calm intelligence. His brown legs were knotted and gnarled from activity but the sight of his knees made her shiver in the watery sunlight.

For most of the journey from Bedlam-le-Beans, he'd been reading a recent but well thumbed copy of *Wrainwright's Guide to the Wold*, and she smiled when she noticed that, as soon as he'd been able to, he'd dipped into it again.

"How does the search for the Black Orchid go?" she asked him.

"The first objective has been achieved. I have safely arrived in Wormton."

"There were times when that seemed in doubt."

"They do say that to travel hopefully is better than arriving."

"And I've heard it said that the word travel is derived from the French word for work."

"Hmm," said Professor Cluttercrap. "Probably said by different people then."

"Pip, pip," went the tram and they began to rumble out of the station, past Slake looking the other way as he squinted into the low afternoon sun.

Covetousness had a homely smell of soot and damp carpets, except that it didn't have any carpets. Gloria decided it must be the upholstery and endeavoured to hover over it.

"Of course, I was forewarned by Wrainwright what to expect," went on Professor Cluttercrap, "but four de-railments and four re-railments certainly breaks the ice between passengers."

"It's an extraordinary service, isn't it?"

"Remarkable. So tenacious."

"What's the next item in your programme?"

"I intend to establish myself in a comfortable boarding house for a few days and acclimatise myself to the Wold. And after that, I shall venture beyond the walls of Wormton into the vastnesses of the Woldernesse."

They rattled past the post office, which had two large letterboxes let into its wall. One was marked "Wormton" and the other simply said, "The Rest of the Wold."

Gloria shivered a little. "Having just gained the protection of the town walls, I am loath to leave them again."

"I am an experienced rambler, and the wide-open spaces hold no fear for me."

The Wormton tram had been superimposed on a medieval town. Here and there, the corners of houses had been whittled away to allow the tram-cars through. Altering the roof had obviously been considered too difficult, so the bevelled walls rose up and over to meet the bottom corner of the roof in half a Gothic arch as if, whenever a tram approached, the houses swung their hips out of the way but not their roofs. It was often such a tight squeeze, the tram would get stuck if the walls were repainted.

"Where are you staying?" asked Professor Cluttercrap.

"*The Alhambra* in Conduit Street," Gloria replied

Professor Cluttercrap consulted the street map in the back of Wrainwright. The tram shuffled between the hip-swinging houses as if participating in a parlour-game where the music and dancing had just stopped.

"That's the stop after mine," said Professor Cluttercrap. "I'm staying at *Shangri-La* in Pig Midden Alley. In fact, what's the name of this street?"

The street names were displayed on rusting blue enamel signs over the ground floor windows to pass at eye level with the tram passengers.

"We're travelling along Tainted Well Lane," Gloria told him.

"In that case I had better alight at the next request stop. It's surprisingly fast, this little tram."

He pressed the bell for the tram to stop and it pulled up outside a typical Wormton town house, built out of limestone. It also had the characteristic roof built from similar stones except that these were much flatter. Big wide ones sat above the eaves but each row above became progressively smaller as the roof rose.

On the wall next to the big oak door was a nameplate.

"Look at that!" marvelled Professor Cluttercrap. "*The Alhambra*! Delivery to my door!"

The driver and fireman of the engine came and helped him extricate his rucksack.

"Good hunting, Jeremy," called out Gloria.

"Thank you, Gloria," he called back as the tram pulled away. "Enjoy your stay."

"Thanks," Gloria said to herself as she waved from the door of *Covetousness*. "I think I just might."

CHAPTER 24

Over the next few days the weather worsened. The River Mither turned brown and stayed brown. Water frothed and foamed over obstacles, such as the little clapper bridge over the Wilber Mere. After prolonged heavy showers a dead cow or sheep would occasionally bob downstream, which depressed the drinkers in *The Young Farmers*. They didn't like to see stock being washed away, and removing the bloated carcasses from the grilles under Wormton's walls was a grisly task.

Despite her original opinion of his incompetence, Mrs Gaffathwaite decided at length to summon Dr Worstedwright.

"So what exactly is the problem, Mrs Gaffathwaite?" Dr Worstedwright asked her over the telephone.

"He's tekken to his bed, doctor."

"Well, that isn't like your husband, I grant you, but what precisely is wrong with him?"

"He just sleeps, doctor."

"And when did these ... this symptom first manifest itself?"

"Last Thursday."

"Hmm. Did he exhibit any other strange symptoms?"

"Nay. But he had fallen int sheep dip earlier that day after one of t'sheep butted 'im."

"Ah. And you think that becoming immersed in a trough full of oregano phosphate might have something to do with it, do you?"

"Well, it might, mightn't it? And when ah say he fell in, well, he were pushed."

"Pushed?"

"Aye. Butted! By that bloody great lamb of his! Ah nivver liked that beast."

"It escaped, I heard."

"Good riddance to bad rubbish, ah say."

"Look, Mrs Gaffathwaite, it is quite clear to me that the only thing wrong with your husband is wounded pride and disappointment at the Giant Lamb's escape. While I grant you that it must be demoralising, I'm sure that any shepherd worth the name could come to terms with what is a relatively minor loss."

"Minor loss! Minor loss! Ee's been in bed ever since!"

"Mrs Gaffathwaite, I know very little about farming. But I know my business well enough to realise when someone is malingering."

"Malingerin'? He's not reet, ah tell thee!"

"Tell your husband to pull himself together. He will just have to show the customary phlegm," and here Dr Worstedwright broke off in a fit of coughing to demonstrate that phlegm was something he was not short of. His smoker's cough racked him whenever he became annoyed, and the disgusting sound of some glutinous liquid popping and crackling inside his lungs had ensured that none of his patients had ever smoked.

"Apothecary, heal thysen!" Mrs Gaffathwaite shouted into the receiver.

There were some horrible acoustic effects and what sounded like Dr Worstedwright's pipe clattering against his mouthpiece. Daisy could hear it from the other side of the room.

"There's nothing wrong with your husband, Mrs Gaffathwaite!" he spluttered.

"Tha doesn't knaw owt till tha sees him!"

"I don't need to see him. He's malingering, I tell you, and that's that. I'll stake my reputation on it."

"Ha! What reputation!"

"Madam! This interview is at an end! Good day to you!" and he hung up.

Mrs Gaffathwaite stared incredulously at her handset. "Useless! Absolutely bloody useless! No wonder nubuddy's ever ill around 'ere! They just pop their clogs!"

"Mrs Osmotherly would only have said, 'I told you so,'" said Daisy.

"Daisy. That sort of remark helps no-one. Dr Worstedwright refuses to investigate ma husband's illness!"

"Yes, mum," said Daisy.

"Ah'm going to see Mrs Osmotherly! Send for the car!"

"Yes, mum."

Mrs Gaffathwaite went upstairs for her hat, coat and gloves.

Daisy put on some galoshes and escaped to the outdoors to round up some suitable farm labourer who could act as chauffeur. She was crossing the farmyard when a candidate hove into view driving the biggest and blackest Wolseley tractor she had ever seen. For a working tractor it was immaculate.

Tractors were a measure of wealth all over the Wold. Sheep farmers didn't really need very big tractors to go about their business, but tractors were a display of wealth and an important part of a courtship ritual that, unfortunately, female Woldspeople didn't always fully appreciate.

Despite a succession of ever bigger and shinier Wolseley tractors, Mr Heckmondwike had succeeded in remaining steadfastly single.

"Mr Heckmondwike! Are you busy?"

"Aye. Ah'm allus busy."

"Mum wants to go to Mrs Osmotherly's. Would you drive her?"

Mr Heckmondwike considered this for a moment, the vibrations of the big diesel engine rippling his jowls.

"Aye. Appen ah will. Ah'll be reet there."

He parked the tractor in a corner of the yard and squelched his way over to the farmhouse.

"I've sorted out the car, mum," Daisy told Mrs Gaffathwaite, who was preening herself before the mirror in the hall.

"Thank you, Daisy. Ee, that man does annoy me! It takes a lot to get me aeriated but today ah became reet vexed with him. Confound t'man!"

Mr Heckmondwike paused on the threshold.

"Oh, not thee, Mr Heckmondwike. Dr Worstedwright! He's got me gnawing away like a dog wi' an old bone! Ah wouldn't normally bother with him, but I reckoned that seeing as my husband's a man, he might be able to offer some sort of help with a man's problem."

"Man's problem?"

"Well, he's useless at women's problems."

"Women's problems?"

Mr Heckmondwike looked at them helplessly for some sort of explanation.

Daisy widened her eyes at him by way of a hint.

"So," went on Mrs Gaffathwaite, "seeing as how Dr Worstedwright's useless, ah was going to get Mrs Osmotherly to look at him again."

"Good idea," said Mr Heckmondwike, feeling he was on firmer ground. "Yon apothecary's cough can be heard reet across town."

Mrs Gaffathwaite turned towards him with closed eyes. "No, not Dr Worstedwright. Ah was going to get Mrs Osmotherly to examine ma husband." She opened her eyes again. "Mind you, heck as like as 'appen as mebbe tha's got a point there, Mr Heckmondwike. Perhaps she could get Dr Worstedwright medically retired."

"How's Mr Gaffathwaite fettlin?" he asked.

"Just the same. Come on up and see for thysen."

Following a withering look from Daisymaid, Mr Heckmondwike took his boots off on the doormat in the porch and followed Mrs Gaffathwaite upstairs.

However, when they opened the door to the bedroom, instead of an unconscious Mr Gaffathwaite he looked wide-awake.

"Sidney!" exclaimed Mrs Gaffathwaite. "Thou art awake!"

"Aye," replied Mr Gaffathwaite, querulously. "And ah'm reet hungry n'all."

She rushed over to him and gave a great big wet kiss. There was an eclipse of the daylight caused by the seat of her tweed skirt.

"Maybe we should leave them," suggested Daisy.

"Nay," said Mrs Gaffathwaite, standing up. "Ah want tha both to see ma recoverin' husband!"

Mr Heckmondwike and Daisy had a good look.

"Ow ta fettlin?" asked Mr Heckmondwike.

"Fair to middlin'." Mr Gaffathwaite had a curious downy pallor about him and he wore an air of innocence that was somehow deeply troubling.

"Glad to see thee awake again," said Mr Heckmondwike.

"Yes, me too," agreed Daisy.

"Aye! It's marvellous!" said Mrs Gaffathwaite. She looked so happy she could cry.

"Er, will tha be needing the car, then?"

"What?"

"To visit Mrs Osmotherly."

"Oh nay, nay thanks, Mr Heckmondwike. Ah'll give her a ring in a moment."

"Right," said Daisy, "we'll leave you alone but I'll be up again soon with a nice piece of roast lamb for you Mr Gaffathwaite."

Mr Gaffathwaite suddenly looked very strange. He was too pale to go any paler so he went green instead. "No meat for me, thanks," he said quickly. "Just bring me the vegetables."

Everyone stared at him in surprise.

"Nay lamb?" asked Mrs Gaffathwaite softly.

"Aye, nay lamb, thanks very much."

"Awreet." Mrs Gaffathwaite turned to Daisy. "Just vegetables then, please, Daisy."

"Gravy?"

"Nay thanks," he replied quickly.

"Okay. Coming right up."

Daisy closed the door rather hastily.

They made their way along the corridor and began to descend the big polished oak staircase. Portraits of previous Gaffathwaites gazed down upon them.

"Ee's still not hissen, then," mused Mr Heckmondwike. "Could take him some time to get ower a shock like that."

"Still," said Daisy, after some thought, "at least he's back in the land of the living."

CHAPTER 25

Slake needed some carburettors. Or, rather, he'd decided the cottage hospital ambulance needed three large Skinner's Union carbs to fit the rather splendid manifold he'd designed for it.

He liked Skinner's Union carburettors. Many Horsepower Whisperers used them and he liked the way they looked, lined up beside an engine. They resembled smooth aluminium bells from above, but underneath screws and levers and springs bristled meaningfully. Old ones could be tall and elegant, more like an upturned wine glass than a bell, topped off with a brass knob on their dashpots. Newer ones were squat and broad-shouldered with hardly any stem and black plastic knobs.

Mr Grandlythorpe's ambulance had two carbs feeding six cylinders. This wasn't too bad, but whenever an SU carb fed three cylinders the middle one ran rich while the outer two ran lean. Another carb on his special manifold would balance the mixture across all six cylinders. Just like the Steam Sorcerers a century earlier, Slake wanted perfect combustion.

He had a vague recollection from his childhood that a similar ambulance had once misjudged the Wormton tram. If this was correct it was probably lying in one of Wormton's scrapyards. He visited two minor dealers in scrap metal, but he was really only eliminating them from his enquiries. He was fairly certain it would lie within Bessie Dooker's yard.

Bessie was even more taciturn than usual. She wasn't in her office but sat in the back of a laid-up Wolseley 25 limousine and watched him from inside, with all the windows wound up. He had to use gestures but he was fairly certain he failed to mime carburettor very convincingly. At first she ignored him. Then she just stared at him. In the end, he gave up and decided she was having one of her funny turns.

The scrapyard had been founded by Bessie's grandfather, but not much had been scrapped because Wormton was such a long way off from any iron furnace. So the Dookers had concentrated on the more valuable metals such as lead, bronze, copper and silver, which were still worth shipping. The rest of the scrap metal just lay around in heaps and accumulated as the fortunes of Wormton had dwindled.

Slake always made a little ritual in Bessie Dooker's to bring him good luck in his search. This involved swinging on the starting handle of the oldest car in the yard and turning its engine over a couple of times.

Old Number One did not start. It was generally accepted to have been the first Wolseley in Wormton, and was a 1904 10-horsepower model that had backfired whilst on the Mithering road many years before, setting light to the rear of its bodywork. Despite the driver, Old Mr Gaffathwaite, throwing mud from the roadside at it, the car quickly burned out, fortunately without injuring anyone. It was then dragged into Wormton behind a horse and dumped in disgrace in the Dookers' yard. Nobody locally had the expertise to mend it at the time, and although this situation changed over the years, *Old Number One* remained there. Apart from the lack of any bodywork, it was still largely complete. What was more, the attentions of generations of Bessie Dooker's customers had ensured that the engine had not seized.

The idea of resurrecting *Old Number One* appealed to many of the old men who frequented the *Agricultural Mechanics' Institute* but Mr Heptonstall was the obvious candidate for the job. Slake decided it was time to have a word with him. It would look good restored in his showroom.

Having paid his respects to *Old Number One*, he walked off between the rows of the other, progressively more modern, cars that had followed it into this great resting place. No matter how many he times he visited Bessie Dooker's, he never came to know it all and there were always surprises tucked away in corners or exposed for the first time after being hidden for years.

It could be a desolate place, for it was full of degradation, but here and there were real treasures in the undergrowth.

Some of the exhibits were old friends, and Slake had started to enlist the help of some of the legions of disaffected gremlins who inhabited the yard to stop these old cars degrading any further. Among the serried ranks, Slake frequently stopped to renew the sigils protecting one of his favourites from rust or seizure, but most gremlins just got up to mischief in Bessie Dooker's yard. They picked at scabs of rust, flattened any battery with a charge in it and left oily hand and footprints, which only a skirrow could see, on everything. Sumpghouls and sparksappers lurked deep in most engine bays. Ion ladies tangled and shorted their way through wiring looms. Ringwraiths wailed from deep inside seized cylinder blocks, and Slake heard the pattering of tiny feet as he disturbed rebellious grunnions as they benighted tired suspension systems.

Slake penetrated deeper into the yard, until he reached an elderly and gremlin-infested group of Wolseley trucks. Mechanically similar to the ambulance he sought, these might contain the SU carbs he wanted, but they didn't. They just had Solexes and Zeniths, and unlovely ones at that.

A big, black Vincent motorcycle leant against one of them. It was a brutal machine but clearly the work of an artist. Anything not associated with going very fast had been whittled away, sometimes to nothing, and it was either chrome, polished aluminium or a primeval black that reflected light with the vibrant spectrum of petrol on water. Its generous tank featured beautiful scallops for knees and elbows and also to allow the low-set clip-on handlebars to turn on full lock. The raven-feather paint swirled as the clouds passed overhead, and its name, *Nosferatu*, was written on the tank in Gothic script.

It had no registration plate but somehow it had been ridden into town and parked in Bessie Dooker's yard. It was still warm and ticked quietly to itself as it cooled. Slake felt he should know it already from somewhere.

Slake looked around for the rider but found instead another incongruity. He frowned. It was the tail end of Mrs Osmotherly's Citroën 2CV, poking out between longer-term residents of the yard. He knew she'd bought a new car, but not what had happened to her old one.

Then he realised that he was not alone.

He squeezed through the discarded Wolseleys, Jowetts and Armstrong-Siddeleys to get a better look. Somebody was peering under the 2CV's bonnet.

Down came the bonnet and up came a head, wearing a crash helmet and a black one-piece visor of the sort that Horsepower Whisperers might wear in The Petropolis.

The Horsepower Whisperer grinned at him.

"Marvellous!" he exclaimed. "Fantastic!"

"Really?" said Slake.

"Oh yes. This is very well done. And the more you look, the more you see. It's clear there are more than just two horses to this little car. I don't suppose you know who built it, do you?"

"Well, yes. I did."

"Then I compliment you!"

Slake beamed at him and began to point out all the little problems he'd overcome to fit the four-cylinder engine under the bonnet.

The Horsepower Whisperer nodded appreciatively and asked several informed questions. "Q cars always appeal to me," he said. "With this car, I particularly admire the way there's no obvious sign of the bigger engine under the bonnet. Apart from the bigger bore exhaust, of course."

"And the noise," said Slake.

"I have a lot of time for the Citroën flat four engine," went on the Horsepower Whisperer. "The hemi-heads have outstanding breathing potential and I see you have endowed it with twin downdraught Webers!"

"Yes," said Slake.

The Horsepower Whisperer laughed. "The gremlins are still all in support as well, I see."

There they were, a complement of four, lined up on the dashboard like a little rock band.

"There's just one thing wrong."

"Oh, yes?" asked Slake, suddenly nervous.

"Yes. It shouldn't be here."

"Ah. I suppose the woman who owned it brought it here," Slake ventured after a little thought.

"That can't be right can it?"

"Well ..."

"Then we are agreed," said the Horsepower Whisperer. "It must come out."

Slake remembered little after that. There had been a good deal of that 'Trouble's going, trouble's gone,' business. He had a vague recollection of them getting an old Wolseley truck running again and loading it up with the 2CV. He also thought that, once they'd arrived at Frogheat, the Horsepower Whisperer lifted *Nosferatu* down from the truck as easily as if it were filled with air.

They worked well together and it wasn't long before the reprieved 2CV was doing laps round the deserted block in Park Bottom.

Slake couldn't remember if Bessie Dooker had been a party to their activities or not, so felt it best not to say anything.

They'd parted in the Wild Hunt manner, punching arms and wishing for good fuel, free running and bad women.

Then a sudden torpor came over him and he fell into bed and a deep, dreamless sleep.

But his final thought, as he lost consciousness cuddling the two-inch SU he'd been given, was, "What an idiot! I never asked him his name!"

CHAPTER 26

Time was playing tricks on Mrs Osmotherly. Twenty years ago seemed fresher in her mind than twenty minutes ago, and sometimes she couldn't recall anything that had happened that very morning.

The evenings always came around too suddenly for her liking. Now that she was in the twilight of her years, she hated twilight.

As a wise woman of long experience and formidable reputation, in addition to predicting Dark Time for the WPC, she contributed a column to *The News of the Wold* newspaper. On Tuesday and Thursday evenings, she dispensed wisdom to paying customers at her cottage, and she also practised heckupuncture, which involved applying knitting needles to out of the way parts of the body while the patient uttered oaths.

And at least once a week she went down to *Where the Rainbow Ends*, the teashop where everyone could benefit from some gossip and a little rumour therapy.

But it was her work on her motorscope that really marked her out from the other wise women.

Tonight, when the last of her clients had left, Mrs Osmotherly still felt as if there was some unfinished business to attend to. She restlessly fed the fire, although it was late and more visitors were unlikely, and tidied up her wisdom dispensing room. She became so distracted with thoughts of what the motorscope could hold that as she plumped up the upholstery on her settee she mistook her old grey cat for a rather listless cushion.

She quickly put him down again, before he stirred.

"If I am in the twilight of my years, then you are past the bedtime of yours," she told him. "In fact, Old Grey," she added, leaning a little closer, "sometimes, I think you might have turned out the light altogether."

Indoors flicked an ear as he lay with his head upside down, his lips drawn back from his ivory fangs. At least twice as old as Mrs Osmotherly was in cat years, Indoors Food now sought to transcend death in an orgy of sleep, and devoted his every waking hour to dozing.

"Something should be happening," she told her old cat, who silently disagreed with her.

Unable to go to bed or settle to anything more constructive, Mrs Osmotherly took up position by the shutters inside the windows and peered out through one of the gaps. This simple act gave her an enormous sense of well-being. Out there were the vastnesses of the Wold, and somewhere in the darkness lay Wormton. Inside, her home was an oasis of warmth and calm and wisdom, but she looked out into the darkness from time to time to savour the delicious contrast.

In the valley below, two headlamps were approaching. Made solid by the mist, they groped along the dry stone walls beside the road. They paused at the junction with the track up to Diggle Farm and then continued, even more cautiously, up the hill to her farmstead. When at last they turned into the farmyard, Mrs Osmotherly saw the illuminated radiator badge that marked the car out as a Wolseley, and the roof light showed it was a taxi from Wormton. It pulled up on the glistening cobbles. A hooded figure alighted and stepped delicately across the yard while the taxi switched off its lights to wait.

Mrs Osmotherly opened her front door to a muffled-up figure holding up a gloved hand on the point of knocking on her door. It was a small hand and the glove was made from fine leather.

The outside light plunged the newcomer's face into darkness.

"Are you Mrs Osmotherly?" asked a young woman's voice with not a hint of a Wormton accent.

"I am."

"Good. I hope I'm not too late."

"Is it an emergency?" asked Mrs Osmotherly, reaching for her coat.

"No. I just need some advice."

"You seem in a hurry."

"Only on account of Mr Melliver in the taxi." Mrs Osmotherly's visitor turned, and her face was revealed for the first time. She was in her early twenties, and a romantic novelist might have described her as beautiful in an entirely conventional manner had not her personality set her apart.

"Although he's not charging me for the wait, he has a very bronchial cough and I don't want to keep him any longer than I have to. I was just concerned that it may be a little late for you to receive visitors."

"Not at all," Mrs Osmotherly reassured her. "Come in," and she stood aside to let her visitor cross her threshold.

"Thank you." The stranger threw back her hood, and Mrs Osmotherly saw that she was a nurse, still in her uniform.

"You're Gloria Gubbergill, aren't you?"

Gloria flashed a dazzling smile at her. "It seems I am famous already."

"Wormton is a small place. You work at the cottage hospital."

"That's right."

Mrs Osmotherly called out to Mr Melliver.

"Ow do, Mrs Osmotherly!"

"You can wait in the waiting room, if you like."

"Ah'm listenin' to a programme abowt wormuts ont Wold Service."

"Well, you can listen to it in here. It'll be warmer and you can have a cup of tea. Come along, now!"

Mr Melliver joined them arthritically. "Heck as owt!" he said. "Wormuts ont radio! Whatever next?"

Mrs Osmotherly firmly shut the studded oak door behind them and pulled a heavy curtain across the arch. She threw open her waiting-room door and poured more coal on the fire while Mr Melliver wound up her wireless set and settled down to listen. He gripped the arm of the chair with one hand and the seat back with the other in a pose of rapt attention.

"I never knew you were so interested in wormuts, Mr Melliver."

"Me? Ah love me wormuts," he assured them. "Such variety! Such colours!"

"Do follow me," she said to Gloria, and turned down the passage that led past the waiting room.

The fire in her study had just noticed the new coals and was licking around them with interest. Mrs Osmotherly shut the door behind them. It closed with a muffled sound that suggested secrets that had been well kept. She took the nurse's coat from Gloria, hung it up on the door and bade her to take a seat.

"Now then. What can I do for you?"

The nurse smiled. She had a very clear complexion, but there was a woldliness in her clear blue eyes that interested Mrs Osmotherly deeply.

"I'm not sure if you can help," she began. "I knew of your reputation before I came here and I have read about your work in *Wise Woman's Realm*."

"*Wise Woman's Realm*? I would have thought *Cognopolitan* was what you young things read."

Gloria gave her a smile, a gentle smile that Mrs Osmotherly would have liked to be able to give to someone herself. It had great warmth in it yet it contained great wisdom. "*Cognopolitan* is only interested in one thing."

"Isn't that why we buy it?" asked Mrs Osmotherly.

"If we do, then it doesn't disappoint. But I've moved on from *Foreplay for Foresight* and *Twenty Top Tips To Spice Up Your Tea Leaves*. I am beyond the help of magazines altogether."

"Oh? Before we start, perhaps you would like some tea?"

"Ooh, yes please."

"I could spice up your tea leaves if you like," said Mrs Osmotherly, who always had the materials to hand.

"Oh no, thank you. Mine are quite spiced up enough as they are."

Mrs Osmotherly could believe it.

She made the tea with her customary quiet efficiency. It was amazing what a difference this small ceremony could make to the proceedings, and she could already feel the tension and uncertainty leeching out of her visitor. She handed her a cup and a biscuit.

"So where are you from, Gloria?"

"Lanson."

Gloria paused a little awkwardly and Mrs Osmotherly expertly filled the gap.

"You have swum against the tide, then. Most Wormtonians leave here for Lanson and The Petropolis."

"I feel more at peace here than I have anywhere else. At least, I did. Recently, I've had cause for concern."

Mrs Osmotherly sighed. "That is the unfortunate lot of wise women everywhere," she said.

"Or, rather, the cause for concern found me."

"Oh?"

Gloria produced a well-thumbed copy of *Cognopolitan* from her bag. "Have you read this?" she asked.

Mrs Osmotherly produced some reading glasses. "No," she said, "but I am not exactly a subscriber."

She read the article out loud.

" 'Ever felt you're being followed?

" 'That's okay if it's a tongue-tied hunk who's worshipping you from afar. But here we're talking about unwanted attention from the less corporeal sort of follower.

" 'Many women who possess second sight can attract unwelcome attention from entities from The Other Side. They see enough already for their sanity to be questioned, so a supernatural stalker is most unwelcome.

" 'So here is a brief self-help guide to help you deal with any nasty elementals you might unwittingly pick up along the way.

" 'First, don't encourage them but acknowledge their presence. It's better for them and better for you, too. Sometimes the mere knowledge that you can see them is enough to scare them away. Fortunately, this is often true with the most malicious types of spirits.

" 'Do view their behaviour with a sense of detachment but don't ignore any behaviour that could endanger your own Space/Time continuum.

" 'When, rather than if, you get covered in ectoplasm, try to enjoy it.

" 'If circumstances persist, consult your local experienced wise woman and get some more exorcise!' "

She put the article down and took off her reading glasses. "Vacuous idiots!" she snorted. "Can't they take anything seriously?"

"The thing is," Gloria began slowly, "the thing is, Mrs Osmotherly, that, well ... I see things. There, I said it."

"Things?" repeated Mrs Osmotherly, slowly.

"Yes."

"What sort of things?"

"Well … Not things, really. Beings."

Mrs Osmotherly nearly echoed "Beings?" but she realised this was not a good idea, and instead said, "Oh. I see."

"Ah," replied Gloria, with a wry smile, "but you don't. And I envy you."

"What sort of beings do you see?"

"Hateful, horrible, fat, ugly little beings. About this big." She held her hands apart by eight centimetres. "Oh, they're horrible, Mrs Osmotherly! They have little coats and baggy trousers and big heads, but short arms and legs. They have disgusting habits, carry fishing rods and sometimes push little wheelbarrows. They sit on bright red cushions covered with yellow spots but that's only until they can grow a fungus with the same décor."

"Go on."

"If they drink too much, they pull down their trousers and bare their horrible little bottoms at each other and this often ends in a fight. You can see their bottoms anyway when they bend down to put bait on their little fishing rods. And the colours of their clothes clash so frightfully! They must see a completely different spectrum!"

Mrs Osmotherly patted her hand. "There, there, Gloria. Have some tea."

"Oh, thank you, Mrs Osmotherly! It's such a relief just to tell someone about it. Do you think I'm mad?"

Mrs Osmotherly smiled her own smile at Gloria. As smiles went, it wasn't much worse than Gloria's. "No, you are not mad."

Gloria uttered a tremendous sigh of relief. "Thank goodness. I was really beginning to wonder!"

"A few hundred years ago they would have burned you alive, of course, but they would've warmed things up for me before now as well."

"My parents knew something was odd about me. Childhood was pretty miserable until I learnt to keep quiet about what definitely weren't imaginary friends. They don't smell very nice. I really want to get rid of them. Do you know what they might be? I wondered if they might be imps."

There was a strange pinging in Mrs Osmotherly's mind, as if a visiting idea was being paged by reception.

"The study of homunculi is not my field I'm afraid," she said, "but I think you will find that imps look completely different." As she spoke, she remembered the Bedlam Imp, the Hillman Imp. Could there be a link with the motorscope? She made a sly entry in her notebook for later, while Gloria stared thoughtfully into the fire.

"So what are they?" Gloria asked her. "They congregate in the cottage hospital and, occasionally, they tickle the old people with their fishing rods like a fly annoys a horse. Of course, the patients can't see this, but it makes them a little agitated all the same. I'm really worried they'll pull the life out of an old person in the wee small hours and make off with it in their wheelbarrows."

"Hmm," said Mrs Osmotherly. "I have heard that when someone's death approaches entities can gather to fish for their soul. Usually that soul's guardian angel comes to guide it during the next stage of its journey."

"A sort of spirit guide?"

"Kind of. Not all souls have a guardian angel. There are those that forfeit them. My guess is that these harbinger gnomes are fishing for them speculatively."

"Sometimes there are little women, too."

"Somebody has to propagate the species."

Gloria pulled a face. "Both are good cases for celibacy. But, so far, I have hope for my frailest patients, because, at the very end, I glimpse something benevolent come for them."

"Really?"

"Yes."

"So that's all right, then."

"I suppose so. So far, anyway."

"You are very privileged to witness this phenomenon."

"I don't feel privileged. It's more like a curse. I suppose I will just have to learn to live with it."

"I'm afraid so. Perhaps you would like to get in touch with the Department of Homuncular Research at the Polyversity of Summercourt. They specialise in this field."

"Ah, Mrs Osmotherly, I feel so relieved, I can't tell you!"

"Let me see. I can lend you some old texts that might help." She stood up to search her bookshelves. "They are a little out of date. Professor Van Hellstorm was a leading hom010cuologist in his day. I met him once," and Mrs Osmotherly showed Gloria his signature on the flyleaf of *Elementals and Their Habits*. "He came here to search for trolls."

"Did he find any?"

"I don't know. He disappeared."

"But what happens when a guardian angel doesn't appear?"

Mrs Osmotherly thought for a moment. "Do you know any of your elderly patients that are not worthy of a guardian angel?"

Gloria thought hard and then shook her head. Then she smiled and so did Mrs Osmotherly.

"So long as you can come to that conclusion, Gloria, I think you will be spared finding out. If you ever do come across an unworthy elderly person, you can always encourage them to repent. It depends on what they've done, of course, but any sort of atonement can reduce the danger."

Gloria sighed. "I'm so happy I came tonight! It all sort of makes sense!"

"Don't forget your tea."

Gloria noticed the cup of tea and the digestive biscuit that Mrs Osmotherly had given her. She picked them up.

"Oh! A chocolate digestive!" she said in pleasure but then guilt flashed across her face.

"A virtual chocolate digestive," Mrs Osmotherly quickly assured her. "You can't see the chocolate. So is it really there?"

Gloria peered underneath it and then bit it. "I can taste it."

"But you can't see it."

"I can definitely taste it."

"But you can't see it. Surely that must plant a seed of doubt in your mind. Whether it tastes of chocolate or not, could it contain any calories? Or maybe you associate the taste of chocolate with all digestive biscuits."

Gloria looked closely at Mrs Osmotherly. She was slim to the point of thinness. "I think I like virtual chocolate," she said, with her mouth full.

"I know I do," replied Mrs Osmotherly.

"Sometimes I don't know what I see. Or whether to believe it."

"Here. Have some more. You just need a bit of practice, that's all."

"If I recognised a soul being taken away in one of the gnomes' horrible little wheelbarrows, is there anything I could do?"

"I rather doubt it. I think the die is cast by then."

"Couldn't I grab a crucifix or something?"

"Maybe – but only if you really, genuinely believe in the use of such things."

"I don't think I do. Except … except that if these elementals really do exist, then I suppose I have to believe. Call me a Doubting Thomasina if you like, but I suppose you can't have one without the other. Perhaps I will keep a crucifix handy, just in case."

"That sounds sensible."

"Yes. Sometimes I am very sensible. Quite clever, even."

"A clever girl is a wise woman in waiting," said Mrs Osmotherly, gazing contentedly into the dancing flames of the fire.

However, when she turned to look at Gloria again, she froze.

Gloria was no longer looking at her. She was staring in disbelief at something behind her. Mrs Osmotherly's scalp began to prickle. She was far from the first flush of youth, but she hoped she had still had a long and candlelit twilight ahead of her. And now this girl, who could see harbinger gnomes and angels, was staring right behind her.

"What is it?" she whispered. "What do you see?"

Gloria did not answer but continued to stare straight past her.

Mrs Osmotherly made an effort to control the volume and pitch of her voice. If the gnomes and angels had come for her, what had she, a diviner of the future, missed? What mortal error had she made?

"Tell me, Gloria," she hardly dared to whisper, "tell me what you see!"

"Hmm? Oh, nothing really. It's just that, unless I am very much mistaken, that grey velvet cushion on the chair behind you appears to be breathing."

Mrs Osmotherly swallowed hard.

"That's Greymalkin. He does that a lot."

She stood up, activity helping to hide her quaking limbs, picked up her ancient cat and carried him back to her chair to introduce him to Gloria.

"Do you have a cat?" she asked her.

Gloria reached out to stroke the old grey cat, and he looked at her blearily. "I'm not supposed to because I live in the nurses' home, but a black kitten is trying to adopt me."

"Let her. If anyone gives you any trouble, let me know. But they shouldn't, so long as you keep her away from any expectant mothers. Not that there are very many of them around Wormton these days."

"How long have you had Greymalkin?"

"Oh, years and years. He's become part of the furniture. Old women who live on their own often commune with cats, but I'm no hermit and nobody could feel threatened by a familiar as slothful as this indolent old animal. My visitors often sit on him by mistake but it doesn't seem to do him any harm."

Greymalkin was giving Gloria's fingers a good sniff. In the right circumstances, insight could be smelt.

"Most of the time he just dozes, and he's getting very deaf nowadays. He can always hear Indoors or Food, though."

Indoors suddenly became quite animated.

"I see what you mean. Perhaps you should call him that instead of Greymalkin."

"Oh, no, not after all these years. He's far too old to change now. You can't teach an old cat new tricks, can you, Old Grey?"

Indoors Food appeared incensed.

"On second thoughts, you can't teach cats tricks at all," mused Mrs Osmotherly. She put him down. "They just do things if the mood takes them."

Gloria reached out to stroke him now that he had sniffed her. "You should go back to sleep, old fellow," she told him. "You don't want to waste your energy on us."

Mrs Osmotherly beamed at him. "If he wasn't so deaf, I'd say that he understood every word you said to him."

"Perhaps he can read minds," suggested Gloria.

Indoors Food looked up at her with evident approval.

"I find that very difficult to believe," replied Mrs Osmotherly.

Gloria watched the old cat regard his mistress disdainfully before making his way stiffly back to his chair. He jumped into it very lazily and sat down.

"He's got an incredibly expressive face," she said.

"Do you think so?"

"Oh, yes. It's truly remarkable. He's looking at you in a mixture of frustration, incredulity and, now, pity."

Mrs Osmotherly shrugged her shoulders and refilled their cups. "One thing, though, Gloria. Don't let on about what you can see at the time of death. It could be unsettling for some people."

"Like the elderly, you mean?"

Mrs Osmotherly squirmed.

"Or my patients?"

"Exactly."

"I suppose it could make them uneasy, especially if they are getting on a bit."

Mrs Osmotherly assured Gloria that this might be so.

"All right, I'll keep it to myself. But I've told you, and I'm delighted I have. I'll let you know if I see anything strange."

"Yes. Do that."

"So you don't think I should worry?"

"No."

"Even though I am seeing angels and daemons?"

"You're not the only one," grunted Mrs Osmotherly.

"I beg your pardon?"

"I wonder if there may be a link with a little problem of my own. I saw a figure I didn't like the look of at all, recently."

"Was he a daemon?"

"I fear he was."

"So you see daemons, too?"

"Not like yours. But then I'm not a seer. Not like you."

"What manner of daemon did you see?"

"A man. A stranger in these parts, although there's nothing wrong in that. He is a man who is an ordinary man no longer. Have you heard of horsepower whisperers?"

"Yes."

"They ride in The Wild Hunt."

"I saw that when I lived in Lanson."

"Horsepower whisperers can exhort their engines to great feats of power and endurance, and they race against each other in the Wild Hunt. They are not inherently wicked and some are quite benign. But not this one. This one is Nicholas Eldritch Hob. He is The Metal Guru and The Lord High Priest of The Engine Henge. He is the most successful horsepower whisperer of all but he was seduced by the power he wrought and became a Soul Trader."

Gloria shivered. "And you have seen this Soul Trader?"

"I have," answered Mrs Osmotherly, gravely.

"What's he doing here?"

"I don't know. But I mean to find out. The game is awheel, Gloria. I'd keep what I've told you to yourself if I were you."

Gloria nodded. "Do you think my gnomes are connected with him in any way?"

"I fear they might be. Strange things have been happening around here recently. I may not know much about homuncuology but I have made a life-time study of autology."

"Ah, yes! I've heard of your work on the motorscope! What does it tell you?"

Mrs Osmotherly sighed. "I'm still learning what it tells me. My latest discovery is that the motorscope is interactive. It would appear that to some extent we can alter the course of fate."

"I have always thought that ultimately we have control of our own des-tinies," said Gloria with feeling.

"But I made a serious mistake with the motorscope a few days ago. I misread the traffic signs completely."

"Perhaps it would help if you told me about it. Talking to you tonight has certainly helped me."

Mrs Osmotherly smiled. "Thank you, Gloria. I rather think it might. But we ought to do it another time."

A gentle snoring came from the other room.

"We shouldn't keep Mr Melliver waiting too long, wormuts on the radio or not."

CHAPTER 27

The next fine day found Mr Heckmondwike high up by the eaves of Riddaw Lodge, clearing out his gutters. Although massively constructed, it took a great deal of upkeep. A building is a living thing, albeit a very sleepy one, and over its life it goes through many changes. Walls bulge, floors sag, and doors stick. Once-smooth surfaces show cracks and ivy and algae grow in the most unexpected places.

Not everyone had a tied cottage like Mr Heckmondwike's. Riddaw Lodge was more of a small castle at the very edge of the Scar Fell Farm estate. It had originally been built as a base for hunting in the surrounding forest. The forest had subsequently been pushed back to allow cultivation, but the outlying farms had since been engulfed by the unchecked trees, and Riddaw Lodge was now an outpost of the civilised Wold. From here, Mr Heckmondwike tended the wild and woolly Outland flocks.

His mood did not match the sudden warmth of the weather, and it only lightened a little when he heard the unmistakeable exhaust note of a well tuned V8 approaching. Out here, the noise of some mechanical contrivance was always welcome. On really gloomy days, Mr Heckmondwike would fire up his Wolseley tractor just for the hell of it. It was a defiant blast against the advance of the wild Wold.

He turned his back on the gutters and gargoyles, and sat on the mossy crenellations to gaze over his flock and watch for the V8 to crest the horizon. The forest had drawn up in a line on top of a nearby cliff known as Nibley Edge, like Indians ranked on the horizon. The cliff ran roughly east to west for several leagues, and acted as a natural barrier to the onward march of Riddaw Forest, which had not yet found a way down. This didn't stop them filling up his gutters with pine needles, however, and on stormy nights, wet pine cones would get thrown down the great chimney to land, hissing and spitting, on the hearthrug, like damp grenades.

The exhaust sound suddenly grew louder, and a stripped-down, tuned-up Mudlark, with Slake theoretically in control of it, came hurtling up to Riddaw Lodge, and Mr Heckmondwike nearly fell off the battlements.

Slake pulled up outside its great wooden gates, shook the ground with a blip of his throttle, and gave a completely unnecessary blast upon the horn.

He noticed Mr Heckmondwike dangling nonchalantly and yelled, "Ow ta fettlin, Mr Heckmondwike? Look what I've got!"

Mr Heckmondwike looked.

"It's my very own Mudlark!" Slake shouted up to him. He opened the bonnet. "Look at that! This represents the proceeds of all my stationary engine work. I must have been around every farmstead in this part of the Vale since I came back. I reckon this is the quickest Mudlark this side of Bedlam, and soon folk'll be clamouring for replicas! Come on down and have a closer look!"

It took some time for Mr Heckmondwike to pull himself back inside and wend his way earthwards, but at last a Judas gate let into one of the great oak doors opened, and he emerged into the daylight.

"What were you doing up there?" Slake asked him.

"Cleaning out ma gutters."

"You ought to have a word with Reverend Chunderclough. There are masonry gremlins to prevent that sort of thing and I reckon his reverence has 'em in his thrall."

"Oh aye?"

"Yeah. Ever seen him do anything to his church?"

Mr Heckmondwike thought hard and frowned.

"No, neither have I," said Slake, not waiting for an answer. "Might be worth getting him out here and having him 'Bless this house.' Anyway, take a look at my new wheels!"

Mr Heckmondwike peered at the engine and made some approving noises about how it differed from his own. Then he said, "Ah wonder what Mrs Osmotherly would make of this."

Slake stiffened at her mention. "I hear Mr Gaffathwaite's taken the loss of the Lamb to heart," he said, quickly.

"Aye, well, mebbe he has, mebbe he hasn't."

"Is he any better?"

"He's regained consciousness but he's still not hissen. Mrs Osmotherly visits him regularly. Now that he's awake and able to utter oaths, they tried some of that heckupuncture stuff on 'im."

"Blimey. Usually just the prospect of heckupuncture provokes a full recovery."

"Not for Mr Gaffathwaite. Mrs Osmotherly said that as soon as she tried to apply t'fust knitting needle to him, he took a turn for the wuss. Reckons t'mere sight of one filled him with terror and t'room wi' terrible oaths. She brought that new young nurse with her t'other day. Gloria was her name."

"Oh yeah? In my experience, Mr Heckmondwike, all girls named Gloria or Desireé are right tugs."

Unable to reconcile this view with his own observations of Gloria, Mr Heckmondwike asked Slake directly if he had seen Mrs Osmotherly recently.

"No."

"Ah suppose she'll notice thine Mudlark soon enough."

"Yeah, well not a lot misses Mrs Osmotherly. Only the occasional Giant Lamb."

"Everyone makes mistakes," Mr Heckmondwike pointed out.

"Not everyone tries to pin them on others, though. Can you remember the last time you made a mistake? Bet you didn't blame somebody else for it."

Mr Heckmondwike thought about it.

"Not so very long ago," went on Slake, "I can remember feeling as if everything I did was wrong. It's all part of being a kid. I couldn't do anything right. I couldn't get to grips with animal husbandry, I couldn't build walls and I couldn't grow vegetables. I couldn't play sport. It was only later that I found out what I was good at and it's this. Everything fell into place. I got to know Mr Heptonstall, then Old Mr Macklefract. Suddenly, I could create power. It took me to The Petropolis, where I learnt a lot, but now I'm back and it seems I'm still being held responsible for anything that goes wrong. Slake the scapegoat. It's like being thirteen all over again."

"The only mistake tha made, lad, was souping up Mrs O's car without telling her."

"Okay. That was a mistake. But I don't go around saying it's your fault, do I?"

"Hast tha nivver spoken in haste, lad?"

"Of course I have, and I've immediately regretted it and then for some time afterwards. But I still think it was ridiculous. She blamed me for her own negligence."

Mr Heckmondwike sighed. "Ah went after t'lamb, yest'day."

"The lamb? The Giant Lamb?"

"Aye."

"How did it go?"

"It went reet enough."

"Whaddya mean?"

"Bloody beggar just ran off."

"Couldn't you catch it?"

"Nay, lad, t'bloody beast has grown too bloody big!"

"How big?"

Mr Heckmondwike glanced up at Riddaw Lodge behind them. "Too big for these gates."

"Bloody hell! I thought it had stopped growing."

"Nay, lad, it has not. And take a look at this." They squeezed through the little door in the gates, and Mr Heckmondwike showed Slake the ragged remains of a tyre that adorned the wheel of a Mudlark. "What does tha make of that?"

"That's a very nasty blow out."

"Can tha tell it was a blow out?"

"What else would it be?"

Mr Heckmondwike sighed. "Ah dunnaw. Ah might be getting paranoid in ma old age but ah reckon it could've been sabotage."

"Sabotage? By whom?"

"Mithering Brethren."

"Ah. Yeah. Of course."

"Ah heard what could've been a rifle shot as the tyre exploded."

"Fair dos, Mr Heckmondwike, that could have been the tyre giving out."

"Nay, lad, ah've had blow outs before now. This one sounded different. And t'timing couldn't have been any wuss. Ah was just within a gnat's whisker of catching the lamb."

"Really?"

"Aye, Slake. Ah've been trying to do summat about it on the sly for days, weeks even. And all the while it's getting bigger. A sheepdog can't handle it naymore."

"What? Not even Widdershins?"

"Nay." Mr Heckmondwike stroked his sheepdog's noses. "Widdershins has lost its nerve. And who can blame it?"

"Oh no!"

"Anyroad, yesterday, ah devised a kind of noose on a pole and ah had it ont blighter's neck when ah had this blow out."

"What speed were you doing?"

"About 45 to t'hour!"

"Over the moors?"

"Aye, lad!"

"Driving a Mudlark and trying to noose a bloody great lamb?"

Mr Heckmondwike nodded.

Slake was trying to imagine how it could be done. "One hand steering and another noosing?"

Mr Heckmondwike shook his head. "Both hands noosin' and both knees steerin'."

Slake's face broke into a grin at the idea. "Now that I would have liked to have seen."

"But somebody else did see me and that's why ah were thwarted! It were reet at t'critical moment; they couldn't have timed it better." Bright sunlight was finding its way through cracks around the doors and one cast a long stripe across Mr Heckmondwike's face and highlighted his fierce pale eyes. "Ah saw the flash of reflected light afterwards and reckon it were their gloatin' glasses."

"Well, the next time you go after that lamb, let me know. There's no point in struggling on your own and I'm sure my Mudlark would catch it."

"Nobbut a word to anyone about this, lad."

"Don't worry," Slake assured him. "They won't hear anything from me. And I doubt they'll hear anything from the Brethren, either. It'd give their game away."

"Aye," said Mr Heckmondwike, dubiously.

Slake suddenly felt great pity for his friend. An engine blowing up in the Wild Hunt wouldn't do as much damage to his standing in the community. If word got out that the Lamb had evaded Mr Heckmondwike again, his good name might never be recovered.

"This must be what the Great Shepherd was on about," Slake told him.

"Aye. Appen tha's reet."

"Okay. That's settled then. We go after the Lamb together, shepherd and skirrow!"

CHAPTER 28

Mrs Osmotherly was not entirely surprised to receive an invitation to dinner at Wormton Castle. Enquiries soon revealed that it was to be a select gathering, with just Mr Heckmondwike and Mrs Gaffathwaite also attending. Usually, Mr Gaffathwaite would have been invited as well but Mr Quirkmaglen had let it be known that he did not want to impede the encouraging signs of recovery.

The fact that Mr Gaffathwaite was still suffering from a mysterious illness was clearly by the by.

Mr Heckmondwike and Mrs Gaffathwaite collected Mrs Osmotherly in the newest of the Scar Fell Farm Wolseleys, a dignified 6/110 in black, just like Constable Arkthwaite's police car but without the blue lights. They exchanged pleasantries but quickly fell silent until they reached the outskirts of Wormton, when Mr Heckmondwike casually asked Mrs Osmotherly if she had seen anything of Slake recently.

"No," she replied. "Why?"

"Just wonderin'."

"Nothing bad's happened to him, has it?"

"Nay, nay, nay. Slake's as reet as rain." Mr Heckmondwike applied the windscreen wipers.

"Oh. Good." She sighed and sank back into the leather seat, surprised at how tense she had become at the mention of his name.

"That one's not meant to grow old," said Mrs Gaffathwaite.

There was a heavy silence.

"He's built himself a V8 Mudlark," said Mr Heckmondwike. "It's got t'most powerful engine this side of Bedlam."

"Mr Heckmondwike, you are well aware that Slake and I did not part on good terms recently."

"Aye."

"I would hate anything bad to happen to him."

"Ah reckon tha would knaw bayforehand," said Mr Heckmondwike. "So would tha tell 'im?"

"Of course, I would."

"Tha'd speak to him, then?"

"If it was necessary, yes."

"If it were necessary," said Mr Heckmondwike. They entered the gates of Wormton Castle. "If it were necessary."

Mr Quirkmaglen lived a life of gracious ease in the thickest part of the old town walls, which was all that was left of his castle. The towers had long since gone – dismantled to pay the gambling debts of his dissolute forebears – but the bailey still existed, and many elderly people lived here on a grace and favour basis, thanks to some past connection with Mr Quirkmaglen's family.

His own apartments featured a row of deep windows, the only ones in the whole of Wormton's old walls, with a view to the north west. Unfortunately, this was Wormton's gloomiest prospect, perpetually in shadow and looking out over dank, unproductive pasture and unfruitful orchards. A view like that didn't colour one's view of the Wold. It drained it of what little colour there was.

For one of Wormton's most prominent citizens, Mr Quirkmaglen's business affairs were shrouded in mystery. There were rumours that he was sufficiently clever to make a handsome income by simply 'moving money around'. Quite how this was achieved was beyond the ordinary Woldspeople. They'd tried it for themselves in *The Tin Cur* but, sooner or later, somebody started to hang onto it. It seemed to work for Mr Quirkmaglen, though, as he ran an Armstrong-Siddeley Sapphire, and whenever the collieries at Hettup and Stingey needed some extra capital it was Mr Quirkmaglen they approached for a loan to tide them over.

Although he'd never married, there were stories of kept women in Bedlam and Mithering.

Mr Heckmondwike parked the car in the outer bailey. The outer gates were so sagged and swollen with age that they were now immovable, but on the inside wall was another, smaller, set. These were better maintained and the nail heads were freshly blacked. Mr Heckmondwike knocked hard to make himself heard and they could hear the muffled echo inside.

As they waited, everyone checked each other's appearance. Then Mrs Gaffathwaite said, "All this for his benefit. What's he want to see us for, any-road?"

"I really couldn't say," replied Mrs Osmotherly. She wished Mrs Gaffathwaite had voiced these thoughts in the car. Walls have ears, especially those with alert gargoyles.

Windows with stone mullions and leaded lights peppered the ancient stonework. As clouds cleared the low sun, little diamond-shaped patches of sunlight were reflected around the courtyard.

An old man showed them in and guided them silently up steps and along passages big enough to take a Wolseley Hornet until they reached another set of doors. Here the old man knocked on the beautifully carved mahogany, waited for a murmured reply, and ushered them into Mr Quirkmaglen's private chambers.

The effect, after the darkness of the old castle passages, was dramatic. The pale evening light gently leaked into the room but it still had enough energy to light it unaided. Mr Quirkmaglen sat in a chaise longue, silhouetted against the silvery landscape outside.

He looked up, snapped shut a small volume he'd been reading, smiled and stood up to greet them.

"Thank you for coming," he said. "Do, please, take a seat." He indicated a table laid for dinner. "What wet weather we've been having recently, haven't we? Would anyone care for an *aperitif*?"

An elderly butler came forward and passed a bottle around in a refined silence. As he withdrew, Mr Quirkmaglen grew concerned and asked how Mr Gaffathwaite was keeping. Mrs Gaffathwaite started to describe the course of his illness and Mrs Osmotherly added how pleased she was with his progress.

They were called to table shortly afterwards and an elderly maid served them their soup.

"And you honestly have no idea what ails him?" Mr Quirkmaglen probed gently.

"No," admitted Mrs Osmotherly. "It's unlike any other illness I've seen before."

"And he's still off his meat?"

"Aye," Mrs Gaffathwaite answered, in between deftly eating her soup without a slurp.

Again Mr Quirkmaglen appeared concerned. "Curiouser and curiouser," he said.

The candles were lit and, over deliciously tender lamb with new potatoes and luxuriant green beans, they discussed a number of subjects, including the incompetence of the local medical profession and flock market trends, but eventually Mr Quirkmaglen raised the topic they suspected most exercised his mind.

"Mr Heckmondwike," he said, "could you tell me something of the Giant Lamb? It seems to be exercising the imaginations of so many people at the moment."

"Well, Mr Quirkmaglen, there's nobbut much to tell. It was injected with all manner of chemicals by a growth hormone salesman from Bigga-Beast. After that, it just grew and grew. When we dipped t'flock it butted Mr Gaffathwaite int sheep dip and escaped."

"I see. And it has proved elusive ever since?"

"Aye."

"Are you going to go after it?"

"Of course."

"Is it still growing?"

"Aye but it must stop some time."

"Do you suspect the involvement of the Mithering Brethren?"

Mr Heckmondwike considered this for a moment. "In what way?"

"Simply that it is common knowledge they have been trying to adulterate the pedigree flock of Scar Fell Farm for many years."

Mrs Gaffathwaite was beginning to twitch. Although they had all caught some of Mr Quirkmaglen's inscrutability, some had it less than others.

"Do you have any grounds for this suspicion, Mr Quirkmaglen?" asked Mrs Osmotherly.

Mr Quirkmaglen gave her a mild smile. "I was merely thinking out loud."

Mrs Osmotherly and Mr Heckmondwike exchanged glances.

A clock chimed, except that it was not the hour.

Mr Quirkmaglen said, "Do excuse me," and rose from the table. He went over to an elegant writing bureau, unlocked it and opened it.

Inside, instead of pigeonholes and drawers, there were lots of little screens of figures.

Mr Quirkmaglen pressed some buttons on a keyboard and spoke into a slim microphone. "Well?"

He picked up an earpiece, and a lens in a cubbyhole moved slightly towards him.

"Smelly River Ordinaries? Very well. Sell sixty per cent. I'll take twenty thou in cash and buy… buy …"

He scrolled through columns of figures, occasionally calling up graphs that changed colour rapidly and not always to his satisfaction. Then he found a different coloured graph.

"Buy Blue Hills Bonchancers. Yes that's right. Well, I appreciate your concern, but those are my instructions. Kindly comply. Thank you. And you."

When he had locked up his bureau and returned to the table, Mr Quirkmaglen was slightly flushed. "More wine anyone?" he asked.

As the steamed treacle pudding arrived, Mr Quirkmaglen asked how valuable an animal that big would be, and Mr Heckmondwike explained the intricacies of hornswoggling to him at such length that Mrs Osmotherly found it hard not to smile. To Mr Quirkmaglen's credit, he weathered the next half an hour with considerable fortitude, but neither of the two women thought he was really paying any attention.

"So," summed up Mr Quirkmaglen over cheese, "although there is a considerable quantity of meat and wool on the Lamb, you have severe doubts about the merchantable quality of the produce it would yield?"

Mr Heckmondwike saw no harm in admitting that this was true.

"Simply because of the large quantities of growth hormones it might contain?"

"Aye."

"And the same would hold true of its milk, I suppose, once it reached maturity?"

"Aye."

"Does Mr Gaffathwaite share this opinion?"

"He has nay opinion these days."

"He has no opinion," echoed Mr Quirkmaglen, thoughtfully. "But there would be no point in breeding from it because its size results merely from the injection of artificial chemicals?"

"Aye. That's reet."

"I wonder if you could clear up another point for me, Mr Heckmondwike. "The Lamb escaped after it had been dipped?"

"Nay, Mr Quirkmaglen. Bayfore."

"So it was not dipped?"

"Aye."

"Would it be vulnerable to disease, then?"

"Aye, it would at that."

"So would you say it was a very healthy animal?"

"To be honest, ah do not believe that growing so quickly to such a size is good for any animal. Ah would not be surprised if it died young."

"Mm. Thank you, Mr Heckmondwike. But my final question is this. If it remains – ahem – at large, is it dangerous? In a nutshell, should we be worrying about it?"

"Well, Mr Quirkmaglen, it's like this. T' Giant Lamb is nearly big enow to step over a Mudlark but it's still a sheep, a lone sheep. In fact, it's nobbut a lamb still, not yet fully-grown and quite immature. Ah'd say it were harmless."

"I find your opinion very reassuring, Mr Heckmondwike, very reassuring indeed. But other folk within these walls are not so well informed as you and I, and view this animal as a monster."

"Sheep are less of a threat than threatened," insisted Mr Heckmondwike. "It's an aberration, but it's still one of ma flock."

"The good shepherd giveth his life for the sheep," said Mr Quirkmaglen.

Mr Heckmondwike stared at him.

"Of course," went on Mr Quirkmaglen, as the coffee arrived, "there is another aspect of the Giant Lamb that we have not considered yet."

"Oh aye?"

"Indeed. There is a vast amount of symbolism associated with lambs – sacrifice, vulnerability, innocence."

"Stupidity," put in Mrs Gaffathwaite.

Mr Quirkmaglen ignored her. "The Giant Lamb is an enormity of innocence. 'Behold the Lamb of God which taketh away the sin of the Wold.' "

"Are you suggesting some divine intervention in the origin of the Giant Lamb?" asked Mrs Osmotherly.

Mr Quirkmaglen smiled superciliously. "It's an interesting idea. Isn't it?" and soon afterwards they found themselves dismissed.

"Well!" said Mrs Gaffathwaite, as they were leaving, "what did tha make o' that?"

"He was playing poker with us," said Mrs Osmotherly.

"It seemed to me he were assessing t'commercial value of t'Giant Lamb," Mr Heckmondwike told her, "and volunteering me for a sacrifice."

"And what about all that religious mumbo-jumbo!" said Mrs Gaffathwaite.

"I keep going back to his point about the possible involvement of the Mithering Brethren," added Mrs Osmotherly. "That is something none of us had considered before."

"Aye," agreed Mrs Gaffathwaite, "but what game is Mr Quirkmaglen playin'?"

CHAPTER 29

"So," said Hob, to a slight reverend gentleman at the tramway terminus, "what in damnation brings you here?"

"The tram, of course," the little vicar replied, mildly.

"Wormton's a bit off the beaten track for you, isn't it?"

"The track is not beaten but well polished from the passage of wheels. And there are not many services like the Wormton tram."

A train came in and the vicar quickly made a note of the engine's number in a small notebook.

"Have you been here before?" asked Hob.

"Once or twice. But only for pleasure, never on business."

"Not saved any souls around here, then?"

The vicar laughed. "No," he said. "Not yet."

"Any plans to?"

"That all depends."

Another engine approached.

"That's a nice little Manning Wardle," enthused the vicar. Out came his notebook again and he made a note of the number carried on the front of its chimney.

"You know, Reverend, the way that little engine creeps by, peering out from behind its buffers like that, it's almost as if it's trying to hide from us."

"Really?"

"Well, hide from you. Are you going to add it to your collection?"

The reverend gentleman frowned. "My collection?"

"Not the monetary offerings your flock offer you, of course, but your collection of engines."

"I thought you might be referring to my other collection."

"Oh, I see. What you might call your, er, congregation."

The vicar smiled another mild little smile. "Just so. If I did take it on, that Manning Wardle would be the first Wormton Tramway engine to leave here. They come to Wormton never to depart, you know. Every single one of them is still here, typically out of use."

"How is the old congregation? Saved anyone good, recently?"

"Rather. Of course, really good souls, vividly soaked by all the vibrant hues of life's rich tapestry, are always of value."

"I'm quite happy with a little oil stain here or there," said Hob. "Or perhaps some iron filings stuck in the creases."

"I go for coal dust, myself," said the vicar.

"Always? Not even a little diesel?"

The vicar pulled a face. "I just can't get on with infernal combustion."

"As far as we're concerned, Tregaskis, it's all infernal!"

Reverend Tregaskis laughed. "That's very good. Yes, very good. I shall have to tell that to my grease bogles and klinkergeists."

"I doubt if they'll see the funny side of it."

"They will if I tell them to. Oh, they have a good afterlife as far as the eternally damned can expect. Polishing a little brasswork never did anyone any harm."

"But, Tregaskis, it's endless."

"Eternal. Exactly."

"So what *does* bring you here?"

"Locomotives have been interfered with."

"Interfered with?"

"Vandalised." Reverend Tregaskis became incandescent for an instant and then regained his composure.

"But who would do such a thing?" asked Hob.

"The Mithering Brethren. They believe that such petty acts of sabotage can save souls."

"Get on!"

"No. Really."

"But that's perverse!"

"I know."

"A few dark colours in the tapestry of the soul serve to highlight the vividness of full and intense experiences, but a perpetually frustrated soul is virtually worthless."

"That may be the idea. They devalue souls and reduce their desirability. Tell me, Hob. Has anyone tried to save your soul?"

"My soul? You mean my very own soul?"

"Yes."

"No."

"It's not pleasant, believe me. It involves unnatural practices such as self-restraint."

Hob laughed. "I only do indulgence!"

"I quite agree. And I'm sure I could indulge your souls most effectively."

Hob looked at Reverend Tregaskis, sideways. "Even my very own soul?"

"I'd look after it well, you know."

"I'm not so sure. I think I'll keep it for the time being, thank you."

Reverend Tregaskis sighed. "Saving the soul of a Soul Trader would be quite a thing. If I saved a soul like yours, the gates of heaven would assuredly be open for me."

"But it wouldn't really be saving it, now, would it? You'd turn me into some sort of grease bogle to look after your unholy collection of scrapped steam engines."

"Of course."

"Then the gates to heaven would be closed to you, and I'd be doomed to eternal polishing and oiling."

"As a Horsepower Whisperer, that's what you do anyway, reducing friction and polishing cylinder heads."

"You don't polish cylinder heads," Hob told him. "A polished surface collects fuel droplets when you really want the air/fuel mixture to remain an atomised vapour."

"My, what a team we'd make, though!"

"It'd be a very one-sided team, Soul Trader and soul tradee."

"No different from your blessed *Terminal Murrain*."

"Kindly moderate your language! You'd be banned from STANTA."

"Would I?"

"Of course!" said Hob. "STANTA's Rule Number One expressly forbids trading in the souls of fellow soul traders."

"But you're not a member."

"No, but you are."

Reverend Tregaskis laughed. "You're right, of course. The very idea is flawed."

"Still," said Hob, "got any skirrows?"

"Of course. How many do you want?"

Hob opened his rucksack. "I've got thirty-three wheel wights, ten grease bogles and half a dozen klinkergeists."

Reverend Tregaskis peered inside and made approving noises. "Then I'll swap you …" He opened up an ancient leather case and began to count. "Let me see. That's twenty-one skirrows, one Horsepower Whisperer …"

"Well, I never! Buster Bearing! I wondered what happened to him."

Reverend Tregaskis counted out the souls as they stood on the platform. "Twenty, twenty-one, Buster Bearing and a skateboard."

"A what?" Hob looked dubiously at the skateboard as Reverend Tregaskis handed it over.

"A skateboard. Currently very popular on the west coast of Consumerica. It won't be long before many teenagers will be willing to trade their souls for one of these."

Hob shrugged. They shook hands and sorted out their souls, and then Reverend Tregaskis showed Hob how to do an ollie on the station platform.

CHAPTER 30

Where the Rainbow Ends was a teashop in a respectable side street off Wormton's market place. It was an oasis of cultural "refainement" in a bleak and lonely Wold where rumour therapists could hold forth and women of the Wold could anoint themselves in the healing balm of inconsequential scandal. Inside *Where the Rainbow Ends* were many little tables, each with a lamp and a red tasselled lampshade. The interior was rather dark but the pools of light above these lamps invited the patrons – or rather matrons – of *Where the Rainbow Ends* to gather around confidentially, like moths to a flame. The whispering hiss of the gas lamps made eavesdropping very difficult but tantalisingly possible.

The best seats were along the walls in cosy booths that enabled discussions of the most delicate matters. Each one had heavy red velvet curtains that kept out draughts and which could also be twitched shut as an added precaution against lip-reading.

Where the Rainbow Ends was so much more comfortable than the snug in *The Tin Cur*, where flagstones erupted through time-expired rugs. In *The Golden Fleece* – unofficially known as *The Golden Fleas* – Three-headed Wormton Sheep Dogs lay in piles at their masters' feet while the men folk boasted about how they had seen each other off in the marketplace and compared the size of their tractors.

Dogs were not allowed in *Where the Rainbow Ends*, unless they could be carried under one arm. It was a warm and inviting place where connoisseurs of high domestic management could relax and share news with like-minded friends without worrying about the washing up afterwards. It was a place where laughter tinkled like a teaspoon dancing in an impossibly white china cup, a place where nice became "naice" and the waitresses could be complimented on their lovely buns without anyone sniggering.

However, the remainder of Wormton, typically those who were not wise and not women, said, "*Where the Rainbow Ends* the gossip begins."

Mrs Osmotherly gently eased herself into the pleasant gloom of *Where the Rainbow Ends*. There was the usual muted buzz of barely suppressed excitement and faces registered astonishment as one rumourmonger unburdened herself to others.

"My dears," she overheard Old Mrs Skeglathwaite saying, "hast tha heard about Mr Gaffathwaite?"

The circle of other women around the table tightened.

Mrs Osmotherly hovered inconspicuously nearby.

"He were mauled by a sheep," confided Old Mrs Skeglathwaite.

The circle opened up as its members leaned back and looked at each other with horrified mouths, but delighted eyes.

"Horribly mauled," insisted Old Mrs Skeglathwaite.

"My lad were there," insisted Mrs Thorngumbald. "Mr Gaffathwaite were head butted by t'Giant Lamb and fell int sheep dip!"

"He had to be carried home on a bale o' wool because of 'is appallin' injuries," Old Mrs Skeglathwaite told them, demonstrating one of the advantages of deafness.

"Aye, that's reet enough," admitted Mrs Thorngumbald, "but he were nivver carried home on a bale o' wool, it were in Osmotherly's 2CV."

Mrs Osmotherly shrank further back into the shadows.

"And," went on Old Mrs Skeglathwaite, "he had to be identified by his wife from marks on his body that only she could have known about."

There was an exquisite silence as the ladies present considered the marks on their own husbands' bodies.

Not having had a husband for several years, Mrs Osmotherly unobtrusively penetrated deeper into *Where the Rainbow Ends.*

"It is said," Mrs Hammerhulme was saying, "that t'Mithering Brethren 'ave a safe house in Wormton."

"But whoever would give them shelter?" a scandalised Mrs Macklefract demanded. Living far out in the Woldernesse, she had frequently been bothered by the Brethren.

"Who indeed? But they are not stupid. They would nivver confirm our suspicions by openly thwarting Wormtonians in broad daylight."

"They even deny us that!" snorted Mrs Macklefract.

"They are working for t'salvation of our souls from within," Mrs Hammerhulme assured her, "from within t'walls of Wormton!"

A delicious shudder ran through the group of women.

"But we threw 'em out years ago!" protested Mrs Amplepance.

"Well they're back!" Mrs Hammerhulme assured them.

"They've nivver bin away as far as we're concerned," said Mrs Macklefract. "Ah'm just so glad Great Uncle Henry kept up t'walls of our homestead."

"Ah blame t'promiscuous society," said Mrs Amplepance.

"We must all be especially vigilant," went on Mrs Hammerhulme. "They are convinced what they do is right. There's no gainsayin' 'em! Attainin' a goal or fulfillin' an ambition only encourages sins like pride, jealousy, covetousness and all manner of other evils."

"Man was put on earth to sin," agreed Mrs Amplepance, sardonically.

"Well, we all knaw that," quipped Mrs Macklefract, "but what were woman put on earth to do?"

"Housework!" said somebody. Nobody laughed.

"T'only path to certain salvation is complete frustration," Mrs Hammerhulme told them.

"So why don't they frustrate each other then?" asked Miss Periwig, who usually just listened.

"Because thwarting your fellow Brethren …"

"And Sistren!" Mrs Macklefract piped up.

"… only prevents souls being saved. Any act of self-defeating behaviour is as sinful as suicide in their eyes."

"Tha seems to knaw an awful lot about it," said Miss Periwig.

"Well, of course, ah do," Mrs Hammerhulme told her. "Ah have studied them at great length."

"Ah hate it when they regale thee wi' smug quotes," said Mrs Macklefract, "such as, 'If God had wanted us to have clean food, He wouldn't have invented t'fly.'"

" 'Consider t'fly,' " Mrs Hammerhulme began.

"And 'If He'd wanted us to have clean water, He wouldn't have invented dysentery,'" quoted Miss Periwig.

"The crosser they make us, t'happier they are," said Mrs Amplepance. "Ah hate 'em!"

"Ah'd like to see them ont pot wi' tummy upsets," said Mrs Macklefract.

Nobody shared her enthusiasm. She was in danger of being shown a red or yellow doyley by the management, for indelicate remarks.

"If t'desires of t'soul are denied, so t'soul is saved," said Mrs Hammerhulme, adroitly moving on.

"We must be vigilant," insisted Miss Periwig. "Look out for saboteurs or anyone who gleefully predicts failure!"

"Tha would think they would have difficulty recruiting," said Mrs Amplepance. "Can't be much of a life. Nubuddy likes 'em."

"Ah do not believe we should feel sorry for 'em," said Mrs Hammerhulme. "And they have surprisin' resources. Ah am convinced they have some wealthy benefactor behind 'em."

"Malefactor more like!" snorted Mrs Macklefract.

"But who?"

"What does thee think, Mrs Osmotherly?"

"Perhaps the Outlanders have become too well defended," suggested Mrs Osmotherly, entering their circle. "Wormton was always their main target. I think you're right, Mrs Hammerhulme. They are among us in Wormton, possibly at this very moment."

Her companions froze and then, as inconspicuously as they could manage, leaned back and looked around to check if the Mithering Sistren had penetrated *Where the Rainbow Ends*.

"Tell me, Mrs Macklefract," went on Mrs Osmotherly, "have the Mithering Brethren been active recently in your part of the Wold?"

"Nay, Mrs Osmotherly. Nay, they have not."

"I thought so. They used to target the shepherds but not any more."

"Sheep were their allies," said Mrs Macklefract. "Their self-destructive tendencies were a gift to t'Brethren."

"Aye." Mrs Hammerhulme sighed. "And now we 'ave t'Giant Lamb."

A waitress arrived with their meals and there was a pause in the discussion until plates and customers were matched up. A fresh pot of tea also arrived.

"So," said Mrs Hammerhulme, reaching for it, "who's going to be mother?"

"Well," said Mrs Amplepance, "it's funny you should say that ..."

But Mrs Osmotherly was staring at a small pot of green jelly that accompanied some lamb cutlets, and an extraordinary idea was forming in her mind.

CHAPTER 31

"The souls here are very concentrated," said Hob, as he strolled through Wormton with Reverend Tregaskis. A skateboard was strapped to his rucksack.

"Yes," said Reverend Tregaskis, who swung his leather case nonchalantly from one hand, "concentrated but not refined."

"Exactly!"

"However, there are a few who might be of interest to us."

"Few but some," conceded Hob.

"Did you come here on *Nosferatu*?"

"Of course."

"Hmm. In that case, I wouldn't be at all surprised that your presence has been noted by Mrs Osmotherly."

"Who?"

"Wormton's wise woman. She's developing the motorscope."

"Is she?"

"Yes. It's like the horoscope but it uses traffic to predict the future."

"I know full well what it is. I've used it myself."

"It's a bit like locomancy except there are no stations and no timetables."

Hob looked at Reverend Tregaskis. "Is she any good?"

"I think so. Mind you, *Nosferatu* is many things but discreet is not one of them."

Reverend Tregaskis gave Hob a large book.

"Here you are, old chap, a copy of *Bradshaw's Railway Guide to The Wold*. Mrs Osmotherly finished using railway timetables to divine the future decades ago. She'll have no idea of your movements if you use public transport."

"I can't do that. But what about *Nosferatu*?"

"*Nosferatu* can travel in the brake van. There's usually plenty of room."

"Now look here, Tregaskis, you know I can't ride on public transport, at least, not very often."

"Only because you can't read the timetables properly."

"That's not true. I'm just a little out of practice."

"Use the roads, then, but reconcile yourself to the certain knowledge that she'll be watching you."

"She can't watch all the roads all of the time."

"She doesn't need to. Do astrologers look at the stars all the time? Not if they're any good, they don't."

"Let's just think about this," said Hob. "Can she know why I'm here if she is still learning how to interpret the motorscope?"

"I don't think we should underestimate her."

"I reckon she'd be very keen to be able to interpret it correctly, don't you?"

"I can see where your train of thought is leading."

"It's just a question of what price enlightenment. You don't have plans for her soul, do you?"

Reverend Tregaskis shook his head. "She has renounced locomancy."

"I might have it then."

"You might. But you have something of mine already."

"Eh? Ah. Yes. I'm glad you reminded me."

"I'd like it back, please. Only, I had it on a borrow, myself."

"I should have mentioned it earlier," began Hob.

"Stop trying to look sincere," said Reverend Tregaskis, "and you never did guilty anyway."

"Now look here, Tregaskis. I'm afraid I've lost it."

"You've lost it?"

"Yes. It got out of its box."

"Oh dear. Dora will be cross."

"It's not the first time it's happened."

"That, my dear Hob, was entirely different. You never did tell me why you wanted it in the first place."

"It's rather a long story."

"You can tell me while we look."

"Look for what?"

"Why, the G-gnome, of course!"

"Well," began Hob, "it's all to do with a sheep. Or rather, a not-so-little lamb."

CHAPTER 32

Mr Heckmondwike was tired. Usually the soundest of sleepers, he'd lain awake for most of the night, pondering on the ideas Mr Quirkmaglen had put to him. When he did sleep, he dreamt of the Great Shepherd.

The Great Shepherd was becoming a frequent nocturnal visitor. Mr Heckmondwike would dream that he was going about his usual business but then realise that he was not alone. He would turn around to find the Great Shepherd watching him in troubled silence.

When at last He spoke, He turned Mr Heckmondwike's blood into water.

"Thee and thine are about to be sorely tried."

The following morning, he half expected to turn and find the Great Shepherd gazing at him sadly.

Delayed in his routine by such distractions, it was much later than normal when Mr Heckmondwike left Riddaw Lodge for Scar Fell Farm. By then, the gloomy day was as bright as it ever would be. It was an exceptionally misty morning, even for the Wold, and visibility was not good, so he drove his Mudlark cautiously down the familiar road.

He had not gone far, however, when he came across a sheep lying in the road. This was not unusual because the tarmac retained heat better than moorland and it was always drier, whatever the weather. Mr Heckmondwike pulled up by the sheep and got out.

As soon as it didn't run away he knew it was in trouble. Sheep would ignore a thundering Mudlark down on them completely. In fact, they often stepped out in front of them to provoke emergency stops. Only when the driver got out would they sprint away. Something about creatures walking on two legs put them into a blind panic.

When Mr Heckmondwike looked closer, what he saw made him gasp. It was not so much a sheep as the external wrapping of a sheep, little more than a fleece with its head and limbs still attached. Mr Heckmondwike passed his hands over it although it took all his self-control to touch it but all he could feel were bones. There were some vital organs within the bag of skin, but without the blood they were shrivelled and useless.

The worst thing, however, was that it was still warm.

There was a wound on the neck that looked vaguely familiar but Mr

Heckmondwike couldn't say why.

With a heavy heart he picked up the corpse, which was disgustingly light, and carried it back to the Mudlark. He ordered the fascinated Widdershins out and laid the dead sheep down in the back.

Widdershins ran off, barking. Not far away they had found another one. Three curious noses examined it closely but Mr Heckmondwike saw it was just the same as the last one.

Widdershins fell ominously silent. Three pairs of eyes and three pairs of ears became fixed on a point some way off in the mist.

"What is it?" asked Mr Heckmondwike but Widdershins ignored him. They didn't growl or whimper but just looked and listened and sniffed hard. It was a bit like "the look" collies give a sheep. But there was a terrible degree of uncertainty in all three of Widdershin's expressions. Mr Heckmondwike felt they were looking at something entirely new to their experience. And as he peered into the mist he saw other corpses of dead sheep lying around them.

He began to gather them up, two sickening bags of wool in each big hand, and threw them into the back of the Mudlark.

The dogs, however, remained rooted to the spot, now whining a little as they tracked the movement of something in the mist.

Mr Heckmondwike could only make out dead sheep.

"What is it, Wid? Der? Shins? What's happening to the sheep?"

Widdershins looked up at him with wise sorrowful eyes and wagged its tails in encouragement.

"It's not the Giant Lamb, is it?"

By way of confirmation, Der gave an embarrassed sneeze. She only did that when Mr Heckmondwike asked her a question to which she knew the answer and he did not.

Mr Heckmondwike stood up. "Ah knew it! The ground's not shakin'! So what is it out there?"

Widdershins didn't know for certain the answer to that but obviously had a better idea than he did.

"We can't leave these like this."

He took a few steps forward and then stopped.

He found his wrists were held in the mouths of Wid and Der. They gripped him softly but firmly while Shins stood in front of them, baring his teeth and growling at something unseen in front.

Mr Heckmondwike peered into the mist again.

"What is it?" he whispered.

Der rolled her eyes at him, a gesture she could have learned from Daisymaid.

"Ah think mebbe we go down to Wormton," he said softly.

Three tails began to wag. It wasn't vigorous, it was discreet. Shins looked back at Mr Heckmondwike, tongue lolling out of his mouth in a grin of approval.

Mr Heckmondwike took a step back and Wid and Der released their grip. Cautiously, the four living creatures made their way back to the Mudlark. Mr Heckmondwike opened the cab door for them and then climbed in himself. As soon as they were inside, the dogs pressed up against the passenger door window, looking into the mist with cocked ears.

He started up the Mudlark and drove on. It was the most depressing journey he'd ever made. Everywhere, there were dead sheep. Whenever the mist lifted a little, it revealed more bodies, right up to the limits of visibility.

Despite the damp chill of the mist, Mr Heckmondwike found that he was sweating. Feverishly he began to try to calculate how many dead sheep he'd seen so far. He realised that it must have been about a hundred.

He felt physically sick. Wid was looking at him with a worried expression on her face. She whined and pushed her nose under his arm as he drove.

"Typical collies," he said softly. "More worried about my well-being than thine own."

Shins barked and Mr Heckmondwike brought the Mudlark to a halt. Something had run across the road in front of them. He opened the door and the dogs leapt over him and darted off into the mist, living up to their name again with their contrary nature.

He stood beside the Mudlark, transfixed. Then he heard a wondrous sound above the silence. It was a bleat. He followed the sound and Widdershins emerged out of the mist with a sheep, acting as a kind of moving collie sheepfold. The poor sheep was clearly terrified and worn out. When Mr Heckmondwike walked up to it and picked it up, it made no resistance. Compared to the corpses, this animal was reassuringly heavy. He carried it back to the Mudlark.

He unloaded the dead sheep and put the live one in the back.

"Does tha reckon there's any more nearby?"

Widdershins leapt and barked at him joyfully.

"Go on, then! Find them! Bring them to me!"

Widdershins disappeared again. Mr Heckmondwike strapped a dead sheep to the bonnet of his Mudlark. He would bring one corpse home at any rate.

The dogs soon returned with half a dozen terrified animals. They almost seemed relieved to see Widdershins, and Mr Heckmondwike squeezed them into the back of the Mudlark, wishing for once that it were a long-wheelbase version.

Thankfully they didn't see any more bodies lying on the moor. The mist began to lift a little as they descended from the Outlands. As more of the Wold became visible, Mr Heckmondwike could see heafed flocks grazing contentedly. However, as the Mudlark drove by, something spooked them.

When they came to Scar Fell Farm, the dead sheep on the bonnet of his

Mudlark made workers coming out of the barns and milking parlours stop and stare.

Mr Heckmondwike drove up to the house and pulled up. He said nothing. The condition of the sheep did that for him. The Teds undid the tailgate and escorted the survivors away. George stared at the dead sheep on the bonnet.

Mrs Gaffathwaite came running out of the house in her apron. "Whatever's going on?"

"Strewth!" said Mr Kindlysides. "What 'ippened, mite?"

"Dunno lad. There's summat wrong wi' our fecund sheep."

"Lit's git the flock off the moors!"

CHAPTER 33

That evening, before work, Gloria visited Diggle again. She had not seen any more gnomes. None of her patients had died. They all seemed hale and hearty and likely to last for ages. The cottage hospital had assumed its familiar, pleasant atmosphere again.

Since her return from *Where the Rainbow Ends*, Mrs Osmotherly had been watching the roads and was now hunched over her notes.

Although comfortable in her armchair, Gloria was aware of an uneasy silence that had filled the room. "How did your chat with the editor of *Cognopolitan* go?" she asked.

Mrs Osmotherly replied slowly without looking up. "Dorinda?"

"Yes."

The clock ticked and the flames of the fire could actually be heard lapping against the coals on the fire.

"You did speak to her today, then?" Gloria persisted.

Opposite Gloria by the fireplace was another armchair, and on that was a velvet grey cushion with ears and legs. It opened two rheumy yellow eyes and stared at her blearily in a silent request for quiet. Then Indoors Food gave himself a half-hearted head massage with one paw to relieve his sudden tension.

Gloria's words had set up a spell that Mrs Osmotherly eventually found irresistible.

Although she didn't want to answer she looked up and put down her pencil. She slumped back into her great winged armchair that was nearly big enough for two people and, complete with its roof, resembled an upholstered cave. Across its arms was an angled table on wheels like those used by patients in the cottage hospital.

She stared at Gloria, lost in thought. Gloria curled her legs under her, snuggled deeper into the upholstery of her winged armchair and wrapped herself around a large mug of cocoa, even though she was not cold.

At last Mrs Osmotherly spoke. "She said I should be thankful to Slake for his interference."

Gloria sipped from her mug and said quietly, "I suppose without him, we wouldn't know the motorscope is interactive."

Mrs Osmotherly turned her head so that she looked sideways at Gloria. "You didn't speak to her as well, did you?"

"Me? No. I don't know her."

"Hmm," said Mrs Osmotherly. "It's just that those were her very words to me this morning."

"She has a point I suppose."

Mrs Osmotherly was suddenly electrified. "But without him we wouldn't have a Giant Lamb!"

Indoors was outraged by this outburst. He stared at Mrs Osmotherly with his paw up by his face as if appealing for calm.

Gloria waited for Mrs Osmotherly to subside again. "Is that really true?" she wondered.

"Without his interference, I would have been able to interpret the motorscope more accurately and perhaps done something about it."

"Like use the interactive motorscope."

"Yes! No! Stop tricking me, Gloria. It's been a long day and I am old."

Indoors Food gave Gloria what could only be called a knowing look and stretched out with his head upside down. His eyes remained open, however.

"What else did she say?"

"That we ought to enlist the help of all the other autologists throughout the Wold to watch for similar clues."

"That would give us the womanpower we need but it could still take ages."

"It will," Mrs Osmotherly assured her. "It's taken the best part of my life to get this far."

"Let's enlist their help through *Cognopolitan*. What does the motorscope tell you tonight?"

Mrs Osmotherly sipped her sherry, virtual sherry probably. "All that I saw was as it should be," she said.

"Mostly Wolseleys then," summed up Gloria. She began counting on her fingers. "Wolseley motorbikes, Wolseley cars, Wolseley trucks, Wolseley buses. Big ones, little ones, old ones, new ones, Wolseleys on their own and Wolseleys in little groups. All with subtle variations of meaning, but so long as there are Wolseleys on the roads all is well in the Wold. Wolseleys are the control in the experiment."

"Exactly! Like the ravens in the Tower of Lanson and the choughs on the cliffs of Anarchadia, their disappearance means trouble. It's the rest of the traffic we have to watch. Wormton doesn't have much anyway, which is why it's such an ideal place for me to work."

Gloria nodded. "It can't be easy, developing a new system of foretelling the future."

"No, it is not," agreed Mrs Osmotherly, "but it's coming along! At the moment all the indications are normal to good. So, why, Gloria, do I feel a chill in my bones?"

Gloria was suddenly looking at Mrs Osmotherly very intently.

Mrs Osmotherly stiffened. "Gloria? You're making me nervous, staring like that. You don't see any gnomes around me do you?"

"No, no. I was just thinking. You haven't seen the Horsepower Whisperer again, have you?"

"No. Nothing but Wolseleys with the occasional Armstrong-Siddeley and a couple of Jowetts."

"But what happens if he's driving a Wolseley?" Gloria asked. "What happens if he whispers to it and changes it into something else?"

"Like what?"

"There are rumours at work that one of cottage hospital ambulances is being altered. It is said they're making it much faster."

"Slake will be behind that."

"Is this Slake in league with the Soul Trader?"

Mrs Osmotherly considered this for a moment and then said, "No. I don't think so."

"People living close to Park Bottom have heard engines roaring."

"That could have been *Simurg*."

"Who?"

"*Simurg* is a what, not a who. It's a trike made out of a resurrected Wolseley that got squashed by a tree."

Gloria looked at Mrs Osmotherly very intently. "Brought back from the dead, you mean?"

"Yes. By Slake."

"I'm not sure I like the sound of this Slake. Don't you ever wonder what effect something reborn in another form could have on the motorscope?"

Mrs Osmotherly looked puzzled. "Reincarnated you mean?"

"Maybe. Either that or resurrection, in the case of *Simurg*."

"When you are my age, you may find yourself approving of reincarnation. I have analysed *Simurg*'s movements but found nothing sinister in them."

"So far," added Gloria.

"Every type of vehicle has its part to play in the motorscope," said Mrs Osmotherly. "Here, Wolseleys are normal. And ambulances that get help where it's needed must be beneficial. A Hillman Imp or a Dodge Demon are not in themselves evil, but only from association with the Horsepower Whisperer."

"We still don't know why he's here."

"No." Mrs Osmotherly sighed. "There's definitely something going on that we don't know about."

"Maybe he has a deal that was struck years ago," said Gloria.

"Like when the Wild Hunt came through here?"

Gloria shrugged. "That was before my time."

"So it's not your soul then."

"I hope not!"

Mrs Osmotherly shuddered at the idea of souls being bargained for before they were born.

"Although it's not my calling, maybe I ought to know some more about the motorscope. Perhaps I could help you in its development."

"Perhaps you could. I have worked on it alone for so long. One of us might spot something the other has missed."

"And I have seen the Wild Hunt more recently than you have, too."

"The last time I saw it was years ago when it came through here. I think there are still ripples from it in the local Journey Time/Road Space Continuum. Its road conjunctions can have a long-term effect."

"Some would say terminal," Gloria added. "What a challenge that would be! To analyse the Wild Hunt. We would need a whole team of Wise Women!"

Mrs Osmotherly snorted. "We would never run with the hunt! We would be strictly non-participating observers."

"Wouldn't we be better placed to observe it if we were in it?"

"Certainly not!"

"Of course." Gloria helped herself to another virtual chocolate biscuit. "We need to understand the effects by observing the road conjunctions. If we participate, we mess things up."

Mrs Osmotherly nodded ruefully.

"Generally speaking," Gloria went on, "Wolseleys give Wormton reliability. Jowetts and Armstrong-Siddeleys are also beneficial."

"The Wold is a happier place for all three," concluded Mrs Osmotherly.

"But in the current context, Hillman Imps and Dodge Demons are not so good."

"Again," said Mrs Osmotherly, "it depends on one's journey. Convert a ruined Wolseley 18/85 into *Simurg* and Mr Heckmondwike is convinced he will die if he rides in it. When Slake runs in the Wild Hunt he usually meets with success. Imps and Demons can be benign. So can souped-up ambulances. But it is said that the road to hell is littered with good Imp engines."

"So I've heard," said Gloria. "But how does the motorscope work?"

Mrs Osmotherly thought for a moment and then began to explain some of the basic principles.

"In its simplest terms," she said, "the motorscope works like this. If you're in a traffic jam, you're going to be late.

"When a little red van pulls up outside your house, you'll be receiving a letter soon, and if it's a big red van then it might be a parcel.

"If you live in a built-up area near some traffic lights that are frequented by poorly maintained diesel engined lorries, then you could soon suffer from asthma."

From these beginnings, she had developed the principles of autology. Progress in the early days had been slow. Often, she made no headway for months but, gradually, her copious notes and observations began to show some sort of subtle relationship with what was going on around her. Slowly, she began to recognise the signs, the road signs, which govern everything everywhere, and she passed this hard-won knowledge on to the other Wise Women in the Wold via the letter pages of *Wise Woman's Realm* and *Cognopolitan*. Wise women armed themselves with the latest editions of *The Observer's Book of Automobiles*, *The Observer's Book of Commercial Vehicles* and *The Observer's Book of Motorcycles*, and slowly the motorscope had been made to work. After a while, when little red vans bumped up the steep lane to her cottage on the side of the hill, Mrs Osmotherly could say fairly accurately who they would be from and what they would be about.

"Without sounding immodest I had always found it fairly easy to predict the next Dark Time. Even the apparently random Erratics or Occasionals were not difficult. Most Dark Time events are controlled by cycles.

"Have you ever have heard of Mrs Bradshaw?"

"Of course," Gloria replied. "She was renown for her ability to predict the appearance of people and items of luggage on railway platforms."

"Precisely," said Mrs Osmotherly, with a grin. "Most people are familiar with Bradshaw's published works, many of which illustrate her principles in the crudest possible terms, but I was lucky enough to discover the more refined developments that she achieved in later life. The cause and effect of alterations within the interwoven railway timetables can have quite dramatic effects, and for a while I was a devoted exponent of locomancy."

"Ah," said Gloria. "I've seen people on railway platforms practising locomancy."

"Were these people men?"

"Always, I think."

"Hmm. They are not true locomancers. Although they might be familiar with Bradshaw, they do not fully understand the signals associated with railway movements. They might be working for their wives, I suppose, for analysis of the data at home. You sometimes see them at coach stations or freight depots as well, undertaking similar work. Omnibusology and lorrymancy were the next developments. Timetables and logistics hubs have much to answer for."

"So do you need to be an omnibusologist to understand the motor scope?"

"Of course."

"And a lorrymancer?"

"Yes. While learning these arcane arts, it occurred to me that perhaps there was another system that was not so ordered, that did not run to a timetable, and that was, through being less structured, a much subtler yet more significant means of looking into the future, one that stretches beyond the next change of driver."

"Were you the first autologist of all?"

"As far as I know, yes. But believe me, Gloria, there have been many times when I wished that I was not!"

"Has your training in predicting Dark Time helped you in your studies?"

"Sometimes."

"Can you apply the cyclist philosophy to the motorscope, for instance?"

"Oh yes, but only as far as commuter traffic is concerned. Although there has already been all this work before on Bradshaw's and the fluctuations in bus punctuality ..."

"Ah, yes! The omnibusoscilloscope!"

"I was really starting out with something completely new, and I soon discovered that the motorscope doesn't have much apparent structure to which I could apply cyclist philosophy. It took me a long time to identify any sort of relationships beyond that, and only after recording countless observations."

"I can imagine!"

"Fortunately, I am very good at shorthand and have a photographic memory."

"It must still have been a lot of work."

"I think it was worth it. The results are more credible than anything gleaned from watching the stars."

"An imperfect system by any means," Gloria agreed. "The information is out of date by millions of light years."

"And yet the horoscope still has its devotees. That thought alone was enough to keep me going. The underlying principles of the motorscope convinced me that success must be ultimately achievable."

"Did you have many setbacks?"

"Yes! But I had many breakthroughs as well. The biggest one was concerning people's road signs."

"Road signs?"

"Yes. Everyone is born under a road sign. Not literally, you understand, but close to one, and this can have a profound effect upon their destination."

"And destiny follows on from destination?"

"Exactly!"

"What road sign am I, then?" asked Gloria.

Mrs Osmotherly studied her for a moment. "I would say that your road sign, Gloria, is Hospital."

"That's amazing! I was born just to the north of the sign of the Hospital!"

"It's not so remarkable. Hospital is the most common birth road sign."

"It could have been a lucky guess."

"It could have been."

"But it wasn't!" exclaimed Gloria. "I am a typical Hospital. I have all the characteristics."

"Apart from being full of illness."

"Well obviously! But I'm a nurse. It stands to reason. So which road sign are you, Mrs Osmotherly?"

"I am a Tram Pinch."

"Wow. What's that then?"

"It's a very old sign. It warns of a congruence of the road kerb and the rails of a tram. There is always a danger in such situations of narrow-section tyres getting caught in the rails and steering bicycles and old-fashioned cars off the road."

Gloria studied Mrs Osmotherly. "Yes, I think I can see it now."

Mrs Osmotherly swelled with pride. "There's not so many of us about now," she said. "I was born at home for one thing."

"And trams are getting rarer nowadays."

"Yes, although Wormton still has them."

"It's interesting how tram pinches can disrupt the course of cyclists."

"Yes. I've often wondered about that. Another course of research when I have time."

"Can the motorscope be applied to pedestrians?" wondered Gloria.

Mrs Osmotherly thought for a moment before answering. "Maybe. You would have to undertake a different process of observation, for one thing."

"Another potential area for development?" asked Gloria.

"For someone else," agreed Mrs Osmotherly.

"Some motorscope principles might apply to it," suggested Gloria. "The future could be predicted by the way they walk."

"Or where they walk."

"Like if they walk under a ladder."

"Or pass upon some stairs. Are you interested in developing the new science of – let me see – plodology?"

"I am, actually. I've heard of the mischief that the Mithering Brethren can cause. That's one thing the motorscope can't help with, because they don't drive."

"The Mithering Brethren know about the motorscope," seethed Mrs Osmotherly. "They walk everywhere to thwart me in my attempts to predict when and where they will strike next!"

"What happens if we thwart them?" mused Gloria.

"That I've never understood."

"Their souls are not saved, then?"

"Put it this way. They do not seem to appreciate the gesture."

"Perhaps it is holier to be the thwarter than the thwartee."

"To save rather than be saved? Who knows?"

CHAPTER 34

Later that same night, something stirred in Park Bottom. An old ambulance emerged from the trees and bushes around Frogheat and burbled its way purposefully towards the main road out of town. Although it moved slowly, there was a muted urgency about its exhaust note and it sat lower on the road, as if it were about to leap. Otherwise, Wormton was quiet. Many of the older inhabitants didn't see too well after nightfall, and most Wormtonians were tucked up in bed. They only noticed nocturnal traffic if their windows rattled enough to disturb their sleep. And as a lot of them rattled their own windows with their snoring, the ambulance passed by largely unnoticed.

After a dismally misty month, the night sky was suddenly clear. The moon was a full one and seemed determined to outdo the sun. Deep shadows like solid blocks of darkness propped up the jumble of houses, while the other side of the street was bathed in silver. The street lamps were unlit because they would have been quite unnecessary and the ambulance drove on sidelights, as headlamps seemed superfluous.

Slake muted the ambulance's highly tuned engine as he drove between the houses. He was letting the oil circulate and warm up properly. He'd spent a long time accurately matching engine parts. Now the carthorse had become a racehorse.

At this hour, only two town gates were open, one on the Mithering road to the west and the other on the road to Bedlam in the east, both manned by a skeleton crew of volunteers to keep the Mithering Brethren out.

Through the West Gate, the open road stretched out into the Wold. In some of the hollows around the riverbanks, wisps of mist still lurked, but visibility was generally good.

Slake pulled up at the barrier beside the gatehouse, stopped the engine and alighted. The chill of the moonlit crispness made his heart thump and he savoured the sensation. Within the embrace of Wormton's walls, all was safe and secure, and deep within the bulk of the gatehouse would be a brightly lit hearth and armchairs for the elderly volunteer constables.

He heard the sound of a radio playing music. It was *A Hundred Best Tunes*, broadcast by the Wold Service. None of them were any of his best tunes but it was still good to hear them.

He knocked on the studded oak door to the right of the main gateway and opened it. The warmth, light and music fell over him as if the room had been full to bursting. His eyes hurt with the sudden brilliance.

"Hallo, Slake!" A little silver-haired old lady had been captured by an enormous armchair and was being toasted alive by the roaring fire.

"Hallo, Mrs Amplepance. Are you keeping well?"

"Ah'm keeping very well, thanks lad. The important thing is to keep warm," and she wriggled deeper into the cushions. "Close t'door behind, thee, and come in. What's tha doing out toneet?"

"I'm going to test one of the cottage hospital ambulances. I've been working on it for Mr Grandlythorpe."

Mrs Amplepance sucked her teeth. "Make it go faster, tha means."

"That's what you want in an ambulance, isn't it," Slake retorted with a grin as he approached the roaring fire.

"That all depends. That all depends on whether tha's getting out of t'way of it or being rattled daft int back."

"I reckon we'll have to agree to disagree."

"Aye, lad, ah reckon tha's reet. Ah, here's Daddy."

Mr Amplepance emerged from a small doorway that led to a stone spiral staircase.

"Ow do, Slake. Is tha goin' out toneet?"

"I am."

"It's a beautiful, clear neet for a drive."

"He's testing that ambulance outside," his wife told him.

"Oh, aye. Goin' far?"

"Not too far. Just enough to give it its head, let it sing its song. You know."

"Ah remember when t'Wild Hunt came through." Mr Amplepance fell into the clutches of an armchair similar to that which had his wife in its terrible grip. "That were quite summat."

"If tha enjoyed it so much why doesn't tha go with him?" his wife wanted to know.

"Nay, lass. We're on duty toneet, t'pair of us. We can't leave! Besides," he added, turning to Slake, "it's a young man's game."

"Not necessarily," he said. "I've seen loads of old codgers race in the Wild Hunt when I was in The Petropolis."

"Ah'm built for comfort me, not speed," replied Mr Amplepance, and his wife giggled. "How long does tha think tha'll be? Our watch ends at six."

"Nowhere near that long. I just want to hit the open road and see what it'll do. I don't have much brew, and it's likely to be a juicy beast."

"Ah love the smell o' high octane brew," enthused Mrs Amplepance. "It makes the backs of ma eyeballs go cold!"

"Reet, then," said her husband. "We'll look out for thee on tha return."

"Ow's tha getting' on with our old Wolseley?" asked Mrs Amplepance.

"Ah saw thee driving it the other day."

"It's far too good for me," said Slake. "It drives like new."

"Aye. It allus were a good little car."

"You're right there. I quite fancy making a special out of a Wolseley 8 one day but there are plenty of rougher examples down at Bessie Dooker's. I'll just keep that old car as it is."

Mr Amplepance stared at Slake. "Well, ah nivver thought ah'd hear the like! Did tha hear that, mother?"

"Aye! Seems like the lad's turning into a reformed character!"

"You been racin' along t'road to Damascus?"

Slake laughed. "No! Don't worry. I just recognise the merits of keeping your old car together, that's all."

"Good for thee, lad," said Mr Amplepance.

"Ah'm glad to hear it," agreed his wife.

"Keep the home fire burning," Slake told them and he drew himself away from the gatehouse fire. "I'd better get a shake on. Good night." And with a chorus of "Goodnight, Slake," he was outside again.

Back in the cab of the ambulance, Slake said, "Trouble's going," and thumbed the starter. The starter motor struggled to turn over the high compression engine. Slake grinned when the big six-cylinder motor caught and he rattled the foundations of the gatehouse for the Amplepance's benefit. He turned on the lights, and the dashboard lit up his face.

From within the gatehouse, Mr Amplepance pulled the finely weighted levers to raise the barrier.

"Trouble's gone!" said Slake and he snicked the ambulance into first gear and drove it out into the Wold.

It revved easily and the exhaust sounded suddenly loud as it bounced back from the town walls, which shrank back on either side. Quickly he selected second and the same thing happened. Third saw him accelerating steadily away from Wormton. He didn't want to disturb anyone and waited until he was well clear of the town before really stirring things up. He gently tried a test of the roll-on acceleration, and the exhaust note hardened and became more purposeful.

Then he was into fourth, much earlier than would have been possible with an ordinary ambulance, and he nailed it. He had waited long enough. The ambulance simply sprang forward as if it had been in a catapult. He found himself about to negotiate a corner. Was he here already? His uprated brakes allowed him to scrub off the excess speed. The tyres were nothing special, being of an old design with high, flexible sidewalls, but they gripped well enough and did not feel too soggy. Slake's face was hurting from grinning. He pressed the loud pedal and the back end of the ambulance stepped out of line as if it wanted to lead the procession.

Slake whispered as he conducted the ambulance with indecent haste.

"Don't slacken off and we just hang the tail out around the corner," and the Wolseley did as it was told.

He whooped with delight. "Perfect! So communicative! My guesses at tyre pressures are just about right!"

Another corner came up and he didn't brake so much, just tugged at the wheel and then laughed out loud as the ambulance adopted its cornering posture in a finely balanced tail slide.

The next thing he knew, the passenger door flew open and a dark figure leapt into the cab. An attractive young woman with great swirling tresses of black hair was thumbing through a personal organiser beside him.

Slake throttled back in surprise.

"Reynald Thorngumbald?" she said, glancing at him for a moment.

"What?"

"Reynald Thorngumbald? That is you, isn't?"

"Yeah, but nobody calls me that. I'm Slake to everyone these days."

"Okay. Slake then. Why Slake? Forget it. We don't have much time. Slake. Listen to me. Turn this ambulance around now and return to Wormton before you crash it."

"What?"

"You heard. Don't argue."

"Who are you?"

"See these?" She opened the door and unfolded a pair of enormous wings. "I'm your guardian angel. Bye," and she leapt out of the ambulance and disappeared.

Slake stood on the brake pedal and the ambulance screeched to a halt. He jumped out and ran back down the road to where his skid marks started but there was no sign of her. Everything was quiet. There was just the reassuring throb of his ambulance at idle.

Still looking all around, Slake stomped back to the ambulance.

"Double weird!" he said as he climbed back into the cab. "Must have sniffed the brew a little too much. Trouble's goin'!" He re-engaged first. "Everybody trying to tell me what to do!" He flicked out a stopwatch from the pocket of his leather jacket. "Time for a proper test! Trouble's gone!"

He floored the throttle and the rear tyres lit up in clouds of rubber smoke. The ambulance shot forward and the needle on the tacho he'd bolted to the dashboard swung around. He snatched second, snatched third. He hung on and saw the speedo needle swing past sixty. He pressed the stopwatch and gasped.

"Nine and a half seconds! By the spanners of St Bendix, that's brilliant!"

The next thing he knew he was opening his eyes and seeing what appeared to be another angel.

CHAPTER 35

On a bend in one of the old and infrequently used mountain passes, Hob gazed out over the Vale of Wormton. He sat on a dry stone wall by his bike in the moonlight, sucking a blade of grass as if he were Mr Heckmondwike. Mist lay in the hollows below but on the high ground everything was clear.

"No doubt you have heard of Fortunato?" he murmured.

His rucksack squeaked that it had. It was perched on the saddle of *Nosferatu* and moved about very slightly as if it was alive, which it wasn't.

Hob removed his blade of grass. "The Terror of the Targa Florio? The Scourge of the Carrera Panamerica?"

Each question brought another squeak.

"He was the quickest of the Quick, the fastest of the Fast. We had a deal that he would ride with us in the *Terminal Murrain*."

The rucksack squeaked again.

"But when he at last splashed his brains out in the Mille Miglia, I found that the Foundling of Rauschenberg had prior claim."

Hob paused and the curious rucksack wriggled for him to go on.

"Fortunato sold his soul twice over. He believed the two deals would cancel each other out but the Foundling's deal predated mine. Fortunato's soul belongs to him."

The rucksack quivered like a bag full of kittens on their way to being drowned.

"I suppose I could have ignored the technical niceties," mused Hob. "The Foundling may be a member of STANTA but I'm not."

The rucksack piped a question.

Hob shot a glance at it in disbelief. "You don't know?" He thought for a moment. "Well, I suppose I shouldn't be surprised. You're just skirrows and obsessed with the Wild Hunt. STANTA is short for the Soul Transference and Necromancy Trade Association. It's an incorporeal self-regulating profess-ional body that issues guidelines and advice – none of it at all ethical – for those who trade in souls and commune with the dead. It recommends a code of malpractice and offers a mediation service."

The rucksack became quite animated. It sounded as if a great many squeaking entities inside it were clamouring to be heard.

"Don't be ridiculous," sneered Hob, above the din.

The rucksack subsided into dejected hopelessness.

"Mediation between disputing soul traders, not between them and the possessed. The situation created by Fortunato's double dealing is by no means unique and is one of the issues covered by STANTA's guidelines. The prior claim is upheld."

The rucksack's next squeak was very subdued.

"Well I could have disputed it, but it wouldn't have helped. Deutz is a fully paid-up member whereas I am not even affiliated. I've barely been trading for a quarter of the requisite century. And you only have to do a soul count in there to see that I'm doing quite nicely, thank you. Even when I have been trading for long enough, I don't think I'll bother joining."

The rucksack evidently thought that joining would be a good idea.

"Why? I'm not the joining sort of chap. STANTA can't do anything for me that I can't do for myself."

There was another squeak from the rucksack.

"Well, I could try to steal Fortunato's soul from Deutz but he's a mate. I'm sure you understand."

So – Hob's souls in torment wanted to know – why were they in the middle of nowhere waiting for the Foundling of Rauschenberg?

"I've asked Deutz here tonight to trade for the soul of Fortunato."

The rucksack considered this for a moment, but before it could ask the next obvious question Hob answered it.

"I have a soul he might like. Or, rather, I can get it for him. You see, while I trade for Wild Hunters, he trades for souls with some special talent or peculiarity. He's a bit like that himself. That's what comes from being locked up on your own in a darkened tower for most of your life. Do you know? He can identify different alloys merely by passing his hands over them. That's an elemental step in thaumetallurgy, that is."

The rucksack twisted around on *Nosferatu*'s saddle to study Hob more closely. He was still gazing out over the valley, waiting for the Foundling to come, but every so often he looked the other way, back towards Wormton.

"Yes, it's one hell of a soul, this one," mused Hob, talking to himself as much as to those in his possession. "I've never seen the like before, and I'm pretty certain old Deutz hasn't either. And any minute, with a stroke of luck, they shall both be here and Fortunato's soul will be one step nearer to being mine."

They continued to wait. Clouds raced across the moon like razor blades slitting eyeballs, and the glittering humours poured down and gathered in the river valleys.

Earlier that evening, there had been the distant sound of a highly tuned engine. It clearly sang *The Song of The Machine* and it had the power to stir Hob and each and every one of the souls who raced with him in the Wild

Hunt. It was a pleasant surprise to hear it, out here in the Woldernesse, and all the souls agreed it that was a big capacity straight six and whoever had worked on it had done a very good job indeed. They'd listened to it for some time as it sang its song but then there had been a crash and an ominous silence.

Hob had been tempted to go and have a look but the soul of Fortunato was a prize he wanted too badly.

Eventually, his patience was rewarded.

He spotted a movement far away on one of the old roads to Mithering. Despite his wrap-around shades, he had very good night vision and a highly developed sense of proximity awareness.

Approaching from the east came a horseless carriage. It wasn't a car. It was a horseless horse-drawn carriage. Its shafts were folded back over the empty driver's seat and it bowled along without any obvious means of propulsion. It rattled over the ruts and the carriage body swayed violently on the leather straps that served as its suspension. Its silhouette was truly dreadful and its shadow under the hunter's moon – a wild hunter's moon – was far larger than it ought to be. Behind it flew a small flock of large black birds.

Hob threw away his blade of grass and stood by his bike. He watched the horseless carriage approach, and when it went below the brow of the hill he waited for it to reappear.

As the horseless carriage crested the hill, it seemed to rise up out of the very ground itself. It slowly rolled up to Hob and a large number of ravens settled on the dry stone walls nearby but kept a respectful distance. A door flew open of its own accord and a gaunt figure alighted, dressed in what had been fashionable in 1830s Germany. He bowed slightly to Hob, clicked his heels and Hob returned the gesture.

"Good evening, Deutz," said Hob

"*Guten abend*, Hob," said Deutz. "Although it is the mittel of the night. How goes it with you, my young friend?"

Although they looked about the same age, the Foundling of Rauschenberg was over a hundred years older. It was a fringe benefit of soul trading.

"It goes very well, old chap," said Hob. They shook hands. "Thank you for coming this evening."

"The ravens brought me your message. You might have a soul for me."

"Yes. I rather think I might. It should be here very soon. I'm glad you came when you did."

"*Ja*, I'm sorry I'm late. The Karmawallah was having a post-soultaking sale."

"No problem," said the accommodating Mr Hob. "Keep your eye on that rocky promontory over there."

Below them a large flock of sheep grazed contentedly. The mist along the river was beginning to climb up towards them.

"Whatever it is we are waiting for," said Deutz, "it should be something out of the common mould."

"I can assure you it is. You still have Fortunato's soul?"

"Of course."

"Good."

Deutz nodded. "I know you want his soul to ride against in the Wild Hunt."

"You gave him proximity awareness."

"He was the best, you know. After you, of course."

Hob smiled.

As they watched, a strange shape appeared on the rock. It seemed to have arrived on all fours but then it stood on two legs and looked out over the flock below.

"Hob! What manner of creature is this?"

"Wait!" whispered Hob.

The strange animal seemed to shrink. It was breathing out as far as it could. Then it began to expand as it drew in as much night air as possible. It paused and opened its mouth. There was some delay over the distance but soul traders can compensate for that sort of thing. Even before the sound travelled to them, Deutz heard it.

It was loud and defiant in a sheepish sort of way. It spoke to the sheep below and they responded with similar cries of their own. They ran away from the mist, around the base of the rock and out of sight.

"A weresheep!" gasped Deutz.

"Impressed?"

"It's bleating at the moon! How did you find it?"

"I can't possibly tell you that."

"Do you have a claim on its soul?"

Hob shrugged enigmatically.

Deutz grinned. "So what's to stop me going and getting it myself?"

"Nothing," replied Hob. "It's just that it's easier for me to do it than for you. In exchange, I want Fortunato's soul to race against in the Wild Hunt."

"I understand. You act as my soul agent and Fortunato keeps your reactions honed to those of an amphetamised cat."

Hob gestured to the rucksack on *Nosferatu*. "Behold, the quick and the dead."

"Not just quick, either. As *blitzen* you will be!"

Hob grinned wolfishly.

Deutz considered Hob's proposal. "Very well," he said. "Fortunato's soul in return for that of the weresheep. We have a deal," and they spat on their palms and shook hands.

Both grinned at each other. Both were going to get what they wanted.

CHAPTER 36

"Hello," said the angel. Unlike Slake's guardian angel, this one had a halo.

"Have I died and gone to heaven?" Slake asked her.

The angel laughed but flushed a little. "Well, we do try to make our patients as comfortable as possible but hospitals," she said, offering him a massive clue, "are generally not about sending people to heaven."

"I thought you were an angel."

The angel really blushed this time. Slake realised that he suddenly felt very much better.

She made to tuck him up but he was just lying on the bed, not in it, so she settled for smoothing out the flares of his jeans.

She moved her head and the halo disappeared. The light in the ceiling she had been standing under suddenly hurt Slake's eyes.

"Haven't I seen you before somewhere?" he asked her.

"Oh, come on!" she said. "I know you've just regained consciousness but you don't know how corny that sounds!"

Slake looked down at himself, expecting to see white jeans and a white leather jacket, but he was still wearing his old clothes.

"I'm not dead then."

"Not yet. From what I understand, though, it's only a matter of time."

"That's true for all of us."

"Some sooner than others. What's that say on your tee shirt?"

Slake mumbled, " 'The faster I get, the better I was.' "

The nurse angel gave him a look not unlike that Daisymaid might give George or the Teds when they dared to enter her kitchen with their boots on.

"I *have* seen you before, though. I'll remember in a minute."

"How about you telling me your name?"

"Reynald Thorngumbald."

"You're kidding!"

"No, really."

"It says Slake here."

"Ah. Yeah. That's … that's … that's my name as well."

"I see."

"No. Really."

"And where do you live?"

"Frogheat, Park Bottom."

"I don't have to do this, you know."

"Honestly. It's true."

"Well, you'll be spending the rest of the night in the cottage hospital, as soon as we can find you a pair of pyjamas."

"Last thing I remember I was driving an ambulance."

"Well, you were found in an ambulance."

"A lot of hospital patients are, I imagine. You make me sound as if I was tucked away in the glove box."

"Maybe you were. I understand the ambulance was quite a mess."

"Whaddya mean, quite a mess?"

"There's no need to get excited."

"I'm okay. Really. Just tell me about the ambulance."

"Well, I haven't seen it myself, of course, but I gather that you rolled it end over end."

"Oh no!" sighed Slake and he put his head in his hands. Some of his fingers were bandaged.

"Cheer up. You had a miraculous escape. You must have a guardian angel looking over you. Besides me."

"I did. She appeared out of nowhere, told me off about something and then jumped out."

"Really?" The nurse angel's eyes were as round as saucers.

He nodded. "You don't believe me, do you?"

"Look, Slake, I really think you'd better get some rest."

"Yeah. No worries." Slake frowned. "I've definitely seen you before somewhere. And you know my name."

"I know both of them."

"So what's your name?"

"Gloria. Go on. Say it. Say 'That's a pretty name!'"

"I could, of course, but I was just wondering, actually, what the N stood for?"

Gloria frowned. "What?"

"I was just wondering what the N stood for."

"What do you mean?"

"Gloria N Excelsis," explained Slake.

Gloria laughed. Then she stopped. "It stands for nurse," she said. "Here, you might need this."

He took it from her. "Aha! Bedpan humour."

"I definitely think you need some rest. I know I do."

"I remember now! You were at the station while I was waiting for some of my containers to turn up. You were unloading an enormous trunk."

"That must have been the day I arrived in Wormton. We had three derailments and three re-railments. I thought it was all rather fun."

"Thanks to you I bought myself a rather nice six-cylinder Wolseley Hornet, completely unseen."

"I do what I can for all my patients."

"Really?" said Slake, giving her what could only be described as a sly grin.

"Within reason," Gloria replied pointedly, "and with one or two possible exceptions. And now I must go and attend to them. I don't think there's much wrong with you."

"I have to confess that I've never felt better."

"I'm so pleased. My job is done then. Good night."

CHAPTER 37

Mr Grandlythorpe stared at five pieces of paper on his desk. Usually, these pieces of paper, if there were any at all, came singly.

"Five missing persons already this year," he muttered.

"What's that, Mr Grandlythorpe?"

The only other sound was Miss Pickeridge on her typewriter in the next office. The steady tattoo of her fingers on the keys hindered his thought processes.

"Five missing persons already this year," he repeated more loudly.

"It was only two this morning. Who are they?"

"Ramblers."

"Oh dear." She appeared in the doorway, a thin, efficient woman who was wasted in her job but happy enough to plod along with it. "That's not good, is it?"

"Nay, lass, it is not. If word gets out that ramblers are vulnerable, they'll cease to come."

"And the season's only just starting."

"Ah knaw."

She picked up a copy of *The Wormton Respondent*. "I thought so. Mrs Thorngumbald, President of the Landlady's Association, was saying only last week what a promising season we were having. She's currently hostess to that eminent Professor who's searching for the Black Orchid."

"The Black Orchid?" Mr Grandlythorpe sighed. "Appen he'll be next. Our landladies are getting restless. Too many of their guests have ventured out into the Woldernesse and not come back."

"No Woldspeople have disappeared yet, then."

"Nay, lass. We don't traipse about idly."

Someone entered the outer office and Miss Pickeridge ducked out of the doorway. He heard her exchange pleasantries with someone and then she cleared her throat and announced, "Constable Arkthwaite to see you, Mr Grandlythorpe,"

"Ah ha! Show him in!"

Constable Arkthwaite filled the doorway; his dark blue arms the thickness of another man's thighs.

"Now then, Mr Grandlythorpe."

"How ta fettlin', Constable?"

"Ah'm awreet. It's all them other beggars. Fettlin' well thysen?"

"Aye, nobbut graidly, tha knaws."

"Appen? Wormton is fair to middlin' these days, despite everythin'."

"Aye. Heck as likely as happen as mebbe tha's reet. Not too shabby e'en tho it's me that says so as shouldn't."

They gripped each other in a Woldsman's clench and then sat down, surreptitiously nursing their aching hands.

"What can ah do for thee?"

Constable Arkthwaite nodded at the reports on Mr Grandlythorpe's desk. "Ah see tha's heard about ramblers disappearin'."

"Aye," said Mr Grandlythorpe gloomily.

"And there's summat bleeding t'sheep dry."

"Appen?"

"That's not at all. Has tha spoken to Slake this morning?"

"Nay, Constable. What's to do?"

"Ah might as well tell thee straight, then. Ee's written off thine ambulance."

"What!"

"He hit summat last night and rolled it end over end."

"Badly?"

"Aye. It's wrecked. Mr Heptonstall's attempting to salvage what he can as we speak."

"Then the bill will go to Slake and not the parish council."

"Fortunately, he 'ad lightened it by takin' out all t'medical equipment so it were spared the crash."

"Wouldn't've bin much use as an ambulance, then."

"Oh ah dunnaw. It woulda got there quickly. It just wouldn't've bin able to treat anyone."

"Ah don't reckon he understood the question."

"I were wonderin' if he might 'ave a look at ma police car."

"Er, how is Slake, by t'way?"

"He's awreet, considering. He was knocked unconscious and has cuts and bruises."

"Mrs Osmotherly usually prevents accidents with that motorscope of hers, but she fell out wi' t'lad."

"Aye. The point is, though, that Slake hit summat big on the Mithering road. He was travelling at a hell of a lick, mind. He must a done a champion job on thine ambulance and nay mistake."

Mr Grandlythorpe grunted.

"There's nay sign of another vehicle being involved," went on Constable Arkthwaite, "and he can't remember what happened, but he musta hit summat. Summat big. And whatever it was isn't there any more. There's summat odd about t'site, too."

"Oh, aye?"

"Aye. There's a big pile of what looks like white wire. Except it's not wire. It could be plastic, but it's oily and stinks when tha burns it."

"What does thee make o' that?"

"Tekken wi' t'giant hoofprints, ah think there is only one explanation."

"Which is?"

"Slake crashed into t'Giant Lamb."

"Aw naw!"

"There's more. Summat attacked t'Scar Fell Farm flock, yesterday. Bled a lot of it dry. Mr Heckmondwike's greatly troubled by it."

"Aye, ah'll warrant!"

"Not t'heafed Tablebacks, tha knaws, but some of t'outland flock up by Riddaw Forest."

Mr Grandlythorpe shivered, which for such a big, bluff man was a terrible thing to see.

"All t'shepherds have been warned," went on Constable Arkthwaite, "and as many sheep as possible 'ave been moved down to t'lower pastures."

"But it's t'highland pasture t'farmers need to exploit at this time o' year."

"Ah knaw," said the constable. "And t'Landlady's Association need t'ramblers n'all."

"So what have we got?" asked the town clerk. He began to count out misfortunes on the prizewinning carrots he called fingers. "Ramblers are disappearin', there's summat bleeding t'sheep dry on t'high pastures and t'Giant Lamb is big enough to be a threat to traffic."

"There's summat else, lad."

"What else?"

"Just a small thing. Some of t'Scar Fell flock somehow moved themselves from one field to another. And t'same thing 'appened to t'Gout Leg Pike flock, n'all. It's as if they thought t'grass were greener."

"That sounds like Mithering Brethren to me," said Mr Grandlythorpe.

"Ah bloody well hope it isn't! Nay, if owt, t'sheep movements kept t'death rate down. They were moved away from t'areas where sheep were bein' killed."

"Is there a link?" asked Mr Grandlythorpe.

"Ow should ah knaw?"

"T'WPC will have to act," said Mr Grandlythorpe, grimly.

Constable Arkthwaite just snorted.

"Somehow we've got to contain this," went on Mr Grandlythorpe. "If word got out to the Wide Wold, nubuddy will come here or buy our meat."

"So we keep it quiet."

"As far as we can. We'd best let Wormton folk knaw."

"Reckon *Where t'Rainbow Ends* is buzzin' about this already."

CHAPTER 38

The next Dark Time was exactly as Mrs Osmotherly had predicted. It lasted for ages, and after the recent events many Woldspeople found themselves wondering what they would find after its passing.

Mr Heckmondwike lay awake throughout. It was often difficult to sleep through these periods of intense magnetic activity, and although he didn't have much hair to stand on end what he did have bristled energetically. And when he put his flat cap on, to face the next uncertain dawn, it levitated a few millimetres from his scalp.

He hated it when that happened.

At last the dark sky and strange lights began to fade, and as soon as they cleared Riddaw Lodge his clockwork two-way burst into life.

It was Slake. "How ta fettlin', Mr Heckmondwike?"

"Ah'll be frank with thee, lad. Ah could be better. Summat's up wi' our fecund sheep."

"What the flock?"

"Aye."

"What's wrong with 'em?"

"Summat's bleeding 'em dry."

Slake's effervescent enthusiasm evaporated. "I'm sorry to hear about that."

"Thanks, lad. Sorry to hear about thine ambulance."

"Thanks. Huh. It wasn't mine, it belonged to the WPC."

"Does that make it any better or worse?"

"Worse, I guess."

"They're not ma sheep, ayther. It's ma job to look after 'em."

"So, are we going after the Giant Lamb or not?"

"Aye. Ah have nay choice, Slake. Ah'm a shepherd."

"Then so am I. Is everything in place?"

"Aye."

"See you shortly, then."

Mr Heckmondwike had laid his plans carefully. He knew a large but roofless byre that had been abandoned many years ago to the Woldernesse. It stood a few leagues to the west at the head of a narrow valley formed by a curious twist of the sheer cliff faces of Nibley Edge. All they had to do was spook the monster into running up the valley until it was apparent that it was a dead end. There they could restrain it progressively with a large amount of cables, ropes and nets that he'd assembled beforehand. Once they'd caught it, they work out what to do with it.

Slake at last leapt over the horizon in his enraged V8 Mudlark with a great "Yump!" and Mr Heckmondwike immediately felt a small weight removed from his still leaden heart.

"Tha's late," he said as Slake slid to a halt outside Riddaw Lodge.

"I went for another burn. Seemed silly not to on such a splendid morning. Watch this," and Slake blipped the throttle. The body of the Mudlark twitched to the right with the torque reaction.

Mr Heckmondwike found himself grinning, too.

Slake switched off the engine, unbuckled himself from his bucket seat and jumped out. "I suppose you'll be wanting one now," he said.

"Ah've got a Wolseley stationary engine if tha wants to do a swap."

"Nice try, Mr Heckmondwike, but no thanks. There's a lot of work gone into this machine and not just on the engine, either. I've uprated the suspension and the brakes to suit. It's still under development, of course, but a replica to this stage of tune will still set you back quite a few hundred quid. They take a long time to build, y'see."

Mr Heckmondwike could tell the danger signs. The bonnet was already up and Slake was talking rapidly about dual quads and high lift cams. Unless he acted quickly he would receive another blow-by-blow account of how the latest Slakespeed V8 Mudlark had been put together.

"Come on," he said, squinting at a bright patch in the clouds. "We're burning daylight."

"So. What's the plan? Leave it alone, and then it'll come home, bringing its tail behind it?"

Mr Heckmondwike wagged his finger at him. "Thee! Thee! Tha should be ashamed of thysen!"

"All right, all right, all right! Keep ya flat hat on!"

Mr Heckmondwike reached up for his flat hat to check it wasn't still levitating, took it off, looked at it and put it back on again. "This is nay time for nursery rhymes, lad!"

"I get the message. You regard my last remark with all the contempt it deserves."

"Aye. Ah do at that. Besides," Mr Heckmondwike added a little ruefully, "we tried that fust of all."

They stood examining each other's faces for a while, and at last finding what they were both looking for barked out a staccato laugh and slapped each other around the shoulders.

Mr Heckmondwike looked at Widdershins. "Let's go get that Lamb!" he said, and the three-headed sheepdog bounced and cavorted all around them.

"Thanks for helping, lad," he said, as Widdershins leapt into the back of his Mudlark.

"I just wanted to watch a master at his work," said Slake, climbing behind the wheel of his Mudlark. "Besides. It shouldn't be difficult. It's only a sheep."

"Aye. And a lamb at that. And ah am resolved to bringin' it in."

"Dead or alive!"

"Alive, Slake, and don't tha forget it. A dead sheep before its time is nay use to anyone."

"All right!" said Slake. "Let's get this show off the road!"

They drove for several hours, heading east and a little way south but always, it seemed, in a steady climb. This was probably the highest part of unforested moor and, once the cliff face of Nibley Edge had disappeared over the horizon, it felt as if they were being squashed by the flat-bottomed clouds that floated above them in a sky so thin Mr Heckmondwike could almost see stars.

They pulled up by some peaty pools of water and Slake took the opportunity to refill the fuel tanks of his Mudlark from some jerry cans. "That's the downside of having a more efficient engine," he explained. "There's always the temptation to make use of the greater power. It's not an overly thirsty beast. It's just that I am weak and can't resist booting it."

Mr Heckmondwike wasn't paying him much attention. He was examining the peaty pools of water very closely.

"Anyway," went on Slake, "do you know where the Giant Lamb is?"

"Aye."

"Anywhere close?"

"Not yet. Ah've been tracking the Giant Lamb for some time and it's started to act like nay sheep ah've ivver knawn."

"I suppose we shouldn't be surprised," said Slake. "It's not natural."

They pressed on, avoiding the peaty scabs in the grass as they went. This was the part of the moor that the shaggy red cattle frequented, an isolated place that the shepherds of Wormton would normally only see when one of their flock with a particularly poor sense of direction, distance and self-preservation had wandered off. However, the cattle had recently developed an inexplicable preference for more civilised areas and moved down closer to Wormton.

Mr Heckmondwike could read the subtleties of the moor like a dog could read scents on a breeze. After several more hours of travelling, they at last noticed a white dot in the distance amongst the purple of the heather and the green of the spring grass.

"Aha!" said Slake but Mr Heckmondwike did not reply. They burbled over the gentle undulations of the open moor and began to approach the Lamb.

It took an awfully long time to get to it. There was nothing to measure distance against except speed and time.

Sceptics used this effect to explain away the occasional sightings of the Big Grey Man. He was usually just an indistinct shape in the fog and most Woldspeople had sensed his enormous presence just beyond what they could see but closer than was really comfortable. One school of thought was that he was another manifestation of the Great Shepherd. Occasionally, he was seen up here in broad daylight, always a long way off, but always a giant. Sceptics who knew the Outlands said he was just another traveller on the moor and that the lie of the land had made him seem further away and hence bigger.

As they approached the Lamb, the opposite seemed to be happening. The lie of the land was making it seem smaller and nearer.

They pulled up their V8 Mudlarks beside each other and switched off the engines so they could talk.

Overhead, a skylark sang, fit to bust.

"So," said Slake. "We found it."

"Aye."

They watched the Giant Lamb for a while. It was trying to graze but every time it took a mouthful of what it hoped would be grass, it excavated a small hole in the moor and had to spit the earth out.

"Hasn't it got a big head! Do you suppose it's full of brain?"

"What else would be inside it, lad?"

"Well, wool like any other sheep."

"Bigger doesn't allus mean better," said Mr Heckmondwike.

"But do you think it's cleverer than an ordinary sheep?"

"Can't be any less of a deep thinker. Mebbe more of a wool gatherer."

"The point is, can it reason? What sort of intellect are we up against here? If it has developed physically so rapidly, has it also grown intellectually?"

Mr Heckmondwike suddenly felt very uneasy. "What a time to start thinkin' about that!"

"You've got to admit, it's a point worth making," said Slake.

"Aye, but not now, lad! Not when we're trying to corner t'beggar!"

"I suppose it might have been more appropriate to raise this question earlier. I mean, I don't want to sound alarmist or anything, but have you ever been outwitted by a sheep?"

"Nivver!" said Mr Heckmondwike with some feeling.

"Not once in all your dealings with lambkind?"

"Not once," Mr Heckmondwike replied emphatically.

Slake considered this for a moment. "There's always a first time, I suppose."

"What's tha mean by that?"

"Well, it's a matter of statistics. The more you do something, the greater the likelihood of the occurrence."

Mr Heckmondwike suddenly felt like a very damp firework. The issue of the Giant Lamb's intellectual capacity had escaped him up to now and he began to wonder if he should re-consider his carefully laid plans, but everything was in place and the Giant Lamb was growing all the time.

"Not necessarily. T'more tha does summat, t'better tha gets at it!"

"Are we going to do this or not?" replied Slake.

Some shaggy red cattle came plodding over the hill, holding their heads down as if the weight of their horns was too much even for their thick necks. They slowly became aware of the Giant Lamb and looked up. The Giant Lamb didn't notice them but the aurochs came to a decision and turned around to walk away, somewhat stealthily.

Mr Heckmondwike and Slake fired up their engines and rumbled cautiously towards the Giant Lamb. They spread out a bit but then they felt exposed so they spread back in again. True to its normally sized forebears, the Giant Lamb ignored wheeled vehicles completely.

Slake later told Mr Heckmondwike that he was reminded of a painting he'd once seen in The Petropolis. He'd been dragged around an art gallery by one of the well-bred arty young things who had decided he needed "improving". The painting was by Klimt, although he didn't know it then, and was a landscape in which everything appeared to be on the same plane. He'd stood in front of it for some time and his companion, when she found him, had said how impressed she was that he liked it so much, to which he replied that it just made his eyes go funny. Seeing the Giant Lamb was exactly like looking at Klimt's *Field of Poppies*.

At last, when their senses were screaming at them that they had sunk into the ground and would collide with the Giant Lamb at any moment, they stopped, and Mr Heckmondwike ordered his three-headed sheepdog out of his Mudlark. Widdershins had been strangely subdued throughout their approach. It fell on its bellies as normal but did not attempt to round up the Lamb. It just lay in the heather, licking its noses. Mr Heckmondwike issued a few more commands and Widdershins made a half-hearted attempt to draw a little closer, clearly very unhappy about this mission. When it glanced back at him, it seemed to be questioning his judgement that this thing should ever be rounded up. It also seemed to be doubting his courage as well its own.

This cut Mr Heckmondwike to the quick. He undid his safety harness and climbed out of the truck.

Sheep are not known for their risk-management skills. As Slake was keen to remind him, one theory was that they had come to rely too heavily on their shepherds. They can stand and gawp in front of an incoming car but it needs the driver to get out and show that he is a biped for them to take flight. And very often that biped is their protector. Goats had more wits and more careless goatherds.

The Giant Lamb noticed Mr Heckmondwike and immediately took flight. The ground shook as it ran, turning his legs to jelly, and he found it helpful to sit on the ground for a moment. Any satisfaction he might have felt at provoking such a reaction was soon replaced by the realisation that big, nervous animals are the most dangerous of all.

They followed the Giant Lamb at a respectful distance until it renewed its attempts to graze again. This time they drew a little closer before stopping.

"Stay in thine truck," he told Slake.

"No worries," said Slake.

"We don't want it to run away again," said Mr Heckmondwike, "at least not yet."

"Yeah, I get the message. Bloody hell, Mr Heckmondwike! It's enormous!"

"Aye! Hast thou ever seen the like before?"

"Never!"

"Ah hope we don't ivver again."

"You can't tell near from far with that thing."

Mr Heckmondwike's sense of distance was lost. The only reason he knew the hills were behind the Giant Lamb was because they bordered the sky. He felt giddy and wanted to reach out and fall on his face and hug the ground, just to prove it was not a wall of colour before his nose. "We've got to lift the Lamb," he said.

"Come again?"

"We've got to get it moving before we can trap it."

"Okay. I'm just checking for Mithering Brethren." Slake twisted around like a corkscrew from within the confines of his racing harness.

"See anything, lad?"

"Negatory."

"Ready to go?"

"Affirmative. Ready as I'll ever be, I guess."

"Go over to t'far side of it and wait for me to start it moving."

"How are you gonna do that?"

"Walk towards it. Ah reckon once it's movin' we can keep it goin' if tha keeps on its heels with thine engine at full bore. T'Giant Lamb's nivver heard a V8 Mudlark cranked up really high before. All we've got to do is funnel it up t'valley to Mopp's Head Stymie. Ah've placed all t'cables, ropes and nets ah could lay ma hands on to restrain it there, and then we can keep t'beggar int byre until we've worked out what to do with it."

"Is the byre going to be big enough?" asked Slake.

"It doesn't 'ave a roof," said Mr Heckmondwike.

"Yeah but will it be long enough?"

Mr Heckmondwike said nothing. He was beginning to wonder. Judging the size of the creature had become very difficult.

CHAPTER 39

Slake was not entirely sure how one lifted a normally sized sheep. The only stage of the plan he felt completely confident about was the middle bit where he terrified the Lamb and chased it at speed to confuse it.

He burbled across the moor to where Mr Heckmondwike wanted him. He parked up but left his engine running. He watched the shepherd through a telescope, who looked reassuringly far away, but whenever the Giant Lamb obscured his vision the monster seemed heart-stoppingly close.

It was not eating grass industrially as a normal sheep would do but picking up great mouthfuls of turf with an air of distaste. He could see that it, too, must have great difficulty in judging distances.

Slake chuckled. He'd had a particularly awkward clumsy stage. Seeing the problems the Giant Lamb was having didn't so much put his own gawkiness in perspective as put it beyond the vanishing point.

Slake's clockwork two-way buzzed. It was Mr Heckmondwike.

"Ready, lad?"

"Yeah."

"Graidly. Ah'm gonna get it moving," and the shepherd rang off.

Slake looked through his telescope again. Mr Heckmondwike undid his harness and slowly dismounted from his Mudlark. Viewed from between the legs of the monster, he looked terribly small.

The Giant Lamb, searching for something palatable amongst the heather, turned its head towards him out of curiosity.

Mr Heckmondwike paused and then walked deliberately towards the Giant Lamb. Widdershins waved him on with its tails. The Giant Lamb turned around and began biting its rump, irritably. Mr Heckmondwike looked at the Giant Lamb. Then he began shouting and flapped his arms up and down.

The Giant Lamb turned and fled. Slake whooped with joy until he realised it was running straight for him. He put down his telescope and found he didn't need it to see that the Giant Lamb was rapidly approaching. His first instinct was to rev up his engine and get out of the way but then he remembered their plan, which seemed to be working remarkably well so far. All he had to do was wait for the Giant Lamb to come past him but, suddenly, doing nothing seemed very hard. However, he managed it.

The Giant Lamb, about the size of a Dutch barn, stepped over him. Slake threw his Mudlark into gear and floored the loud pedal. The Giant Lamb leapt into the air at the sudden sound of the V8 underneath it.

Slake's Mudlark shot out four great rooster-tails of mud behind it as it dug in. It took all Slake's skill to avoid Mr Heckmondwike as he tore past in his Mudlark with Widdershins' tongues and tails streaming out in the wind. Slake got a bit crossed up before he could align his Mudlark properly, but when he did he cranked it up through the gears and began to catch up.

Giant hooves carved up the moor and sent enormous divots hurtling into the sky. Too far away from the Giant Lamb, and Slake and Mr Heckmondwike found they had to dodge the tumbling islands in the sky. Too close, and although the vast clods of earth sailed in graceful arcs above them, it was more difficult to steer out of the Giant Lamb's hoofprints and avoid a pitch-in.

The Giant Lamb began to accelerate away from them. Desperate to keep up and ahead of the fallout from the monster's flying hooves, both men buried their feet in the toe-boards of their Mudlarks, and the landscape flashed by, under their wheels and over their heads.

Inevitably, Slake began to pull away from Mr Heckmondwike, and he yelled in pleasure as he rejoiced in the power of his Mudlark. At this rate, they would soon be at Mopp's Head Stymie. Their plan was working perfectly. All he had to do was gun his engine and keep the panic in the Giant Lamb so that it blundered into the trap set for it.

CHAPTER 40

Mr Heckmondwike felt near-death elation. Slake timed his entry into the chase beautifully and Mr Heckmondwike laughed to see the colossus jump as the big V8 bellowed underneath it. While Slake filled the Giant Lamb with fear, Mr Heckmondwike set about steering it by placing his Mudlark to either side of its great shuddering flanks.

Vast lumps of the Wold fell around them from the Giant Lamb's flying hooves, and a direct hit from a small parcel of land nearly broke his windscreen, bringing Mr Heckmondwike's euphoria under control. He realised he was going to need all of his shepherding skills although he was reasonably confident that he'd second-guessed everything a sheep might do to escape.

But Slake's earlier comment about the size of its brain came back to haunt him. Mr Heckmondwike didn't like this talk about statistics. He used to think that the more he worked with sheep the better he got at it, but now it seemed it was only a matter of time before one would, someday, outwit him.

Mr Heckmondwike despised himself for this most inopportune idea. He tried to mentally stamp it out but it just wriggled away and multiplied.

Slake was right. It had a massive brain. Who could say what thought processes went on inside it?

This is not the way I think, he thought, feeling surprised and aggrieved. I am more focussed and positive than this. Where are these ideas coming from? That colossal intellect upon those woolly shoulders up there couldn't have developed a mind-reading capability, could it?

Mr Heckmondwike had very mixed feelings about having his mind read by a sheep. On the one hand, he felt ashamed that if it was happening he wasn't mentally robust enough to block it out and prevent the Lamb understanding his plan. But if it could read his mind then it would know how determined he was to catch it. And this thought dispelled his doubts.

Mr Heckmondwike shouted his defiance above the roar of the engine and Slake, seeing him, did likewise. Widdershins barked and Mr Heckmondwike felt proud of doing all these mental and philosophical gymnastics whilst in control of a thundering V8 Mudlark, travelling at full speed over such treacherous terrain in pursuit of a monstrous and unpredictable freak. And if that freak could read his mind then it, too, would surely be impressed.

Now they were between the cliffs of Nibley Edge, funnelling the Giant Lamb towards Mopp's Head Stymie. The exhausts of two highly tuned Mudlarks reverberated off the sheer cliff faces and added to the terror of the Giant Lamb. It ran even harder and the clods of earth became more frequent, but they were smaller for here the soil was thinner. The terrain became rougher but Slake never throttled back. He sped recklessly over the bumps and spent a good deal of time in the air while Mr Heckmondwike and Widdershins followed the Giant Lamb more doggedly.

Then Slake's Mudlark coughed as it yumped.

Mr Heckmondwike's heart skipped a beat.

Slake's Mudlark coughed again. Its nose rose as the engine cut back in again and it squatted like a farm cat about to pounce, but then its exhaust note stuttered and it began to misfire as it slowed.

The Giant Lamb stiffened and slowed as well. Mr Heckmondwike willed both Mudlarks onward, but as he overtook Slake he could see him pounding on the steering wheel. Mr Heckmondwike overtook him and looked back to see Slake's agonised face. Then, realising he had throttled back as well, he buried his boot in the toe board and accelerated after the monster alone.

They rounded the final corner and found themselves at the end of the valley. The Giant Lamb broke its stride and raised its head as if in surprise. It saw the snares around the byre but instead of appearing confused it skipped before them playfully. Mr Heckmondwike had seen sheep do this before, in front of very elderly sheepdogs that had become too arthritic to chase them. He pressed onward, cranking his own engine up higher than ever, but still the monster just gambolled before him.

It was taunting him.

The next moment it wasn't even in the valley. It had skipped over the sheer rock face of Nibley Edge on the left, like the spring lambikin it was, and scampered grotesquely along the cliff top, provoking falls of rock below it.

Mr Heckmondwike pulled up and great echoes of engine noise bounced off the cliff faces around him. When they failed to subside, he realised that it was his own heartbeat. He caught the eye of the Giant Lamb and thought he glimpsed some sort of deeper awareness in its expression. The Giant Lamb smirked at him and shook its woolly head, just as its mother had done after she had butted Billy Brockhouse.

Widdershins barked from the back of the Mudlark. Mr Heckmondwike had forgotten about the poor animal during the chase but was pleased to find that it hadn't been shaken overboard from the Mudlark. Then he remembered Slake. He turned the Mudlark around and headed off back down the valley.

He found him under some oak trees that grew taller and straighter in this sheltered place. The bonnet was up but Slake was leaning idly against the wing of the Mudlark, whittling a branch with his pocket knife.

"What happened, lad?" asked Mr Heckmondwike as he drew up alongside.

"Ran out of fuel," snorted Slake.

Widdershins bounced and barked all around him.

"Is that all?"

"It was enough."

"It were just one o' those things, lad."

"I suppose so," said Slake. He whittled the last piece from the branch and looked at Mr Heckmondwike. "I'm sorry."

"Next time tow a small bowser behind thee."

"I take it that you couldn't manage to trap the Lamb."

"Nay. It worked out an escape route, all by itself, and jumped out of Mopp's Head Stymie as easy as tha pleases."

"Bloody hell!"

"It seems there's nowt trickier than a lone sheep."

"It doesn't need an enormous brain to leap up a cliff, just long legs."

"It still played me for a fool, Slake."

"We'll both know better next time. Don't be too hard on yourself, Mr Heckmondwike. It was bound to happen sooner or later."

"Does tha want a punch up t'bracket?"

"Not particularly."

"Too fast to live, eh?" said Mr Heckmondwike, glancing at Slake's favourite tee shirt. "Too fast to keep goin' more like."

"I was just pointing out the law of probabilities. Cheer up. Now that you have been outsmarted by a sheep, statistically, it's unlikely to happen again." Slake punched him on the arm. "Besides. Nobody would ever believe me if I told them."

Mr Heckmondwike grunted.

"Look at the state of us," said Slake. "Sons of toil covered in tons of soil."

"Come on," said Mr Heckmondwike. "We can get some brew from Old Mr Macklefract."

CHAPTER 41

An ignominious procession arrived at Topwack Farm later that afternoon.

Mr Heckmondwike pulled up outside the gates with Slake's fiercer Mudlark behind him on the end of a towrope. He banged on the gates and Mrs Macklefract answered to say that her husband was digging up potatoes. She handed out two battered tin helmets.

"Summat weird's happened to his tatties," she explained.

"Oh aye?"

"Go and have a look for thysen. But don't get too close."

Slake and Mr Heckmondwike pulled faces at each other. They left the Mudlarks safe inside Topwack's gates, under the watchful gaze of Widdershins, just in case there were some Mithering Brethren lurking nearby. As they made their way to the enclosure where Mr Macklefract grew his potatoes, the sun came out and it was almost difficult to believe there were troubles anywhere in the Wold.

"There he is," said Mr Heckmondwike softly.

"What *is* he doing?" asked Slake.

"He's digging up potatoes."

"No, he's not, he's digging up potatoes very carefully."

"This early int year? Ay up, Mr Macklefract!"

Old Mr Macklefract took no notice.

"He's not using his ear trumpet," said Slake. "We'll just have to wait until he sees us," but try as they might they couldn't attract his attention.

The old man just carried on, digging up potato plants with exaggerated care.

"He's making a meal of it, isn't he?" said Slake.

"Must be t'secret of good potane," grunted Mr Heckmondwike.

Old Mr Macklefract had a Wold wide reputation as a brewster of the highest quality potane. Traditionally, hill farmers had been crippled by high fuel prices, but about twenty years ago they had miraculously become self-sufficient. Old Mr Macklefract had cracked how to make good quality brew from organic material, something Wormton had in abundance. Many farmers through-out the Wold had already adapted their tractors to run on methane using Gas-o-gene converters and soon, following Mr Macklefract's example, illicit stills sprang up everywhere. Mr Macklefract even made diesel substitutes from vegetable by-products, calling it Friesel because it cost next to nothing. Demand for conventional fossil fuels dwindled until the oil companies decided it wasn't worth their while to supply the Wold. So the tankers stopped coming and the garages would have run dry had they not entered into local arrangements with farmers to sell local produce to the general public.

To avoid the interest of levy-raising bodies, it was called brew so that anyone not in on the secret of potane would think people were talking about tea, which was also consumed in large quantities throughout the workshops of the Wold. The WPC, however, like many local authorities, didn't mind these activities at all because they had never benefited from the fuel tax revenues anyway.

All manner of organic materials found their way into brew. Old Mr Macklefract developed a special recipe using potatoes, which he cultivated himself in dedicated allotments at Topwack Farm. This particularly heady variety of brew became known as potane and many people strove to emulate it.

Soon there were many different recipes and regional variations. As well as Topwack Potane, there was Spitfire, Old Speckled Hen, St Alamo's Fire, Old Peculiar, Rodweiser and Chateau Lafite-Sparnauldswick '59. Some skirrows began to boast that they could tell what farm had made which brew simply by the way their engine was running. But there had always been something special about Topwack Potane. Some referred to it simply as OAB, which stood for Original And Best. At Topwack, potatoes grew like nowhere else in the Wold.

"Now what's he doing?" asked Slake.

"He's picking up a potato as if he's scared of it."

"Let's join him on the potato patch."

"Nay, lad. Mrs Macklefract told us not to get too close and ah've got a funny feeling about this."

Old Mr Macklefract straightened up and held a very small potato aloft to look at it closely. He stared at it for some time and then, without warning, threw it over the hedge.

Immediately there was a bang and a sheet of flame.

"Ay up, lads!" cried Mr Old Macklefract, pointing his ear trumpet at them. "Ow ta fettlin?"

Mr Heckmondwike and Slake picked themselves up, dusted themselves off and nonchalantly shouted back assurances that they were "fettlin' well enow."

"I'm a bit plashed off, though," admitted Slake. "Me Mudlark's run out o' brew."

Old Mr Macklefract just laughed.

They began to walk towards him but he became agitated. "Don't step on ma plot, lads! Walk around t'edge!"

They did as they were told and joined him on the far side.

"What was that explosion just now?" Slake asked the old man, as he produced an ear trumpet.

"Summat weird's happened to me tatties," he told them.

"Appen? Tha wife said as much."

"Ah shouldn't really be doin' this int sunshine, tha knaws. Tha needs a fine drizzle to raise these in greater safety."

"Weird in what way exactly?" asked Slake.

Old Mr Macklefract looked at them intently. "Me tatties have become reet volatile. See this pooser? That's what we call these little chaps. Well, watch this."

He threw the tiny potato and when it hit the ground it exploded.

"That's not supposed to happen," declared Slake.

"'Ave a go, thysen, lad! Go on!" and Mr Macklefract took Slake's right hand with his left and planted another pooser into it unerringly. "Careful now! Don't drop it!"

Slake lobbed it over the wall. Again, there was a bang and a great gout of flame.

Mrs Macklefract appeared on the other side of the field with a saucepan on her head. "Is tha awreet? That's three pops ah heard."

"Aye, we're awreet, awd lass. Ah'm just showin' t'lads 'ere our latest crop o' tatties."

"What are they like?" she asked.

"Livelier than ivver!"

"Exploding potatoes?" murmured Slake, still trying to take in the concept.

"Aye. Day before yesterday, one of t'kittens ran across t'potato patch and used up about forty-five of its lives detonating half of it."

"T'little beggar!"

Slake laughed at the picture of one of Topwack's big-footed kittens running about, just ahead of a series of explosions. Then another idea hit him. "Wow! Just think what you could do with a fuel made from potatoes such as these!"

"Aye, ah have!"

"One false move and tha'd be in orbit," said a horrified Mr Heckmondwike.

"Aye," chorused Slake and Mr Macklefract with glee.

"Speakin' o' fuel," said Mr Heckmondwike, "we were hopin' tha might see thine way to lettin' us 'ave some of thine special brew."

"Nay problem, lad."

Slake grinned to hear Mr Heckmondwike being called lad.

"Just give me a hand wi' this lot and tha can 'ave as much as tha likes."

They waited as he wrapped each potato up in cotton wool, placed them in a wrought iron box and stacked them carefully in a wheelbarrow.

"Is it safe?" asked Slake and Mr Heckmondwike, together.

"Oh aye," replied Old Mr Macklefract, dismissively. "So long as they don't go off. But be careful. Ah didn't get to be this age without treating ma tuber's wi' respect."

There weren't many other skirrows in the Vale of Wormton but Old Mr Macklefract was the most venerable. He had turned his slight build and light weight to advantage in the night races and it was rumoured that he'd been in the Wild Hunt since it had begun. Even in his dotage, Mr Macklefract exuded a rubbery, boundless energy. He was only called old by those who ruefully felt the weight of their own years and saw how lightly he carried his. He freely admitted to falling asleep suddenly at inopportune moments, particularly after meals, so had recently retired from serious competition. His wife said he only ever had two speeds – full power and off.

According to *The Vrooms Day Book*, he rarely had a class win but he'd never failed to come home, which was more than could be said for a good many skirrows in the Wild Hunt. He also had a significant entry in *Whose Watts?*, the guide to Wild Hunt engine tuners, where he was listed as an expert on supercharging Jowetts and latterly as a Villiers engine tuner. His associations with the legendary Wolseley enthusiasts Mickleness, Loncaster and Dobson were well known.

Eventually he had become a Wild Hunt scrutineer. This was like being a second in a duel, and rumour had it that the bad-tempered outcome of a particularly prolonged grudge match had prompted him return to the anonymity of the Vale of Wormton and the peace and quiet of Topwack.

Slake slowly wheeled Old Mr Macklefract's potatoes from his allotment to the gate of his farmstead.

"Up 'ere," said Mr Macklefract, as they took in the view, "tha can hardly believe there's any trouble int Wold."

The moor around Topwack curved over hills that looked like inflated bubbles of closely cropped grass. It was especially green that day, and shadows from the clouds raced over the hills so that the landscape seemed to be moving gently, like a rolling sea. Visibility was so good they could almost see Bedlam in one direction and Mithering in the other.

Then the Giant Lamb appeared on a distant hilltop. It stopped cavorting and scratched its ear with a hind leg. It seemed to be scratching a lot lately. Off it went again, bucking and prancing, into a valley and out of sight.

"Does that come up here often?" asked Mr Heckmondwike.

"The Giant Lamb? Aye. Ah've seen it and, although ah'm deaf as a post, ah can feel it comin'."

"Feel it?" said Slake. "What does it feel like?"

"An earthquake."

"We've decided it's unworthy of the name of lamb, haven't we, Mr Heckmondwike?"

"Aye. That monster is an aberration."

"We were trying to catch it when I ran out of fuel."

Old Mr Macklefract brandished his ear trumpet. "Oh aye?"

"Yeah and we would have succeeded, too."

Mr Heckmondwike glanced at Slake. "Nay we wouldn't!" he hissed. "T'monster would have jumped out of t'valley anyroad."

"We don't know that," Slake whispered back. "You'll be a laughing stock if word of this gets out."

"Aye, ah fully expect to be one n'all."

"But I was the one that ran out of fuel. Look. Mr Heckmondwike. Your reputation in Wormton was damaged on the fateful day at the sheep dip. It's not just the Lamb that you stand to redeem."

"Ah'm nivver gonna protect ma good name at the expense o' thine!"

"Look at it dispassionately, Mr Heckmondwike. I can afford it. You can't. My good name has not existed for as long as yours. Some might say I haven't got one. I've got more years to rebuild a reputation than you have."

By now, with a drying wind and some sunshine, the mud that clung to them after chasing the Giant Lamb had largely fallen away.

Slake carefully bumped his way into the farmyard and then adroitly avoided detonation on the threshold of the shed where Old Mr Macklefract kept his still. When they came out of the shed, carefully rolling large drums of Topwack OAB , they noticed a brand new Wolseley Hornet parked behind their Mudlarks.

"Oh aye," said Mrs Macklefract from the farmhouse doorway. "Ah forgot to say. Mrs Osmotherly's here for her home visit."

"Or rather your home visit, Mr Macklefract. Good afternoon, Mr Heckmondwike."

"Art noon."

"And Slake."

"Hallo."

"And she's brought another young nurse with her as well," added Mrs Macklefract.

"Hello, everyone," said Gloria.

There was an awkward pause.

"Well, what's everyone waiting for?" asked Mrs Macklefract.

"Ah feel reet graidly," Old Mr Macklefract told Mrs Osmotherly, and he stood up really straight.

"They've just bin diggin' up tatties," Mrs Macklefract explained.

"Well, he has," corrected Mr Heckmondwike.

"Digging up potatoes?" asked Mrs Osmotherly. "This early?"

"Ah knaw, ah knaw. Ah was just tellin' these lads."

"Summat weird's happened to his tatties," chipped in Mrs Macklefract.

"They've become reet volatile. If tha steps on 'em they explode."

"Ee, they gave Mr Tibbs 'ere a bit of a freet, dint they?" Mrs Mackle-fract picked up a young cat that was evidently indestructible.

"And ah've made some special fuel out of 'em," said Mr Macklefract. "Ah've diluted it wi' paraffin. Try some int bomb calorimeter, lad."

Slake produced a small cast iron cylinder from a pocket in his leather jacket and filled it carefully with a measured amount of Old Mr Macklefract's most volatile potane. Very gently, he put the lid on, wound it up, pressed the button and then looked at the dial.

"Wow!" he said. "Right off the scale!"

"Take whatever brew tha needs, lad," Mr Macklefract told him. "There's plenty o' biomass round 'ere."

So Slake filled his Mudlark up with it and borrowed a number of jerry cans just in case. As he decanted the fuel, Mr Heckmondwike told the others about their adventures with the Giant Lamb.

"The more setbacks we have, the more determined he becomes," said Slake as he rejoined them.

"Aye. It's ma duty. T'monster is that rare thing, a lone sheep, one that doesn't run wi' t'rest of t'flock. It's still one o' mine, though, and ah'm responsible for it."

"Why doesn't tha organise an off-road Wild Hunt?" suggested Old Mr Macklefract. "Slake'd make a small fortune from building V8 Mudlarks if that caught on. And tha might run t'Lamb down."

Slake shuffled his feet. "That's not such a bad idea, Mr Macklefract."

"Surely it's not that difficult to kill a lamb, even if it is a big one," put in Gloria. "From what I know of them, they often do the job for you."

"Huh," said Slake, "it's like no lamb I've ever known."

"There's a lot of eldritch creatures about at the moment," said Mrs Os-motherly.

"Aye," mused Old Mr Macklefract.

There was an awkward pause.

"Er, Slake," said Mrs Osmotherly, "I feel I have to apologise for losing my temper with you the last time we met."

"Well, I can understand your annoyance, Mrs O. I should never have souped up your 2CV without letting you know."

"I'm still sorry for what I said, Slake."

"I'm sorry, too, Mrs Osmotherly. I realise how important your research is to you and how I must have messed it up for you."

They hugged a big bear hug and Old Mr Macklefract was omnipresent with glee. "Ee, that's what ah like to see!" he said, as he skipped about. "Two of ma favourite people reconciled!"

They released their clench and beamed at each other.

Mrs Osmotherly looked at Mr Macklefract. "You seem very well," she told him.

"Oh aye," he replied, "although a nice dish o'tay and a sit down would be just the ticket. Let's go inside."

Mrs Macklefract had been baking. On the kitchen table was an impressive spread of Topwack cakes.

Slake reached out and she good-naturedly slapped his hand away.

"Don't worry!" laughed her husband. "Nothing here will explode!"

"Nowt 'cept Slake's stomach!" said Mr Heckmondwike.

"Pineapple fritter?" asked Mrs Macklefract.

"Ooh, yes, please!" Slake replied.

"Make thysen at home," Mr Macklefract told them and he fell gracefully into a button-backed leather arm chair.

"Seen anything of the other King Pins recently?" Slake asked him.

"Aye, last month down in Bedlam. There's just the four of us now, tha knaws."

"There can't be many colonial and perpendicular teams left."

"There's fewer every year."

"I like this idea of a Yankee V8 in an ambulance, you know."

"Aye. There's nay substitute for cubes! A Chevy big-block would do the trick – 454 cubic inches!"

"Have you ever seen the Giant Lamb up here?" Mrs Osmotherly asked Mrs Macklefract.

"Oh, aye, many times."

"Ah expect tha's glad not to have any livestock to take care of any more."

"Aye, Mr Heckmondwike! Beasts are nobbut trouble."

Mrs Osmotherly and Gloria then went into a huddle and everyone else fell silent.

"Okay, you tell them," said Gloria as they turned to face their audience.

"We've made one or two discoveries," began Mrs Osmotherly. "The first one is that the motorscope is interactive. Without your help, Slake, we might never have found that out."

"My help? What did I do?"

Mrs Osmotherly blushed. "You souped up my 2CV, that's what!"

Everybody laughed.

"Any time, Mrs O, any time! Only I'll let you know you're going to be interactive next time."

"As I said, thanks to Slake, we now know the motorscope is interactive. Meanwhile, Gloria here has been developing the talent she has for seeing lares and penates."

"What?" said everyone.

"Lares and penates."

"You know," said Gloria, "the household deities around one's home or household effects, gremlins, gussages, pugwoppits, woolverteens and pullykins."

"What the hell's a gussage?" demanded Slake.

"It's like a gremlin except it does the washing up," Mrs Macklefract explained.

"What! You mean no more doing it in the bath with a shower attachment and a box of Ajax?"

Gloria looked at him in horror.

"Only kidding," he added hastily, "I don't do it like that really!"

"I know you have influence over gremlins, Slake," went on Mrs Osmotherly. "Maybe they can offer us some clues as to what is going on."

"So while I'm communing with gremlins," Slake said to Mr Heckmondwike, "you can do the shepherding equivalent."

"Ah've nivver clapped eyes on a woolverteen and only ivver seen a pullykin once."

"But surely now, with a bloody great brobdingnag bleating belligerently outside the walls of Wormton, you'd be sure to see them, wouldn't you?"

"Nay. Woolverteens are supposed to look like little centaurs wit torso of a Greek god ont body of a sheep. Ah've nivver seen owt like that. But ah seen a pullykin once, which was enough. It was like a small pot-bellied were-sheep."

"The point is," said Mrs Osmotherly, "there is an unprecedented amount of supernatural activity at the moment. There must be a link to the appearance of the Giant Lamb. The common daemonator – I mean denominator – in all our enquiries seems to be Hob, the Soul Trader."

Slake started.

"You awreet, lad?" asked Mr Macklefract.

"Er, yeah. Yeah, I'm fine. It's just that, er, I remember you telling us about him some time ago."

"That's right. I'd only seen him once at that stage, and that was before the appearance of the Giant Lamb. Hob, as Horsepower Whisperer, has dominion over the gremlins. Do you think you can discover anything about him from the gremlins under your control?"

"Well, I can certainly try but I'm not what you could call fluent in gremulin. Maybe we should involve Reverend Chunderclough. Pugwoppit is a similar dialect, I believe."

Mrs Osmotherly clapped her hands. "Brilliant, Slake! Good idea!"

"But I imagine it's not a good idea to have anything to do with Hob."

"No," she said, becoming suddenly very serious. "He is extremely dangerous. I've seen the Metal Guru again since we last spoke and I have reason to believe that the Foundling of Rauschenberg and Reverend Tregaskis are here, too."

"Who are they?" asked Mr Heckmondwike.

"Reverend Tregaskis is another Horsepower Whisperer, this time with steam engines."

"Whoa!" exclaimed Slake. "Just wait until I tell Mr Charabangwrath!"

"He doesn't know, and I want to keep it that way," said Mrs Osmotherly.

"Okay. Who was the other one?"

"The Foundling of Rauschenberg," put in Gloria. "He's another Soul Trader. He's – erm – a bit odd."

"In a way that the others aren't?" asked Slake.

"If you like."

"So what does all this add up to?" asked Mrs Osmotherly.

"Well, we were rather hoping tha would tell us that," said Mrs Macklefract.

"That's a pity, because I can't."

"The game is awheel," Gloria added.

"Let's just think about this carefully for a moment," said Slake. "The Giant Lamb is still at large."

They all groaned.

"That's rather an unfortunate expression in the circumstances," said Mrs Osmotherly. "But yes, none of us can argue about that."

"And we've summat that is bleedin' sheep and ramblers dry," Mr Heckmondwike reminded them, "until they are nobbut skin and bone."

"Does tha reckon t'Giant Lamb is responsible?" asked Mrs Macklefract.

"Ah dunno what to think nay more. Ah've been wondering if whatever was pumped into that innocent little lamb might have other effects, like changing its basic feeding habits."

"We've seen it feeding from t'tops of t'trees int Riddaw Forest," Old Mr Macklefract told them. "It can't eat grass nay more."

"So," said Mrs Osmotherly, "we have the Giant Lamb and a vampire."

"Or vampires," put in Slake, with his mouth full.

"Which may, or may not, be one and t'same thing," said Mr Heckmondwike. "My guess is they aren't."

"And we have the weresheep," said Gloria.

"The what?" chorused Slake and the Macklefracts.

"The weresheep. Something is running with the flock by the full moon, leading it astray to lie down in new pastures, having eaten all the best grass along the way."

"How do you know?" asked Slake.

"One of the Transwold bus drivers saw it," explained Mrs Osmotherly. "I expect you know him, Slake. Mr Dungey? I've had to put him to bed under sedation."

"Did it attack him?" asked Slake.

"No, just put the wind up him. Afterwards, the sheep were found miles away from where they should have been, absolutely worn out and completely gorged on all the best meadows. But the sheep shifting was done well. It moved them away from areas where the blood-sucking activity occurred."

"And it's a weresheep that's doing all this?" asked Slake.

"We think so," said Gloria. "It's been heard to bleat at the moon."

"Very often?"

"Quite often. Often enough."

"Correct me if I'm wrong," began Slake, "but that doesn't sound particularly life-threatening."

"It's not," Gloria replied. "It's just another weird thing."

"I suppose there must be a link with the Giant Lamb," said Slake. "I mean, for centuries we never used to have a monstrous lamb gambolling about the place and when we do, wallop, we get a weresheep."

"It could be a sort of super bellwether," suggested Gloria.

"And overwhelming evidence of some blood-sucking agency."

"No, I'm afraid I really have to disagree with you there, Mrs Osmotherly," said Slake.

"Really?"

"We've had insurance salesmen for years."

Mrs Osmotherly sighed. "There is a time and place for levity," she told him, "but this is not one of them."

"This weresheep," said Mr Heckmondwike. "Any idea who he is when he – or she, ah spoase – takes on human form?"

"No," said Mrs Osmotherly.

"So," said Slake, licking his fingers clean to count on them, "we've got the monstrous lamb, vampires …"

"Oversized grasses," put in Mr Heckmondwike.

"Oversized grasses, exploding potatoes, a weresheep, sheep shifters and three Soul Traders. Anything else?"

"Hob," said Mrs Osmotherly. "He must be the common daemonator in all this."

"The common what?"

"Sorry. I meant denominator. It worries me that Hob is usually interested in just trading souls for horsepower. This is not his usual behaviour."

"So, do you think he is in league with the other Soul Traders?" asked Gloria.

"Yes, I rather think he is."

"Then what can we do?"

"I don't know," said Mrs Osmotherly. "Remain vigilant?"

They tucked into Mrs Macklefract's cooking a little gloomily.

Gloria sat next to Slake. There seemed to be a natural space just when it was needed. She leaned across and whispered to him, "Have you always been able to see gremlins?"

Slake frowned. "I think so. I can't remember not seeing 'em."

"Do you understand how the motorscope works?"

"No. I understand how engines work but the motorscope is beyond me."

"I wish I knew more about it," said Gloria.

"It might be useful," agreed Slake. "We sometimes laugh at Mrs O and her strange ways but she's very clever really."

"She has quite a high opinion of you, too," Gloria replied with a mischievous smile.

"Really?"

"Yes, but she told me not to tell you in case you got big-headed."

"Better to be damned with faint praise, eh?"

Gloria looked up at the ceiling and rolled her eyes a little.

Slake's heart stopped for a moment.

"Or praised by faint damnation, I suppose," she said, allowing Slake's circulation to continue normally. "Mrs Osmotherly is teaching me about the motorscope but it's difficult without any transport."

"You could take a Transwold bus," suggested Slake.

"That's omnibusology. It's completely different. Besides, services have been suspended until Mr Dungey's better."

"Well, it's not that difficult to get some wheels. Cars are cheap if you know what to look for."

"I'm like Mrs Osmotherly. I'm learning what the traffic means, but I don't know anything about it."

"I know! You could have Mrs Amplepance's old car. It's a really nice Wolseley 8."

"What? That little black car you drive around in?"

Suddenly she blushed, just as she had when the'd met the second time. Slake realised that she'd just admitted to watching out for him. Quickly, like the true gallant that he was, he moved on, but made a mental note to revisit the pleasant warm glow he was now experiencing.

"That's right. She gave it to me but, to be honest, it's a bit too good for me. Have it with my compliments."

"Oh, no, I couldn't."

"Why not?"

"Well ..."

"Would it help if I said it was in the way and you'd be doing me a favour?"

"Maybe."

"It's yours. Have it."

"Okay. If you insist."

"I do insist."

"Thank you."

Gloria looked at Slake and then gave him a little kiss.

"What was that for?"

"Nothing. You just did me a favour."

This time it was Slake who began to burn up.

CHAPTER 42

On his way back to Riddaw Lodge early that evening, Mr Heckmondwike met a big black police Wolseley.

Constable Arkthwaite looked particularly grim. "Ow do, Mr Heckmondwike," he said. "Fettlin' well thysen?"

"Aye, nobbut graidly, tha knaws."

"Appen? Most o' those hoggs o'thine look reet fair to middlin' these days."

"Aye," said Mr Heckmondwike, wondering where this was leading. "Heck as likely as happen as mebbe tha's reet. Not too scabby e'en tho it's me that says so as shouldn't. Most of 'em at any road."

"Would tha just come wi' me for a bit?" Constable Arkthwaite asked him. "Ah've got summat to show thee," and Mr Heckmondwike dutifully fell in behind him and followed him over the moors for many miles until they were well on the way towards Mithering.

Eventually they came across a Wolseley 8 with Special Constables Sopp and Blenk on guard.

Constable Arkthwaite stopped, and as Mr Heckmondwike pulled up alongside he said, "Now then, Mr Heckmondwike, "what's tha make o' that?"

He nodded towards a truck in the distance, parked up on the side of the Mithering road. The sun beat down on it and detail was lost in the glare but he could see its doors were all open. It might have stopped for a picnic but something suggested it had pulled off the road in a hurry.

They got out of their cars and approached the truck. Ever since his last run-in with the Giant Lamb, Mr Heckmondwike didn't trust his sense of distance. It was a big truck, a three-axled Wolseley, and it took some time for them to reach it. He mentally turned up his sensory acuity and immediately noticed a sickly smell that was vaguely familiar. He paused and concentrated on it, inhaling deeply, aware that Constable Arkthwaite was waiting for his reaction. He sniffed like a sheepdog. Widdershins, still in the back of the Mudlark, could smell it, too. Neither of them liked it. The last time he had smelt it, the mist had watered it down, but in the sunlight the stench of something familiar, yet out of place, was stronger.

Constable Arkthwaite stopped and raised a quizzical eyebrow. "Is tha awreet Mr Heckmondwike?"

Mr Heckmondwike nodded. "On a day like this, ah should be smelling meadowsweet," he muttered.

"But tha doesn't smell it, ah'll warrant."

Scattered around the truck were many dead sheep and the bodies of three men. They lay slumped on ground that had been torn up by something immense. Clear rain water had gathered in irregular pools.

"Knaw who they are?" Constable Arkthwaite asked him.

"Sheep shifters," he hissed.

"We've not had rustling in the vale since '63," said Constable Arkthwaite. "If they were sheep shifters, why did they kill the sheep?"

Mr Heckmondwike bent down to examine a dead hogg. It belonged to Mr Ollerenshaw who farmed near the Bedlam road, and consisted of skin and bone just like the ones he'd found before. And there was the puncture mark again.

"Does tha knaw these men?"

Mr Heckmondwike climbed over the torn-up earth to the corpses and looked at them in turn. "Nay," he replied. "Nubuddy ah knaw. It's not a local truck." Instead of a number and a W the registration plate began HMD. "How did they die?"

"Look closely at 'em. Carefully now."

Mr Heckmondwike was not squeamish but there was something disturbing about the way their clothes hung on their bones and the way their skins sagged across their faces.

"They look old before their time," he remarked. He knelt down beside a corpse that lay near the back of the truck.

He found its expression in death particularly disquieting. He carefully examined the surface of the skin, without touching the body.

"Nay blood," he said.

"Nay, nay blood. Nay blood anywhere."

"Hang about? What's this?"Mr Heckmondwike pointed to a curious mark on the wrist. "His skin was punctured by something here. See?"

"Aye, ah see it."

"And here, n'all. Wrist, ankle and – by gum! – on his neck!"

Constable Arkthwaite peered over his shoulder. "Aye. Well then. He's been bitten where ivver the body emerges from t'clothing."

"Ah knaw this mark," Mr Heckmondwike muttered grimly. "Ah'll warrant the dead sheep have it as well." He leapt up and checked a nearby carcass.

"Reckon Mithering Brethren could do this?" ventured the constable.

"Nay, they don't go in for killing. It's live souls they're after. It has to be summat else." Mr Heckmondwike clenched his fists. "Ah should knaw t'answer."

"So," said Constable Arkthwaite, standing up again with creaking knees, "whativver killed t'hoggs, killed t'sheep shifters."

"Looks like that. The question is what. Or who."

Mr Heckmondwike looked around them.

The Wold here was very flat and stretched out in every direction. There was just the ribbon of road and the high moor; no cover of any kind.

"Why did they stop here?"

"To gloat over their haul?" wondered Mr Heckmondwike.

"Mebbe. But why here?"

"Who can knaw t'workings of t'criminal mind?"

"But tha's a policeman!"

"Aye. We don't have criminals in Wormton," said Constable Arkthwaite proudly.

Mr Heckmondwike sighed. "So tha's a policeman," he said.

"Aye but ah dunnaw owt about t'criminal mind. That's for detectives. Me? Ah police. In ma book, tha doesn't have to detect if tha gets the policin' reet."

"So," began Detective Inspector Heckmondwike, "they lifted the sheep – where are their dogs ah wonder? – and drove to this spot."

"Then," went on Constable Arkthwaite, "they opened up t'truck to see what they had tekken, as if they couldn't wait nay more. And while they were doin' that, summat came along 'n' killed 'em, man and beasts alike. Killed 'em by suckin' 'em dry."

"Mebbe summat made 'em stop here," suggested Mr Heckmondwike. "How long would tha say they've bin 'ere?"

Constable Arkthwaite considered his answer carefully. "Since before t'rain stopped," he said at last. "Dr Worstedwright might be able to say more accurately."

"Ah wouldn't bet on it. Now, ah'm still racking ma brains about those marks ont necks and wrists. I knaw them from somewhere. But here's summat ah do recognise." He pointed at the torn-up earth around them.

Constable Arkthwaite stared at them blankly.

"These are t'hoofprints of t'monster."

"Monster?"

"Aye. Tha knaws! T'Giant Lamb!"

"Appen!"

"Aye."

"Nah, let's be quite clear about this, Mr Heckmondwike. Is tha sayin' t'Giant Lamb went after t'sheep shifters?"

"Ah'm not sayin' it did and ah'm not sayin' it didn't. All we can be sure of is that t'monster were 'ere. And summat killed these creatures at around t'same time."

The two men glanced at each other's neck, wrists and ankles for puncture marks as if something unseeable was attacking them while they were talking. Then they checked their own skin.

"So what does that leave us?" demanded Constable Arkthwaite. "A vampire sheep?"

Mr Heckmondwike frowned but said nothing.

"Ah don't believe in vampires," muttered Constable Arkthwaite with an encouraging degree of conviction. "Leastways not in broad daylight." The big man shivered. "And neither will t'Doc. Now tha's seen t'sheep, ah'd be grateful if tha could help us clear this lot up."

"Aye but isn't tha worried about destroying any clues?"

"Mr Heckmondwike, ah do t'policin' round 'ere and ah've had a bellyful o' clues."

CHAPTER 43

"So," said Professor Cluttercrap's guardian angel, "is there nothing I can say or do to dissuade you from this expedition?"

In many ways she reminded him of his favourite lecturer at university. She wore a white lab coat over a tweed jacket and skirt, and had the most extraordinary calf muscles. Her sensible shoes made him want to help her with her experiments a lot.

But he was starting to get annoyed with her. She'd been following him all the way from the water meadows, and although he found it comforting that someone was trying to watch over him, her constant complaining did not make her a good travelling companion.

"Madam," he replied, "just walking from my guest house to the West Gate of Wormton I spotted gallworts, slutroses, throsselknaves and three new varieties of hart's tongue. The water meadows were full of magnum moss, bladdercups, inkberrows, kiddy-come-down-the-road-jump-up-and-kiss-mes and, thanks to the wonderfully pure air hereabouts, some very rare bird-eating lichen. There is enough work here for a chaos botanist to last a lifetime."

"If you continue in this direction," said his guardian angel, "that will not be so very long."

"Nevertheless, in answer to your question, no. There is nothing you can say or do to stop me."

She pouted at him in a way that no college lecturer should. Then she took out a blackboard rubber from her chalky jacket pocket and began to pat it on the flat stones on top of a dry stone wall.

It was so reminiscent of Miss Trubshaw that he had to look away before his resolution weakened. "I am intent on reaching Riddaw Forest by nightfall," he told her, to convince himself as much as anything. "I am resolved to find the Black Orchid, if it exists."

She narrowed one eye at him, fixing him with the other, and echoed, "If it exists," and for a horrible moment he thought she might know if it existed or not.

It would have made life simpler if she had told him, but guardian angels, he now realised, were not here to make life any simpler.

"In that case," she said, pocketing the blackboard rubber in a puff of chalk dust and opening her lecturer's briefcase, "I'd like you to sign this."

"What is it?"

"It's an indemnity, absolving me from any further responsibility for you while you're in the Outlands."

"And when I come back?"

"Normal service will be resumed as soon as divinely possible."

"When I come back."

"If you come back. Some would say that prognosis is – how can I put this? – entirely academic."

Professor Cluttercrap forced himself to ignore her. "And if I sign this, it will make your life easier?"

"Much easier."

"You won't be pestering me any more?"

"No. I've got others to look after, y'know."

"Where do I sign?"

She held out the most beautiful fountain pen he'd ever seen and gazed at him with a mixture of relief and sorrow as he signed her form in red ink that must have marked a thousand essays.

"So now I am free to search for the Black Orchid," he said, handing back her pen.

"Yes," she said. "And I am hereby absolved of all responsibilities with regard to your welfare."

"It would appear that that suits both of us."

"Until if you come back."

"When I come back." He began to walk away and this time she didn't follow him.

"Even if you don't find it, that won't prove it doesn't exist, you know."

He bowed his head to her and continued walking away. When the path doubled back on itself as it climbed a hill and he faced the moor he'd just crossed, there was no sign of any other human figure for miles around.

Now that she was gone, he realised she had a point. If he found the Black Orchid then all well and good, but what if he didn't? Where would that leave him? Would he come back again next year? Would he keep coming back year on year? How many more forms would he be signing?

But he hadn't gone much further when he spotted something unlike anything he'd seen before.

A small bush had grown into the shape of a bench.

It stood on the apex of a bend in the road that wound its way up into one of the high mountain passes. At first, as he approached it from below, he took it to be a wickerwork seat placed for the benefits of sightseeing ramblers, but a few steps closer and he realised it was upholstered with foliage. By the time he drew level with it, it was obvious that it was a living thing.

He was standing in the middle of the road, trying to take it in, when a

V8 Wolseley Mudlark burbled up the valley and stopped behind him.

"By the crook of St Mary, our Lady of Lapurdo! What the blood yell does tha think tha's doin'?" demanded an irate Woldsman.

Professor Cluttercrap looked around.

Three black and white faces regarded him with interest from the back of the Mudlark

"Aye! Thee!" yelled the driver. "Ah'm talkin' to thee!"

Professor Cluttercrap blinked. "I am rambling," he said. "And you are not talking to anyone. You are shouting."

"'Eck as like as 'appen as ah am but wi' good reason!" yelled Mr Heckmondwike, dismounting from his rumbling Mudlark. "Does tha have any idea 'ow dangerous t'moors 'ave become?"

"No."

"Of course, tha doesn't!" said Mr Heckmondwike more quietly, but still with feeling. He glared at the vastness of the Outlands around them. "T'Wold was nivver as dangerous as it is nah."

"Tell me. What manner of plant is that?"

"That's a bodged bush."

"A bodged bush!" exclaimed Professor Cluttercrap. "I have neither heard nor seen the like before!"

Mr Heckmondwike gave him the most peculiar look.

"Are they common in these parts?"

"Common enow if tha knaws where to look."

"You mean there are others? Would you be so kind as to show me?"

"Tha's that idiot scientist! Isn't tha?"

"Scientist, yes, idiot perhaps," replied Professor Cluttercrap. "I am a chaos botanist and my enthusiasm can sometimes run away with me."

"Nature has a marvellous way of compensatin'," said the irate shepherd.

"And you must be Mr Heckmondwike," said Professor Cluttercrap. "I've heard about you, too. Nothing bad, of course."

"Dint thine landlady not warn thee of t'threats out 'ere?" Mr Heckmondwike hunched his shoulders again and looked suspiciously around them.

"I've heard rumours of a giant lamb."

"They're nay rumours and it's nay a lamb nay more. It's a monster."

"I've faced far greater dangers, I assure you."

"Ah am not assured! There's a terminal murrain out 'ere and nay mistake."

"Hmm. Wormton may be full of stories about the Giant Lamb but they haven't put you off venturing out here."

"Aye well it's ma job!"

"Then we have that in common. I am a man of science and monsters hold no fear for me."

"But why does tha have to ramble out 'ere, of all places?"

Professor Cluttercrap smiled and pulled out his copy of *Wrainwright on the Wold.* "This," he said, finding the page. "This is the reason."

Mr Heckmondwike peered suspiciously at the cover of the book before delving inside it. Professor Cluttercrap guided him to the paragraph that had bewitched him.

Mr Heckmondwike read it out loud, and despite the passage of many years the words still caused a shiver of excitement through Professor Cluttercrap's wiry frame.

" 'It is also said that some remarkable black orchids grow hereabouts yet the locals regard these as just yet another flower, as if it blossoms in profusion throughout the Wold. However, a particularly striking specimen will occasionally inspire some interest from a passing shepherd or herb gatherer and they might pick it up and take it home out of sheer curiosity. Indeed, I myself chanced upon a Bleeding Heart, an arresting purplish-red variety, which I discovered by the roadside purely by joyous happenstance as I answered the call of nature. An eminent visitor was once shown a Bleeding Heart in *The Golden Fleece,* and was sufficiently moved to pay several guineas for this handsome specimen, only to be thrown into a state of agitation by the dismissive comment of an ancient shepherd who voiced the opinion that the Bleeding Heart was but a mere weed compared to the Black Orchid. This, the old gentleman went on to say, was common enough in his youth all over the Outlands yet was still to be remarked upon for its jet velvet petals. Since then it had become rare and nobody else present could recall ever having seen such a specimen. In short, the whole affair strikes this writer as smacking strongly of humbug.

" 'And yet and yet. What if there were a Black Orchid waiting out there in the Woldernesse for someone to appreciate it properly? What a marvellous counterpoint one would make for a fancier of the vanilla genus!' "

Mr Heckmondwike handed Wrainwright back to Professor Cluttercrap, took off his flat cap and ran a hand the size of a wheelbarrow over his scalp. He replaced his cap and asked, "Where's tha headed, lad?"

"I am bound for the forest of Riddaw."

"It's a mad scheme, tha knaws."

Professor Cluttercrap inclined his head slightly and smiled. "And where are you headed?"

"Ah work at Scar Fell Farm. Ah tend t'flock hereabouts."

"Would that flock include the Giant Lamb?" asked Professor Cluttercrap, although he knew the answer already.

Mr Heckmondwike looked at him for some time before answering. "Mebbe it does and mebbe it doesn't. Appen one thing's for certain. Scar Fell Farm's ont way to Riddaw Forest and there'll be plenty more bodged bushes along t'way. Ah'll give thee a lift."

CHAPTER 44

"T'Wold is not what it was," declared Mr Heckmondwike as he drove Professor Cluttercrap towards Scar Fell Farm. "Everything's turning into summat else."

"Change is the only constant," said Professor Cluttercrap, appreciatively. "You live in a chaos botanist's paradise."

On either side of the road were spread the magnificent Outlands. Professor Cluttercrap felt he should be walking through it. That was the best way to really appreciate it. That was the best way to get what he called "on all fours with nature" if an interesting specimen attracted his attention.

But Mr Heckmondwike had been most insistent about the dangers of the modern Wold, and his promise of more bodged bushes, as he called them, had proved too much to resist.

Professor Cluttercrap was the antithesis of Slake. He could make anything grow but hardly anything go. He preferred to trust his own limbs than the wheels of some mechanical contrivance. Public transport usually wasn't affected by his adverse aura but his recent experience on the Wormton Tramway had made him believe in Shanks's pony even more. Fortunately, Mr Heckmondwike's Mudlark remained largely unaffected by his presence and they drove along under the watchful gaze of the three-headed collie in the back.

They came to a bend in a hill pass and on its apex was a spectacular bodged bush. It was an inviting settee and Professor Cluttercrap began to wonder if it was shaped that way to attract people to sit in it. He couldn't be sure, but he had a nagging suspicion that there had been something resembling a low coffee table in front of it.

Mr Heckmondwike paid it no attention. He just carried on, glaring at the far horizon, daring the Wold's problems to come over it and face him.

Before Professor Cluttercrap could ask to turn back, they came to another hairpin bend, this time with a three-piece suite, complete with footstools, commanding spectacular views over the valley. And was that a nest of tables as well?

"Pardon?" asked Mr Heckmondwike.

"Er, nothing," replied Professor Cluttercrap who had not been aware that he had spoken. He just wondered furiously how such plants could ever grow. Were they carnivorous? Did they feed off weary walkers in the Woldernesse? Or were bodged bushes pollinated by aching legs and buttocks? How could Wrainwright have missed such curiosities if they were around in his day? Were growing numbers of bodged bushes behind the demise of the Black Orchid?

Then the Woldernesse unfolded to reveal a sheltered valley and a handsome farmstead nestling among its sheepfolds.

"If it's bodged bushes that interests thee, this is t'place to visit," Mr Heckmondwike told him.

They turned off the main road and passed a sign that said Scar Fell Farm. There were walled gardens in front of the house and to either side were impressive farm buildings. Farm workers bustled through the farmyards as hundreds of sheep in the nearby fields cheered them on with their bleating.

But, as they approached Scar Fell Farm, Professor Cluttercrap noticed how much ivy hung from the splendid Regency façade and he began to wonder if the whole manor house hadn't been bodged. It certainly looked very leafy and organic.

Mr Heckmondwike added their Mudlark to a large collection of estate cars, trucks and tractors.

"This is Scar Fell Farm," he said, "and ower there are some bodged bushes that might interest thee."

Professor Cluttercrap followed Mr Heckmondwike's pointed sausage of a finger and saw what appeared to be a badly trimmed thicket growing on the otherwise immaculate oval lawn in front of the house, but even as he looked at them the small bushes re-arranged themselves into familiar but out-of-place items of furniture.

He stepped down from the Mudlark and approached them slowly as if they might take flight. There were chairs and tables and loungers and stools and what looked like the beginnings of quite large wardrobes and cupboards. Even the fence cordoning them off consisted of regularly spaced and shaped branches, and he gazed with increasing disbelief upon the exquisite tracery of a wrought wooden gate. It was attached to one gatepost by a thick convoluted branch designed to not only transmit life-giving sap to the gate as it sat on its mechanically correct hinges but also to act as a return spring to close it.

"This is incredible," he muttered.

Mr Heckmondwike stood beside him. He wasn't smiling but he was clearly amused.

"Do you grow these here?" Professor Cluttercrap asked him.

"Mr Ransomes is the one to ask owt about bodged bushes," he replied and he went off to find him.

Professor Cluttercrap edged a little closer to the garden furniture.

The bushes grew contorted branches that served as the frame for the chairs. They seemed to grow up from four corners and then interlink. The foliage served as upholstery, and as far as Professor Cluttercrap could make out each item was made up from one plant.

Three sheepdog pups came bounding up to him and piddled over his walking boots.

Professor Cluttercrap looked up to find an affable Woldsman grinning at him.

"Does tha like ma chairs?" he asked him.

"Oh! Are they yours?"

"Well now, they belong to Mrs Gaffathwaite but tha could say ah'm responsible for 'em. Ah'm George Ransomes. Tha can call me George. And thee must be t'famous Professor Cluttercrap."

They shook hands.

"Cluttercrap's a graidly woldly name," said George.

"Ngyah," replied Professor Cluttercrap, who after the handshake had his hand in his armpit and didn't care if it showed. "I'm from the Petropolitan Polytechnic but my father's family came from this region. Am I famous, then?"

"T'whole of *Where t'Rainbow Ends* is talkin' about thee. Mither thee! They talk about *everyone* there. Ask ma wife!"

"I came here in search of the Black Orchid."

"So ma wife tells me."

"But these plants ... they're remarkable!" exclaimed Professor Cluttercrap. "I have a particular interest in chaos botany and these are the most outrageous examples I've ever seen."

George grinned. "Chaos botany, eh? That's nivver chaos botany! That's high-class bodgery, that is. And ah should knaw 'cause they were bodged by ma own fair hands!"

"I beg your pardon?"

"Ah did all this," said George waving towards the garden furniture.

"You mean these are artificial? You made them?"

"Sort of."

"This is incredible!" cried Professor Cluttercrap, examining the tables and chairs closely. "This is not so much bodgery as something between bonsai and topiary!"

"See here? Ah bent the branches down low so they touch t'ground and then they send out roots. Int supernature wonderful?"

"Are there many bodgers around Wormton?"

"Not nowadays. Hedgerow carpentry's got a bad name these days, but it takes years o' practice to do it reet. It's not easy bodgin' a chair out of nowt but twigs so it can support t'weight of a man. Or even some women. Folk used to need bodgers 'cause they could nivver afford timber cut to shape, but there's nay call for it nowadays. Ah cannot claim to have bodged professionally for nigh on a quarter of a century. Now ah'm a shepherd. As soon as folk could manage it, they turned their backs on us poor old bodgers, and bodgin' became associated wi' poor workmanship. They burnt their old bodged tables and chairs. And very well they burned, too, for they were all well seasoned."

He sat down and motioned for Professor Cluttercrap to try a chair. He did so, and beamed from ear to ear at how comfortable it was.

"Ah allus thowt there were more to bodgin' and as soon as I weren't makin' ma living from it, ah saw a better way of doin' it. Ah wanted to mix the art of bodgin' wit discipline of cultivation and, e'en though ah says so meself as shouldn't, ah reckon naybody would throw owt a *living* piece of furniture."

"What happens if you want to move them?"

"Tha grows 'em in a pot. 'Course, eventually they'll die but that doesn't mean tha can't still use 'em. Their leaves'd just fall off and tha'd have to make some proper cushions for 'em."

Professor Cluttercrap was lost for words.

"The best part of it," explained George, "is that t'grain is allus int reet direction."

"Naturally!" quipped Professor Cluttercrap.

"Aye! It takes a long time to grow a chair, but ah reckon t'results are worth it. It's not much more effort when all's said and done. Tha just needs patience. And what time tha spends on shaping t'plant as it grows is saved when it comes to shaping pieces of wood into furniture. Tha has to grow it anyway, so why not get it to grow int reet shape int fust place?"

Professor Cluttercrap agreed and admired the tabletop.

"T'hardest part o' that, said George, leaning forward, "were getting' a branch to grow flat. Course, ah'll nivver get it zactly flat but wi' a combination of weavin' 'n' graftin' ah managed to get it summat like it."

"Do they need much maintenance?"

"Just an occasional trim."

"But I expect there is great skill in the trimming."

George shrugged modestly. He reached down to a recently blossomed cupboard and produced a bottle and some glasses. "Elderflower cordial?"

"Don't mind if I do."

"I expect my wife will, too. Dilys!"

"Hallo?"

"We've got a visitor!"

From the far side of the formal herb garden, a woman came striding over. She wore a long, rather old-fashioned skirt and many freckles.

"This is Professor Cluttercrap," said George as they stood up to greet her. "He's from T'Petropolis."

"Really? Not one o' t'Grisedalemiddenstead Cluttercraps is tha?"

"Grisedalemiddenstead? Er, no, I don't think so."

"This is ma wife, Dilys."

"Pleased to meet you, Dilys."

"George is from Bedlam-le-Beans originally," explained his wife. "Consequently, he's got the only remotely sensible first name in t'whole of this part o' t'Wold."

"Me and Ted Totteridge," he reminded her.

"Oh aye." She paused. "It's funny 'ow they've both got t'same Christian name, int it?"

This was lost upon Professor Cluttercrap who didn't know Ted. Or Ted for that matter.

"But Dilys is a nice name," he said.

"Oh aye, Dilys is awreet. It's what it's short for that's t'problem."

"What is it short for?"

George leant over and whispered it to Professor Cluttercrap.

"Daffodilys!" he burst out. Then he added, sheepishly, "Perhaps I'll call you Mrs Ransomes."

"Dilys will do nicely," she said a little stiffly.

"I was just admiring your husband's handiwork."

"Aye. It's not too shabby, is it?"

"I am very impressed," he assured her. "I came here searching for the Black Orchid, but I never dreamt I would see anything quite as remarkable as your furniture. I wonder. Have either of you ever seen a Black Orchid?"

George and Dilys shook their heads.

"Ah dunnaw anyone who 'as," said Dilys. "Ow did tha come to hear of it?"

He showed them the passage from *Wrainwright on the Wold.*

"Ah," they said.

"He goes on a bit, don't he?" said George.

"He were deeply moved," Dilys told him. She turned to Professor Cluttercrap. "Ah'm sorry to say, though, that ah agree wi' Wrainwright about the hornswoggling."

"That goes for me, n'all," said George.

"I beg your pardon?"

"They just spun him a yarn about it int lounge of *T'Tin Cur.*"

"I still have hopes," sighed Professor Cluttercrap. "I've seen so many strange things since I've been here."

"Aye. We've got plenty of outlandish plants around these parts."

"Well, we do live int Outlands, petal."

"Ah knaw!" Dilys turned to Professor Cluttercrap. "If tha asks me, things are getting' weirder!"

"Tha's not wrong there, lass!" said George. "Ah reckon now's a good a time as any to search for t'Black Orchid."

"Is it me or are earthworms getting bigger these days?" wondered Dilys, pausing to examine some wriggling thing in the grass that a sheepdog pup had found. "Then there those gurt great grasses down by Best Meadow," she went on. "They're downright peculiar and nay mistake."

"Oh really?" asked Professor Cluttercrap.

Behind them someone began ringing a bell.

"Aye. There's a connection wi' Giant Lamb, int there George?"

"Reckon as 'appen as likely as mebbe there are connections wi' every bloody weird thing," muttered George.

"Anyroadup," said Dilys, rising, "tha's invited to tea."

The sheep in the fields around Scar Fell Farm were very noisy. Professor Cluttercrap was reminded of perpetual broadcasts of manic communist propaganda that he'd experienced in repressive regimes during his earlier travels abroad. Piped everywhere, it seemed, the voices of amphetamised party workers urged everyone on to surpass every glorious production target. The constant bleating seemed to have the same purpose.

However, at the ringing of the bell, the farmworkers, who had been working so heroically up until then, began to stop what they were doing and converged on the kitchen door of the manor house.

The sheep carried on bleating regardless.

George and Dilys showed him into a large dining hall. Appetising smells wafted in through a doorway and Professor Cluttercrap could see an enormous range in front of which whole lambs were roasting on spits. Other gears and shafts wound down oven doors or moved pots from the hottest parts of the hot plates according to adjustable bi-metallic strips that monitored temperatures.

In charge of everything was not some dumpy, gravy-stained cook of advancing years but a lissom young woman, barely out of her teens, with the nicest set of ankles Professor Cluttercrap had ever seen.

"Daze?" said George. "Ah've brought a guest."

"We'll put him here, then," said Daisymaid, serenely.

Other farmworkers helped finish laying the table and in a quietly relaxed process, grown out of a long and easy association with each other, the staff of Scar Fell Farm served up a huge meal and sat down to eat it.

"This is Professor Cluttercrap," announced George. "He's t'chaos botanist from T'Petropolis."

There were many oohs and ahs.

"Does tha knaw, Slake, then?" asked a well-fashioned woman who was introduced as Mrs Gaffathwaite.

Professor Cluttercrap said he felt he did know him although he had never actually met him.

"Aye," replied Mrs Gaffathwaite. "He's Wold famous round 'ere. Mither thee, so's thee. Ah just wondered if thine paths had crossed int Petropolis."

"Alas no," Professor Cluttercrap replied.

"So, what's a chaos botanist when he's at home?" asked Mr Heckmondwike with a smile.

"Same as he is when he's on holiday, actually," said Professor Cluttercrap. "It's a vocation more than a job," and he went on to explain about his interest in dandelion trees, prune bushes, drupe nettles, bunbury plants and wake-me-nots.

"Hmm. Tha ought to visit Old Mr Macklefract," said Mr Heckmondwike. "His potatoes have become reet volatile. T'awd chaps makin' rocket fuel out of 'em. Slake tested some in his bomb calorimeter and t'bloody thing went off t'scale."

"Language at t'dinner table!" cried out Mrs Gaffathwaite, imperiously.

"Anyroad, we tried some in Slake's V8 Mudlark and it went like sh … very fast."

"That's not all, mite" put in Mr Kindlysides. "Rimimber those tall grisses in the field where you kipt the Giant Limb? They're not normal, either."

"Biological gigantism is not so rare," said Professor Cluttercrap.

They all gave each other a knowing look and after one or two stragglers had turned up Mrs Gaffathwaite said Grace.

"Thank Thee God for life so sweet, thank Thee God for t'food we eat, thank Thee God for t'birds that sing, thank Thee God for everything. Amen."

"Amen."

Professor Cluttercrap took Mr Gaffathwaite to be the pasty-faced gentleman with the spectacular mutton-chop whiskers who sat next to her. He gathered that ever since a recent accident he wasn't quite himself. He no longer liked to lead the Grace but was quite happy to follow.

The first course was a warming broth and this was followed by roast lamb with all the trimmings.

For a long while nobody spoke. There was just a contented silence in the room that made the noisy bleating outside more noticeable.

Occasionally Mr Heckmondwike stood up and took a look outside, but each time he returned fairly promptly.

"The sheep are restless," Professor Cluttercrap said to George.

"Aye. They should be ont high fells this time o' year."

"No wonder you prefer to park them on the open moor where no-one can hear them."

"Nay, lad! It's not that! They go ont moors for sweeter pasture but there's some bad business out there at t'moment."

"Oh?"

"Aye."

"There's a terminal murrain," Mr Gaffathwaite bleated.

"There's summat wrong wi' our fecund sheep," explained Mr Heckmondwike.

"We had to git the flock off the moors," added Mr Kindlysides.

"Language at the dinner table!" snapped Mrs Gaffathwaite.

"Summat's sucking their blood," went on Mr Heckmondwike, "but we dunnaw what."

"Please!" interrupted Mrs Gaffathwaite. "We are eating!"

Daisymaid passed bowls around the table and they selected helpings from a series of vast steam puddings that were then drowned in custard.

Ted Totteridge leaned back and looked behind her as she passed.

"Yeah. Just look at those little beauties," Mr Kindlysides whispered to him, loudly.

"Stop it!" said Daisy trying not to smile.

"Ankles like swan's necks," replied Ted. "The most under-rated part of t'female anatomy," he added.

"Will you two stop it!" Daisy managed to look quite cross.

"Ah love it when she says stop it like that!" enthused Ted and he suddenly laughed at the thought.

"Just makes ya wanna do it more, doesn't it, mite?" said Mr Kindlysides.

"Ted and Barry and Ted?" said Mrs Gaffathwaite. "Stop teasing Daisy."

Daisy stuck her tongue out at them.

"Daisy? Stop encouraging them."

"I'm not, mum!"

"Just get on with your work. We have a guest today."

"What did you say your nime was, mite?"

"Cluttercrap."

"Ya kidding!"

"No. I'm a lecturer in the Faculty of Chaos Botany at the Petropolitan Polytechnic, and I am particularly interested in your local flora."

"Nice girl, our Flora. Frindly, like."

"Ah. Yes. Ha ha."

"Would tha like another helpin', Professor?" asked Mrs Gaffathwaite.

"Well, I'm not sure I could manage another one."

"She made it herself," hissed Dilys.

"But it's so delicious I think force-feeding myself is not exactly a hardship."

Mrs Gaffathwaite nearly blushed.

George winked at Professor Cluttercrap and Dilys patted his hand.

"My main objective," said Professor Cluttercrap, as he passed his bowl across, "is to find the Black Orchid."

"The Black Orchid!" everybody echoed.

"Has tha been reading Wrainwright?" enquired Mrs Gaffathwaite, as she issued a challenge to gluttony into Professor Cluttercrap's bowl and covered it with custard.

"Indeed I have. Have any of you seen the Black Orchid?"

Everyone looked around but nobody owned up to it.

"Ah well. It doesn't mean it doesn't exist, I suppose."

"Tha nivver knaws," said George. "Tha might be t'fust man to find one."

"About t'giant grass," probed Mr Heckmondwike. "Has tha any idea what could've caused it?"

He winked at George conspiratorially. Everyone waited for Professor Cluttercrap's assessment.

"It could be one of two things," he said authoritatively. "It could be a local mutation, which frankly I doubt, or it could be the result of some external influence that has not affected the genetic make-up of the plant. Personally, I believe the answer lies in the soil."

This brought forth another murmur of approval.

Mr Heckmondwike nodded. "Tha's heard of t'monstrous great beast that's gambolling somewhere out there int vastnesses of t'Wold."

"Somebody did mention it."

"That monster were born ont this farm."

"He refuses to call it a lamb any more," explained Dilys.

"It were injected by a growth hormone salesman in a free daemonstration of his wares."

"Don't you mean demonstration?" Professor Cluttercrap asked him.

"Nay. He called it a daemonstration and, after all t'devilment that's followed, ah would say that's nobbut t'half of it. T'creature grew and grew and when we tried to dip it wit rest o't flock it escaped but not before it had butted Mr Gaffathwaite here into t'sheep dip."

Mrs Gaffathwaite touched the arm of her husband.

"We've tried to corner it since then," went on Mr Heckmondwike, "but it's eluded us and it's still getting bigger. After it escaped, we noticed that some of t'grasses int fold we'd put it in were growin' much taller 'n normal."

"Aha!" said Professor Cluttercrap. "Sorry. Please do go on."

"That's all there is to it," said Mr Heckmondwike.

"You did the right thing to keep the two separated," Professor Cluttercrap told them. "The soil would have been contaminated with droppings from the Giant Lamb. I understand there have been other instances of over-large plants in the vicinity."

"Aye. There were some bloody great dandelions," said Ted, "but tha's just missed 'em. Aye," he went on, "and some enormous plantains, n'all."

"Any other peculiar phenomenon?"

"T'aphids are bigger," observed Ted.

"I rickon the earthworms are growin'," said Barry.

"And ah tripped ower a woodlouse yesterday," added Ted. "Oh, aye, we both did, dint we?" he mused.

"The gigantism is spreading," said Professor Cluttercrap, "but we would expect the effects of the growth hormones to become watered down. There may be something we've missed."

There was a little nervous laughter around the table.

"Like what?" asked Dilys.

"The x-factor – something unknown, the presence of which can only be surmised by the observable effects it has on other things."

They all looked at each other.

"Any ideas what the x-factor might be?" asked Mr Heckmondwike.

"None whatsoever," said Professor Cluttercrap, brightly. "You only know it when you see it, and then it is no longer the x-factor. If you find out what it is, you will let me know, won't you?"

"Tha can count on it," said Mr Heckmondwike.

"Well," said Mrs Gaffathwaite, "despite the x-factor, tha's made me feel better wi' thine eddycated talk! Ah wish thee success in thine search for t'Black Orchid. One and all? Ah propose a doch-an-doris!"

"What's that?" asked Professor Cluttercrap.

"A toast," whispered Dilys. "It's a parting cup."

Chairs grated on flagstones and everyone stood up. Daisymaid went around with a barrel on wheels and filled everyone's glass. When she'd finished she poured a glass for herself, and turned to face Mrs Gaffathwaite, who raised hers in front of her.

Everyone else followed suit.

"Will tha nay come back again?"

"I certainly hope so," said Professor Cluttercrap and for some reason everyone else laughed. But they drained their glasses and grinned at him and bid him to do the same, so he followed their example and nearly expired on the spot.

"Pa-ch-ow," he said softly and everyone applauded. George slapped him hard on the back and this helped dramatically.

"What is that stuff?" he wheezed.

"Some of Old Mr Macklefract's potane," said George. "Not t'new stuff they run engines on, mind, but t'old stuff made for drinking, long before his tatties took to explodin'."

"Now I really must be on my way to search for the Black Orchid."

"Ah'll give thee a lift, lad," said George, "as far as Riddaw Lodge."

"T'Black Orchid is calling you, Professor Cluttercrap."

"That's right, Mrs Gaffathwaite. Do you know how many others it has called in this fashion?"

"Reckon there's been at least one a year since Wrainwright were published."

They all trooped out to see him off. He felt a little light-headed as they helped him into George Ransomes' car, which was, when he thought about it, exactly what a bodger would have owned. It was a small and surprisingly organic-looking motorcar. It could have been as old as the Wild Hunt itself but it had been sympathetically modernised. Every fitting flowed out of the main shape. Only the radiator featured any appreciably abrupt angles but this served to highlight the way the other components melded together. Had it been accomplished on the west coast of Consumerica it would have been called a hot rod, but here it was simply a Wild Hunt special, not so far removed from a wolf in sheep's clothing.

"Thank you for your hospitality," he said to Mrs Gaffathwaite.

"Oh that were nowt. Ah'd like to thank thee for thine assurances in these troubled times."

"I hope your husband soon feels much better."

"Ah'm not mysen, tha knaws," Mr Gaffathwaite replied hesitantly.

"Good luck in thine quest," his wife added.

"And if tha spots t'x-factor," said Mr Heckmondwike, "let us knaw."

"Trouble's goin'!" said George starting his car.

"Goodbye, everyone."

"Trouble's gone!"

"Fare well."

The light was falling as they climbed up into the Woldernesse. At one point, fresh prints of cloven hooves crossed the road but they arrived at Riddaw Lodge without seeing anything more untoward.

Along the way, George explained how his car had once been a perfectly ordinary Wolseley Stellite until it fell into the hands of a skirrow and became, by degrees, lighter, lower and faster. George, as befitted a hedgerow carpenter, had found it in a hedge and taken pity on it. That had been over twenty years ago and now it was more or less as he wanted it.

"Tha could stay with us toneet, tha knaws," he told Professor Cluttercrap as he alighted.

Professor Cluttercrap considered his offer and then said, "Thank you, George, but I really must go."

"Aye, well then. Tha's better get a shake on." George extricated his rucksack from the furthest recesses of the Stellite's pointed tail and then shook his hand, making a special effort not to crush it, a gesture that was not lost upon Professor Cluttercrap. "If tha runs into any difficulty int Outlands," he said, "lemme knaw ont old clockwork two-way and ah'll come and git thee."

"Thank you. That is most comforting to know." Professor Cluttercrap who didn't like to tell him he was deliberately not taking a clockwork two-way. "Well I must be on my way. It looks like it's going to rain again tonight."

George turned to follow his gaze. "Aye. It's gonna come in reet nasty in an hour."

"Is there an easy way up that escarpment?"

George described the best way in the greatest possible detail, short of actually taking him there himself, and then Professor Cluttercrap was off.

"Good luck," he heard George say, but then he heard him mutter, "Reckon tha's gonna need it," which rather spoilt the effect.

CHAPTER 45

"What do you think's wrong with it?" Gloria asked Slake as he peered under the bonnet of her car.

"It's running on three cylinders," he said, looking up.

"Is that why it sounds different?"

"Yup." Slake removed the distributor cap and something jumped out of it, making Gloria squeal.

"What was that?"

"A luddite!"

"What's a luddite?"

"It's a gremlin gone bad, I'm afraid."

"Where's he gone?"

"I dunno." Slake peered into the depths of the engine bay. "Ah, I tell a lie. He's hiding under the control box. Fortunately, I have some of Reverend Chunderclough's Holy Water hooch," and he chased the luddite all over the engine bay with the specially blessed aerosol, squirting Holy Water everywhere. Eventually, he scored a direct hit. The luddite slumped and would have fallen to the ground had not Slake grabbed him in time.

He held him up and showed Gloria an ugly little figure in dirty blue overalls. "We can use this little chap for good," he said. "Y'see, your basic gremlin is very misunderstood."

The gremlin between his thumb and forefinger had already regained consciousness and was gesticulating and wriggling and uttering vigorous oaths.

"Do you know what he's saying?"

"Hmm? Not really," Slake lied.

The gremlin made an explicit gesture with his hand and forearm.

"Gremlins are essentially neither good nor bad," Slake went on. "A bit like people really."

Gloria thought the gremlin understood every word and at this terrible slight it seemed to become almost incandescent with rage.

"One of the tricks of horsepower whispering is to get these little fellows on your side."

The gremlin began to struggle furiously.

"How?"

"In here for instance," and Slake pointed at the glove compartment of the little Wolseley.

Gloria found a service history booklet.

"Each page contains the necessary sigils against this little chap's mischief." Slake waved the apoplectic gremlin at the booklet. "Take Mr Heptonstall's dealer stamp, fr'instance. It's especially good at warding off evil, but I bet the service record hasn't been added to for some time even though this car is low mileage."

"No, you're right, it hasn't."

Slake rummaged in his toolbox with his free hand. "See this inkpad and stamp? Alter it to today's date and stamp the service record."

Gloria did so and straight away the gremlin stopped struggling.

"And now we make some special marks on the works plate."

Slake sat the dormant gremlin on the wing beside the engine bay.

The gremlin began to look around. He appeared a little dazed.

Slake scratched some strange signs on the embossed chassis plate, and by the time he had finished the gremlin had produced a small rag and was polishing the sidelight lovingly, whistling while he worked.

"There you go, my fine little fellow. No more mischief from you." Slake opened the distributor and popped the beaming gremlin inside.

"So what made him go bad?" asked Gloria.

Slake shrugged. "I dunno. A poor start? Lack of recognition? Boredom?"

"The devil finds work."

"That's right. And not just for gremlins, either. Trouble's goin'!"

He pressed the starter. The engine churned away.

Slake shot a glance at the gremlin.

"C'mon," he muttered, "shake you sinner!"

The little car burst into life and Slake grinned widely as it ran sweetly.

"Anyway, this engine will be much happier now. So will you, I hope."

Gloria smiled at him, strawberry lips parting to reveal peppermint teeth. "Yes. I am. Awfully."

Slake returned her smile with interest.

"I wonder where they come from," she said.

"Who knows?" Slake closed the bonnet. "I have heard it said that they are lost spirits that succumbed to temptation, so now they have great labours to perform during a kind of earthly purgatory. Maybe that is what awaits us after death."

"Do you see only gremlins?"

Slake nodded. "But I see lots of different sorts. Ringwraiths, sump ghouls, sparksappers, ion ladies, pyroblins, grunnions, grease bogles and electrognomes, I can see every sort of gremlin and stop their squabbles." He paused. "I do see one other sort of homunculi, actually."

"Really?" Gloria's eyes widened.

"Yes. I can see cherry bums."

"What? Cherry bums?"

"Yeah. Those fat little children with wings. One of them's pointing an arrow at me right now. There! He's shot me! The bastard!"

Gloria laughed and then she kissed him.

CHAPTER 46

"Engine's going well, dad," said Percy.

The Wormton tram was rattling along towards Bedlam. In its youth it had blithely skipped over the rail ends but, over the years, had become sadder and wiser about falling in between the rails. Bad things happened to little trains that did that.

Pa Coppitt couldn't remember when *Jane*, an old engine built by George England & Co. well over a hundred years before, had ever run any better. Their progress was nearly recklessly good and, as the unfamiliar feeling of being on time grew, Pa Coppitt became uneasy.

"Ah don't like it, lad," he said.

"Oh, garn, Pa! *Jane's* never ran this well before! We'll make Hettup in nay time!"

"Taint natural," grumbled Pa Coppitt, and the better *Jane* ran the more morose he became.

Percy toyed with the whistle.

"Leave that alone," growled his father.

"Aw, Dad. Reckon they'll hark that in Wormton?"

"Whistles are for warnings or cries for help."

Percy scowled at him.

Pa Coppitt couldn't help himself from adding, "Save the steam. We may need it."

Percy looked pointedly at a gauge and tapped it as if it were a barometer. Instead of barely showing anything, the needle was set fair at 130 psi. There was no slackness in *Jane's* motion and the old engine's wheels and cranks whizzed around, ringing gently like happy little bells.

Neither of them knew anything about gremlins, so they could never have guessed that some of Reverend Tregaskis's grease bogles were behind *Jane's* rejuvenation. If they had, they would have started to wonder why. And that would have made both of them very depressed.

Pa watched Percy feeding coal into the firebox. Thanks to Reverend Tregaskis's klinkergeists and pyroblins, flames danced gleefully over a perfectly banked-up fire instead of sulking and refusing to come out to play.

They were even riding much smoother than usual, too. During the night, track fairies had been at work and now all the passengers were having a lovely ride. It made such a pleasant change to relax and look out of the window, instead of steeling themselves for a sickening crunch and another re-railing exercise.

"Was that thunder?" Mr Whimsleypleat suddenly asked his fellow passengers.

"Don't think it was a sonic boom, mite," quipped Mr Kindlysides.

Everyone laughed, even Mr Whimsleypleat. This was just the sort of run needed to re-establish the good name of the Wormton tram. Today it could show just what it could really do.

Around Slatey Grave, the fog thickened profoundly.

Pa Coppitt almost felt reassured. He cracked the regulator back slightly as they began to descend the hill and approach a dense patch of fog.

The tram rounded the bend and Pa Coppitt blinked. He'd never seen a cloud sitting on the track before. His hand fluttered disobediently around the brake wheel but he knew this part of the line like the back of his hand. He'd re-laid most of it, anyway.

Percy stopped stoking the firebox and looked up. "What's that, Dad?"

Pa was about to say it was just a cloud when they both realised it had eyes and was growing two small horns.

"Blood yell!"

"Language, Percy!"

"Hit t'brakes, dad!" but Pa Coppitt would rather crash than get flats on his tyres.

They hit the Giant Lamb at about thirty miles an hour. This was unbelievably fast for the Wormton tram. Mr Charabangwrath couldn't believe his terminal velocity calculations when he came to enter the incident in the latest volume of the Wormton tram's accident book

They didn't hit the Giant Lamb hard. The wool absorbed most of the impact but the shock was still enough to upset the worn flanges of the little train and it stepped sideways off the rails.

The Lamb bleated and stood up quickly. The ground shook and the leading carriage lost its balance and keeled over onto the low bank beside the track, as if the old saloon was swooning theatrically.

For the passengers, it felt anything but dignified. As soon as gravity had been switched somewhere to the north they slid or fell until there was a big pile of everybody stretching from one end of the carriage to the other.

Jane had been engulfed by wool and there was a strong smell of singeing. Pa Coppitt emerged from the cab holding his ears, which ached from the great bleat the Giant Lamb had just uttered. Percy followed with a nosebleed.

Pa Coppitt climbed onto the side of the passenger saloon and peered through the windows at the tangle of limbs and faces inside.

"Is everyone awreet?" he shouted.

But before any of the passengers could answer sensibly, they all began yelling and screaming. Unbeknown to Pa, plunging down out of the mist above him, was the head of the Giant Lamb.

Pa Coppitt soon realised they were not screaming at him and turned to look up. The head of the Giant Lamb, without any visible means of support, fell to earth until it seemed it would smash through the very windows of the saloon. Pa slid off the saloon and flattened himself in the heather.

The Giant Lamb snorted. Its little horns made it look even more wicked than ever and its foetid breath was as full of malice as the yellow vortices of its eyes. It steamed up the windows of the leading saloon and breathed in to deliver another earth-shattering bleat, but just then, as if in delayed shock, *Jane's* safety valves lifted and a column of steam shot up into the mist. The Giant Lamb snapped its head back into the clouds onto unseen shoulders, and the ground trembled as immense hooves carried it away, but not before it had blundered through the telegraph poles that lined the track and marked its course in blizzards.

Mr Whimsleypleat emerged from the saloon with his coat-tails over his head and asked, "O, who will spare us from this troublesome lamb?"

CHAPTER 47

The news that the Giant Lamb had attacked the tram hotfooted across the Wold before the truth had even got its boots on. The Mithering Railway immediately suspended all services to Wormton, and Transwold motor coaches stopped setting out to the old town, too. Rumours spread and clockwork two-way springs broke. Horrified housewives gathered on the street corners of Mithering, and stranded enginemen and miners from Hettup and Stingey held court in the public houses of Bedlam.

An overloaded Transwold coach struggled into Wormton, full of its own passengers as well as the women and children from the Coppitts' little train. The agitated driver was none other than Mr Dungey, who had only just returned to work the day before after witnessing the weresheep bleat at the moon. By the time they made it back home, he was ready for some more sedation, which some of his passengers could have benefited from, too.

The menfolk hitched lifts from the traffic on the Hettup road and steadied their nerves in *The Golden Fleece* and *The Tin Cur* as soon as their adventure was over. On the East Gate, Constables Sopp and Blenk thought people were skylarking them until Mrs Ollerinhulme, the guard of the Coppitts' train, turned up.

It was some time before enough volunteers could be found to send out a rescue train. By then, an even thicker mist had rolled across the Wold. Mr Charabangwrath and his crew made cautious progress, seeing not just the Big Grey Man but also something else lurking in the mist. It might have had horns and four legs, and when darkness fell they felt the tremor of hoof beats through their jittery rails.

They reached the stranded train in darkness and were relieved to find that the Coppitts had lit a fire to act as a beacon and had kept *Jane's* steam up. Thanks to years of practice, they soon had the train back on the rails, and occasional thunderous bleats helped to concentrate their efforts. Then, as watchfully as the weary crew could manage, the combined train, with *Old Number Seven* leading and *Jane* at the rear, carefully returned to the security of Wormton's stout walls.

Before they had left, somebody had already written, "Tram rams lamb" on the blackboard outside the normally quiet offices of *The Wormton Respon-*

dent. By the time the rescue train returned, this had been changed to "Lamb attacks tram" and the printing presses ran through the night on special editions.

The whole affair of the Lamb and the tram became the source of much ribaldry enjoyed by everyone except shepherds and tramway staff. An excitable mob found Ted and George and Ted in *The Tin Cur*, and gleefully broke the news to them about what had happened.

"Did tha raddle t'engine?"

"Nay need, it's oily enough!"

"Or did it singe t'wool away?"

"Imagine t'progeny!"

"Aye, it'd go like a locomotive!"

The following morning, Mr Amplepance's nephew managed to take a rather indistinct photograph of the Giant Lamb, gambolling about the Water Meadows. It was not a good photograph technically, but it gave an impression of scale and soon the fuzzy image of the cloven-footed monster, growing little tumps of horns and obviously travelling at great speed, was flashed all over the Wold, from The Petropolis down to Lanson and from Solion to the Filth of Froth.

Shortly afterwards, the Giant Lamb materialised out of the mist right outside the walls of Wormton and, it was said, threatened to gobble up some onlookers on the towers on either side of the East Gate. This was interpreted as further evidence of its savage nature and satanically bad breath.

Parents sought the help of the Giant Lamb to get their children to behave. Schools were closed and kids gathered around the gatehouses. They were expressly forbidden from climbing the town's battlements because these were considered to be unsafe at the best of times. Instead, they would sneak outside, much to the consternation of the extra Special Constables on the gate, and whenever one of them thought they saw the Giant Lamb, they would run, screaming deliciously, for the safety of the same town walls they were forbidden to climb.

The Giant Lamb was nothing if not a great sport. The Vale of Wormton sloped away to the east and west, and the mountain passes to the north and south leaked into one another behind the high hills. So the Giant Lamb might stroll nonchalantly across the moor in the distance, disappear from view behind a hill and then reappear, sometimes at great speed, from a completely different direction. Sometimes it wouldn't appear at all, but juvenile panic could still break out over a cloud or a normally sized sheep that perspective seemed to have placed on the horizon.

Static built up as Dark Time approached. Mrs Osmotherly grimly prowled the Wold, and the staff and patients at the cottage hospital grew restless. Gloria thought she was catching sight of harbingers out of the corners of her eyes and Mr Heckmondwike's cap was levitating again. The coats of the sheepdogs bristled aggressively when they fetched the shearlings down from the moors and blue sparks arced across the backs of the equally impressive sheep. Slake, with his long dark hair, bristled like the negative of a dandelion seedhead.

Everyone turned to their wireless sets for news but the Bedlam transmitter grew weaker and more difficult to pinpoint. The querulous voices of the Wold Service became suffused with fear but, gradually, all output from the Bedlam Broadcasting Company was replaced by static. Clouds tore across the darkening sky, regretfully stroking some of the highest hills as they went, as if in farewell.

The civilisation that had created the Giant Lamb turned its back on the old town.

Wormton was on its own.

CHAPTER 48

Mayor Naseby convened an all-night sitting of the privy council and the WPC went through the motions of evacuating the moors from the security of their privy chamber. Mayor Naseby hammered his little hammer and called for order but everyone else indulged in a full and frank exchange of views. Everyone else, that is, except Mr Quirkmaglen, who sat with a thinly veiled look of amused distaste as he watched their descent into uproar, and Mrs Osmotherly, who at that very moment wanted to be away from Wormton and observing the traffic conjunctions for up on the moors she had spotted something most peculiar.

Mr Grandlythorpe had only just managed to contact her on her clockwork two-way as Dark Time closed in and he'd had to use all his powers of persuasion to reel her back in to Wormton in time to attend the emergency meeting. Now that she was in the privy chamber, she contributed nothing to the argument. She just sat and brooded on what the motorscope had shown her – a glimpse of a pink Mudlark.

Pink Mudlarks were so rare they came with automatic suspension-of-belief. Militia men used them when they trained in exotic desert locations where outrageous pastel pink paintwork acted as camouflage. However, here in the upper reaches of the green Wold, pink Mudlarks looked nervously embarrassed by their surroundings.

Even in the gathering Dark Time, she had barely been able to look at the Mudlark's vaguely obscene pinkness. It seemed to fluoresce in the gloom. It had no roof and was covered in equipment. Even the bonnet was loaded.

An armed man with a blackened face sat in the driver's seat. He looked very cross and she noticed that he had disguised his scent, as a dog might do, by rolling in something really smelly.

"Oy," he said, "you ain't seen me. Uhroight?"

She smiled and retreated a little.

"Dark Time is coming," she told him. "Soon your engine won't work."

He looked at her doubtfully. "You ain't seen me. Uhroight?"

She smiled and nodded and left him.

Shortly afterwards she received the faint summons from Mr Grandlythorpe. As she hurried to where she had parked her Wolseley Mini, she rang Gloria at the cottage hospital.

"Mrs Osmotherly! You're terribly faint!"

"I have just made an important discovery, Gloria. I have just seen a pink Mudlark high on the moors to the south of Diggle!"

"What can that mean?"

Mrs Osmotherly paused before answering for she could scarcely believe the implications herself. "It can only mean that the SAS are operating in this area."

"What?" replied Gloria. "You mean – the Special Agrarian Service?"

"Precisely!"

"But why?"

"Something is awheel, Gloria! And I think I know what it might be!"

"Have you heard about the Giant Lamb attacking the tram?"

Mrs Osmotherly snorted. "Is that what they're saying? Yes, Mr Grandlythorpe told me. And, no, he doesn't believe it, either. The mayor has called an emergency meeting of the WPC to argue about the situation and frankly achieve nothing. I'll call you again as soon as I can. Bye."

And now here she was in the privy chamber, with the WPC living down to her expectations.

"Wait a moment!" cried the mayor. He'd mis-hit his hammer and hurt his hand. "What are members of t'public doin' int chamber?" He raised his hammer high over his head. "This is t'meeting of t'Wormton Privy Council and privy means private!" and he struck the desk in front of him as hard as he could.

The shouting stopped.

"Ah'm not a member of t'public," his wife said quietly.

"Ah," said Mayor Naseby, in the face of a sudden constitutional crisis.

He was used to having his great wife behind him. Despite never participating in them, she lent weight to his arguments. Now she was in front of him, emphasising a point to Mr Floridspleen with her knitting needles.

"Er. Then tha must be ma guest," he suggested.

Mr Floridspleen looked like he might object, but in the face of Mrs Naseby's lethal weapons he thought better of it.

The mayor turned to address the others. "It is unconstitutional for privy councillors to pass motions ont floor of t'chamber!"

Sullenly, the privy councillors returned to their seats. Only Mr Quirkmaglen and Mrs Osmotherly possessed the good grace to keep out of such ugliness, but Mr Quirkmaglen sometimes had a very disdainful way of exhibiting it.

Mrs Naseby did not return to the public gallery of the Privy Council Chamber but stood behind her husband with her knitting in her hands and glared at the councillors.

"Ah think we are agreed then," ventured Mayor Naseby, "that t'Giant Lamb poses a serious threat to Wormton. T'question remains, what we are gonna do about it?"

"Kill it!" snapped Mr Grandlythorpe.

"Drive it away from here!" said Mr Floridspleen.

"Capture it!" suggested Mrs Hammerhulme.

"Stop people coming here until it's safe," said Justice Jaglinlath.

"What?" cried Mrs Thorngumbald

"Incontestably!" replied the judge. "We owe a duty of care to our visitors. We could be liable for the tort of negligence should anything happen to them."

"What about t'rest of us, then?" Mr Floridspleen wanted to know. "Or are we second-class citizens in our own home town?"

Mr Floridspleen grabbed Justice Jaglinlath and they had to be separated, with some difficulty, by Constable Arkthwaite.

"Order!" roared Mayor Naseby's wife and she grabbed her husband's hammer and hit it so hard she broke it.

There was a sudden silence. The head of the wooden hammer bounced somewhere on the stone floor of the Privy Council Chamber.

Constable Arkthwaite let go of Justice Jaglinlath who let go of Mr Grandlythorpe who let go of Mr Floridspleen.

The judge straightened his wig.

"This is getting us nay where!" declared Mayor Naseby. "We cannot dissipate our energies by this internecine squabblin'. So t'fust thing to do is to contain t'problem."

Everyone started shouting again.

"Contain it? We wanna get rid of it!"

"We have to destroy t'monster!"

"And t'vampires!"

"And t'weresheep!"

"Ah may not knaw owt abowt giant lambs or vampires or weresheep," said Mayor Naseby, "but as a businessman this ah do knaw. We need to protect our livelihoods."

There was a sudden silence of consent that took him completely unawares.

"Er. Our economy could suffer. Mr Whimsleypleat?" He searched in vain for the town treasurer. "Where is Mr Whimsleypleat?"

"He's still having a lie down, Thine Indulgence," Mr Grandlythorpe told him. "He were nivver very good durin' Dark Time and ee were ont tram at t'time when ... well, tha knaws."

Mayor Naseby rolled his eyes. "Anyroad, we need to keep our visitors comin'."

The other councillors hadn't thought about this. They were suddenly impressed by the mayor's insight and Mayor Naseby sensed this.

"To that end ah propose we erect a sign to warn them, yet not overstate t'case for danger."

"Oh aye?" said Mr Floridspleen.

"Aye. A warning sign depicting a giant lamb."

"No!" Mrs Osmotherly suddenly shouted.

"Aye," agreed Mr Grandlythorpe. "Just above where it says *Wormton does not welcome careless drivers.*"

"No!" shouted Mrs Osmotherly. "That's the worst thing you could do!"

"We already have signs warning about sheep," Mrs Hammerhulme pointed out. "How do we get t'message across that it's a giant lamb that's abroad int Wold?"

"We 'ave a much bigger sign!" replied Mayor Naseby.

Mrs Osmotherly could barely believe her ears. "No! Listen to me!"

"But it ought to be a lamb," pointed out Mr Grandlythorpe, "not a fully grown sheep."

"By the time a shower like thee decides owt, it will be bloody sheep," said Mr Floridspleen, "and it'll be more than fully grown, n'all!"

"No!" repeated Mrs Osmotherly, jumping up and down. "You don't know what you're meddling with here!"

"Mrs Osmotherly," said the mayor, "does tha have some objection to what seems to be an entirely sensible plan?"

"I most certainly do. The last thing you need is a new road sign depicting a giant lamb! The motorscope is interactive! If you adopt the Giant Lamb as your road sign, you will alter your destiny."

"Will tha still be able to predict Dark Time?" asked Mr Grandlythorpe.

"I very much doubt."

"So – are we all born under a road sign?" asked Mayor Naseby, incredulously.

"Yes!"

"One that governs our destinies?" asked Miss Reeth.

"Of course."

"So, if somebody was born under the road sign of t' Giant Lamb, would that make 'em an Aries?" she asked Mrs Osmotherly.

"I thought that was a goat," said Mrs Hammerhulme.

"Not according to Wrainwright's photos of Cost-is-lost it isn't."

"That's the horoscope and totally different," snorted Mrs Osmotherly.

"Seems to me tha doesn't understand t'motorscope at all!" said Mr Floridspleen. "Ah propose we add Mrs Osmotherly to t'vote of nay confidence in our mayor."

Again there was uproar.

"Tha can't sack t'town's wise woman!" shouted Mr Grandlythorpe.

"There's allus a fust time!" insisted Mr Floridspleen.

"Ladies and gentlemen, please!" Mayor Naseby appealed.

His wife had returned to the public gallery. Even she knew it was wise not to cross Mrs Osmotherly.

"Raise the sign of the Giant Lamb and I resign!" Mrs Osmotherly declared.

"There's nay cause for alarm!" insisted the mayor.

"Do you really think not?" asked Mr Quirkmaglen.

There was another surprised silence.

"If there is no reason for alarm, Your Indulgence, then why are you panicking?"

"Ah am not panickin'," Mayor Naseby insisted. "Ah may be very intense about things but ah am not panickin'!"

"So tell us what t' plan is," said Mr Floridspleen.

"Ah would if tha would stop arguing about me panickin'!"

"Ee is panickin'," said Mr Floridspleen to Miss Reeth.

"We're not arguing about you panicking," Mr Quirkmaglen said urbanely. "We are agreeing upon it."

"How many more times? Ah am not panickin'!"

"Oh but I think you are," said Mr Quirkmaglen. "It's understandable of course. Most people would be alarmed by monstrous sheep, some eldritch blood-sucking agency and whatever bleats at the moon these nights. But panic in a mayor is unseemly."

Mayor Naseby tried to stare him down but his right eyelid kept fluttering.

Mr Quirkmaglen smiled. "What is the expression?" His hand stole to the side of his face. "Ah yes. You have the breaking strain of a Mars bar."

"Ah have not!" retorted Mayor Naseby.

"In fact you aspire to the breaking strain of a Mars Bar, a Mars Bar on a hot day."

"Stop it!"

"A Mars Bar on a hot day in the afternoon. Near the equator."

Mayor Naseby finally lost his temper. He threw the remains of his battered gavel at Mr Quirkmaglen but just then Mr Whimsleypleat entered the chamber.

"Had a nice lie down, then?" asked Mr Floridspleen.

"Aye, it were graidly," said Mr Whimsleypleat. "And then ah made a phone call that could solve all our problems."

He smiled and Mrs Osmotherly had an intense feeling of *déjà vu*.

"Well, t' problem of t'Giant Lamb at any rate." He smiled nervously. "Aye. Ah've, er, decided to summon t'militia."

"What?" demanded the WPC with one voice, all except Mrs Osmotherly who, from her most recent work on the motorscope, said, "Of course!"

"Ah've summoned t'Rural Marines."

"Councillor Whimsleypleat," said Mayor Naseby, "does tha formerly wish to raise this recommendation for debate?"

Mr Whimsleypleat suddenly looked very odd. "No, ah do not," he snapped. His voice sounded strange.

"Ah, well," said Mayor Naseby, "that's the end of that then."

But Mr Whimsleypleat said, "But it's not! They're comin'! The militia are comin'! Ah have acted unilaterally."

"What?" cried the mayor.

"Well done lad!" said Mr Floridspleen. "So much for being crap durin' Dark Time!"

"They said they could fit us in next Thursday."

"What?" repeated the apoplectic mayor.

"They're doin' adventure training int mountains 'til then."

"But this is unconstitutional!" fumed Mayor Naseby.

"That's as maybe," said Mr Floridspleen, "but he's the only one of us to actually do summat about t'bloody Lamb!" and he stepped over and shook Mr Whimsleypleat's hand.

"Won't it cost a pile o' brass?" asked Mr Grandlythorpe.

"Oh aye," replied Mr Whimsleypleat, "but if it rids t'Wold of t'Giant Lamb then it'll be cheap at twice t'price."

"But we've had nay need for militia for ower two hundred years!" ranted Mayor Naseby.

"Do they still exist?" asked Mrs Hammerhulme. "They've not been seen here since t'advent of t'Horsepower Wars."

"Obviously they exist," replied the mayor, "since Councillor bloody Whimsley-bloody-pleat's bloody well summoned 'em!"

"Wait a moment!" cried Miss Reeth. "Mercenaries! And they are here to fight a giant lamb! Don't you see? Under t'sign of t'Giant Lamb! Aries! Mercen-aries!"

"That's a goat, woman!" shouted Mr Floridspleen.

CHAPTER 49

Dark Time embraced the Wold again. As Slake examined diagrams of old Wild Hunt Wolseleys by sulky candlelight, there was a knock at his door. When he opened it he found a figure, not on his doorstep but by the gate.

"Dark Time is upon us again," said his not entirely unexpected visitor.

"Mmyes," said Slake. "Funny that. Isn't it?"

The cowled figure inclined its head in a rather supercilious manner.

"Mind you," added Slake, mischievously, "it's fading fast," and Mr Brother looked around nervously.

"You have the car?" he asked quickly.

"Do you have the rest of the money?"

Mr Brother plonked a heavy duffel bag of coins on the path and then retreated. "Is that sufficient?"

Slake stubbed his toe on it and it chinked expensively. "Yeah, that'll do. The car is this way."

He led the well-muffled stranger to one of his garages and opened the door. Inside was Mr Brother's Wolseley 24/80 Blue Streak. "Of course, as it's Dark Time I can't start it."

"No matter," said Mr Brother. "If we push it just outside your gate I can arrange for its collection."

"Just the way it was delivered?"

"Yes."

They pushed the car out and Slake said, "I have anticipated this situation. Here are starting instructions and a servicing routine. These must be followed to the letter but if you have any problems let me know."

Mr Brother bowed.

Slake opened the bonnet.

"What are you doing?"

"I'm showing you the engine."

"Oh. Have you done much to it?"

"Mr Brother, I've done everything to it. Of course, you can only see the external changes like the snake-pit exhaust and the alloy air box. And I didn't just touch the engine, either. It's got a roll cage and polycarbonate side windows. There's a de Dion back end and the whole suspension setup is adjustable so you can tune it for different courses. I've written it all down in the accompanying notes."

"Excellent." Something about Mr Brother's body language indicated that Slake's pride was deeply distasteful to him. "Sounds just what we require."

"Who's we, then?"

"I beg your pardon?"

"We. You said my proposals sounded just what you required. You, plural. Are you part of a team?"

"In a way, I suppose you could say we are."

"What's the name of this team, then?"

"It's a secret."

"Ah well. Good hunting."

And Mr Brother left without shaking hands.

CHAPTER 50

Mrs Osmotherly strode southwards, as the hills subsided under her furious feet. She wound up her clockwork two-way and spoke again to Gloria.

"It's as I thought," she said. "Mr Whimsleypleat has summoned the Rural Marines. The militia are coming to the Wold for the first time in centuries.

Gloria whistled involuntarily.

"But that's not all!" went on Mrs Osmotherly. "The WPC are going to erect a road sign depicting the Giant Lamb outside the walls of Wormton!"

"What! Why?"

"To warn people about it, the fools! There's no telling what harm will follow!"

"What can we do?"

"Stop them, of course!"

"But how?"

"I don't know yet. Oh, and I've resigned as the WPC's wise woman."

"I don't blame you!"

Mrs Osmotherly laughed. "I can't tell you what a liberating experience it's been. I am free to work on the motorscope unimpeded. And this recent incident with the pink Mudlark shows that we are closer than ever to discussing its secrets! Let's meet tomorrow."

"Yes. I'll call you after work."

"Okay, then, Gloria. Bye."

She strode northwards for home, and by the time she reached the outer slopes of the Vale of Wormton a full moon as bright as a chrome hubcap had risen, brightening up the Wold as if it were daylight. After the gloom of Dark Time, the contrast was striking. Mist that had gathered in the river valleys and over the water meadows bounced the moonlight around, darkening shadows but creating such a glare it was possible to see colours instead of just silver and grey.

She paused by an outcrop of rock and sat down. She felt tired, now. Another couple of hours and she would be back at Diggle, in an armchair by the fire with her lazy old cat for company. No, he probably would have let the fire out already and would be slumbering sternly for her return. Or he would have infiltrated the airing cupboard and the only way to get him out of there would be to starve him out.

On a night like this, in happier times, she could have contemplated the heavens for hours, but there was so much to do. All she wanted was to get home, but now that she'd stopped for a rest she felt so stiff. She began to wish she hadn't sat down. There was a limit to even her endurance. And it was such a beautiful night. It was at times like this that she had gained sudden flashes of inspiration into how the motorscope worked. She was a lunatic, but not the mad unstable kind. She was the brilliant and inspired sort. That's how the moonlight felt this evening, but she was too tired, too old and too far from home for the magic to work properly.

There was a movement nearby and, before she could do anything about it, she felt a soft mouth close about both wrists. She looked down and found that she was surrounded by a Three-headed Wormton sheepdog.

"Widdershins?" she whispered.

Three tails wagged. Wid and Der held her wrists while Shins stood guard in front, looking at something intently.

"What is it?" she asked but Wid and Der began to gently pull her off her seat and towards the ground. Shins crouched down on his belly in front of them and, unsteadily, Mrs Osmotherly lay down as well.

Wid and Der looked at her, then at each other, then at her again. Slowly, as if presenting her with a stick to throw, they let go her wrists and waited.

Mrs Osmotherly stayed very still.

Widdershins turned its three heads towards the valley below.

They didn't have to wait long. A strange figure appeared on a cliff down in the valley. It crouched on all fours and let out a terrible bleat.

A dry stone wall keeled over nearby and her head swam.

Sheep began to flow across the valley floor. Widdershins raised its ears, all six of them, perplexed by the unnatural ritual.

The weresheep vanished into the shadows gambolling like a spring lambikin.

The flock passed silently across the valley and went out of sight behind the hill.

Mrs Osmotherly looked at Widdershins, but the three-headed collie was waiting for something else.

The something turned out to be Mr Heckmondwike. He was sweating and Mrs Osmotherly felt a pang of sympathy for the slack-limbed shepherd as he climbed wearily to where she lay with his dogs among the heather.

"What's going on?" she asked him.

"Did tha see 'im?"

"Who?"

"Bloody Mr bloody Gaffa-bloody-thwaite! He's a sheep shifter and a weresheep!"

"Of course," she breathed. "The tumps of horns, the white woolly hair, and the flat cap – how long have you known?"

"Too long. A knew before ah were prepared to admit it, tha knaws. Come on. Let's follow those sheep!"

CHAPTER 51

They followed the sheep to higher pasture, but when they caught up with them the weresheep was no longer with them.

"Perhaps he's going back to Scar Fell Farm," suggested Mrs Osmotherly, but despite the brilliance of the moonlight they couldn't see any movement on the moor in that direction. "Come on!" she said. "We can get my car and drive there."

They hurried back to Diggle and Mrs Osmotherly got out her little Wolseley Mini.

Mr Heckmondwike looked at it dubiously. "This won't be as good ower t'rough stuff as thine 2CV."

"I don't intend to take it off road. I've still got legs for that. Get in!"

Although Mrs Osmotherly insisted Slake hadn't been anywhere near it, her car went very well.

"There was an extraordinary meeting of the WPC today," she told Mr Heckmondwike.

"Oh aye?"

"Mr Whimsleypleat has summoned the Rural Marines to deal with the Giant Lamb."

In the darkness she couldn't see his face but she could feel his expression had become thundery.

"And I have resigned from the WPC as their Dark Time adviser."

Mr Heckmondwike turned to look at her. "Why?"

"They are going to erect a road sign of the Giant Lamb. I warned them of the consequences but they won't listen."

"Aye," said Mr Heckmondwike.

They were not surprised to see lights blazing in the farmstead as they approached Scar Fell Farm, and when they pulled up outside Mrs Gaffathwaite came running down the steps.

"He's gone again!" she wailed.

"Mrs Gaffathwaite," began Mrs Osmotherly, "there's no easy way to tell you this but you have to know. Please prepare yourself for a shock."

Mrs Gaffathwaite nodded expectantly.

"I'm very much afraid that your husband is the weresheep."

"In ma heart of hearts ah believe ah knew it all along," she sobbed.

"However," explained Mrs Osmotherly, "he is in no way responsible for any of the deaths of sheep or people."

"Aye," said Mr Heckmondwike. "The weresheep is benign. Ah reckon it guided us away from t'mist toneet."

Mrs Osmotherly put her arms around Mrs Gaffathwaite. "Let's go inside shall we?"

They went downstairs into the kitchen and Daisymaid handed everyone steaming cups of cocoa. "I hope Mr Gaffathwaite comes home soon," she said.

"Bringing his tail behind him," murmured Mr Heckmondwike, which prompted a dark look from Mrs Osmotherly, but Mrs Gaffathwaite was lost in her own thoughts.

"It's not t'first time," she said.

"At least we know what's wrong with him now," sighed Mrs Osmotherly.

"How does one cure a weresheep?" wailed Mrs Gaffathwaite.

Mrs Osmotherly patted her hand. "We'll find a way," she said.

A muffled sound upstairs made them all start.

"He's back!" exclaimed Mrs Gaffathwaite and she ran out of the kitchen. The others all leapt up too, but then fell back a little so she could find her husband alone. Slowly they ventured upstairs and found them in each other's arms.

"Ah just had t'strangest dream," he was saying querulously. He was sitting up in bed but looked out of place.

"Oh look at you!" his wife scolded, her eyes burning bright with tears. "Another pair of pyjamas ruined!"

"The best thing for you is rest," said Mrs Osmotherly.

"That's reet!" said Mrs Gaffathwaite fiercely and she pulled the bedclothes tight across his chest and arms so that he was trapped, and tucked him in, hard.

As quietly as they could, the others stole from the room.

"Thanks for coming out, Mrs Osmotherly."

"Think nothing of it, Daisy."

"Mum'll be in touch with you tomorrow, I'm sure."

"Tell her to do so at any time."

"Yes. I will."

"Now I think we all deserve some rest."

CHAPTER 52

Mr Heptonstall was reading the latest edition of *The Wormton Respondent* in the calm of his workshop. Anything that entered it would either be fixed or used to mend something else. It was just a shame the outside Wold couldn't be like that.

On a work bench nearby, Slake was finishing off a Wolseley Walrus lorry engine, surrounded by a fairy ring of empty tea mugs.

"Ah see Mr Whimsleypleat has lost his seat ont Privy Council," mused Mr Heptonstall.

Slake looked up from his work. "What's he gonna do now?" he asked.

Mr Heptonstall considered this for a moment and then said, "Stand again ah spoase."

"Does it say much about Mrs O resigning?"

"Nay, lad. Appen t'WPC is too embarrassed."

"I suppose you don't resign from the Privy Council, just ask to be excused." Slake fitted the cylinder head bolts and began to torque them down, by degrees, in their special sequence. "Heard about Ted's pig?"

Mr Heptonstall lowered his paper. "Nay? That prize-winning Glamworth he owns jointly with 'imself?"

Slake nodded. "It got out and was found foraging in the sheepfolds where the Giant Lamb was, before we tried to dip it."

"The ones wi' giant grasses?"

"That's right. Well, it's disappeared now."

"Appen? Could it be at large int Wold like t'Giant Lamb?"

"Probably."

"Blood yell! A giant pig 'n' all! It doesn't bear thinking about it."

"Well you can't get bacon from a sheep," Slake pointed out.

Mr Heptonstall sighed and folded up his paper. "Fancy a wander ower t'New Gate? T'militia's due to arrive today."

Slake finished off and they caught a tram outside the garage. It had been sauntering up and down all morning so it was only a matter of time before somebody caught it. Pa Coppitt and Percy were delighted to see them. Pa said they'd been getting bored and dizzy confined to the town's tracks, and the excitement of passengers was a real tonic for them.

They climbed aboard the empty saloon, which bore another of Mr Quirkmaglen's euphemisms for desire. As the houses of the besieged town went by, they stretched out on either side of *Concupiscence* and gazed languidly out of the windows.

"T'awd town looks much t'same," observed Mr Heptonstall, as the empty streets went past.

"Mmyes," mused Slake, "but it feels different."

Mr Heptonstall looked across at him.

"Yeah," Slake continued. "Now we're under siege it feels much smaller."

"More confined, like?"

"Yeah, not so much a town as a very spread out house."

They turned the corner of Ram's Bottom Row and clanked their way up Pig Midden Alley.

"Is that how tha feels in Park Bottom?"

Slake frowned. "No. No, not really. It's too overgrown to be inside the house. I suppose I would be in the conservatory."

Mr Heptonstall laughed. "A hothouse flower!"

Concupiscence carried them along Conduit Street by the glue factory.

"Maybe I'm in the rough patch next to the compost heap."

"Nay, lad," said Mr Heptonstall sucking in his cheeks, as they approached their stop. "Tha's not int bloody garden. Tha's int bloody garage."

Wormton's New Gate was several hundred years old. It had been let into the town walls at the height of Wormton's prosperity, and a new road had been started on the south side of the River Mither. However, fortunes had waned and the new route remained a rough one. Fewer feet and wheels made for a less comfortable road, and experienced travellers chose the old ways. Visitors from Bedlam-le-Beans continued to enter by the East Gate while those from Mithering used the West. Traffic through the New Gate never reached expectations and, as Wormton's wealth declined over the following years, tradition insisted that only good fortune had ever passed through it, and not in the right direction either.

Slake and Mr Heptonstall alighted from the tram outside the empty Forrester's Hall and wandered up to the oaken gates, which were nearly as hard as their black iron studs. Outside, an army was massing.

Civic memory had not forgotten the marauding bands that had plagued the Wold centuries before. The WPC was determined that the Rural Marines stayed outside the town walls.

From within the gatehouse, Constable Arkthwaite peered out through a glazed arrow slit. Mr Heptonstall asked him if they could watch from the battlements, and he said any extra eyes to oversee the continued safety of Wormton would be most welcome, but they had to be careful where they trod. They climbed up the spiral staircase and peered out from the crumbling battlements.

"They don't look owt special," remarked Mr Heptonstall.

"They're just ordinary blokes," agreed Slake, clearly disappointed.

Another convoy arrived. It was led by a motorcycle with its headlamp on and consisted mostly of trucks. It was surprisingly colourful. The trucks were green, grey, khaki, white and at least two different shades of blue. There were even three bright red trucks and three pink Mudlarks.

"I hate to say it," said Slake, giving notice that he was going to say it anyway, "but I think they have yet to grasp the principles of camouflage."

"Mebbe t'colours confuse t'enemy," mused Mr Heptonstall. "Ah wonder what Mrs Osmotherly will make o' this lot."

A movement inside the walls caught Slake's eye. "There's Gloria down there!" He waved and gestured for her to join them. She nodded, disappearing from view only to reappear shortly afterwards in the gate tower doorway.

"Hallo," said Slake, a little self-consciously.

"Hello, Slake. How are you fettling, Mr Heptonstall?"

"Ee, graidly, graidly tha knaws. Ah see t'lad's been telling thee about some of our Wormton ways."

"Yes, he has. I'm starting to feel quite at home here." Her gaze lingered on Slake just a fraction too long and Slake felt himself swell with pride.

"Has tha come to see t'militia, lass?"

"Yes, I have."

"I'm surprised Mrs O isn't here," said Slake.

"She's started worrying about the Soul Trader again."

"Really? Why?"

"She says he's the beginning and end to it all. She reckons the Soul Trader is after a soul."

"Whose?"

Gloria gave him a special look, the look that all young men receive when pretty, intelligent girls are exasperated by their obtuseness. "Yours," she said.

"Mine?"

"Yes, yours. Hob's gone right out of his way. The best reason either of us can come up with is that he is after a special soul. And it could be you."

"Blood yell!"

"Tha should be flattered," chuckled Mr Heptonstall. "A special soul, eh? He might want thee for t'*Terminal Murrain*. It's an honour, tha knaws! Hob needs t'quick and t'dead to race against int Wild Hunt. No matter how good a skirrow thou art, t'more tha practices, t'better tha becomes."

"Does he ever cheat?" asked Gloria.

"Cheat? He'd nivver cheat. He's a skirrow fust and a soul trader second. Ah dunnaw how a soul trader thinks but a skirrow wants to go t'distance. T'whole point is about speed, covering as much ground in as short a time as possible. Nay. Hob wouldn't take any short cuts."

"What about cheating with his machinery?" persisted Gloria.

"Ah, well, int open classes, owt goes."

Gloria was looking at them both, thoughtfully. "I don't suppose you know anything about horseless carriages, do you? Not veteran cars, but carriages that don't need horses."

Slake frowned. "I'm not sure what you're driving at."

Gloria sighed. "I'm not sure either. Mrs Osmotherly saw something very strange on the roads the other night and I just thought I'd ask if you'd ever seen anything like it in the Wild Hunt. It was a carriage that looked as if it should have had horses before it but didn't. Something else propels it. Silently."

"Sounds like something to do with the Soul Trader," said Slake. "Wouldn't you say so, Mr Heptonstall?"

"Aye. T'Almighty is not t'only one to move in mysterious ways."

"She's also seen a souped-up Wolseley. Only at night, she says, and once in the presence of Hob."

"You don't know what type of Wolseley, do you?" asked Slake.

"No but there can't be so many of them around here, can there?"

Slake and Mr Heptonstall exchanged glances.

"She reckons she saw the driver making a pact with Hob."

Below them, Rural Marines were clambering out of trucks and saluting each other. Gloria studied them intently with a troubled look.

"There's a lot of them to kill a lamb," said Slake.

"Aye but there's a lot o' lamb to kill!" pointed out Mr Heptonstall.

"The Lamb isn't really the problem though, is it?" replied Gloria.

"Isn't it?" asked Mr Heptonstall.

"No." She pulled herself away from gazing at the men below. "It hasn't actually done anyone any harm."

"What about t'tram?" Mr Heptonstall asked her.

"And me?" pointed out Slake.

"You all survived," said Gloria, flushing a little. "And you all drove into the Lamb. It was just minding its own business."

"Ah see thine point," conceded Mr Heptonstall. "T'Lamb is innocent."

"Yet people are dying," said Gloria, "and those that survive see a connection of sorts." She turned to look again at the militia. Tents were going up and things were starting to be organised. "People understand so little," she said pensively, "and in the end the actions they take are so predictable."

"I still reckon there was no need for them to come," said Slake. "We should be able to sort this out ourselves. I don't understand how they can help."

"If we understood everything," said Gloria, without looking at either of them, "then there would be no need for armies."

CHAPTER 53

Slake was not alone in feeling that the militia should not have been summoned.

Mayor Naseby insisted that the WPC had not been involved and that Mr Whimsleypleat had acted beyond his authority. He tried out this argument on Justice Jaglinlath who began to outline the niceties of *Gaffathwaite vs. Macklefract, 1765.*

Mr Floridspleen said that the problem wasn't so much that Mr Whimsleypleat had acted beyond his authority but rather that he had acted at all.

Justice Jaglinlath had asked him to expand upon this point and Mr Floridspleen then gave them more examples than were really necessary of their combined ineffectuality.

"Seein' as they're gonna be camping on our doorstep," he said, "we should bloody well make use of 'em!"

"Nevertheless," replied Mayor Naseby, "t'very presence of an army in t'Vale of Wormton makes us all very nervous. Ah need hardly say why. T'walls of Wormton are old and have long memories."

"It does seem rather a shame sending them home without having a pop at the Lamb," said Reverend Chunderclough.

"While they're here, they might as well do summat useful," said Mrs Hammerhulme.

"And if it's a question of cost, then Mr Whimsleypleat said we can just about afford it," Reverend Chunderclough pointed out, in his capacity as emergency treasurer.

Mayor Naseby could feel himself being persuaded. "Let's hear what they have to say, then!" he said, testily.

Mr Grandlythorpe ushered the captain of the militia into the chamber.

He was a bright-eyed, fresh-faced fellow who looked much too young for his moustache. He appeared to have borrowed it from a much older gentleman, probably because the moustache was developing too much personality of its own. Quite who was wearing who was unclear.

However, despite his evident youth, it was obvious that he was born to lead and very eager.

"Hello!" he said. "Captain Keen. Delighted to be here."

"And we are delighted to sithee," Mrs Hammerhulme assured him.

"Now, steady on," said Mayor Naseby, disappointed to see the immediate effect a uniform could have on the womenfolk. "There is a small matter concerning t'manner in which tha were summoned."

"Oh yes?"

"Aye. Tha must understand that t'treasurer, Mr Whimsleypleat, was acting far beyond 'is authority when ee asked thee to come 'ere."

"And what exactly does that mean?"

"Captain Keen, ah shall pay thee the compliment of being blunt. He shouldn't've asked thee to come."

"That's as maybe," said Captain Keen, "but we are here, as you can see."

"Ah think what His Indulgence is trying to say," went on Mr Grandlythorpe, "is that we are not bound to pay thee for thine services if tha goes after t'Giant Lamb."

"I see," said Captain Keen. "I also see that the situation is becoming progressively more desperate for you."

"Tha can't argue wi' that," said Mr Floridspleen. "Ah say flog the mayoral Armstrong-Siddeley and pay t'lads!"

Everybody, apart from Mr Quirkmaglen, began talking at once. Mayor Naseby, having broken his hammer, had to call quite loudly for order.

"So it wasn't a unanimous decision to invite us?" asked Captain Keen.

"By nay means," said Mayor Naseby.

"But we've not yet had a vote on it," said Mrs Hammerhulme.

"All those in favour say 'Aye!'" shouted Mr Floridspleen.

"Aye!"

"Motion carried."

"Now 'ang about!" protested Mayor Naseby.

"We'll make a trophy of your Giant Lamb," Captain Keen promised him. "Or perhaps we'll keep it ourselves as regimental mascot."

"If Mr Whimsleypleat said we could afford it, then that's good enough for me," persisted Mr Floridspleen.

"But this is ratepayers' money!" protested the mayor.

"Aye and ratepayers want shot of t'Lamb so we'll get shot of it!"

"Ah say we send in t'militia," said Mrs Hammerhulme.

"How does tha propose to deal wit Giant Lamb?" asked Mr Grandlythorpe.

"We intend to attack it with helicopters," said Captain Keen.

"Helicopters?" There was an urgent funding discussion between Mayor Naseby and Reverend Chunderclough.

"I thought you'd be impressed!" went on Captain Keen with a dazzling smile at Mrs Hammerhulme. "They're not here yet, of course. We're just setting up a base from which to operate our Hueycobras."

"Thine whats?"

"Our Hueycobras. Our choppers." Captain Keen looked a little perplexed at all the blank faces around him. "Our helicopters?" he tried again.

The civilians at last appeared to understand.

"So," he went on, clapping his hands together, "where is Larry?"

"Larry?" echoed Mayor Naseby. "Larry who?"

"Larry the Lamb," said Captain Keen, without batting an eyelid.

"We don't knaw where t'Lamb is," said Mr Grandlythorpe.

"So we need to locate the objective as well, hmm?"

"In a nutshell, aye," said Mayor Naseby.

"Fine." Captain Keen did not seem put out by the extra task.

"Er, is that gonna make things any more expensive?" asked Mr Grandlythorpe.

"I don't think so. It doesn't sound very difficult. You can ask my budget manager, if you like. Miss Bookings?"

A tall, fair woman with spectacles and a long plait joined them. Captain Keen introduced her to the WPC and asked her whether there would be a search fee.

Miss Bookings pursed her lips. "We can account for it as a training exercise," she said.

"Splendid!" said Captain Keen. "I think a Mark 1 Eyeball is in order."

"A what?" asked the privy council.

"He would like to look around," explained Miss Bookings.

"Certainly," said Mayor Naseby, "anywhere outside t'walls of Wormton, as we agreed."

"Yes, of course" said Captain Keen, although it was obvious he didn't like being kept outside.

"Look, let's not get carried away wit past," said Mrs Hammerhulme. "Let's invite t'Rural Marines into Wormton so that t'townspeople can see 'em and show them some gratitude."

"They are getting paid!" retorted Mayor Naseby.

"All in favour say, 'Aye?'"

"Aye!"

"Just about carried, ah reckon."

CHAPTER 54

Slake and Mr Heptonstall wandered around the outside of the wire-fenced compound.

"Ah don't like t'look of this lot," said Mr Heptonstall.

"Why not?"

"They're not Wolseleys. Ah reckon they're Land Rovers."

"Oh dear. No wonder Mrs O's so worried."

"She told me she has no truck with badge engineering."

"She didn't mention Logo, the little-known god of badge engineering, did she?"

"Aye. She did at that. Ah reckon he has many followers as well as many faces. Typically, those who worship at his altar disguise their own ineffectuality by continually re-naming things. They don't understand brand loyalty. They lose t'true identity of everything and she says it plays havoc with her motorscope. And ah fear that t'Nuffield Organisation has been infiltrated wi' disciples of Logo."

"Oh dear. I suppose it's a graphical form of camouflage."

"Camouflage is a form of disguise and disguise is, int eyes of our Mrs O, a trick."

Wolseleys had begun with sheep-shearing machines that were so well-engineered and effective that the antipodean sheep shearers who visited Wormton wouldn't use anything else. It was then a foregone, and quickly fostered, conclusion that everything produced by Wolseley must be of a similar quality. Under vigorous and well-informed questioning, Mr Heptonstall might admit that he was a dealer for other products of the Nuffield organisation, but if anything labelled as a Morris or an Austin ever entered his garage, it left re-badged as a Wolseley.

"Ah don't want any challenge to our carefully laid premise that Land Rovers are Mudlarks manufactured under licence from Wolseley," said Mr Heptonstall. "Ah spoase we could re-badge 'em. Reckon anyone would notice if we did?"

"It's a bit late to lay all that 'Buy wisely, buy Wolseley' stuff on the militia."

"Better late than nivver, lad."

"Illuminated Wolseley badges could give their positions away."

"Aye. Ah believe they are a major contribution to road safety."

"Not when you're trying to sneak up on someone under cover of darkness, they aren't."

"Well 'appen they still look champion, thoughbut!"

"I still think illuminated radiator badges look silly on stationary engines."

"It's t'brand identity, lad! A shining talisman that cuts through the mist and murk of the Woldernesse in winter. Tha can nivver fully knaw what thrill of pleasure such a small thing gives t'owner of such machinery in such circumstances. T'Wolseley range begins wi' engines wi' nay wheels and extends to motorbikes ..."

"Re-badged Francis-Barnetts," put in Slake.

"Through to cars, tractors, trucks and buses."

"You're on safer ground with the cars, but how Mrs O can condone you calling the commercial vehicles Wolseleys I'll never understand."

"It's because Wolseley is a power for good!" Mr Heptonstall replied, proudly. "Anyway, it were partly 'er idea. It protects thee and me when t'Logomaniacs embark upon their orgies of re-badgin' and re-namin' at head office, whatever that may be called nowadays – may t'nemesis of Logo glow between t'headlamps at night to guide us! Ah just hope this lot don't stay long. There's no tellin' what effect Land Rovers'll have ont motorscope."

"Yeah," said Slake but he wasn't thinking about Wolseleys. He didn't like the searching looks Gloria had been giving the militiamen.

CHAPTER 55

Mrs Osmotherly sat beside her fire, warming up in preparation for another night of nocturnal wanderings. She pursed her lips as if she was about to ask a question, but then thought better of it. "I'm sorry, Gloria, but I still want to keep asking you if you're certain."

Gloria sat opposite her. "I know what I saw," she said. "Every militia-man has a group of harbinger gnomes around him."

"Then they are doomed," said Mrs Osmotherly.

"Is there nothing we can do?"

"Nothing I can think of."

"Why would anyone want to be wise in this situation?" asked Gloria.

"Wisdom may be a burden but it's usually preferable to ignorance," Mrs Osmotherly assured her.

Gloria consoled herself with another virtual chocolate digestive. "Perhaps the motorscope can offer us a means of changing the future."

"All we need is to set up the right combination of traffic signs."

"Exactly!"

"The trouble is, we don't know what that combination is."

"Then we'll have to experiment," Gloria said grimly.

"I have a strong presentiment about that new sign outside Wormton."

"What would happen if we destroyed it?"

"I don't know."

"Do you think it's about time we found out?"

"The only problem is, the gates of Wormton are now so well guarded it's going to be very difficult to do it."

"But they wouldn't suspect us." Gloria suddenly grinned. "How about if I get some explosives from the militia and we blow the sign up?"

"Brilliant! But how will you get explosives out of the militia?"

Gloria just grinned even more.

Mrs Osmotherly started to giggle. Then she stopped and said, "What about Slake?"

Gloria looked a little uncomfortable. "He would never understand."

"Then he must never know."

"I am not happy about deceiving anyone."

"Sometimes our talents lie heavily upon us."

"If only he could be distracted in some way."

"How many days do you think the soldiers have to live?" Mrs Osmotherly asked her.

"Three at the most. The gnomes were riding with them in the trucks."

"Let's blow up that sign!"

CHAPTER 56

Once the militia had established their camp to the satisfaction of their commanding officer, the WPC formally invited the Rural Marines to carouse within the walls of Wormton, and Captain Keen graciously accepted. The Town's Women's Guild was delighted by the prospect, but the men folk of Wormton became even more enthusiastic with the arrival of the next convoy, for this was crewed by the Rural Marinas.

Mrs Hammerhulme requested an emergency sitting of the Privy Council to discuss the situation, and when Mayor Naseby asked for her reasons she said she had changed her mind about inviting the militia into Wormton.

"But why?" he wanted to know, secretly glad that she had come over to his side.

"Historical precedence," she said. "Every time t'militia have come within our walls we've got into trouble."

"Oh aye?" said a curious Mayor Naseby.

"But that were years ago, lass!" scoffed Mr Floridspleen.

"And these are civilised men, Mrs Hammerhulme," insisted Reverend Chunderclough.

"And women," put in Mr Floridspleen.

"However, ah must say that ah agree with thee about t'need to keep them outside," said Mayor Naseby. He paused. "'Ang about. What did tha say about women?" he asked Mr Floridspleen.

"Hasn't tha heard? T'Rural Marinas have arrived."

In the public gallery, Mrs Naseby became a little agitated.

"T'Rural Marinas?" repeated her husband.

"Aye!" said Mr Floridspleen, "a squadron of very healthy young women wearing tight white blouses, figure-hugging black skirts and t'very latest in black-stocking technology."

"Fighting women!" exclaimed Mrs Hammerhulme with evident disapproval.

"In uniform!" added Mr Grandlythorpe, gleefully.

"Luscious long-legged lovelies!" gushed Reverend Chunderclough. "Firm-buttocked young Amazons!"

There was an awkward pause.

"Ah beg thine pardon?" asked Mrs Hammerhulme.

"Er, I'm terribly sorry," said Reverend Chunderclough. "I think I'll just step outside and get some fresh air," which was a Woldish euphemism for taking a cold shower, for in Wormton the two are much the same.

"I really would advise against withdrawing your original invitation," said Mr Quirkmaglen, "especially now that it has been accepted."

"Ah see thine point," said Mr Grandlythorpe, scratching his chin. "Perhaps we could restrict festivities to *T'Tin Cur*."

"It is not the most salubrious of establishments, is it?" said Mr Quirkmaglen, who had never set foot in it. "Wouldn't *The Golden Fleece* be more appropriate?"

"Ah think we've just made a decision," said Mr Floridspleen. "We're in danger of getting good at this."

Mr Quirkmaglen offered to act as intermediary. There was something about his old Wold authority that the militia responded to, and the following evening a large group of them, conspicuously dressed in full ceremonial rig, trooped into Wormton and crowded into the snug of *The Golden Fleece*.

Many Wormtonians had let it be known that they wished to welcome the militia personally, so Betty decided that she would need some extra bar staff. However, there was no shortage of volunteers and she had to use some sort of selection criteria. This merely infuriated the Town's Women's Guild, many of whom had already served tea to the dashing Captain Keen in *Where the Rainbow Ends*. They could not, for instance, understand why she had chosen Daisy from Scar Fell Farm when so many of them were more conveniently placed.

"How's she going to get home afterwards?" asked Miss Periwig, but the other ladies just sucked in air and tutted.

Mayor Naseby made a speech that was instantly forgettable and then Mr Quirkmaglen announced that he would foot the militia's bar bill, which everyone remembered.

Very soon a party, the like of which had not been seen in Wormton for many years, was in full swing.

Mr Heckmondwike had just sunk a couple of pints with Mr Floridspleen when Mr Grandlythorpe interposed and announced that if it helped with the funding situation Captain Keen was willing to waive his own salary. "It seems he's got private means."

Mr Floridspleen frowned in concentration. "Private Means?" he said. "Ah think ah met him. Big chap, scar on cheek, machine gun, drives a tank."

"I think you can do a lot with Private Means," agreed Mr Heckmondwike.

"Then there's Chief Able," went on Grandlythorpe.

"Oh aye. Ah knaw him n'all. Short chap, wears a hat and an eye patch, only one arm but salutes a lot."

"Looks like t' Rural Marines have a positive attitude to disability."

"Some would say they turn a blind eye to it."

"Others that they actively encourage it."

Captain Keen was rather predictably holding court to the Town's Women's Guild, while many of the WPC's male members were squeezing up to the Rural Marinas at the bar and expressing concerns for their safety.

"Captain Keen," said Miss Periwig, as she allowed him to buy her another half pint of milk stout, "have you tried The Usual?"

"Er, no, I haven't. What is it exactly?"

"It's a local speciality," she assured him.

"Is it always called The Usual?"

"Usually!" she burst out, and Miss Periwig giggled so much she got hiccups and had to retire to the ladies.

"They call it that because it's most people's favourite," explained Mrs Osmotherly. She was drinking water. Sherry was for the home. "Its real name is Wapenhulme's Kidney Sneeze."

Captain Keen regarded her glass as if it were undiluted gin. "Got any lager?" he asked.

"Oh there's Nurse Gubbergill," Mrs Osmotherly said loudly, but it seemed that Captain Keen had already noticed her. "Allow me to introduce you. In the event of any casualties you would become acquainted anyway but let's do it properly while we have the chance."

"How are you fettling?" asked Captain Keen taking Gloria's hand.

"I am fettling very well, thank you, Captain."

"Call me Crispin."

"May I compliment you on your Woldish speak."

"It's nothing but fair to middling, you know. The ladies of the Town's Women's Guild have been coaching me."

"I'm sure they have."

"Allow me to get you a drink. What would you like?"

"A mineral water, please."

Despite the crush, Captain Keen got her drink easily. "I must say it's very refreshing to meet someone who doesn't drink pints."

Gloria glanced at the ladies of the Town's Women's Guild, who were watching her like a tweedy flock of hawks, and smiled. "Please excuse the uniform," she said. "I've come straight from work."

"It suits you," he said and gave her an admiring glance.

"Thank you. And I think your uniform suits you."

"I have to say that I don't think you're the only one. I must thank you for saving me from them," and he threw a glance back at the ladies of the Town's Women's Guild, many of whom were already a little worse for wear.

"Do you have a jukebox?" a burly Marine asked George Ransomes above the din.

The bodger looked non-plussed. "There are nay dukes round 'ere," he shouted back.

Slake, who was talking to a pair of very lively Rural Marinas nearby, intervened. "Yeah mate," he told the Marine. "It doesn't get a lot of use but I sorted out some music in case it was needed."

He put a coin into the record machine and it played the opening bars of a song.

"Brilliant!" cried the Rural Marinas. "We love The Prisoners!"

Everybody in *The Golden Fleece*, young or old, began dancing to *Say your prayers*.

Although he didn't usually do this sort of thing, Mr Heckmondwike had an acute sense of occasion and asked Mrs Osmotherly for a dance, and she laughingly accepted. However, for a man of the Wold he was actually a very good dancer.

"I didn't know you liked the psychedelic Medway garage sound," Slake said to him.

"Oh aye!" said Mr Heckmondwike. He was getting quite carried away.

"Why've you got such long hair?" the Marine asked Slake as the song ended.

"The girls like to run their fingers through it," he replied, bending some notes on his air guitar.

The Marinas tittered and tried it.

"Good answer," said the Marine.

"Why are you nearly bald?"

"It's the rules, innit? Fancy a drink?"

"Cheers. Just ask Betty for a pint of Usual."

"More Prisoners!" squealed the Rural Marinas.

One of them hugged Slake and shouted, "Oh, this is my absolute favourite! *Hurricane*!"

Slake turned and caught sight of Gloria dancing with Captain Keen. Their eyes did not meet.

"You don't talk like the others, do you?" Marina number one shouted to him. She was a dark-haired girl whose buttocks looked extremely firm.

"I spent some years in The Petropolis," he explained.

"Really? That's where I'm from!"

Mrs Osmotherly was enjoying herself and was particularly impressed with Mr Heckmondwike's air drumming, but then she caught sight of some very worrying figures on the other side of the bar. One, dressed as a German gentleman from the 1830s, was hand jiving with a Rural Marina. Next to him was a slight reverend gentleman who was miming along with Miss Periwig. Miss Periwig was playing the air Hammond organ complete with air Leslie speaker for that authentic garage sound. It seemed she took them everywhere with her. Finally, in the darkest corner of the pub, a tall figure wearing a crash helmet, a black visor and a scuffed leather jacket was energetically getting it on down with Daisy and the bar staff. He looked like he was into garage music more than anyone.

She only had a fleeting glimpse of them. Everyone was jiggling about so much to *Hurricane* that the crowd obscured her view for a moment, and when it subsided again the strange figures had disappeared. Instead of pulling Horsepower Whisperers, Daisy was pulling pints. Miss Periwig had put down her air keyboard and was holding onto one of the pillars to stop the room from spinning and all the Rural Marinas seemed to be dancing around Slake and Mr Kindlysides.

So Mrs Osmotherly could only assume that she had been mistaken.

Gloria glanced around nervously. Slake had to be here somewhere but it was such a crush of people. Then she saw him with his back to her, dancing with a very attractive black girl who was surrounded by harbingers.

"I say, are you all right?" asked Captain Keen, as *Hurricane* reached its climax.

"Yes," she said, a little too quickly. "Yes, I'm fine. It's just rather hot in here."

"Especially if you're in uniform," he said, adjusting his collar but not unbuttoning it. "Why don't we go outside for some air?"

Suddenly, a voice bellowed for silence. A disorderly hush descended and Slake halted the next song on the jukebox while everyone craned their necks to see who had shouted.

Then the same voice cried out, "Naked Drinking!"

CHAPTER 57

Reverend Chunderclough had stayed away from *The Golden Fleece*. He would have felt uncomfortable in such surroundings.

However, he still had work to do and churches don't maintain themselves.

That was the job of the pugwoppits and gargoyles.

When Wormton's parish church was built, the masons worked in harmony with their lares and penates. By honouring them with carved likenesses, the pugwoppits, splintergeists and gargoyles could be influenced to watch over the building in the centuries to come.

Unfortunately, during the age of enlightenment, the ability to invoke the co-operation of the gargoyles and pugwoppits had almost been lost. Wormton was one of the isolated communities where it had survived, and Reverend Chunderclough had become expert in it. He regularly practised his homuncular communication skills and was highly regarded by the pugwoppits and gargoyles. His church was festooned with them and he was determined to keep them gainfully occupied. If he didn't, the devil would surely find work for them.

He stood at the transept of his church, dressed in his finery and with all the symbols of his office. He gazed up at the vaulted pillars. The stained-glass windows were darkened tonight, but during the morning great pools of light moved around the flagstones of the church. He took a moment to study the paintings on the rood screen and looked up at the altar.

Then he did a little dance.

Immediately, a small group of ugly creatures emerged from the fabric of the building and descended from the ceiling on stony wings. They bobbed and jigged around him and, niceties over, it was down to business.

Communicating to a three-inch high humanikin was never easy. Their voice boxes made a different set of sounds, usually in parallel frequencies to ours. Consequently, mime was the *lingua franca*.

Reverend Chunderclough blessed some baby guttersnipes, complimented the gargoyles on their work to date and asked for reports on all aspects of the building's structure and decoration. A long, glistening, wormlike sewer wraith wriggled around on the floor outlining how the problem with the drains had been cleared up, and a group of lead-spattered shinglers gave a presentation in the form of an elaborate tap dance how sound the roof was. The larger gargoyles crept forward on their clawed feet and explained about the masonry by flapping their wings with the noise that only membranes made of stone can make.

From a distance came the sound of *The Golden Fleece*'s jukebox.

As the discussion went on, new contributors emerged from the foundations or belfry to join the bacchanal. Not all of the pugwoppits or gargoyles attended these church fabric meetings. Some were holding the structure up, like lots of little Hercules within the arches and pillars, while others were chasing away deathwatch beetles and other pests. If they had any issues for the vicar, they would brief a representative.

Reverend Chunderclough had a long dance with a very pretty glasgal who was in charge of the stained-glass windows. Before long, all the transformed humanikins whose role it was to represent the Biblical characters and saints were gyrating around the vicar as well.

Eventually, the meeting concluded and Reverend Chunderclough asked if there was any other business, not expecting there to be any.

Immediately the assembled throng stopped gyrating, just as something similar was occurring in *The Golden Fleece*.

An elder guttersnipe explained that they had some important news for him.

"News?" exclaimed Reverend Chunderclough, reverting to speech.

"Yech, newch," mimicked the guttersnipe with a sly grin.

There then followed a painstaking explanation of an astounding discovery. Reverend Chunderclough had to concentrate very hard, for there were all sorts of new gestures. Although fluent in architectural terms, his vocabulary was actually quite restricted. The gargoyles and pugwoppits had to repeat themselves several times before he understood.

"The Mithering Brethren?" he said out loud.

The elder gargoyle clicked one set of talons together and pointed at him.

"Here in Wormton?"

The homunculi nodded.

The elder guttersnipe nodded and grinned as only a water spout can.

"I can't believe it!" replied Reverend Chunderclough, break-dancing in the aisle.

He stood up. The elder guttersnipe and the glasgal were conferring. The elder guttersnipe looked at him and pointed down the church. Using the numbers from the *Today's Hymns* board a pugwoppit counted down 5,4,3,2,1 and the glasgal showed him an animation of what they'd just told him in the stained-glass windows.

Reverend Chunderclough's jaw dropped.

There were the Mithering Brethren in their safe house, wearing self-righteous halos. There they were, sneaking out of Wormton in disguise and worshipping what was obviously the Giant Lamb. There they were sneaking back into Wormton and there was their mysterious benefactor with his back to them. And there he was, turning his head to look back at everyone in the church.

Reverend Chunderclough wondered if anyone outside had noticed the animated stained-glass windows but he needn't have worried. If they had, they'd probably just been Naked Drinking and wouldn't have remembered in the morning anyway.

"Is that the person behind the safe houses?" he asked the expectant pugwoppits and gargoyles in a hesitant limbo.

The glasgal grinned impishly and asked if he wanted a repeat by doing a brief salsa with the elder gargoyle.

Reverend Chunderclough sat down heavily on a pew and shook his head.

"You'll have to excuse me," he said, "but I have momentarily lost the power of mime." He thought for a moment. "Could I just see the bit with the souped-up Wolseley Blue Streak again?"

The glasgal grinned and obliged after the pugwoppit had done his count down again.

"I'm afraid I don't know what they're doing," he said. "Do you?"

The pugwoppits, splintergeists, guttersnipes and gargoyles all shrugged as if their first language was French, and waited patiently for Reverend Chunderclough to compose himself. While he did so, the elder guttersnipe began to scratch out a name on a piece of slate.

Reverend Chunderclough nodded slowly and took the piece of slate from the elder guttersnipe. He looked at the glasgal and said, "You really have captured a very good likeness of this man."

She beamed back at him but a splintergeist had brought the *Church Times* edition of *Old Maureen's Almanac* that hung on the back of the vestry door and was pointing at a date that was rapidly approaching.

"My goodness!" said Reverend Chunderclough. "It'll soon be Mithering Sunday! I do hope it's not Dark Time!"

CHAPTER 58

Professor Cluttercrap was beyond Wrainwright's advice now. He had penetrated further than anyone else into the Forest of Riddaw. He felt that if no living person had seen the Black Orchid, then the obvious place to go was where they never ventured. The only trouble was, he now understood why they never came here.

This was the true Woldernesse, the ancient foe the stone men had fought as they had cleared the high ground to allow them to gaze upon the sky, the face of their terrible but sometimes benevolent god.

While he found the plant species encouraging, the darkness of the forest was beginning to alter Professor Cluttercrap's mood, which was usually placidly cheerful. Once the forest had been alive with the shouts of foresters and settlers carving out farmsteads and settlements, but now he had stumbled across the ruins of their labours and plunged even deeper into moss-covered groves that had never heard the sound of an axe or the tread of human feet.

He was rather surprised, therefore, to find that a great swathe of forest had been felled recently and very messily. The exposed forest floor was freshly churned up in places and on the ends of the shattered stumps were many strands of what looked like thick white wire. It was also snagged in the broken branches of the forest canopy.

As he gazed up at the sky and the ragged ends of the trees, his foot struck something of a different texture to the roots and pine needles. He glanced down and saw the remains of a dead fox. To call it a body would have been an exaggeration – it was little more than a bag of fur. It was difficult to say whether there were any internal organs within it and he felt sure that if he picked it up and shook it, the bones inside would have rattled, not that he was going to touch such a grisly specimen. The fox's teeth were bared in a snarl but, even in death, the expression was more of fear than aggression. Flies could hardly be bothered with it and there was a conspicuous puncture mark on the side of its neck.

Around it, the ground had been disturbed by what looked like many feet. Professor Cluttercrap was not an expert tracker but his Boy Scout training told him that there were tracks belonging to the fox and lots of other peculiar marks that were not so much footprints as scrapes in the earth.

He made copious notes and then pressed on, since daytime was slow to arrive and went quickly, as if delving into the forest made it nervous. The unenthusiastic sunlight only served to make the interior of the forest even gloomier, so, as he pondered on the fate of the fox, he chose to follow the trail of destruction.

That night he struck camp by a small stream, lit his gas stove for another boil-in-the-bag curry and put up his tent. He ate his meal quickly and without much pleasure for he was becoming sick of boil-in-the-bag curry. By then it was quite dark so he decided to go to bed, but once he was lying in his sleeping bag the forest, which seemed so empty in daylight, became full of little scamperings.

Of course, he'd heard all the normal night sounds of the forest before but tonight there was some quality about them that made him uneasy.

At one stage he was relieved to hear the familiar "To-wit, to-woo," of an owl but after a few reassuring cries, the owl just went "To-wit." This was followed by muffled squawk and a soft thud. Professor Cluttercrap couldn't be sure but he thought he could hear a soft slurping sound afterwards.

There was no chance of sleep after that. The slightly wrong sounds of the forest continued. The pattering and scratching gradually seemed to focus itself close to the tent and Professor Cluttercrap realised that only its fabric separated him from the source of the noises.

His curly hair and beard began to stand on end.

Something tested the fabric of the tent. Professor Cluttercrap was sure there no trees near enough to touch it with a branch. Besides, it was a quiet, windless night. He lay rigid as the fabric above him was furtively stretched. His ears strained for some more clues as to the nature of the beast outside, but now he could hear nothing apart from the blood in his ears. He felt a curious desire to hear the thing breathing, and when he realised that despite its evident size he could not, his heart began to deafen him anyway.

Now the tent was being touched differently. There was another prod into the fabric and then the sound of the flysheet being punctured, followed by a furtive ripping.

Without thinking, his hand stole silently out of his sleeping bag and found his torch, as if his body could think for itself without him.

He sat up and held the torch towards the cleaving tent fabric and switched on the light.

"No!" he yelled. "The law of surface area to volume ratio! This cannot be!"

CHAPTER 59

"Beware of false prophets," said Brother Guy, "who come in sheep's clothing, but invariably they are ravening wolves."

"*Matthew Chapter 7, Verse 15*," said Sister Elspeth automatically.

"So what happened, Brother Eric?"

"Nothing really," said Brother Eric, nonchalantly.

"Did you thwart the Soul Trader?"

"Not exactly, no."

"So Hob's soul is still his own."

"Yes."

"And you?"

"What about me?"

"Do you still have your soul?"

"I do."

"Good!" said Brother Guy, with visible relief.

Brother Eric shuffled his feet. "For the time being."

Brother Guy sighed. "Don't tell me."

"Okay."

"You've got irresistible preaching skills on a free trial basis for thirty years?" suggested Sister Elspeth.

"No. I'm going to be impossibly righteous for thirty years."

"That's a new one," snorted Brother Guy.

"If you become impossibly righteous you won't survive thirty years," threatened Sister Elspeth.

"It's a risk, I admit that," Brother Eric replied, "but if I am not completely satisfied with my impossibly righteous status at any time within those thirty years, then I can return and owe nothing."

"Yeah, yeah," said the other Mithering Brethren.

Brother Guy turned his back on him and went into a huddle with Sister Elspeth. "How many does that make?"

"Half a dozen. We're still not sure about Sister Millicent."

"We're running out of volunteers, and by now Hob must be wise to our little game."

"This is our strategy," Sister Elspeth reminded him. "So long as we succeed in the end, it doesn't matter how many souls Hob gets. As soon as he repents, they will all be returned to their rightful owners."

"But it's going to take a long time!"

"Have faith!" said Sister Elspeth. "All we've got to do is keep using the car as bait. So long as there is a soul with the car, Hob can't stay away. And all it will take to thwart him is that little word No. If we all say it whenever we meet him he'll soon be completely frustrated and give up. The next person just has to be more resolute."

"More resolute? So far they've been anything but."

CHAPTER 60

It took a lot to waken Mr Heckmondwike, especially after the chaos that follows a bout of naked drinking.

Blearily, he registered something passing over Riddaw Lodge, something unusually rhythmic that provoked a strange dream about rubber bands. He had a vague recollection of rolling out of bed and going to the narrow window.

He didn't remember getting back into bed but he was in it when a similar noise awoke him. It seemed that he was in the no-man's land between sleep and consciousness, where small loops of reality can be mistaken for dreams and vice versa.

The third time he awoke, however, it was much quicker. This time he was definitely awake and listening to the thunderous silence that follows a really loud bang. His sheepdog was barking: three times as much as any normal dog. There was a red glow on the ceiling of his bedroom and, when he looked to the north, part of the moor was ablaze. Even as he watched there was another gout of flame, a little more to the east, followed by another loud bang. Dimly he realised that if he'd been counting he could have worked out how far away it was. Then a third and more distant explosion occurred and he began to pull on his clothes.

He dressed quickly, punching the wall as he pulled his shirt over his head, and went downstairs to collect his agitated dog and fire up his Mudlark. The roar of the big machine brought instant reassurance. After carefully closing the big doors behind him, he headed north.

He travelled without lights. If there were a danger out there in the Woldernesse, he would rather see it than be seen by it. Besides, the red glow provided more than enough light and when he came across the monstrous hoofprints he was able to steer around them.

From his knowledge of the moor he made good progress, but the sky was beginning to lighten a little by the time he reached the rocky outcrop known as Kiss-and-tell. Tonight, it was lit by a hundred small fires and there was an acrid smell.

He wondered if the other explosions had left similar scars, and in the gathering light of the morning found that they had. In each case, the heath had been blasted by fire and he could see scattered fragments of wreckage lying on the smouldering moor.

Thoughtfully, he turned around and made for home. It was quite light by then, which meant he was late for his normal routine. There was no sign of the Giant Lamb anywhere but there was still that awful smell. It made his eyes and nostrils smart.

Back at Kiss-and-tell, he saw many approaching headlamps. Militia vehicles were swarming up from Wormton. As he watched, a pink Mudlark appeared beside him and the passenger ordered him to stop.

The soldiers' teeth and eyes were white in their deliberately darkened faces. "Who are you and what are you doing here?"

Mr Heckmondwike told them. He wasn't used to being treated like this but it was common knowledge amongst the off-road fraternity that it was bad luck to argue with anyone in a pink Mudlark, especially if it might be a badge-engineered Land Rover.

"A shepherd? How long have you been here?"

"Ah've just come back from t'north."

"What were you doing there?"

"I heard a bang and saw t'fire."

The soldiers stiffened. "And?"

"Just t'same as this."

Quickly, they radioed someone. Then the radio operator said, "Could you take us there, sir?"

Mr Heckmondwike led them to the next patch of burnt heather, which looked even worse in the full light of dawn.

In grim silence, they pulled up and began to poke about the fragments of machinery that lay everywhere. Mr Heckmondwike became aware of some non-verbal communication going on between the soldiers.

One of them beckoned to him. "We would be very much obliged, sir, if you didn't mention this to anyone," he said.

Mr Heckmondwike nodded.

"Did you see any sign of the dead sheep anywhere?"

Mr Heckmondwike frowned. "Come again?"

"The dead sheep," persisted the soldier. "You know."

"T'monster, tha means? Nay, lad, nay sign of it."

"Any idea what this bloody awful smell is?" asked one of the others.

"Aye. It's burnt wool. Lots of it, n'all."

CHAPTER 61

Overnight, the militia became less ceremonial. More helicopters arrived, bristling purposefully with rockets, cannons and antennae. Ground crews attached pods and more missiles to them, making them look even angrier, and then they flew off, like their fellows, never to return.

There was a lot of loose talk in *The Golden Fleece*, *The Tin Cur* and *Where the Rainbow Ends* about the failure of the militia to destroy the Giant Lamb. The Rural Marines implemented an unpopular curfew and, avoiding any questions about progress, forbade anyone to approach Riddaw Forest.

Morale was lifted by the arrival of 2 Para – the Second Paraphernalia – and another party was held in the extended wire compound outside the walls of Wormton by the New Gate, one to which no civilians were invited and at which naked drinking certainly went on.

Later, reconnaissance parties combed the moors, and platoons of mechanised armour moved into the Outlands. As quickly as these left Wormton, reinforcements flooded in from the east and the west, mostly by truck convoy but also on the Mithering Railway in special troop trains.

The Giant Lamb stayed away from the town. It kept close to the forest where it fed off the leaves of the taller trees.

Mayor Naseby visited Captain Keen in the official Armstrong-Siddeley. He was driven out through the West Gate and then back to the Rural Marines' camp outside the blocked-off New Gate. Along the way, he passed the WPC's new warning sign. After a great deal of debate they had settled on something about four times normal size, to give an appreciation of the scale of the problem, and consisting of the usual red triangle containing an exclamation mark. Underneath this was another sign that simply read, "Bloody Great Sheep."

There was much activity in the army camp. Captain Keen looked tired. "Good morning, Your Indulgence," he said. "Can I help you?"

"We 'ave some concerns ower t'campaign against t'Giant Lamb."

Captain Keen, never a very supple man, became surprisingly rigid. "I'll write you a report," he said.

"Nay, nay, nay, lad, there's nay need for that.

"You might say things have not as graidly as I had anticipated. However, let me assure you that if I fail to kill this sheep, my career is over."

"A verbal brief will do."

"Nevertheless, I would prefer to give you a full written report. Much has happened since we last spoke."

"Very well. If tha insists."

"I do insist. One other thing," said Captain Keen. "The information contained in my report must not be disclosed to the general public."

"Privy means privy in Wormton, tha knaws."

Captain Keen was as good as his word. His report took some digesting, and Mayor Naseby came late to the next WPC meeting and was ashen-faced. The councillors fell silent as he took his place and sat down.

"Does tha need more time to collect thysen, Thine Indulgence?" asked Mr Grandlythorpe.

"Collect 'imself?" retorted Mr Floridspleen. "It looks like he's gonna have to pick up t'pieces before he does any re-assembly."

"Ah have Captain Keen's report," said Mayor Naseby at last. He held it up with a trembling hand. "There's nay good news. Far from it. T'militia are having lots of problems in attacking t'Giant Lamb. They were initially confident of a swift conclusion to this sorry business, as indeed we were. T'helicopter gunships should've dispatched t'monster quickly and relatively humanely."

"Ah hadn't reckoned on them being humane," whispered Mr Floridspleen, loudly.

"However, for reasons that are still not entirely clear, t'helicopters are running into difficulties. Many have crashed before releasing t'full force of their attack. Captain Keen's experts believe t'Giant Lamb's bleat triggered some sort of harmonic resonance that shivered t'aircraft apart and t'Giant Lamb escaped unharmed."

"What? Not even wounded?" exclaimed Mr Grandlythorpe.

"Aye. It seems that t'missiles dislodged tufts of wool that clogged t'air intakes of t'helicopter engines but, according to t'black boxes, it were t'Giant Lamb's bleat that downed 'em."

"What's a black box?" whispered Mrs Hammerhulme.

Mrs Thorngumbald considered this for a moment before replying "Appen it's summat to do wi' chocolates."

"Do they 'ave a revised plan of attack, then?" asked Mr Floridspleen.

"Aye. Several. Captain Keen has told me t'Wold is not big enough for t'militia and t'Giant Lamb."

CHAPTER 62

"So you can predict Dark Time," said Captain Keen.

"Yes," replied Mrs Osmotherly. Although she no longer acted on behalf of the WPC, her professional curiosity ensured a visit to the Rural Marines. "Don't they have Wise Women where you come from?"

"I don't really come from anywhere. The army is my home. Mater and pater live in the Dyfnent. Our family has for years, in fact. I suppose, if I come from anywhere, it's there, but I've always been more interested in where I'm going."

"Any orientation is a good thing," said Gloria.

"Can you predict Dark Time as well?" Captain Keen asked her.

"No. I have other abilities."

"Hence your interest in fireworks."

"Er, yes."

"I suppose you want to let them awff during Dark Time."

"I might do."

"It must be jolly useful to predict Dark Time."

"There's probably a wise woman forecasting it close to your family home," explained Mrs Osmotherly. "You often find that country people are closer to nature."

"Funny thing to speak of mater and pater," said Captain Keen, producing a letter from his breast pocket. "They wrote to me the other day and d'you know what? The family banshee's been heard again!"

"Really?" said Gloria, wide-eyed.

"Oh come along, you don't believe in all that rubbish, do you?" scoffed Captain Keen. "Put the wind up pater, though, I can tell you!"

"When was it last heard?" asked Mrs Osmotherly.

"When my grandfather died, I think. I would have been away at school."

"While we're on the subject of warnings," said Mrs Osmotherly, "we ought to explain about the Mithering Brethren."

"Oh yes? And who are they?"

"They are a religious sect who believe man was born only to sin. The only way to redeem souls is to ensure nobody does anything. I am sure they are determined to thwart you."

"Hmm. I've dealt with religious fundamentalists before. Do you know where they're based?"

"I'm afraid not."

"They just traipse around the moors in waterproofs doing no good," said Gloria.

"Forewarned is forearmed," said Captain Keen. "Thank you, Mrs Osmotherly. Your brief has been very instructive. You too, Miss Gubbergill." At the sound of voices outside his tent he looked out. "Ah! Now here's a more helpful religious sort! How are you fettling, your reverence?"

"Good morning, Captain Keen," said Reverend Chunderclough. "How goes the good fight?"

"We may have lost the odd battle or two but the war is not over yet!"

"Good."

"What brings you here, your reverence?" asked Mrs Osmotherly.

"I'm acting as padre for the Rural Marines and Marinas," he explained. He flushed a little at the mention of the Rural Marinas.

"We've had some problems with our helicopters," said Captain Keen. "Reverend Chunderclough is here to bless the Jesus Bolt."

"What's that?" Gloria asked him.

"It's the bit that holds on the rotor arms," he replied, airily. "I'm of a more rational frame of mind, y'know, but, the way I see it, a little religious ceremony such as this can only give my men the psychological advantage."

They followed Reverend Chunderclough out into the compound and found a large contingent of air and ground crew waiting for them.

"Could I have your attention please?" began Captain Keen. "We are gathered here today – oh, sorry padre, that's your line! We're here today to witness the blessing of the, ah, Jesus Bolt. Chief Able? I understand you've experienced some deficiencies that you've had to put right."

The maimed engineer stood to attention. "That's right, sir! Gremlins on the Jesus Bolt, sir!"

Captain Keen leaned forward and spoke to him in a low whisper. "Now look here," they just managed to hear him say, "that's enough of this superstitious nonsense. You're an engineer, man, and must think like one. There is no such thing as a gremlin, do you understand?"

Chief Able stared resolutely ahead. He offered no acknowledgement of what Captain Keen had said, and Captain Keen, although he paused a moment longer to look into his face, said no more, either.

"Carry on, your reverence."

"Thank you, Captain Keen. Dearly beloved, we are gathered here today in the presence of the Lord God Almighty to bless these helicopters and the critical components thereof."

They sang *Who would valiant be* and *For those in peril under rotary wings,* and then Reverend Chunderclough read a lesson from the bible about Ezekiel watching the angels climbing a ladder to heaven.

Then he emptied a bottle of water into a little bowl and produced a small pastry brush. Aluminium ladders had been propped up against the helicopters, and in silence he climbed each in turn and anointed something in the centre of the rotor blades, saying, "I bless this Jesus Bolt in the name of the Father, the Son and the Holy Ghost. May He protect it and keep it and all those who dangle in peril under it. Amen."

"Amen."

"That should do for the gremlins," said Gloria to Mrs Osmotherly, "but I'll ask Slake for his rubber service stamp."

"Have you seen anything of him recently?"

Gloria reddened. "No, I haven't."

After Mrs Osmotherly and Captain Keen had gone back into his tent, Gloria lingered, ostensibly to help Reverend Chunderclough with his things but really to speak to Chief Able.

"I believe in gremlins," she told him. "Do you think they might be luddites?"

Chief Able did not reply but looked at her in open-mouthed amazement.

"If you suffer any more trouble with them," she said, "get in touch with Slake of the Slakespeed Tuning Emporium, Frogheat, Park Bottom, and tell him I sent you."

"Very good Miss, thank you Miss."

As she re-entered his tent, Captain Keen was saying, "Mr Quirkmaglen's an old family friend. His family are very ancient, too. Er, not personally, you understand. He's descended from the original warrior caste that overran this region centuries ago."

Mrs Osmotherly snorted.

"He's taken great pains to brief me about the situation here."

"I'm sure he has," said Mrs Osmotherly.

"Ah, Mrs Osmotherly," said Reverend Chunderclough, as he entered Captain Keen's tent behind Gloria. "I have to speak to you about a matter of the utmost delicacy."

CHAPTER 63

"This isn't going to be easy," said Reverend Chunderclough. He was driving with Mrs Osmotherly towards Wormton Castle in his regularly serviced Wolseley. "I suppose it has to be done."

"I still think we should tell the Privy Council," replied Mrs Osmotherly.

"I know, I know." He held up a hand in a placatory gesture.

Mrs Osmotherly fidgeted. She wasn't used to being a passenger.

"All I ask," he went on, "is that we give Mr Quirkmaglen a chance to answer for himself. We should then allow him to reconsider his position on the council."

"It's his by right!" fumed Mrs Osmotherly. "He just sits there!"

"But if we explain that the pugwoppits have told us about his involvement with the Mithering Brethren, then I'm sure he'll resign."

"He shouldn't even be in Wormton, let alone the Privy Chamber! Think about all the trouble the Mithering Brethren have caused us! No wonder they were so hard to pin down!"

"The problem is also one of evidence. I haven't asked him, but I'm sure Justice Jaglinlath will tell us that homuncular testimony is inadmissible in law. You know what he's like."

"Yes and now we know what Mr Quirkmaglen is like, too!"

As their headlamps swept around the walls inside the old bailey of the castle, she said, "Perhaps it would be better if you left the talking to me."

Reverend Chunderclough looked very relieved.

"Your living in Wormton depends on Mr Quirkmaglen's patronage, doesn't it?"

Reverend Chunderclough looked very uncomfortable.

"Together we need to show Mr Quirkmaglen that the conscience of Wormton cannot be bought."

"My conscience has not been bought!" insisted Reverend Chunderclough.

"Well then. We don't have anything to worry about. Do we?"

They were admitted by one of Mr Quirkmaglen's servants who made them wait while he told his master he had visitors. They didn't say a word to each other as Mrs Osmotherly worked out her strategy.

"Mr Quirkmaglen will see you now," said the elderly servant, and he showed them into the drawing room.

Mr Quirkmaglen was reclining gracefully on a low settee. He was reading the same book that he'd been casually dipping into when he had last received Mrs Osmotherly, and she strongly suspected that it was open at the same page. Opposite the window was his writing desk, the one that trilled and had to be spoken to immediately. Its lid was open and the screens showed graphs that changed their colours periodically.

He waited until they'd crossed the room before he looked up, as if distracted from some reverie, and said, "Mrs Osmotherly. Reverend Chunderclough. What a pleasant surprise. To what do I owe this pleasure?"

"This is not a social call," she began. "We have learnt that you are harbouring the Mithering Brethren."

There was an immediate but very gratifying collapse to his misplaced urbane charm.

Before he could deny anything, she carried on. "Acting on information received," and she glanced at Reverend Chunderclough as if someone had confessed to him, "we arranged for an address to be entered and searched by the parish constables. Two known members of the Mithering Brethren were found, and they have now been banished beyond the walls of Wormton where they belong."

"That was my property," murmured Mr Quirkmaglen, looking away.

"Mithering Brethren are forbidden to enter Wormton."

"True," he said, meeting her eyes again and sighing.

"Then you admit to this?" asked Reverend Chunderclough.

"I admit nothing save that it took you long enough to find out where they were hiding."

"They were being hidden," persisted Mrs Osmotherly. "By you."

"Oh, all right! Yes! I admit it! It was I! Now what?"

"But why?" asked Reverend Chunderclough.

Mr Quirkmaglen shrugged his shoulders.

"Do you have any idea what damage you've done?" demanded Mrs Osmotherly.

"A reasonable one," he admitted.

"Do you share their beliefs?" asked Reverend Chunderclough, but Mr Quirkmaglen just laughed.

"You did it for your own amusement," said Mrs Osmotherly. "Didn't you?"

He didn't answer.

There was a movement at the window. They all saw it and looked.

"Good gracious!" exclaimed Reverend Chunderclough.

It was the Giant Lamb.

It was truly enormous. Its great head had to be lowered to peer into Mr

Quirkmaglen's windows, which must have shone over the moor outside like a beacon. An eye seemed to bulge into the room. Its iris was quite satanic at this size. It tried to adjust to the bright lights inside and experimented with various apertures as it looked around the room before going as quickly as it had come, leaving Mrs Osmotherly doubting that it had ever been there.

"I gather the Mithering Brethren regard the Giant Lamb as the new Lamb of God," said Reverend Chunderclough.

Mr Quirkmaglen yawned. "Then we have been vouchsafed an epiphany."

"You realise that you will not be able to continue with your position on the WPC," said Mrs Osmotherly.

Mr Quirkmaglen gave no indication of whether he realised or cared.

"Not all the members of the council are aware of your involvement," she went on. "If you resign your position, they won't need to be."

Mr Quirkmaglen sighed.

"At least this way your reputation and social standing will be preserved," she added.

"So be it," he said. "Thank you, Mrs Osmotherly. Reverend Chunderclough," and with that they left.

As they got back into the car, Mrs Osmotherly said, "All in all, a deeply dissatisfying experience. I feel no pleasure about this whatsoever."

"Neither do I. It's a bad business all round. But it could have been much worse for him, and I think he knows it. We have set him a moral example and we have avoided the destabilising effect that punishing him would've had on the rest of Wormton's social fabric."

"What about the destabilising effects of harbouring the Mithering Brethren?"

"Mrs Osmotherly. That was not within our gift. Showing Mr Quirkmaglen the error of his ways is something that we *can* do. Be wise enough to receive sound counsel. Withdrawing any more of his privileges will only make him worse."

Mrs Osmotherly was thinking hard.

She looked out of the window and saw the silhouette of a face appear against an illuminated window.

Mr Quirkmaglen was watching them.

"Let's leave," she said.

Reverend Chunderclough started the engine and drove calmly out of the castle's bailey.

"He regards it as his birthright to run the whole town as he alone sees fit," he said. "Who knows how good a job he could have done of it? It would have been only for his own interests, of course, but there are many who believe that a benign despot is the most efficient form of government."

"Considering the achievements of the WPC, it couldn't have been much worse," admitted Mrs Osmotherly.

"Now he's going to be denied the central pleasure in what must be a distressingly empty life."

"His life is what he's made it."

"He was spoilt from the beginning," said Reverend Chunderclough. "We should pity him."

"Maybe. But I still think it would be best for him to leave Wormton."

"Mr Quirkmaglen has a soul as well, you know."

"I think it will be a difficult one to save."

Reverend Chunderclough smiled sadly. "Then the greater shall the Lord's joy be when Mr Quirkmaglen repents his sins."

CHAPTER 64

The following morning, Mrs Osmotherly travelled into town in her Wolseley Hornet to do her shopping. A visit to *Where the Rainbow Ends* would also bring her right up to date with the latest proceedings of Wormton's Privy Council. In fact, she was beginning to wish she'd resigned from the WPC earlier. The communications policy of *Where the Rainbow Ends* had the happy knack of stripping away all the boring bits and leaving only the juiciest morsels.

She had come to know the boys and girls of the militia quite well, and now they let her pass through their patrols with a friendly wave instead of stopping her, searching her car and waking up her cat. They even ignored her breaches of curfew as she observed the motorscope.

There was a palpable buzz about the old town. She saw Mr Heptonstall outside his garage, and he had lost about twenty years. Old Mr Macklefract was circulating in an equally sprightly Jowett two-seater and grinning enough to split his head in half.

She pulled up in the market square and did her shopping. Wormton was virtually self-sufficient in everything so she had no trouble getting what she needed, but everything was more expensive with the monster at large except for locally produced mutton and lamb, which was practically being given away.

In *Where the Rainbow Ends* everyone agreed that something was going on but couldn't say what.

"It's t'engineers," said Mrs Amplepance. "They're ower-excited about summat."

Mrs Osmotherly was just reaching her own conclusions as to what could over-excite an engineer when Mrs Macklefract entered the teashop. From her expression it was obvious that she knew something and knew that they did not.

There was a sudden silence and Mrs Macklefract smiled self-consciously as she removed her hat, coat and gloves, hung them up and sat down with her handbag across her knees.

Nothing was said until Old Mrs Skeglathwaite asked, "Well?"

Mrs Macklefract squirmed deliciously. "It's difficult to knaw where to start."

"Summat's afoot, ma lass, and it's obvious tha knaws summat about it."

"Well, let me see. Nowt is afoot. Summat is awheel."

"Come again?"

"T'Wild Hunt is coming to Wormton."

Pandemonium broke out.

Mrs Skellmersmell came out of the kitchen brandishing her formidable serving wand. The mere sight of this usually restored decorum, but not today. Eventually, she had to bring out a large enamel bowl and rattle a wooden spoon around inside it for calm.

"Ladies! Ladies!" she bellowed. "Let the poor woman be heard. And stop throwing food."

"Thank you, Mrs Skellmersmell. As ah said, t'Wild Hunt is coming to Wormton this weekend. Coded messages have been seen int *Piston Wheel*. Ah'm told there can be nay doubt about it."

"Well, well," said Mrs Amplepance, scraping butter from her chin, "what will Mr Grandlythorpe say about this?"

"Aye," agreed Mrs Thorngumbald, Slake's mother, as she tried to fix Mrs Macklefract with a certain look. "Ah wonder who's behind this."

"And what does Mrs Osmotherly reckon to all this?" wondered Mrs Amplepance.

"Ay up," said Mrs Thorngumbald, turning to look for her, "where's she gone?"

Mrs Osmotherly was nowhere to be seen.

She might just as well have been practising for the Wild Hunt herself. She was driving like a demon to Heptonstall's Garage. When she got there, the showroom was closed so she strode into the workshop.

"Where is he?" she asked an excitable Mr Heptonstall.

"Who?"

"You know perfectly well who I mean. Slake."

Mr Heptonstall and Old Mr Macklefract dropped their eyes in what she interpreted to be shame. But then she noticed a pair of boots sticking out as inconspicuously as possible from under a shiny new Wolseley.

"Slake?"

"Aha, hallo, Mrs Osmotherly."

"Come out from under there."

The boots retreated further under the car and there was the sound of a crawler board rolling across the floor. Slake emerged at the far end of the car, looking desperately innocent.

"What's all this about the Wild Hunt coming to Wormton?"

"Promise you won't be cross."

"And why should I be cross?"

"Ooh," said Mr Heptonstall, hiding behind George Ransomes' car.

"Don't ask, just promise," Slake replied.

"I promise that I won't get cross so long as nobody provokes me."

"That's a bit of a cop out, isn't?"

"What is it you have to tell me, Slake?"

"The Wild Hunt is coming to Wormton."

"Oh yes?"

"If tha think that's provoking thee, Mrs O, ee hasn't even begun yet," Old Mr Macklefract told her, helpfully.

"Mr Macklefract. Do you want to see ninety-five?"

"What? Miles an hour? Or years?"

"Years."

"Mrs Osmotherly! Is tha threatening me? Tha should be ashamed o' thysen!"

"Go on, Slake," said Mr Heptonstall, "provoke her."

"It was an idea I had in hospital," said Slake.

"Tha could be having some more ideas in hospital if tha's not careful," put in Old Mr Macklefract.

"I felt pretty annoyed about being blamed for the Giant Lamb so I took matters into my own hands."

"Like Mr Whimsleypleat?" suggested Mrs Osmotherly.

"A bit. I posted some ads in *The Piston Wheel*, and the rest, as they say, is history."

"Tha might be history as well soon," Old Mr Macklefract advised him.

Slake produced a copy of *The Piston Wheel* and showed Mrs Osmotherly the messages in the personal columns. She'd often wondered why they didn't seem very personal. There was nothing about good senses of humour or attractive single mums but many strange and magical poems about all manner of mechanical things and predominantly whizzing pistons and tyres spitting gravel. And there were quasi-religious texts that didn't read quite properly, as if they had been misquoted in an accidentally-on-purpose sort of way.

"Slake? What *is* this all about?"

"This is confirmation that it's coming, Mrs Osmotherly! The Wild Hunt will flush the monster out and destroy it like any other living thing that gets in its way! One souped-up ambulance wasn't enough, but the way I saw it – the way I see it – at the very least the Wild Hunt will drive the Giant Lamb away from Wormton."

"And at the very most?"

"It would turn it into a giant road kill. Make a bit of a mess, though."

"A bit of a mess? Would that be out of the Lamb or the Wild Hunt? Have you seen the size of the monster recently?"

"More to the point, have you ever seen the Wild Hunt?"

This rather took the wind out of Mrs Osmotherly's sails because she had not.

"Come off it, Mrs O," went on Slake, "what have we got to lose? The militia isn't having much luck against it."

"Your argument is persuasive," she conceded.

"Look," said Slake, walking up to her, "I don't want things to go back to the way they were before between us. I set all this up while we weren't speaking, but now I don't regret what I've started."

Mrs Osmotherly turned to Mr Heptonstall. "Are you taking part?"

He grinned and nodded.

"And you?"

"Aye," said Old Mr Macklefract. "So's George Ransomes 'n'all."

"And I can't believe you won't be," she told Slake. "Won't there be casualties?"

Slake shrugged. "Mebbe. Mebbe not. If there are, the crows will glut themselves on the road kills. That's the Wild Hunt for you. And maybe – just maybe – the Giant Lamb will be among them."

"The WPC won't like it coming through Wormton," Mrs Osmotherly pointed out.

"It won't go through Wormton. It'll bypass it. Keep an eye on the old Wormton cutoff over the next few days."

"We're expecting road pixies," explained Mr Heptonstall.

"Aye. We'll be getting better roads to Bedlam and Mithering an' all," said Old Mr Macklefract.

"And the Wild Hunt won't be here for long," Slake continued. "It'll just flash past the old town and flush the Lamb out of the valley."

"Where does it start from?" asked Mrs Osmotherly.

"Bedlam-le-Beans."

"And where does it go from here?"

"Beyond Mithering. Where else?"

"Indeed. Beyond Mithering."

"We'll pay back the Mithering Brethren with interest."

"I have to admit that parts of your plan have a certain appeal," said Mrs Osmotherly. "Mmyes. It's a long shot but it just might work."

CHAPTER 65

The following Thursday morning, the old Wormton cutoff, or bypass, appeared to have been resurfaced in the night. Throughout the day, small groups of ratepayers went out beyond the walls of Wormton to examine it for themselves.

The militia were just as intrigued. When the mayor and councillors turned up, Captain Keen was standing in the middle of it, with his hands on his hips and with what looked like a violin case stuffed down each trouser leg. He was carrying a riding crop that failed to make sense of his ridiculous breeches and his moustache was bristling at the fairy road.

"How are you fettling, your indulgence!" he said.

"Aye, nobbut graidly, tha knaws."

"Happen? Those hoggs of yours look especially fair to middling these days."

"Eh? Ah don't have any hoggs."

"Oh. Don't you? Oh well never mind. Heck as likely as happen as perhaps you're right, even though it's me saying so perhaps when I shouldn't. Just having a look at your new road, dontcha know."

"It's not our road," replied Mayor Naseby. "We nivver sanctioned any road improvements like this."

"Well whose road is it, then? I'm sure they'll let you borrow it if they're the sort to leave decent bits of black top lying about the countryside."

"Did any of thine men hear owt last night?"

"Sergeant, did any of your men hear anything last night?"

"Not a sausage, sir."

"See anything?"

"Negative, sir."

Captain Keen shrugged. "There you are then. It's a mystery."

"It must be for t'Wild Hunt," said Mr Grandlythorpe, dubiously.

"Really?"

"It's comin' through t'Vale of Wormton on Sat'day night," Mr Grandlythorpe replied.

"Ah would advise thee and thine men to stop soldierin' for a bit," said Mayor Naseby, "to see if t'Wild Hunt can either chase t'Giant Lamb away or run it down."

"Very well. My men could do with a bit of a morale boost. We'll have another concert party!"

CHAPTER 66

"Apparently Ted's pig has turned up again," Mr Heckmondwike told Slake. They sat in the lumpy armchairs at Frogheat before a well-fed fire. Although it was now late spring, they both felt chilled to the marrow by the recent turn of events.

"Bucephalus Epsilon of Riddaw?"

"Aye, t'pedigree Glamworth. It seems it were int sty all t'time. They just owerlooked it amongst t'straw."

Slake frowned. "Overlooked it? Their prize Glamworth?"

"Aye."

"How could they lose a Glamworth? They're like double-decker pigs when compared to the common or garden variety."

"Appen it's shrunk. George's daughter's hamster died and she's lent its cage to Ted and Ted. They say t'shrinking pig loves its little wheel."

"Is it still shrinking?"

"Aye, but nowt as fast as it were."

Slake shook his head. "It just doesn't make sense. Did I mention George's riding with us in the Wild Hunt?"

"Aye, tha did, lad. More than once."

"I'm quite excited about it."

Mr Heckmondwike rolled his eyes in mock amazement. "Appen?"

"Yeah. What was it like when the Wild Hunt came through the last time?"

Mr Heckmondwike struggled manfully not to sigh. It wasn't as if Slake was his son and had just asked him about the birds and the bees.

He gathered his thoughts, peeling back the years from the onion of his memory.

"It were about this time o' year. Life were different back then. Wormton were already on a downward slope but it weren't blown like it is today. There were far more people living here then. And Mr Heptonstall and Old Mr Macklefract had far more customers than they do today. T'Wild Hunt were welcomed. It went all ower t'Wold.

"Folk in Wormton had known abowt it for weeks. They'd seen t'coded messages int *Piston Wheel*. Not many understood 'em but those that did saw to it that all t'appropriate arrangements were made.

"Ah came down from t'moor just in time. You know how tis wi' me when ah'm owt wi' flock. E'en from Scar Fell Farm, ah could tell summat was up and then ah remembered, so ah made ma way down to t'town.

"Wormton lay bayfore me int sunshine and ah could see men, women and children starting to line t'route. There were so many of 'em. They had come from all over t'Wold to see t'Wild Hunt and they were all looking out towards Mithering with their backs to Bedlam. So many folk! Ah'm just a shepherd, a solitary by rights and by nature, more familiar wi' clouds and t'sky and t'moors and at ease wi' ma own company. Around Wormton were more people than ah'd ever suspected lived int whole wide Wold. There were a fair, too, so big they called it a circus, and that stayed for days bayforehand and days afterwards, 'n' all.

"T'shadows were lengthenin'. It were cool and calm int shade of t'western hills but up ont road a great shindig was goin' on. A party was under way and ah felt so happy to've got there just in time. But t'party was getting quieter. Word had come from Mithering; t'Wild Hunt was on its way and would be with us shortly. There had been planes flying ower all day and they could be seen again flying down t'Vale, makin' sure none of t'authorities were tryin' to stop t'Wild Hunt from runnin'.

"And there were all these crows that sat ont telegraph poles along t'road."

"Yeah," said Slake. "They follow the Wild Hunt and glut themselves on the road kills. They'll feast themselves on the Giant Lamb if everything goes according to plan."

"Aye. Well, t'Wild Hunt may be t'most glamorous thing ah've ivver seen but it's also t'deadliest. Once the planes had gone, t'hush were so complete ah could hear our lug holes wriggling. And then ah heard it, faintly at first but getting ever louder, t'first part of *T'Song of T'Machine*.

"It were a flat high buzzin' sound that coulda bin inside ma head to start with, but it were really approachin' from t'west. We shielded our eyes aginst t'setting sun and we could just make out some small shapes moving along t'main road from Mithering. T'cry went up "Trouble's comin'!" and there were a burst of noise as t'first bike came through, followed by another and then another. There was nobbut much between 'em but as fast as they'd come they were away.

"Eh, lad, how we cursed t'sun! Then, as it went behind Blind Ponder and t'shadows bathed our sore eyes, we began to see 'em properly and understood how fast they could travel. T'bikes were getting' bigger and their sounds were changin'. Some screamed by but others boomed. Some felt as if they made thine eyes bleed the noise were that objectionable, but others were like – ah dunnaw – a gulp of Old Sawe's Irascible Anorak for the ears!"

"That good eh?" put in Slake.

"And ah wanted to knaw t'riders, to see what kind of man could go that fast. One chap had a reet bad tank slapper cresting Wooden Leap, that small rise ont approach to Wormton, just up from t'Inner Folds. He didn't slow down at all, he just went straight by, fighting to stay on all t'way.

"Then t'really big bikes began to come by and ah sometimes wonder if mebbe t'Horsepower Whisperer weren't abroad that night."

"It's said he never misses a Wild Hunt," murmured Slake, as he gazed into the fire. "It's certain he was there among them."

"Whenever ah hear Mrs O talk about his bike," said Mr Heckmondwike, "e'en though ah know nowt about bikes – and nayther does she, come to that – ah kinda knaw t'machine she means, as if ah've seen it bayfore."

Slake nodded.

"Ah reckon ah heard it, too. Some bikes roared and others whined. There were one that did both. It made people stop cheering when they saw it, it were goin' so fast. And the noise – it were like the Wold stopped turnin'."

"Some of those bikes were really big," Mr Heckmondwike went on. "They had some sidecars, and then some trikes a bit like *Simurg*. T'last one of t'two wheelers were a gurt big thing, long int wheelbase and not going too quickly. Its motor weren't running reet but this fella still wanted to be int hunt and kept his plot rollin'. He got quite a cheer as he went by and he must have knawn he were t'last bike for he sat up a bit and waved. And ah seen some funny front forks and t'badge on the tank, which read OEC. Hast tha ivver heard t'like?"

Slake nodded. "The Odd Engineering Company."

"Appen?"

Slake grinned. "That's what we call 'em. They still turn out occasionally. OEC really stands for Osborn Engineering Company, but they were certainly odd and not just for their funny front ends, either."

"But t'fust of t'cars were upon us, straight away. It were small and red and very fast, and it weren't long afore all manner of tiny, little, thin-wheeled machines were scampering daintily past us. T'road just filled up with 'em! And they kept on coming, somehow going faster and faster as the evening went on. Some of 'em, well, they made the ground shake and others sounded like tearin' calico!"

"Sounds like the Wild Hunt was a great success," said Slake.

"Aye it were."

"So why is Mr Grandlythorpe so against it coming through the Vale of Wormton again?"

"Doesn't tha knaw?"

"No."

"Ah," said Mr Heckmondwike. "Well it's like this, lad. His sister and fiancée had their heads turned by the Wild Hunt. It does that to some girls, tha knaws."

Slake grinned. "Yeah. I do know."

"They became Mrs Dobson and Mrs Loncaster respectively."

Slake stopped grinning. "Oh dear. Poor old Mr Grandlythorpe. I knew there had to be something, but I couldn't find any mention of it in *The Vrooms Day Book*."

"Aye, there was reet, lad."

"But not the sort of thing *The Vrooms Day Book* would mention, eh?"

"Nay lad. This were wuss. This were personal."

"So the Wild Hunt didn't actually go through Wormton," Slake said.

"Nay, lad. It didn't go through t'town itself, it bypassed it. Ah nivver knew how they managed to build it in time but t'Wormton cutoff appeared outta naywhere ower a couple o' nights."

"It must have been the road pixies," said Slake.

"Come again?"

"The road pixies."

"Eh?"

"Don't tell me you've never heard of the road pixies! They're the lares and penates of the highways. They're inextricably mixed up with the Wild Hunt and it's said that Horsepower Whisperers have dominion over them, just as they do over gremlins. A few nights before the Wild Hunt is due, the road pixies come out and repair the roads. Sometimes they even build new ones. I reckon that's how Wormton got its bypass. The Wild Hunt would never have fitted through the gatehouses or the narrow streets of Wormton."

"So does that explain t'newly surfaced black top ont Wormton cutoff today?"

"Well, what do you think?"

CHAPTER 67

That night, after he'd returned to Riddaw Lodge, Mr Heckmondwike slept badly again. Now that the flock was kept down at Scar Fell Farm, he felt his isolation more keenly, and by the time he'd struggled through the military checkpoints and across the pitch black moors he felt redundant. But to move away from Riddaw would have been admitting defeat.

Although Slake and his nearest neighbours the Macklefracts were always pleased to see him, Mr Heckmondwike was increasingly aware of hostility from other Woldspeople. He felt they blamed him for the Giant Lamb. It was one of his flock so he had to shoulder some responsibility, but he felt like Atlas, with the whole Wold upon his shoulders.

As he lay in bed, aircraft flew over Riddaw Lodge and he listened in vain for their return. Dull crumps sounded in the distance and sometimes he felt the castle tremble. And when he saw a grim glow on the horizon, he knew that lambs did not burn as well as that.

For several days, heavy armour had been moving up to the forest, accompanied by great truckloads of foot soldiers. If it was just a question of weight of numbers, the militia should have succeeded weeks ago but, like the aircraft, none of them ever came back.

Mr Heckmondwike tried not to think about what might be going in the darkness on the moors and began considering life keeping chickens. He wondered if he could be content counting birds in the hand. Widdershins could live in semi-retirement as his hen dog.

No. What he really wanted was to feel the thrill again of rescuing his flock from the jaws of death. He always slept well afterwards – but there was too much death around at the moment, none of it very natural.

He turned over and put his head under his pillow, but it was a windy night and lost souls wailed in the chimney and a loose shutter banged somewhere. On some nights there had been furtive scratchings at the big doors that sent Widdershins into a frenzy of barking. Tonight a gale was blowing outside and it smothered any stealthy sounds around the old walls of Riddaw Lodge. But Widdershins could sense something outside again.

Mr Heckmondwike gradually became aware of the banging and the barking getting louder. In the end he got up, put on some clothes and peered out of his battlements but he could see nothing in the inky blackness.

Then he realised, with the cold sweat of shock, that there was no loose shutter. Someone or something outside was hammering on the doors.

He hurried downstairs and found Widdershins very pleased to see him, flecks of foam at its mouths from prolonged barking.

"Let me in, let me in!" cried a voice that sounded vaguely familiar.

Whatever was outside began hammering with more energy now that the barking had stopped.

Mr Heckmondwike deliberated. The most likely explanation was that it was a militiaman, separated from his regiment and exposed to the new and terrible threats to life that stalked the moor at night.

On the other hand, the threat from the Mithering Brethren was never far away. In his bid for survival, Mr Heckmondwike was determined not to be thwarted.

"Widdershins," he said softly, above the shouting from outside, "ah'm gonna open those gates. Be ready to attack it if it's some eldritch creature."

Then Widdershins had a brilliant idea. Shins scampered up to his Mudlark and jumped behind the wheel. At first he thought the poor creature acted out of fear but then Shins flashed the Wolseley's headlamps at him. He saw the eager face behind the windscreen and grinned back at him.

"Let me in, let me in! For pity's sake, let me in!"

Flanked by Wid and Der, Mr Heckmondwike took up position behind the gates. He looked at each animal in turn, provoking a friendly wag of tails from two and an impatient flash of headlamps from the other.

"Let me in, let me in!"

Mr Heckmondwike lifted the beam across the gates, threw back the great bolts and pulled them inwards.

Shins switched on the headlamps and a dishevelled figure fell between the gates and lay on the ground.

Mr Heckmondwike stared at it. There was something undeniably familiar about it, and Wid and Der sniffed it vigorously.

Then Shins began hooting.

Mr Heckmondwike turned to look out of the doors and saw eldritch shapes running with difficulty towards the open gateway. He kicked the prostrate figure out of the way and slammed the gates shut. There were some dull thumps against the doors and he set the great beam across them again. He threw the bolts home and stooped to turn the figure over.

Widdershins bounced around him joyfully, as if they had just rescued a lost sheep.

"By the crook of St Mary, our Lady of Lapurdo!"

It was Professor Cluttercrap.

CHAPTER 68

Mrs Osmotherly and Gloria travelled to Riddaw Lodge under military escort. As they climbed the stairs, there was a burst of incoherent shouting from above.

"Who was that?" Gloria asked softly.

"Im," said Mr Heckmondwike.

Under the great roof of Riddaw Lodge, Mr Heckmondwike ushered them into a whitewashed bedroom. Professor Cluttercrap lay on the bed. He was fast asleep but so tangled up in the bedclothes he resembled a do-it-yourself mummy. There were feathers all over the floor.

"I blame Wrainwright for the deaths of these ramblers," Mrs Osmotherly muttered. "All that nonsense about Black Orchids!"

"This one's not dead yet," pointed out Mr Heckmondwike.

"No, but just look at his face. Those gone down to the very pit itself never wore a more haunted look."

"And that's while he's still asleep," pointed out Mr Heckmondwike.

"Has he said anything?" asked Gloria.

"Oh aye. He's a noisy beggar, reet enough. None of it makes any sense, mind."

"Really?" said Mrs Osmotherly.

"He keeps shoutin., 'Ah deny it! Ah deny it! The surface area to volume ratio! Ah deny it! Ah deny it!'"

Mrs Osmotherly frowned. "Are you sure?"

"Ah've heard it often enow," said the shepherd with some feeling, "and now so's thee. Mebbe goin' down t'pit and back does that to tha. Anyroad, he survived."

Mrs Osmotherly rolled her eyes at him. It could have been a trick Gloria had taught her, but she brought something of her own to the gesture. "Yes," she said, "but at what price?"

"Oo knaws?" said Mr Heckmondwike.

He watched as the women took over. All through their ministrations, Professor Cluttercrap slept as soundly as a baby. Not once did he cry out or struggle or take a pillow in his mouth and worry it to death like he had before. Mr Heckmondwike had never known anyone who could muss the bed up so quickly and hoped they would see what an energetic sleeper Professor Cluttercrap was, but he didn't oblige.

He picked up a pillowcase and all the feathers fell out of it. "Ah seen many a sick ewe and he looks better than many that turned the corner," he observed.

"Well, it's not exactly a surprise he came through," said Gloria.

"Come again?"

"I could tell he would survive."

"Er, perhaps I should explain," said Mrs Osmotherly. "Gloria has a very special talent."

"Oh, aye?"

"Yes, you see, in addition to being a qualified nurse, she can see the soul pilots who come to guide the spirits of the dead."

"Appen? Where'd they go then?"

"I'm not that good," said Gloria.

"Pity," said Mr Heckmondwike. "That'd be summat else, that would!"

"The thing is, Mr Heckmondwike, I can also see the lares and penates in the hospital. It's a bit like Slake seeing gremlins. Before they arrive, harbingers congregate around those souls that are about to make the final great journey. Mrs Osmotherly was curious to know if I saw any around Professor Cluttercrap."

"And does tha?"

"No. I didn't before, either."

"So that's grand then." Mr Heckmondwike frowned suddenly. "Does tha see them around me, then?" he asked.

Gloria smiled reassuringly. "No. Not yet. You're as much a survivor as Professor Cluttercrap."

"Aye." He poked a finger through one of the many bite-sized holes in the pillowcase and wiggled it, pensively. "The thing is, though, what is it that he has survived?"

CHAPTER 69

Slake was full of wonder at the way a few adverts in *The Piston Wheel* were creating his very own Wild Hunt. He knew how the written spells worked, of course, but he'd never tried it before, and now the personal columns of *The Piston Wheel* were electric with the emerging character of the forthcoming Wild Hunt.

There were only four entrants from Wormton. Slake had his trike, *Simurg*, Old Mr Macklefract was in his supercharged Jowett Short Two, and George Ransomes had entered his much updated Wolseley Stellite. Finally, Slake and Mr Heptonstall had produced a highly non-standard, short-wheel-base, two-door, twin-engined Wolseley 18/85 special. They had taken for their inspiration the Mini Twini-Cooper that had almost cost John Cooper, the Surbiton horsepower whisperer, his life. It featured two warmed-up 1800cc B series engines and a rather elegant fastback interpretation of the standard bodyshell.

"What sort of power does tha reckon that thing's got?" asked George Ransomes as they assembled at Heptonstall's Garage on the Friday night.

Mr Heptonstall pursed his lips. "About 250 brakes," he said.

George made a long low whistle but Slake said, "Rubbish! It must be nearer 300! The standard twin carb "S" unit pumps out 100 bhp. These ones have been gas-flowed to within an inch of their very lives!"

"What's tha gonna call it?" asked George.

"Ow about t'Wolseley 36/170?" suggested Mr Heptonstall.

"I prefer the Slakespeed Special myself," said Slake.

Mr Heptonstall laughed.

"Tha must get the naming of a thing right," mused Old Mr Macklefract, "for using a thing's proper name gives thee control ower it."

"We're underselling our talents calling it a 36/170!" Slake protested.

"Tha means we're underselling thine!"

"Ah reckon, seein' as Mr Heptonstall's drivin' it, ee ought to choose its name," said George.

"Slake," said Mr Heptonstall, "tha won't want it to be a Slakespeed Special if'n it's not successful, will tha?"

"Don't worry, it'll be a primester," said Slake, using Wild Hunt slang for something that wins its class first time out.

There had been a great deal said about Old Mr Macklefract's Jowett as well. It was based on a late 1920s Short Two in which he'd crystallised all his Jowett expertise. He'd given the engine specially cast overhead valve cylinder heads and a supercharger. He'd then fitted the rip-roaring 907cc flat twin powerplant into a much-lowered chassis with cleverly concealed telescopic dampers. It even had independent front suspension provided by very long swing axles that overlapped underneath the cut-down radiator.

"That car is cute enough to wear as a badge," said Slake.

"Ah still reckon it's still too short," remarked Mr Heptonstall.

"Nay!" said Old Mr Macklefract, who was the most senior skirrow by some margin, "ah had a standard Short Two bayfore and that were awreet. This un's bin lowered so it handles e'en better."

On Saturday morning, they gathered outside Mr Heptonstall's work-shops with their racing cars. They'd received their numbers according to the complicated classification system and running order, and painted them on as either black numbers on a white background, white numbers on a black back-ground or black or white numbers with no background according to whatever Wild Hunt convention was appropriate. Slake was No.23, Old Mr Macklefract was No. 145, George Ransomes was No. 357 and Mr Heptonstall was No. 2287, and although their road weapons were familiar enough to the people of Wormton, now they had their numbers on they looked completely different and quite awe-inspiring.

They warmed up their engines, made their last-minute checks and re-membered one or two last-minute things as a large number of well-wishers turned up to see them off.

Gloria gave Slake a scarf, as if she were a princess and he was her champion. It was a very feminine scarf and he confided to Old Mr Mackle-fract that he had rather mixed feelings about tying it somewhere conspicuous.

"Don't worry about it, lad," the old man said. "Tha won't be alone if tha looks hard enough. Tie it somewhere discreet and then wave it to the lass as tha goes by. It'll be worth thine trouble! Mark ma words!"

"Good luck," Mrs Osmotherly told Mr Heptonstall.

"Thanks, Mrs O."

"I'd like you to have this."

"What is it?"

"A St Christopher. Many Wild Hunters have them I believe."

"Thank you." St Bendix was the patron saint of engineers, but Mr Hep-tonstall appreciated the gift, even though he had his lucky orange screwdriver in the glove box.

They kissed but not quite on the lips.

Gloria was kissing Slake.

Dilys was kissing George.

And Old Mrs Macklefract was kissing Old Mr Macklefract.

Mr Heckmondwike kissed no one. He shook all the Wild Hunters by the hand but especially Slake.

"Steady! How am I supposed to drive with this in a plaster cast? Eh?"

"Give 'em 'ell, lad! Splash that sheep across the black top from here to kingdom come!"

"Gentlemen!" shouted Old Mr Macklefract. ""We must get a shake on! Start your engines!"

"Trouble's goin'!" shouted George, Slake and Mr Heptonstall.

The crowd cheered as the engines burst into life, and then fell aside, grinning, with their hands over their ears. The Wild Hunters made their final last-minute checks and then Mr Macklefract made a winding-up gesture with his right hand, mouthed, "Trouble's gone!" and they were off towards Bedlam.

CHAPTER 70

The next day nobody could concentrate properly. Everyone had turned into clock-watchers, so that by mid afternoon many Wormtonians had given up work completely, making Mr Grandlythorpe and Mayor Naseby grumble about lost productivity.

As the afternoon wore on, great crowds assembled along the main road and the newly surfaced cut off. The roads took on a strangely daunting aspect and traffic dwindled. Aerial activity increased conspicuously, and not just because of the militia. Onlookers were treated to displays of mock dogfights from the Wild Hunt planes that made them coo and gasp as if they were watching fireworks.

Closer to the ground, malevolent bunches of black birds gathered on telegraph poles and dry stone walls.

Most of the militia had been granted leave for the evening. Many already knew the Wild Hunt better than the Woldspeople and they settled down by the side of the road with the locals. They had brought part of their soup kitchen along with them, and Mr Heckmondwike had arranged a couple of ram roasts while *The Golden Fleece* had organised a tanker truck of ale. Before long, the pre-race party was in full swing, and the feasting and carousing lasted until about six o'clock when the whisper went around that somewhere to the east of Bedlam-le-Beans, the Wild Hunt had begun.

The road in both directions was now closed.

Wormton was cut off.

Spectators drifted back to the tents and bars until another *frisson* of excitement brought them out again.

"Listen! Something's coming!"

Everyone looked east and strained to hear what Miss Periwig's sharp ears had picked up.

A speck appeared in the sky towards Bedlam and as people shouted and pointed at it, it sank below the horizon as if still trying to sneak up on them. Just before it flew over them they saw it was a Supermarine Spitfire and it waggled its wings in greeting and did a reckless barrel roll over the town before gaining height again in the skies towards Mithering.

"That must have been the last plane," said Mr Heckmondwike.

"What time is it?" asked Mrs Osmotherly.

"About eight," replied Gloria without looking at her watch. She'd only just looked at it.

"When did they set off from Bedlam?"

"Six. Only it wasn't Bedlam. Slake said it was somewhere beyond."

The crowd stood up as something winked at them from the cleavage between the hills.

"Who's going to be first?" Mrs Amplepance wanted to know.

"The bikes," said her husband, who had an old Panther outfit tucked away in his shed.

"Ah wish we had binocklears like the militia," said Mrs Amplepance.

"They're not called binocklears," said her husband, scornfully, "the proper word is biconulars."

The cry went up "Trouble's comin'!" and there was a blast of sound and the smell of burning. Something on terribly thin tyres ripped down the road. On top of these were balanced a pair of very shiny red leather buttocks.

"By 'eck, ee were travelling at a lick!" said Mrs Hammerhulme, whose eyes had been ruined by too much knitting. "Ah thought they were spoased to be slow to start with! Look at the lead ee's got!"

"Ah think tha'll find ee is a she," Mrs Amplepance said to her quietly.

"Get away!"

Similar bikes came wailing past.

"Appen this lot are hangin' back just to admire her rear!" said Mr Melliver.

"Now then, Daze, does tha fancy doin' owt like that?" asked Mrs Gaffathwaite.

"Actually I do."

Further conversation was drowned as other 50cc riders came through, followed by 60s, 75s, 80s, 90s and then 100s. Many of the smallest motorbikes were highly specialised machines ridden by fearless, elfin riders, many of whom were women, exploiting their slighter build to advantage. The next numerically large class after the 50s consisted of the 125s, and the fastest of these were already mixing it with the slower 100cc bikes.

The general rule was slowest first, but by the time the Wild Hunt reached Wormton all the classes were nicely mixed up and the race numbers were all out of sequence. The crowd drew back a little as progressively bigger and faster bikes appeared. Already there was a 500 among the 250s and then a 750 among the 500s.

Gloria had seen the Wild Hunt many times before, but the crowds around Wormton were not as blasé as the ones she'd known before. She found herself becoming more and more excited as the Wild Hunt went by. It glittered and flashed all the colours of the rainbow. There was a profusion of hot smells, some good, some bad, and all manner of engine sounds were present from slow revving four-strokes to ear splitting two-strokes. There were even a couple of sleeve valve motors and the occasional rotary Wankel engine.

To see it, smell it and hear it here, well off the beaten track and somewhere it rarely ventured, made it even more of a spectacle. To her there was always something magical about cars and bikes wearing their race numbers, but the best part was knowing that among them were people she knew. Seeing the race numbers all mixed up together showed a thousand and one little triumphs and tragedies, but they could all be forgotten so long as the riders were still in the hunt.

But her joy vanished when she saw with horror the rider of a rapid 750 motorcycle with harbinger gnomes riding with him.

She glanced around quickly at the rest of the crowd but, of course, nobody else could see them. Then she looked around to see if anyone had seen her sudden change of heart, but of course no-one had. They were all too wrapped up in their own impressions of the Wild Hunt.

The cutoff road had a long straight section allowing really quick bikes to hurtle past slower entries. The new piece of road that bypassed Wormton gently curved away to the south and roughly on the apex of this bend was the watershed point. Before this they were climbing out of Bedlam. After it was the long descent towards Mithering.

Gloria soon regained her excitement but as the 1000cc machines appeared, Mrs Osmotherly froze.

"Gloria!" she said. "Look! There he is! The black rider on the Vincent!"

The whole effect of the Wild Hunt suddenly changed. The crowd heard a thunderous roar but above this was something between a scream and a whine. This was the sound of *Nosferatu* singing *The Song of The Machine* as only a blasphemously supercharged Vincent could sing it.

And the next thing Gloria knew, there he was – Old Weird Wheels himself, the Metal Guru, the Repossession Man, the Crypto-Engineer, His Malign Weirdness, the Grand Whizz-Herd and Master of the Engine Henge, the Lord High Prince of Rock'n'Roll, the Horsepower Whisperer and Soul Trader, that infamous libertine, free radical and road racer of many legends, Nicholas Eldritch Hob.

The Horsepower Whisperer came carving through the pack of slower bikes as if they were traffic cones and was the last of the late brakers at the little wriggle in the Wormton bypass, where the road into the south gate turned off. Everyone saw Hob grinning in his open faced helmet and froze in awe at the angles of lean he assumed as he swept through what must have been like a chicane for him. Both his front and rear tyres seemed to be either sliding or spinning or slipping but it was just the way he rode. He seemed to be accelerating out of the corner before he'd turned into it and disappeared from view even quicker than he'd appeared, riding his bike as if he knew the roads around Wormton intimately.

Everyone looked at each other for reassurance that the rest of the crowd had seen the same display of reckless riding skill. Even the notes of the other engines in the Wild Hunt seemed muted by comparison, and in between there was no longer the sound of any cheering.

Gradually, the euphoria returned to the crowd but soon there was another bike, a lime-green Kawasaki that had a similar aura.

"Another one of Hob's *Terminal Murrain?*" Gloria shouted to Mrs Osmotherly.

The wise woman frowned and nodded. "One of The Quick and The Dead," she replied.

Mr Heckmondwike appeared not to notice, but throughout that Wild Hunt there were other cars and bikes that were set apart from the others by their uncanny speed and apparent defiance of the laws of physics.

Of course, there were loads of other horsepower whisperers in the Wild Hunt besides Hob, but Gloria and Mrs Osmotherly agreed that they could easily spot those who were in Hob's *Terminal Murrain*.

When the partisan crowd spotted the Wolseley Wapenshaw road-racing machines from Bedlam, an especial cheer went up, one loud enough for the grinning riders to acknowledge by a briefly raised hand.

The last of the really big bikes went by and there were already some of the more powerful trikes among them.

"Ooooohwa!" squealed Gloria, jumping up and down. "Slake should be here soon!" She was surprised at how quickly her horror at the sight of Nick Hob had been forgotten.

"There he is!" cried Mrs Osmotherly. An even greater cheer went up and she began jumping up and down, too.

Even Mr Heckmondwike had to admit that *Simurg* looked and sounded fantastic. Slake was showing off in front of his home crowd and looked grimly serious but, as he settled *Simurg* into the correct attitude for the slight dogleg at the end of the straight, he grinned broadly at them, relaxed slightly and raised his right arm making Gloria's coloured scarf stream out like a banner.

She squealed again with excitement and jumped on the toes of Mrs Osmotherly, who then jumped on those of Mr Heckmondwike. He just put his arm out to steady the wise woman, but somehow it found its way around her waist. She turned to look at him, and while everyone was watching the Wild Hunt they kissed, and properly too.

The first of the lightweight four-wheelers came quickly after that. By now, everyone was on their clockwork two-ways, eagerly learning what was to come or telling others what had passed so far.

Another great cheer went up when Old Mr Macklefract's Jowett appeared. The exhaust pipes on either side of his engine were a dull red colour in the twilight. Although the old man couldn't possibly hear the crowd above the roar of the engines, he too waved at his adoring fans in the crowd and even blew a kiss to his wife, who made Gloria's reaction seem quite subdued by comparison.

And then there was George Ransomes moving swiftly in his heavily modified Stellite. The sight of such an elderly car travelling so quickly delighted everyone, and some might have thought that for Dilys this would have been enough. However, it seemed that she had something else up her sleeve, metaphorically speaking.

She had positioned herself by the dogleg at the end of the straight, and as soon as she saw her husband she jumped up and down twice, turned her back, bent down and hoicked her skirt up around her midriff. Underneath she was wearing an old fashioned pair of white "Harvest Festival" drawers of the all-is-safely-gathered-in variety, and across the seat of these, in bright red letters was the single word "Bodger."

A great roar of approval went up from the crowd and George must have moved up several places as he outbraked many of his distracted competitors going into the turn.

Suddenly, Gloria realised she was alone. Mrs Osmotherly and Mr Heckmondwike had disappeared.

Some of the cars were going even quicker now, as fast as the really big bikes. The Wild Hunt was a non-contact affair but an occasional scuff was inevitable. Throughout the close-packed cars the odd little thump or tinkle of glass could just be made out.

All headlamps were on now. Whenever there was another Jowett, the crowd cheered again, and sometimes the Jowetteers heard them and waved back. In the dark the illuminated Wolseley radiator badges were easy to spot and the crowd began to grow hoarse although their enthusiasm remained undiminished.

Some people two-wayed the Outlander farmers towards Mithering and began shouting out news snippets back and forth across the crowd.

"Slake's safely passed the Mortlemains boulders!"

"He nearly lost it at Hettup! Over-cooked it but somehow held on!"

"George Ransomes was lead Stellite through the Wethermask Pass! Only Ebby Ebblewhite in his home-made V8 Stellite was quicker, but he's in the Open Stellite Class."

"The twisty route favours Old Mr Macklefract's Short two. He's still leading the Open Class twin cylinder Jowetts!"

"Mr Heptonstall's coming into view any minute! He was spinning his tyres all the way up Wethermask Pass!"

"Look!"

"Here he comes!"

"There he is!"

"There he goes!"

"Blimey," said Mr Heckmondwike, "ee were motorin'. The crowd didn't even have time to cheer."

"I think they were too astonished," agreed a very impressed Mrs Osmotherly.

"Oh there you are," said Gloria, "where've you been?"

"Oh. Around," said Mrs Osmotherly.

Gloria couldn't read their expressions but in the gathering gloom they seemed to be fidgeting with each other's hands.

"That's all our boys through now," said Mrs Hammerhulme. "Ma goodness, it's nearly ten o'clock!"

Just before the light failed completely the driver of a lone racing car lost control as he came over the Wormton Tramway tracks at Wooden Leap and span, drawing a thick black double helix down the middle of the road and creating a terrible cloud of tyre smoke. Miraculously, he stopped spinning just in time to negotiate the dogleg. The crowd fell back but cheered his recovery and the driver gave them a wave and a sheepish grin before disappearing into the night towards Mithering.

The last two hours passed in a blaze of lights, the roar of engines and the stench of various things nearly burning. Just when the crowd thought that was the last pack, another one hove into view and another little battle in the Horsepower Wars was won or lost. By now all the classes had merged completely, with the late-starting really fast cars carving up through the field of stragglers from earlier, smaller classes.

"Slake's passed Mithering! He's just got another sixty clicks to go and is having a furious scrap with some Citroën-based thingy!"

"Old Mr Macklefract slowed a bit at Mortlemains! He seemed to have some trouble with his goggles but he's picked up the pace again now and is right behind the R4!"

"Aye, ee's still fastest Jowett twin by a long chalk!"

"George Ransomes is passed Mithering! His old car's still sounding strong!"

"One of the 750s crashed heavily between Wormton and Mithering."

"Mr Heptonstall's lost a front headlamp! Ee musta come into contact wi' summat somewhere!"

"Aye but ee's quicker than the Ferrari Dino!"

At last the closure car appeared with its flashing yellow lights, followed by a small convoy of hopeful wrecker trucks, looking out for salvage.

"So that were the Wild Hunt," said Mayor Naseby. "It didn't seem so bad."

"Aye," said Mr Grandlythorpe. He'd been heard cheering as loudly as any.

"Ouef!" said Mrs Osmotherly. "I'm quite worn out."

"Ah'll, er, drive thee home," offered Mr Heckmondwike.

"Thank you."

Gloria was going to say, "What about your car Mrs Osmotherly? It's only round the corner," but something made her stop.

"Yes, I think I'll go home as well," she said instead with a yawn. "Goodnight, everybody!"

"Goodnight, Gloria!" and slowly, but happily, the crowd dispersed.

CHAPTER 71

The Wild Hunters returned to Wormton late on Sunday afternoon. Their cars were travel-stained and showed the odd scuff here and there, but still wore their race numbers. Each man wore a huge grin. A large crowd gathered outside Heptonstall's Garage and they proved a willing audience for tales of derring-do out on the highway.

"Thine wife played a blinder!" Ted Totteridge told George Ransomes as he hugged Dilys. "Aye, we nivver seen owt like it! But did tha have to stoop to such tricks to get by?"

"Nay," said Dilys, "ah was just hastenin' the inevitable. He'd have passed them anyroad."

"Did ah miss owt exciting at home?" George asked Ted.

Ted looked puzzled "Exciting?"

"Aye. Tha knaws. Ont stock-rearing front."

"Eh? Oh! Aye! Here!" Ted produced a matchbox from his pocket and slid it open.

Dilys stifled a shriek.

"Oh ma good gawd!" said George.

Ted closed the matchbox. "We'll have a chat later," he whispered.

"A Ferrari Dino baulked Mr Heptonstall!" Old Mr Macklefract explained as he pointed to a shattered headlamp. "It were quicker int corners but ee could best 'im ont straights!"

"So, was tha a primester?" Mrs Amplepance asked but Mr Heptonstall just grinned, went very red and shuffled his feet.

"Of course he was!" exclaimed Slake disentangling himself from Gloria to slap the garage man on the back. "Now he's in *The Vrooms Day Book*!"

A great cheer went up and Mr Heptonstall looked like he was about to explode with quiet pride.

"Oh, we're all int *Vrooms Day Book* now," Mr Macklefract assured her.

Mrs Osmotherly forced her way to the front of the crowd. "What about the Giant Lamb?" she asked.

The atmosphere imploded.

"Eh?" said Slake.

"Did you kill the Lamb?"

A troubled look came over Slake's face.

"Well?"

"Mr Heptonstall?" Slake called out. "Did you see the Giant Lamb any-where?"

"Ah," said Mr Heptonstall, suddenly no longer in danger of bursting.

"To be perfectly honest," said George Ransomes, scratching his head, "ah forgot all about it."

"Aye," said Old Mr Macklefract, "that goes for me an' all."

"And you Slake? Did you forget about the Giant Lamb?"

"Well, I will admit to being a little distracted by the excitement."

Gloria scowled at him.

"Have any of you heard anything about the Giant Lamb being des-troyed by the Wild Hunt?" Mrs Osmotherly asked them.

"Promise you won't be cross," said somebody.

But the sea of blank faces was answer enough.

CHAPTER 72

Hob threw *Nosferatu* down a couple of cogs to thunder through the Wether-mask Pass. Small stones rolled down either side of the valley as he passed by and the stars blurred a little when he revved his engine. He was on his way back to Bedlam-le-Beans after a very good Wild Hunt. His backpack felt heavier than ever, even though souls don't weigh anything. Even the Karma Walla of Bredanalapur could carry his whole soul takings in the pockets of his baggy trousers.

Up ahead was a lay-by with a dark shape parked in it. A gawky young man sprang out of the driver's seat as Hob approached. Hob pulled into the lay-by, killed *Nosferatu*'s engine and leant it up against the dry stone wall. He walked up to the Slakespeed Wolseley Blue Streak, still wearing his hooded goggles and black crash helmet. Of course, he didn't need either but there was always the look of the thing, especially when everyone else could hardly see anything.

"Having problems?" he asked its jumpy custodian.

"No! Or rather, yes. You see, I don't have enough horse power."

"That's odd." Hob opened the bonnet without being invited. "Something like this should have plenty. Were you in the Wild Hunt last night?"

"No, not really. But I'm thinking about entering it soon."

"But you desire more power."

"Yes."

"You ought to be careful. They do say that absolute power corrupts absolutely."

"I wouldn't care if it did," said the nervous young man.

"Max power and max corruption."

"That's just what I want!"

"The power or the corruption?"

The young man laughed nervously. "Both!"

"Well, it seems that it is your lucky day," said Hob with a grin.

"G-good. That's good."

"Here," said Hob and he gave him his business card.

"There's nothing on this."

"Modesty forbids it."

"And no address on it, either."

"'I'm never at home."

The young man turned Hob's card over again. " 'Nicholas Eldritch Hob,' " he read out. " 'Soul Trader and Holder of Soul Rites. Horsepower Whispering a speciality.' "

Hob took the business card from his limp fingers and tucked it into the young man's shirt pocket. "That's me. And I do exactly what it says on the card. How badly do you want horse power?"

"D-d-desperately badly, actually."

"Badly enough to let me have this in return?" From somewhere around the back of the young man's neck, Hob had produced something resembling a blotched handkerchief.

"Cripes! What's that?"

"Your soul."

"Well I never!"

"It's not very colourful, though, is it?"

"Why? Should it be?"

"Of course! I'm not going to get very much for this, am I? It's virtually worthless. The only thing of value is this thin red line."

The young man peered at his own soul. "What's that then?"

"That is your martyrdom through motordom."

"Ah. Does this mean ..."

"Correct."

Hob had slipped off his backpack and was opening it. "Now if you'll just excuse me, I'd better warn the *Terminal Murrain* of another newcomer. Wouldn't want them to bully you, would we? Look sharp, you lot. Fortunato! How many more times! Leave Fangio alone!"

"But shouldn't we have struck a bargain of some sort?"

"Oh. Yes. Of course." Hob grimaced as if his part of the deal was hardly worth bothering about. He put his new soul into his rucksack, glared at the lively spirits already inside, then spat on his hand and shook that of the young man. "There you go. Signed, sealed and delivered. My word is your eternal bondage. Mind your soul for me while I work on this," and he actually gave the soul back to the devitalised young man, who was so broken by his failure to thwart the Soul Trader that he didn't even think of putting it back where it belonged.

"Ah yes," said Hob from under the bonnet. "I thought I recognised that blower. I've worked on this car before."

It didn't take Hob long to fulfil his part of the deal. He increased the boost of the supercharger and fine-tuned the cam and ignition timing before returning the even more enraged Wolseley Blue Streak into the hands of its keeper.

"Yours is the power, the power and the glory," Hob told the dispirited young man. "For thine is thine martyrdom, arising from my motordom, revs without end, ring-ding-a-ding! It's a pleasure to do business with you."

Dawn was breaking as Hob threw his leg back over *Nosferatu*, but he hesitated before he fired his bike up and looked around him.

An unnaturally large sheep was watching him. It stood awkwardly on all fours and had such an expressive face it looked almost human.

Hob hummed a little tune, the same one he'd played to Billy Brock-house. ""Well, well, well. If it isn't the weresheep. At last. What would you sell your woolly-minded soul for, eh? Some nice grass?"

He gathered some up and the weresheep trotted a little closer.

"I could be your shepherd," said Hob. The weresheep lunged at his handful of lush grass. "Ah-ah-ah. No. First you've got to read this."

The weresheep stood up on its back legs and took the business card from him in a woolly hand. The creature seemed to study it for a moment and then turned the card over. It gave a curious bleat and then turned the card over a second time.

Together, Hob and the weresheep made a curious silhouette against the rising sun.

"Okay," said Hob. "You want some grass. I want this. Know what this is? No? Mind if I have it, then? No? Didn't think so." He put the were-sheep's soul in a separate pocket in the rucksack and climbed triumphantly aboard *Nosferatu*. "Most excellent! Some nights, this job gets too easy."

CHAPTER 73

Mrs Osmotherly was checking the motorscope and tutting occasionally. Gloria was dozing in the armchair by the fireside. Opposite her, Indoors Food was concentrating with his eyes tightly shut.

"Do you still see the gnomes?" asked Mrs Osmotherly suddenly.

Gloria awoke with a start. "Around the militia? More than ever."

"But not around Professor Cluttercrap?"

"No. Never. Not around him, not around you, not around Slake and not around Mr Heckmondwike. Have you seen him recently?"

Mrs Osmotherly smiled. "Who?"

"Why, Professor Cluttercrap of course."

Since the night of the Wild Hunt, neither of them had mentioned what had happened between Mrs Osmotherly and Mr Heckmondwike. Apart from the happy couple, Gloria was the only other person who knew something was going on, and she hardly believed it herself.

"I visited Riddaw Lodge today," Mrs Osmotherly said circumspectly. "His brain fever will subside eventually and then we should be able to ask him about what happened to him."

Gloria couldn't help smiling. They could have been talking about the professor or the shepherd. "Do you think he will get better?" she asked.

"Oh he'll be fine," Mrs Osmotherly assured her, "although I fear Professor Cluttercrap will suffer from terrible qualms for a while."

They fell into silence again but suddenly Mrs Osmotherly's two-way trilled into life. Both women looked at each other with puzzled faces, for few people were blessed with the out-of-hours number of a wise woman. Mrs Osmotherly answered it.

"Ah Mrs Gaffathwaite. Hallo. How is your husband?"

"Ee's just not getting any better!" sobbed the woman on the end of the line. "Ee won't touch his meat and ee tries to eat grass and every full moon ee gets out there int Woldernesse and bleats at t'moon. It's dangerous for him to be runnin' about out there! And ah want ma husband back!"

Mrs Osmotherly listened carefully to Mrs Gaffathwaite's grief-stricken outpouring and chose her moment carefully. "There is something we haven't tried yet," she said.

From the other side of the room, Gloria heard the blubbing suddenly stop.

"We had to wait for the right quantity of medicine to be produced."

"Ah'm prepared to do owt for him!" Mrs Gaffathwaite assured her. "And nivver mither about the cost!"

Mrs Osmotherly looked surprised for a moment and then said, "It's nearly ready. It has to be prepared to a very special recipe."

"Recipe?"

"Er, yes."

"Ah didn't knaw they made medicines to recipes."

"Oh yes they do."

"Ah thought they had formulae and such like."

"Mrs Gaffathwaite, the point is we have a very powerful means to cure your husband. It is the last resort, however."

"Owt to get ma 'usband back!" wailed Mrs Gaffathwaite.

"Very well, then. Be prepared to bring him to Cost-is-lost at short notice. Goodbye, and don't worry."

She put down the two-way and sighed.

"You're going to do it, then," said Gloria.

"There's nothing else for it. But I'm going to need your help."

"All right. But we don't know really know what we're doing."

Mrs Osmotherly snorted. "That's normal. Being a wise woman is all about making educated guesses."

CHAPTER 74

"I haven't got very much out of the gremlins," said Slake.

Gloria sighed. She had come to Frogheat to see him with Mrs Osmotherly. Since either of them had last been in this part of Wormton, Slake had obviously acquired a lot more machinery. Even in his living room, it was everywhere. He wasn't really geared up for entertaining. They were perched on packing cases around Slake's hotplate. He'd offered them some spam fritters but they would have appreciated more skill in basic food hygiene before accepting any.

"They just want to talk about engines and things most of the time." He smiled at them.

"Who does that remind you of?" Mrs Osmotherly grunted to Gloria, but without malice.

"Are they frightened?" Gloria asked him. "Frightened to talk?"

"About the Horsepower Whisperer?" Slake thought for a moment. "No, I don't think so."

"Why don't you both try talking to them?" suggested Mrs Osmotherly. "I can't do it because I can't see them."

"We could do, I suppose," said Slake.

They remained seated and Slake put his plate aside with distressingly oily fingers.

Mrs Osmotherly sighed. "Well, why don't you?"

"What now?" said Slake.

Gloria squirmed uncomfortably.

"Yes! Together!"

Slake looked at Gloria and she couldn't look away.

"Shall we?" he asked her.

She couldn't speak so she just nodded.

"I'll, er, go and find some, shall I?"

"Yes please," said Mrs Osmotherly.

Off went Slake.

A heavy silence fell as they waited for him. Gloria knew Mrs Osmotherly could feel the tension between them. She was a wise woman after all. But if the Horsepower Whisperer was the common denominator – or even the common daemonator as they so often found themselves calling him – then they had to try every avenue of enquiry.

And if that meant working with the bloke she fancied when she knew he fancied her, but when she also knew that he thought she fancied Captain Keen instead when really she only felt sorry for the poor man because, like all the other Rural Marines, he was surrounded by harbinger gnomes, so she only wanted to be nice to poor, dear Captain Keen because he didn't have any future, so she didn't really want to get involved with him, especially when she fancied Slake – then so be it.

But because she knew Captain Keen wouldn't have long to live, it seemed unkind not to be as nice as she could to him, even if it meant jeopardising any chance of future happiness she hoped she might have with the bloke she really fancied, and who really fancied her but who – she knew – couldn't possibly know that she knew he didn't know that she knew he thought – wrongly – that she fancied someone else, especially when she suspected he was apparently trying to commit suicide by poisoning himself with his awful cooking, when really it was so obvious that they were made for each other – well then. They would just have to be professional about it.

She was brooding so heavily about this that she didn't notice Slake return. Suddenly there he was, being very professional.

"Ladies," he was saying, "allow me to introduce some friendly neighbourhood gremlins."

He held up a splendid 1/18 scale model of a Wolseley minibus, packed with very ugly gremlins. He put it down on a shelf and the gremlins opened the side doors. Some got out and sat on the shelf and the book ends, which were fashioned out of melted pistons. Other gremlins sprawled inside on the little seats of the minibus, making the most of the extra space.

"We'd just like to ask you some questions," Slake told them. "You all know me."

The gremlins nodded and grinned. Some greeted him in incomprehensible noises while others made ribald hand gestures at him.

Slake tried not to laugh. "This is Mrs Osmotherly and this, this is Gloria."

"What's going on?" Mrs Osmotherly hissed to Gloria.

"Oh please excuse Mrs O," Slake said to the gremlins. "She doesn't have the sight."

The gremlins waved at her in sympathetic acknowledgement anyway.

"She knows you exist, though. She's the local wise woman."

The gremlins looked suitably impressed.

"Yes," said Slake, "she's very clever."

"I think they like you," Gloria whispered to Mrs Osmotherly.

The gremlins asked Slake a question.

"Who's she?" He looked at Gloria and her heart skipped a beat. "She's just a girl."

The gremlins raised their collective eyebrows.

"Well, she's not just girl. She's a nurse and works with Mrs Osmotherly."

Slake paid close attention to the gremlins and although Gloria didn't understand them she began to get some idea of what they said.

"A clever girl? A kind of wise woman in waiting? I never thought of that."

Slake glanced at her in admiration and their eyes met briefly but Gloria looked away quickly. She didn't want to, it was just that while Slake was looking at her, the gremlins were nudging each other and winking at her.

Slake turned back to them and they stopped their sly behaviour immediately.

"Y'know how interested I am in the Horsepower Whisperer?" he began.

The gremlins nodded.

"Gloria's interested in him, too."

They glanced at her with renewed interest and asked Slake a question.

He reddened. "Well, you could say we're working together."

This provoked more sly looks and gestures, but now they were quite blatant about it.

"We both wonder if you could tell us if there is any link between the Horsepower Whisperer and the Giant Lamb."

The gremlins all began gesticulating and talking at once.

Slake listened very carefully.

"What are they saying?" Gloria asked him.

Slake scratched his eyebrow.

The gremlins gradually stopped communicating.

"They don't know what a Giant Lamb is," said Slake.

"Really?" asked Mrs Osmotherly.

"Well, we wouldn't honestly expect them, too, would we?" Slake replied. "They live in engines. Okay," he said, turning back to the perplexed gremlins. "A lamb is a baby sheep. And, er, a Giant Lamb is a baby sheep that is very big. Hmmm? Well, it's still a baby sheep. No, it's grown up. Well, I suppose it is but … Ah, it got that big by accident. How? It was a growth-hormone experiment. Yes. It went horribly wrong. Well, they are certain chemicals that you inject into animals to make them grow bigger." Slake mimed a syringe. "Animals? Don't you know what … oh well, let me see. They're a bit like us but run around on four legs."

"What do you normally talk about with these gremlins?" asked Mrs Osmotherly.

"Why engine tuning, of course!"

"Just that?"

"Well, there's a helluva lot to be said about it!" Slake replied.

The gremlins were agitating again.

"Cats? Yeah, a bit like cats." He frowned. "How do you know about cats? Can they? Well I never!"

"This is going to take ages," said Mrs Osmotherly.

"Patience, please," said Slake. "We're just starting to make some progress. Just because you can't see 'em!"

He tried again with the gremlins.

"So can you imagine a very woolly cat? As big as a house? No?"

"I think it is fairly safe to say," said Mrs Osmotherly, saying it, "that the gremlins cannot identify any link between the Horsepower Whisperer and the Giant Lamb."

Slake opened his mouth to reply and then shut it again, frowning. He leaned towards the gremlins, "I told you she was a wise woman, didn't I?"

The gremlins nodded appreciatively.

"But can you please tell us," Gloria asked them, "if there is any link between the Horsepower Whisperer and all the strange things that have been going on in the Wold since he arrived?"

She leaned forward earnestly but the male gremlins couldn't bring themselves to look her in the face or answer her. They just lowered their eyes and seemed suddenly shy.

Slake gently touched her arm. "Er, it might be better if you sat down again."

"Why?" she asked, sitting down.

"They were looking down the neckline of your uniform," he explained.

The gremlins that had fallen under her spell had come back to life and were grinning at her again.

"Well can you?" she asked them.

"They've forgotten what the question was," said Slake. "It seems that the, er, prospect of falling into your charms put them under your charms."

The gremlins laughed and slapped their knees and then applauded Slake.

Despite herself, Gloria found herself smiling, too.

"Ah, thank you very much," said Slake, bowing at the gremlins.

"Oh, good grief," said Mrs Osmotherly, folding her arms.

Gloria was surprised what a low boredom threshold she had.

Mrs Osmotherly addressed the gremlins directly even though she couldn't see them. "Is there a link between the Horsepower Whisperer and the weirdness in the Wold or not?"

The gremlins nodded.

They waited.

"So what is that link, then?" asked Slake.

Again, the gremlins all began talking and gesticulating at once.

Slake seemed to be listening very hard to them all, and mirrored some of their gestures for clarity.

The gremlins became even more agitated. Some of them popped out of sight only to return with other gremlins who also began to contribute to the animated discussion.

Slake put his hands out to appeal for calm but the gremlins just became more demonstrative. They winked in and out of vision, brandishing tools, blueprints, spare parts packaging and all sorts of obscure engine components until they were nothing but a blur. Occasionally, Slake reached out to touch something but it was snatched back before he could take it.

Gloria gave up trying to follow the gremlins' convoluted and one-sided argument. All she could do was watch, and gradually she noticed that a packet of sweets was being waved about by various gremlins. It wasn't a gremlin-sized packet of sweets. It was a packet of sweets on a human scale and the gremlins brandished it like a baton or a rolled-up piece of carpet. Sometimes it was there, sometimes it wasn't, but slowly it was there more often than not, and eventually Slake teased it out of their grip only to find that they'd meant him to have it all along but had become distracted from giving it to him by explaining what it was for.

"Look at that," Slake said to them. "Sweeties."

"Don't call me sweetie," huffed Mrs Osmotherly but then she noticed that he held out a packet of sweets. To her it must have seemed that Slake had produced them out of thin air.

With a perplexed expression, she slowly took them from him. "Did the gremlins give these to you?" she asked.

Slake nodded.

She read out the label " 'Uncle Bub's Curiously Strong Mints.' Well I suppose we could all do with a little refreshment," and she made to take one.

The gremlins raised their arms in horror.

"No, no, no," warned Slake, "they really are extremely, curiously strong mints."

"Why've they given us these, then?" asked Gloria.

The gremlins explained.

"Oh!" said Slake "They're to give to the weresheep!"

The gremlins nodded but asked a question.

"Well, a sheep is just like a weresheep but without the "were" bit!" he told them.

"Ah!" sighed the gremlins. Some of them punched their foreheads with their tiny fists.

"I am glad we cleared that up at last," said Slake. "I knew we'd establish some common ground eventually."

"But what's the connection with the weresheep?" demanded Mrs Osmotherly.

Slake grinned at her. "Mint."

"Mint?"

"Mint. What do you eat with lamb?"

"Vegetables?"

"Oh come on! Mint! Mint sauce!"

"Oh my God!" cried Gloria.

"Of course!" gasped Mrs Osmotherly. "Mint sauce! I should've known!"

"So all we have to do," said Gloria, "is give these Curiously Strong Mints to the weresheep!"

"Of course!" agreed Mrs Osmotherly.

"No, no, no!" said Slake and the gremlins.

"If it'll take sweets from strangers!"

"No, no, no!" said Slake and the gremlins.

"You can't get much stranger than a weresheep!"

Slake gently took the packet of sweets back from them and drew their attention to a warning on the wrapper. "Not to be taken internally by mortals." He showed them the writing.

"So what are we supposed to do with them?" Gloria wondered.

Slake grinned. "Dilute them," he said.

"In a sheep dip," said Mrs Osmotherly, and she clapped her hands and stood up. "Thank you gremlins. You have all been a tremendous help." She gave Slake a great hug and walked out. "Of course, they didn't really answer the question but let's quit while we're ahead. Come on Gloria, we've got work to do!"

"Thanks for doing this, Slake," she said.

"That's okay."

"No. I really appreciate this."

Slake shrugged. "Any time. Hey! Think nothing of it."

But Gloria couldn't think nothing of it. As she stood there, nearly ready to leave, she was amazed to see a cherry bum on the lampshade, glaring at her. Its quiver was empty and her heart felt like it had been skewered many times over.

She tried to think of a way of explaining that she knew he thought that she fancied Captain Keen and understood, perfectly well, why he might have thought that, but that she was only being nice to him because he was surrounded by the harbinger gnomes when he – Slake – would never really know how much she really liked him – Slake not Captain Keen – and that she had known for some time that he thought that she knew that he thought that she fancied Captain Keen and didn't care about what he thought. Or thought he knew. And how she was desperate to clear up any possible misunderstanding.

But suddenly it all seemed too complicated and the opportunity passed.

"Mates, okay?" said Slake.

"Yeah," Gloria heard herself say, "mates," and she quietly left.

CHAPTER 75

More militia came and went but only Captain Keen remained. By now, he looked more than old enough for his moustache.

"Our mission is to destroy the monster," he told Mayor Naseby. "We … under-estimated what was involved."

"We're not made of money," warned the mayor.

"We can flex funds from the flags and bunting vote," said Miss Bookings, helpfully.

"I still don't understand why you don't just lump it all together," said Captain Keen, a little testily.

Miss Bookings closed her eyes just like Reverend Chunderclough did when he was being particularly sanctimonious. "And where would the audit trail be then? Do you really want to be called to account before the Rural Accounts Committee?"

Captain Keen shuddered. "As ever, Miss Bookings, I let myself be guided by your good self in these matters."

"Rest assured, Captain, that we can account for everything properly and allow effective capability to be maintained. We are flexing funds from every source to allow this, even the regimental mascot feed account."

Captain Keen had developed an eye tic over the last few weeks, and when she mentioned the word mascot it became quite conspicuous.

"But tell me," Mayor Naseby pressed him, "how does t'operation go?"

"We are confident of every success," lied Captain Keen.

"E'en though tha says so as shouldn't?"

"Something like that."

"Is tha considerin' retreat?"

Miss Bookings gestured frantically at him but it was too late.

Captain Keen flushed crimson. "We never retreat!" he bellowed, leaping to his feet. "Never!"

Mayor Naseby fell backwards out of his camp stool. "Not even in a tactical withdrawal?"

"Never!" exploded Captain Keen.

By now the militia controlled access to the whole of the Outlands. Old Wormtonians filled the church to bless their stout town walls without any prompting from Reverend Chunderclough. Only those with pressing business ventured far beyond them, and when they returned they had to be plied with many pints of Old Sawe's Irascible Anorak at *The Golden Fleece* before their terrible revelations about the state of the Wold could be teased out of them.

Bigger and less sophisticated forces were sent off into the Woldernesse but no militia ever came back. What became of them was a mystery. If the new faces in the camp knew, they weren't letting on, but nobody banked on a return to Wormton. The personalities from the naked drinking incident were now only a fond memory. In the rumour mills of *Where the Rainbow Ends* and *The Golden Fleece* lock-ins, it was said they had met some unnatural fate that left their shrunken corpses bone dry and their equipment smashed or scattered to the four winds.

Although the Rural Marines were not as cheerful as when they first arrived, there never seemed to be any question of not doing what they saw as being their duty. The only half-hearted thing they ever did was trying to persuade Mrs Osmotherly and Mr Heckmondwike to move into Wormton. Captain Keen seemed to know that task was doomed to failure. If he suspected anything else was futile, he never ever showed it.

Captain Keen also made no attempt to dissuade Slake from venturing out into the Wold. The piles of abandoned ordnance were growing. Some items could be seen from Wormton and acted like a magnet for a skirrow like Slake. He was ostensibly doing a lot of business servicing generator sets on the most remote Outland farms, but was blatantly scavenging the abandoned ordnance and materiel on the way home. He often returned to Wormton in a different vehicle but Captain Keen didn't seem to mind.

"Is tha sure t'militia have finished wi' this stuff?" Mr Heckmondwike asked him as he gazed at the trucks and Land Rovers that Slake had collected around Frogheat.

"Not entirely," admitted Slake from under a bonnet, "but they can have it back if they want it."

"Do they knaw tha's got it?"

"Must do. I'm filling up old dundyards with it, right under their noses. I reckon they just can't be arsed about it."

"Does Constable Arkthwaite knaw what tha's up to?"

"Oh yes."

"Oh aye? What does he have to say about t'seven year salvage rule?"

"He's chosen to turn a blind eye."

"Appen?"

"Possession is nine tenths of the law. Besides. Hasn't it occurred to you that we might yet end up doing the deed ourselves?"

It had occurred to Mr Heckmondwike, as every night he'd lain awake listening to the defeat of the Rural Marines by a monster he had reared.

Slake fitted another socket on the end of his ratchet. "Take this GMC truck, for instance. It looked worse than it was and I've pinched a few bits and pieces for it from others scattered over the moors. I swapped some tyres around, filled it with juice, rode my Wolseley Woldsman out to it, threw it in the back and drove it home. I found a magnificent Nuffield tractor that had lost it front axle. They're just down-market Wolseleys, as I'm sure you know, so I got a replacement from Bessie Dooker's. It came off that one that Mr Floridspleen blew the engine on. Look at it! It's got a Leyland truck engine in it. We're gonna need this stuff, Mr Heckmondwike. Soon there won't be any militia left."

"Does Mrs Osmotherly knaw owt about this?"

"Oh yeah."

"What does Gloria think of all this?"

Slake made no reaction except for a sudden jerk of his arm as he was carefully picking up a headlamp. It jumped out of his hand and fell into the mud, finding a stone and breaking its glass. Slake immediately began to pick up the shards but cut himself deeply right away.

Silently, Mr Heckmondwike took Slake's injured hand and began to bandage it with his handkerchief.

"She's more interested in the militia," said Slake. "They say a uniform can turn a girl's head."

"Aye." Mr Heckmondwike tied a knot. "Just like them as ride int Wild Hunt."

Slake stared at him. "I can't compete with them," he said at length.

"Wearin' 'er token int Wild Hunt dint make any difference then."

"Nah. Bloody glory boys."

"Tha knaws what they say."

"What?"

"If tha can't beat 'em, join 'em."

"Me? As a militia man? I wouldn't last five minutes."

Mr Heckmondwike held Slake's arm tightly even though a pressure point wasn't there.

"Ow!"

"As soon as Professor Cluttercrap's up and about, ah'm goin' after t'monster again."

"Then I'm coming with you. You're going to need a driver. And my ordnance."

"T'militia's ordnance," Mr Heckmondwike corrected him.

"Whoever's bloody ordnance we can get our bloody, grubby hands on."

CHAPTER 76

Mrs Osmotherly looked at her watch. "They should be here in a minute." She was waiting with Gloria at Cost-is-lost.

It wasn't long before a big, black Wolseley 6/110 pulled up with Mr Heckmondwike at the wheel. In the back seat were Mrs Gaffathwaite and her husband.

Mr Gaffathwaite hadn't been back to the sheep dip since his accident and he seemed quite agitated as he alighted from the car.

"Why've tha brought me here?" he wanted to know.

"Nothing for you to worry about, dear," his wife replied but Mr Gaffathwaite looked very suspicious.

To placate him, she picked a long stalk of grass but, instead of chewing thoughtfully on it like he used to, he ate it and swallowed it.

"Mebbe we should tell him," his wife whispered to Mrs Osmotherly.

"Tell me what?"

"Further silence might make him more nervous."

Mr Gaffathwaite tried to run away but Mr Heckmondwike caught him and dragged him back.

"See what ah mean?" said Mrs Gaffathwaite.

"Stop talkin' as if ah'm not 'ere!"

"No," said Mrs Osmotherly. She looked at them all in turn. "Let's just do it!" and the four of them wrestled Mr Gaffathwaite towards the sheep dip.

After a few steps, Mr Gaffathwaite, began to struggle and shout, naming his persecutors so they knew he recognised their treachery. Then his nostrils flared and he cried, "By 'eck! What's that smell?"

He stretched his neck and he let out a tremendous bleat. His cap fell off as his hair became white and fluffy. His jacket burst across the shoulders and all the buttons popped off his shirt so that he looked like a badly wrapped bale of wool. His face became longer and longer and he began to grow horns.

Mrs Gaffathwaite became of less use as tears coursed down her cheeks. Horrified, Mrs Osmotherly, Gloria and Mr Heckmondwike stared at Mr Gaffathwaite when they should have been concentrating on holding onto him more securely. His chest deepened and his boots fell off as his feet grew longer and thinner inside them.

He gave a terrible bleat and there was a crack of thunder. Clouds rolled across the sun and an unnatural wind blew up. Mr Gaffathwaite glared at them with satanic eyes as an unnatural strength flowed through his changing limbs. He started to drag them away from the sheep dip. Mr Heckmondwike instinctively grabbed a foreleg and tried to whirl everyone around, back towards the trough. It nearly worked but the weresheep soon realised what was happening and dug his hooves in.

Mr Heckmondwike gasped for breath.

Mrs Osmotherly and Gloria were looking at him desperately. "He's too strong for us," they groaned.

"What's burning?" panted Mr Heckmondwike.

"Mr Gaffathwaite," Mrs Osmotherly managed to say. "The were-sheep is nocturnal – daylight burns him – but as Mr Gaffathwaite – he doesn't have – the strength to fight us!"

"We must get him in the sheep dip before he combusts!" said Gloria, through clenched teeth.

Mr Heckmondwike nodded at them. "One goes, we all go," he panted.

Immediately, they understood. They summoned up the last vestiges of strength and staggered towards the sheep dip, taking the weresheep with them. This time the trough was not filled with oregano-phosphates. Instead there was a thick green liquid that smelt strongly of mint.

Mr Gaffathwaite's nostrils flared and he bleated in terror again.

But this time there came an answering bleat, a distant bleat that was even worse, one that downed aircraft, destroyed armoured vehicles and addled the brains of the militia.

Over the horizon came the Giant Lamb, running as fast as it could.

The liquid in the sheep dip boiled at its approach and the stones of Cost-is-lost began to rattle louder and louder as the Wold began to blur with every monstrous hoof-fall.

They teetered on the edge of the trough, but could go no further. In his ovine form, Mr Gaffathwaite was too strong for them. But then something cannoned into them and they all fell into the sheep dip. Or, rather, they were pushed, for in one last superhuman effort, Mrs Gaffathwaite had taken a run-up and a flying leap at them that was just enough to topple them all into the trough.

And lucky she did, for a moment later the Giant Lamb passed over them.

In the trough, the weresheep gave a final bleat of anguish but he merely swallowed more of Mrs Osmotherly's mint sauce. He struggled briefly as they held his head under the surface and then was still. Mr Heckmondwike grabbed his collar, pushed him into fresh air for a moment and then plunged him under once again.

The women felt Mr Gaffathwaite sheep-shape-shifting again, this time the opposite way, and slowly, cautiously they let go of him as he shrank back to his original shape and size. Mr Heckmondwike still had a firm hold on him, however, and he eyed them warily as they backed away.

He pulled his boss out of the mint sauce one more time to allow him to breathe and was heartened to see that his horns had gone and his bald spot had returned.

After a couple of gulps, Mr Gaffathwaite cried, "By 'eck! This stuff's lovely!" and then he dived under again, nearly taking Mr Heckmondwike with him.

Mr Heckmondwike released Mr Gaffathwaite and caught his breath as he leant against the side of the trough as the women slumped around him. The surface of the mint sauce became calmer, but as it smoothed out Mr Heckmondwike began to look concerned. He leant forward and began to feel around under the surface until he found what he was looking for and pulled Mr Gaffathwaite out again.

By now, all the fight had gone out of him and he swayed a little drunkenly with his shepherd's meaty fist on his collar.

Mrs Osmotherly, Mrs Gaffathwaite and Gloria struggled out and then pulled Mr Gaffathwaite after them, midwives to an oversized mint-fresh baby. Mrs Gaffathwaite fell upon him and began to wash the sauce off his face with her grateful tears while the other two helped Mr Heckmondwike out.

"It worked!" exclaimed Gloria, producing a hose connected to a nearby standpipe.

"What is this stuff?" demanded Mr Heckmondwike.

"Special mint sauce," said Mrs Osmotherly.

"Appen?"

"Very special mint sauce," said Gloria, hosing them off. "Not only is Mrs Osmotherly probably the foremost living expert on lambthropy ..."

"Don't exaggerate, Gloria!"

"She is also a sauceress!"

"Well, a mint sauceress."

"Blood yell!" exclaimed Mr Heckmondwike

"It's a special recipe for the trans-specied," explained Gloria.

"Just don't ask me where I got the curiously strong mints from," said Mrs Osmotherly.

"Is ee cured then?"

"Cured?" spluttered Mr Gaffathwaite, still a little sticky and in tattered clothes. "Ah should blood yell say so! Ah've worked up an 'eck of an appetite. There's only one thing missing now – a nice bit of lamb."

"Let's get thee home then," said Mr Heckmondwike. He shook his employer's hand warmly. "Welcome back!" he said. "Welcome bloody back!"

He helped the Gaffathwaites to the car and once they were safely installed, this time with Mr Gaffathwaite behind the wheel, he turned to Mrs Osmotherly and Gloria. "But ah've got some more good news for thee, n' all. The Professor has regained consciousness."

CHAPTER 77

"So let me get this straight," said Captain Keen, as the Scorpion tank raced back to Wormton across the moors. "My men are being killed by gigantic sheep parasites?"

"Exactly," Professor Cluttercrap shouted down from the turret in which he was snugly wedged.

"It all makes sense, Crispin," said Gloria, who was sitting on Captain Keen's lap.

"In a nonsensical sort of way," added Professor Cluttercrap.

"The Giant Lamb never was dipped," said Mrs Osmotherly. She was squeezed into an empty ammunition rack. "They've been feeding on its blood ever since the Giant Lamb was injected. Now they must look for more hosts."

The radio crackled. The sergeant who was driving passed the headset to Captain Keen.

"Well, what's your report?" he asked. He grunted at the news and seemed neither pleased nor surprised by it. "Okay," he said with a sigh. "Over and out."

He passed the headset back.

"Another bad day?" Gloria asked

Captain Keen ground his teeth. "I'm afraid so."

"Are you going to pull out?" asked Mrs Osmotherly.

"I beg your pardon?"

"Are you going to retreat?"

"Retreat? We don't know the meaning of the word!"

"It means run away, basically," said Professor Cluttercrap, helpfully.

"We never retreat!" bellowed Captain Keen. "We have never retreated! We do not retreat! We will not retreat!"

"Not even tactically?" asked Gloria, surreptitiously trying to brush off the ugly harbingers that still covered him

"Not even tactically," Captain Keen assured her.

"Sometimes we advance to the rear, sir," said the sergeant driving the tank.

"No we do not!" snapped Captain Keen. "You? You keep your eyes on the road," and he waggled one of the skid control levers so the sergeant had to take corrective action. Then he asked, "How intelligent are sheeps?"

"Sheeps?" echoed Gloria.

"I thought they weren't very clever," said Captain Keen.

"Not as a general rule," said Mrs Osmotherly, "but its behaviour is hardly sheepish."

"It's a monster, not a sheep," said Captain Keen. "It seems to be outwitting us at every turn. I wonder if its brainpower has increased in relation to the size of its head? In which case it would be as clever as a whole flock of sheeps."

"That would still make it not very clever," said Mrs Osmotherly.

"We are going to be hard pressed to prevail over it. Still," said Captain Keen looking back up to Professor Cluttercrap behind him, "We've got you now and I'm not altogether surprised."

"Er, thank you. What do you mean?"

Captain Keen reached over and produced a battered and well-thumbed book from the glove box of his tank, which he passed up to Professor Cluttercrap.

"What's this? *Nelson's Jolly Book for Boys?*"

"That's right!"

Professor Cluttercrap thumbed through it. "Adventure stories," he said.

"And in each and every one of them something always turns up in the end!"

"Like what, exactly?" asked Mrs Osmotherly, as Professor Cluttercrap handed her the book.

"Oh, I don't know. A loyal native? A disaffected tribesman? A brave young gel with a Swiss penknife? A scientist with an untried secret weapon?"

"I am none of those things," said Professor Cluttercrap.

"But you are a scientist!"

"I'm afraid I am not that sort of scientist."

"You're still a scientist, though!"

"I am a simple chaos botanist."

"Well, what's that then?"

"I study the apparently inexplicable relationships between plants and their environment. My forte is random agronomy."

"So if there's some aggro, you can sort it out!"

"I have no secret weapon against overgrown lambs."

"Well obviously," said Captain Keen. He gave Gloria a strange look. "It wouldn't be a secret if you told us. But you're a scientist, man! I'm sure you can help!"

"I am quite prepared to help in any way I can!"

"Good man! I knew you would."

"But this is simply not my field."

"Ha ha! Simply not your field!"

"I am the other sort of scientist."

"Animals eat plants, don't they?"

"Some do."

"There you are then!"

"It's no good, Jeremy," Gloria told Professor Cluttercrap. "Crispin regards you as being eminently qualified for anything remotely to do with anything scientific."

"That's right!"

"I can offer you no solution to this problem, Captain Keen," Professor Cluttercrap assured him. "However, I have learnt some things that may be of assistance to you."

"I knew it! Problems attract solutions! You see it time after time in those documentary films about Martians crash-landing in North America."

Gloria and Mrs Osmotherly exchanged glances. How subtle was the military mind?

"There's always a group of nuclear physicists on a fishing holiday nearby," went on the good captain. "Not only that, but they are keen campers, know all about survival techniques and drive woody station wagons. *Nelson's Jolly Book for Boys* serves never to let me forget that!"

"Do you know the rule of surface area to volume ratio?" Professor Cluttercrap asked him.

"No."

"Among other things, it controls the size to which insects and other creatures that use spiracle respiration can grow."

"Oh yes?"

"In normal circumstances, it restricts their size. However, somehow, this rule has been broken with respect to the parasites associated with the Giant Lamb." Professor Cluttercrap paused. "Do you understand what I am saying?"

"Not a bit of it, but carry on."

"Creatures that breathe by means of spiracles are governed in terms of size by the law of surface area to volume ratio. To cut a long story short, these creatures are restricted in size by this law, otherwise they wouldn't be able to breathe. For some reason, the surface area to volume ratio rule does not apply to them any more."

"Why's that then?" asked Captain Keen.

"Well, I don't know. There must be some x-factor we haven't identified yet."

"That's a bit of a bore," said Captain Keen. "How did you work all this out?"

"Some parasites attacked me in Riddaw Forest but I managed to escape by offering them more pleasant sources of food. I discovered that they still prefer sheep's blood to that of humans. By slitting the throats of sheep, I was able to distract them from me, but on my journey back from the forest I saw what these parasites can do to a platoon of Rural Marines. When the Giant Lamb or conventionally sized sheep are beyond their reach, they must sate their burgeoning appetites with blood from your men."

"This changes everything," said Captain Keen. "We'll have to adopt a completely different strategy – once we know what this x-factor is."

"What in the Wold could it be?" wondered Mrs Osmotherly.

"Whatever it is," said Professor Cluttercrap, "it goes beyond the realms of biology!"

CHAPTER 78

On the eve of Wool Purger's Night, an ironed-up Nuffield tractor, resplendent in trademark orange livery, and an ex-militia truck, still in camouflage, slipped out of Wormton by the rarely used North Gate and headed towards Riddaw Lodge. From an autological point of view, both these two traffic movements were extremely significant.

Swapping vehicles according to the terrain, Mr Heckmondwike and Slake found trails of great hoofprints stretching for miles. In some places they even exposed the bedrock, exciting the interest of exploratory miners from Hettup and Stingey.

In Riddaw Forest, something very big and very woolly had evidently eaten its canopy and trampled the trees. Instead of brightening up the gloomy interior, this simply let in more mist. Stripped of their foliage, the larches and pines now sported tufts of wool snagged on their shattered branches, turning the forest from green to white as if it had suffered a profound trauma.

Around the edge of the forest, and sometimes a good way inside it, were piles of discarded ordnance that Mr Heckmondwike and Slake dared not examine too closely. Only if there were signs of freshly dug graves would they pick through the wreckage.

At Riddaw Lodge, they tried to make a feast of Wool Purger's Night but they'd seen too much to be light-hearted. Slake made a semi-circle around the fire out of the armchairs as Mr Heckmondwike listened to the shepherding forecast on the Wold Service. It was so comforting listening to the familiar voices beside the glowing fire that they drifted off into sleep and spent the night in their enormous armchairs.

The following morning they awoke stiff and cold, and breakfasted heavily.

"What does today hold?" Slake wondered in the middle of a pineapple fritter.

"It's going to stay foggy," Mr Heckmondwike, grunted automatically, "for t'foreseeable future."

"Is that some sort of meteorological joke?"

"Wanna knaw summat else? It's Mithering Sunday today!"

"Blood yell! If we didn't have bad luck we wouldn't have any luck at all."

Mr Heckmondwike's weather forecast proved accurate. That morning was foggy in the extreme. They finished breakfast arguing good-naturedly about what the difference between mist and fog was, and when Mr Heckmondwike found it was drizzling he said, "Ah wouldn't want to be a nudist in this weather."

"If you were, no-one would know," Slake pointed out, and for some time afterwards they found themselves fantasising about nudists cavorting just beyond the range of their vision.

They probed the white-out to the west using the ex-militia truck and the Big Nuff because they were diesels and had a greater range. Speeds were low and Mr Heckmondwike was beginning to worry about getting lost although he would never have admitted it.

Near some prehistoric hut circles, they paused for an uneasy brew-up although the silence was complete. Mr Heckmondwike had brought Widdershins along, hoping to benefit from its three noses and six ears. Even if it had lost its collective nerve, which was by no means certain, it remained acutely alert and at one point silently indicated something in the mist.

"Does tha see what ah see?" whispered Mr Heckmondwike

"If it's that size and naked, I'm glad I can't see it properly."

"It's t'Big Grey Man!"

"Holy sheep shit!"

Silently, they watched as the figure in the mist stalked about carefully.

"Wouldn't tha say ee looks a little tense, from t'way ee moves?"

Slake watched the indistinct shape and agreed. "What's he got to worry about?"

"We're used to things being bigger than us but he int. First time ah've ivver seen 'im carryin' a club."

"What's he listening for?" asked Slake.

Then Widdershins started barking furiously.

They listened but felt something instead.

"Look!" said Slake. The tea in his mug was rippling. "Uh oh."

The thumps in the earth became stronger.

Slake pointed to where they'd seen the Big Grey Man. "He's gone!"

"Come on," said Mr Heckmondwike, leaping to his feet.

"Where are you off too?"

"Where ivver t'monster is."

They soon found some more hoofprints. Water was oozing into them from the wounded earth, but as he looked at them, Mr Heckmondwike saw their surface rippling. He called to Slake and flung himself on the ground, accidentally knocking all the breath out of his lungs. Widdershins dived under the truck, but Slake just looked up and up at the approaching darkness in the sky until he keeled over backwards. Thunder passed overhead as well as through the ground. They lay there until the darkness passed and the ground was still again.

"Mr Heckmondwike?"

"What?" grunted Mr Heckmondwike.

"Reckon the Mithering Brethren have become Quakers?"

Mr Heckmondwike sat up "Thee! Tha should be ashamed o' thysen!"

They pressed on and eventually found some enormous craters that steamed from recent impact. While Slake and Widdershins kept watch in case the monster returned, Mr Heckmondwike paced across them and announced that these were the biggest hoofprints they'd yet come across. From time to time, they felt more tremors but saw or heard nothing. They might just as well have been driving through cotton wool.

Eventually, they became aware of the nearby outline of Nibley Edge. They headed towards it and found the ground around its base badly torn up. They took it in turns to winch each other out of the great hoofprints but made slow progress and felt very exposed. Here and there were wads of very coarse wool that rolled like tumbleweed when they knocked them out of the way.

Mr Heckmondwike paced out another hoofprint.

"How big d'you reckon it's got?" Slake asked.

"Ah dunnaw, lad. Not naymore."

Slake looked at the hoofprints. "It shouldn't be difficult to find a monster that size," he said, without much enthusiasm.

At last they reached the foot of the cliff.

"Are we going up?" asked Slake.

Mr Heckmondwike nodded. "One giant leap of faith for us, one small step for lambkind."

The road snaked up the escarpment in a series of switchback curves. The corners were so tight, Mr Heckmondwike and Slake took to reversing along alternate sections, and sometimes the truck's wheels overlapped the edge of the road. Snagged tufts of wool were everywhere, and once they had reached the top they could see that in places the moor was carpeted with it.

They turned off the road and drove cautiously along the cliff edge. Billowing banks of cloud and wool deepened until they were as high as the tractor's bonnet and it was difficult to tell what was mist and what was wool.

Suddenly, Widdershins took Mr Heckmondwike's wrists in two of its mouths while the third gently applied the handbrake. Mr Heckmondwike gazed at Slake in bemusement as the skirrow overtook him on the Big Nuff and began to climb a downy knoll.

Widdershins looked at Mr Heckmondwike and wagged its tails at him but then it looked around at what Slake was doing. To do so it had to release Mr Heckmondwike and the shepherd immediately grabbed his crook, leapt out of the cab and shouted out to Slake to stop, but he might as well have had no voice at all. Slake gave no sign of having heard and Mr Heckmondwike's heart sank as he realised that he could barely hear the sound of the Big Nuff as it forced its way onwards, or the frantic barking of Widdershins, which had, significantly, remained in the truck.

Slake had problems of his own. For all its power, the Big Nuff was becoming bogged down. At last he stood on the clutch and studied the wool intently. "I'm stuck," he mouthed.

Just then the ground gave a great heave upwards.

Mr Heckmondwike hauled himself onto the back of the tractor as beneath them the ground started swaying from side to side.

"We've done it!" he yelled.

"What?" replied Slake.

"We've done it, lad! We've caught t'bloody monster!"

CHAPTER 79

Outside Wormton's East Gate, Gloria loitered by the new traffic sign that warned of the Giant Lamb. She'd managed to hide a satchel full of fireworks in the long grass at the foot of the road sign, but lighting the blue touch paper without being noticed was going to be tricky. In the gateway, Mrs Osmotherly was attempting to distract the attention of Constables Sopp and Blenk but they kept a conscientious lookout.

A vehicle emerged out of the mist and they recognised George and Ted and Ted in the Ransomes' Stellite. "Ow do George," said Constable Blenk as they pulled up. "Ow do Ted. Ow do Ted. Ow's life at Scar Fell Farm?"

"Heck as owt now that we've got Mr Gaffathwaite back," said George.

While Gloria and Mrs Osmotherly shuffled nonchalantly over to the new road sign, Ted leaned forward conspiratorially. "Wanna see summat? Ah but it's not summat we want to spread around, though, is it? Nay, it's not!"

"Perhaps t'ladies should avert their eyes for a moment," began George but Gloria and Mrs Osmotherly were already out of earshot and conspicuously uninterested.

"Come on then," whispered Constable Sopp, looking at the matchbox in Ted's hand, "we're all Men of t'Wold."

Ted craned his head around the two constables to check on the ladies. They smiled innocently back at him. "Awreet then," he said quietly, "but quickly now!"

He gently held up the matchbox and gestured to the constables to lean in closer.

"Now!" hissed Mrs Osmotherly.

Gloria pulled out a matchbox of her own. It didn't contain placid brown-headed safety matches but the dangerous red-headed sort.

"Take a look at this," whispered Ted, and he gently pushed the end of the matchbox until it was about half open.

Constable Sopp gasped and Constable Blenk said, "But that's horrible!"

Ted chuckled.

"Ah've nivver seen one growin' wings before!" said Constable Sopp.

"What!" exclaimed Ted and snatched the matchbox back. The others just laughed at him. "They're skylarkin' us!" he said.

All of a sudden there was a loud bang and a couple of shrieks.

They turned to see the "Bloody great sheep" sign rocket up into the sky.

"What 'appened?" demanded George as the four men ran over.

"A stray shell – must have – hit the sign – from the militia," gasped Gloria.

"By gum, tha both had a narrow escape!" exclaimed Constable Blenk, looking skywards. "Let's get thee inside!"

They picked Mrs Osmotherly up and installed both the shaken women in the two big fireside armchairs that were the chief perk of being on guard duty. Eventually the fuss died down and they were left alone. Gloria and Mrs Osmotherly slumped quietly in their armchairs for a while until Gloria looked conspicuously towards the door, clenched her fist and said, "Yes!"

"Gloria," mumbled Mrs Osmotherly, "promise me next time not to use quite so many fireworks."

CHAPTER 80

A little to the south of Nibley Edge, Captain Keen stood beside his armoured command car watching the Giant Lamb with grim fascination. It often stopped to scrape itself along the cliff and, with Professor Cluttercrap's revelation about the parasites that were feeding off it, Captain Keen realised that it must be itching terribly. To protect his sanity from its hideous bleating he had cotton wool in his ears, but both wads were stained red. His uniform was still clean, but all the other soldiers wore tattered combat fatigues.

On the left flank, a squadron of Chieftain tanks were ready to close in on the Giant Lamb. On the right were his gun batteries and infantry. And somewhere close by were the omnipresent Mithering Brethren.

He hated the Brethren. He'd never understood civilians and these deliberately flouted the normal rules of combat. It was too late to protect their sanity with cotton wool. They didn't shoot at anyone, they just got in the way, and several of his men had been killed or injured trying to save the Mithering Brethren from themselves.

The radio crackled.

"Crab Air calling Pongoes. Do you read me? Over."

"Pongoes calling Crab Air. We read you."

"Have just suffered an air miss with another aircraft. It's definitely not one of ahs. It was red and white and black and of delta-wing construction. It was travelling ebbsolutely vertically at great speed. Could it be Mithering Brethren? Ovah."

"They are particularly active today, Crabs. I am reliably informed by our padre that they regard the Giant Lamb as the new Lamb of God."

"Wait a moment!" interrupted another pilot. "The bogey's falling back dine to earth. Maybe you chaps'll see it."

"Thank you Crab Air. We'll keep an eye out for it and the Mithering Brethren. Are you proceeding to your attack positions now?"

"Affirmative, Pongoes. Estimated time of interception minus five and counting. Ovah and ite."

CHAPTER 81

"That was easy!" enthused Slake. He grinned at Mr Heckmondwike. "Now we've got it, what are we gonna do with it?"

"We've got to get to t'head, lad" said Mr Heckmondwike, trying not to look as surprised as he felt.

Urgently, he wriggled down into the oily wool. Slake grabbed his pack and followed as quickly as he could. The wool was coarse and smelt strongly. Away from the Big Nuff, it sprang up in all directions and was dense and slippery. They tried to stay on the surface, but it was hard work to avoid sinking into it and eventually they both lost their footings and slid into the depths of the fleece. As their eyes grew accustomed to the darkness, they made out a network of tunnels and caverns between the enormous hair follicles. Even Slake could tell that the fleece was not of a very high quality.

"Which way?" he asked.

"That way," replied Mr Heckmondwike, pointing away from the Big Nuff.

The fleece shimmied and they slid down until they came to the skin. As the monster walked, this rippled and heaved but they didn't have to hang on so much and could keep their hands and arms free in case they needed to defend themselves against something. Even so, they staggered about as if they were on one of the steam-powered cakewalks that came to the harvest festival Lamboree in the autumn.

Mr Heckmondwike paused. "We are not alone," he said.

A well-fed sheep tick emerged from the darkness of the fleece.

"Blood yell!" replied Slake. "It's enormous!"

Mr Heckmondwike brandished his shepherd's crook at it but the creature seemed not to take any notice so he hit it as hard as he could. There was the sound of a very thick rubber balloon being struck. The sheep tick seemed a little non-plussed and backed away.

They plunged onwards through the dark, lower layers of the fleece, alternately slipping on grease from oozing hair follicles and scree-running over dry, flaky patches. Little black things stuck to the strands of wool watched them with a curious interest as they passed. Underneath their feet, they could see the purpley-blue veins that transported growth hormones around the creature's vast body.

At one point they were horrified to see something swimming in what would normally have been a blood capillary. It was keeping pace with them and it returned their curiosity with interest.

"That would explain the feeling of being followed," said Slake.

"Nay lad, it could be that," and Slake turned to face appeared to be an enormous hairy, animated potato that tried to embrace him with what could have been either its legs or a set of highly specialised mouth parts.

"Yipe!" said Slake. He leapt backwards and produced a large adjustable spanner from his pack and hit the tick as hard as he could in what was either its groin or its face. The tick fell backwards with a punctured hiss and a painful gait or expression.

Mr Heckmondwike was just about to say "Well done!" when Slake yelled and he turned to find an even bigger sheep tick emerging from behind. Acting entirely automatically, Mr Heckmondwike thrust the end of his crook as hard as he could into its leathery skin. The bloated abdomen split open and the tick's last meal spilled out all over the skin of the Giant Lamb.

Slake watched in gory fascination but Mr Heckmondwike yelled at him to keep away from the blood.

"Don't touch it lad! It's full of that crap from BiggaBeast! " He wiped his crook on the wool. "These well-fed ticks are clumsy and sated. The unfed younger ones are more dangerous."

"More dangerous?"

"Aye."

"What do they look like then?"

"Just the mouth parts, eyes and legs, lad."

"What? Like these?"

Mr Heckmondwike did not reply. He just ran away. Slake followed. As he ran, his rucksack felt like some creature that had landed between his shoulder blades so he took it off. Wool snagged his arm as he brought it over his head and he nearly stumbled but at least he proved there was no creature on his pack. However, his shoulder blades now felt terribly exposed so he began to flagellate himself with his pack, wads of wool catching his elbow as he ran. He barely managed to keep up with Mr Heckmondwike who darted between the hair follicles as if he'd been doing it all his long life.

The monster halted. From somewhere in front, they could hear it snorting as it smelt the air.

"By the spanners of St Bendix!" gasped Slake. "Where are we?"

"Ah reckon we're near t'shoulder blades."

"Are you sure? All this wool looks the same."

"This hill must be its neck!"

"Just a little bit further on and we should ..."

"Stop right there!" An attractive dark-haired Gothic Princess had popped out of the wool. She wore a long, old-fashioned dress and had conspicuously well-developed shoulder blades.

"Who are you?" asked Mr Heckmondwike.

"She's my guardian angel," said Slake.

"Haven't I got one, then?" asked Mr Heckmondwike.

"Of course you have," said a voice. "Here I am."

Mr Heckmondwike found himself looking at a pink and white marsh-mallow, all billowing bosom and bows with a dainty, stylised crook in one hand, a sort of Enormous Bo-Peep but by no means unattractive.

"My dears," she said, "we haven't got long, but then neither will you if you ignore us."

"We've had this discussion before, haven't we, Reynald?"

"Reynald?" guffawed Mr Heckmondwike.

"Is this the one you were telling me about?" Mr Heckmondwike's guardian angel whispered loudly.

The Gothic Princess nodded.

"But he's an absolute dear!" For an awful moment Slake thought she was going to tickle him under the chin. "Shame about the tee shirt. 'Too fast to live, too young to die.' What's that supposed to mean?"

"Anyway, we'll try and get our point across more effectively this time," said the Gothic Princess as the monster heaved beneath them. "Ready? Count of three. Three!"

"You're both going to die, you're both going to die, ee, aye, yatty-oh, if you don't get off the Lamb."

"That should do it," said Enormous Bo-Peep and they vanished.

Slake and Mr Heckmondwike stared at each other.

"Very busy people, guardian angels," said Slake.

Mr Heckmondwike rubbed his eyes.

"Why don't you stick around and actually help us?" Slake shouted into the darkened galleries within the Giant Lamb's fleece. "We're not doing this out of choice, y' know, but duty!"

The guardian angels reappeared.

"I suppose we could," said Enormous Bo-Peep. "If it's their duty."

"Yes!" insisted Slake. "We're are trying to be the guardian angels for Wormton!"

"I see your point," said the Gothic Princess and she punched a sheep tick right between the eyes.

"Take that!" cried Enormous Bo-Peep as she split a tick in half with her crook.

"I think they can take care of themselves as well as us," said Mr Heckmondwike. "Let's do what we have to do and get off this fecund sheep!"

"Language, Thaddeus!" cried Enormous Bo-Peep, imperiously as she fended off a pincer attack from a couple of keds.

"Thaddeus?" sniggered Slake.

"Come on!" said Mr Heckmondwike and he tore off into the fleece, swinging from strand to strand like a low-budget Tarzan.

At last, they emerged just behind its ears, which pointed forward alertly as the monster sniffed the air. Mr Heckmondwike and Slake studied their enormity, as well as that of the appalling ear mites that prowled around inside them.

Gradually both men became aware of what was holding the creature's attention.

"Look over there!" exclaimed Slake. "It's the militia! Hey! They're not pointing those things at us, are they?"

CHAPTER 82

The big guns of the artillery and tanks moved almost casually to point at the Giant Lamb as the Mithering Brethren emerged over the horizon around its feet.

Above the monster was a cloud all of its own.

Captain Keen picked up his binoculars and studied the Giant Lamb. "What's the GS on the weather on the monster?"

"Still fogbound, sir," answered the meteorologist. "Misty in the north."

"Which way is north again?"

"Its head, sir. Light drizzle, force 2 and gaseous in the south."

"Thank you sergeant."

"Picking up the airborne bogey on the radar, sir."

"Where is it?"

"Sir! It's just coming in – vertically, sir! – to land outside Wormton."

"Really? We should be able to see it."

Captain Keen trained his binoculars on Wormton and saw a red and white and black delta-wing aircraft cartwheeling to earth over the nearest gate-house. It clipped the battlements, span out from Wormton's walls and came down to land on its tail by the road.

"Extraordinary," he murmured. "What air force uses an exclamation mark as its insignia?"

"Dunno, sir."

"Wait a moment! There's writing on it. It's a bit scorched but I think I can make it out. Yes. It says, 'Bloody Great Sheep.' " Captain Keen lowered his binoculars as if he might see it better without them. "Oh, for heaven's sake. That's all we need! Unidentified Flying Objects!"

His men looked at him in horror.

"Well, what else could it be?"

"Message from God, sir?"

"He would hardly use the word 'Bloody' now, would He now?"

The radio crackled. "Crab Air calling Pongoes. One and two squadrons are zeroed in."

Captain Keen grabbed the microphone. "And three and four?"

"Three is in reserve and four is trained on the fundaments of the religious fundamentalists by its feet."

"Excellent. Wait for my signal. Okay," Captain Keen said to his bom-
bardiers. "Wait till you see the whites of its eyes."

"Er, we can see them now, sir."

"Oh, can you? Ah. Yes, of course. How about the hairs on its chinny-
chinny chin-chin?"

"Them too, sir."

"What? With the naked eye?"

"'Fraid so, sir."

"Very well. Chap with fleece and horns, eighty millimetre howitzers,
quick fire."

"Sir! There are civilians aboard the Giant Lamb!"

"Hold your fire!"

Captain Keen grabbed his binoculars and scanned the Giant Lamb,
which seemed to be standing at bay.

Between its ears were two very perplexed but undeniably familiar
figures lurking in its fleece who definitely weren't Mithering Brethren.

"I don't believe it!" he said. "Damned civilians! Always getting in the
bloody way!"

CHAPTER 83

"Don't shoot!" shouted Slake and Mr Heckmondwike, despite the fact that they could not be heard.

From behind them came a jet aeroplane, flying low and fast but completely without sound. The jet silently fired some missiles that apparently rammed into the Lamb, although they felt no impact.

Slake and Mr Heckmondwike cheered at the thought that the Rural Air Force had finally discovered a missile guidance system that worked against large amounts of wool, but then they remembered where they were. A great cloud of wool erupted from the monster's flank and engulfed the jet, which promptly sucked it into its engines and sank like a stone as the sound of its approach caught up with it.

To the sound track of its companion's demise, another aeroplane made its attack, but the Giant Lamb just bleated at it and the fighter fell to pieces.

The monster looked around with interest for a parachute and eventually spotted one. It trotted over to intercept it and snapped at it.

"By the socket set of St Bendix!" yelled Slake. "Do sheep do that?"

Mr Heckmondwike looked at the vapour trails the Giant Lamb left behind it. "They don't have their own weather systems, lad, that's for certain."

"Hello," said Enormous Bo-Peep, "have we missed anything?"

Slake's guardian angel karate-chopped an unfed ked away from him.

In front of them, two great ears swivelled backwards to catch their words and, beyond these, they were somehow aware of two giant eyes swivelling curiously upwards.

"Quickly," said Mr Heckmondwike, as the Gothic Princess formed an advance party and cleared the head of parasites, "we don't have much time." He handed Slake his shepherd's crook and then took Slake's pack from him. "When I tell thee, climb up and hook that around one of t'monster's ears."

"What are you gonna do?"

"Ah'm going to lob some of Old Mr Macklefract's poosers down its lug hole."

Slake stared at him in disbelief, a smile playing on his features. "You must be bloody mad if you've been carrying some of Old Mr Mack's exploding potatoes through what we've just been through."

"Ah'm not mad," Mr Heckmondwike assured him. "Ah got thee to do it!" He opened Slake's rucksack and showed him.

"What? But I've batting keds away with that!"

"Reynald," said his guardian angel, "I knew all about it!"

"Fine sort of protector you are!"

"Did they explode?"

"That's not the point! I'm sure something unethical's going on here."

Ignoring his protestations, Mr Heckmondwike produced a Tupperware container from Slake's pack and opened it. It was packed full of cotton wool, but inside were a dozen very small potatoes.

"Go on then," he urged Slake, "hook an ear."

Slake clambered up until he was close enough to hook Mr Heckmondwike's crook around the left ear of the Giant Lamb. He wrestled with it for a moment, but then the Giant Lamb flicked its ear, much as a sheep would do if a fly had landed on it, and Mr Heckmondwike's crook went spinning up into the air, nearly taking Slake with it.

"By the crook of St Mary, our Lady of Lapurdo! That were ma best crook!"

"Oh, pish!" said Enormous Bo-Peep. "Use mine, for heaven's sake!"

She climbed up beside the Gothic Princess and with Slake hooked an ear and tried to keep it in position for Mr Heckmondwike, but the shepherd's aim was not good. Many poosers fell to the ground or landed harmlessly in the wool around his allies. The ear mites were starting to look suspicious and beginning to advance ominously.

Slake braced himself and grabbed a pooser from where it had landed in the wool behind him. He steadied himself and lobbed it right into the monster's ear hole. There was a loud bang and a gout of flame shot out of the ear. The Giant Lamb shuddered and several ear mites dropped into the flames inside its head.

"Again!" yelled Slake and he dropped another one into the same place.

The next bang made the monster really react. It shook its head and bucked. Slake and the Enormous Bo-Peep swung out over nothing as they held desperately onto Enormous Bo-Peep's sheep crook. Slowly they looped upwards and the crook slipped over the ear. Slake began yelling as he fell but Enormous Bo-Peep clutched him to her impressive bosom and rose like a pink barrage balloon before whisking him back to the comparative safety of the parasite-infested fleece. However, the box of poosers burst open and they rained past Mr Heckmondwike and exploded among the Mithering Brethren below.

The militia must have seen this, for all their guns then opened up.

As fast as they could, Slake and Mr Heckmondwike threw any remaining poosers they could find into the Giant Lamb's ear. There was a series of explosions and the Giant Lamb tried to throw its bleat towards them, but they hid in its fleece just in time. The Giant Lamb broke into a run and smoke poured from its left ear, a sight that cheered the onlooking militia greatly. There was also another change that Slake and Mr Heckmondwike did not yet know about. Its left eye was now completely red.

"Advance to the rear!" shouted Slake, but he was suddenly alone. He grabbed his adjustable spanner and disappeared back into the fleece.

This time they met even more parasites.

"Ah would've thought they'd give us a wide berth!" grunted Mr Heckmondwike as he batted one out of the way.

"I don't think they make a conscious decision about it," replied Slake. "I reckon they just attack."

"But we're not their usual source of food."

"Variety is the spice of life, I believe. And a change is as good as a rest. Or maybe …"

"Mebbe what?"

The Giant Lamb bleated one of its terrible deep bleats.

Outside the fleece, aircraft plunged out of the sky, armour plate was shivered to pieces and the minds of any Rural Marines nearby were shattered.

Inside the monster's fleece was probably the safest place to be if it wasn't for the angry parasites.

"Maybe they know we're after their host."

"Oh bloody hell!"

The Giant Lamb bleated again.

"Perhaps they're more aware than we think!"

Mr Heckmondwike brought his boot down on a particularly ugly ked. "That one's not gonna be aware nay more!"

It took ages for the four of them to battle their way back to the rump. The monster was running hard now, so any footing was extremely unsteady and all the parasites seemed alert to the danger their host was in. Just short of the Big Nuff a tremendous battle developed. Mr Heckmondwike nearly fell when a group of keds rushed him, but the next thing he knew The Gothic Princess karate-chopped her way through them and scattered them to the four corners of the fleece.

"Hey!" said Enormous Bo-Peep, grabbing the hand of a surprised Mr Heckmondwike. "This one's mine!"

"So? You rescued Slake just now!"

"That was entirely different. My feelings for the boy are entirely maternal. Who knows what passions you and your martial arts could arouse in an older man?"

"Okay." The Gothic Princess back-flipped incorporating a magnificent reverse kick. "So we're quits!"

Slake grinned from the roll cage of the Big Nuff.

"Ladies! Please!" said Mr Heckmondwike, and the battle resumed.

Mr Heckmondwike felt something in his wellington boot. It had been bothering him all the way through their return journey across the Giant Lamb. Surrounded by the others fighting back to back, he knelt down and took off his boot. Out fell a pooser, and a cold sweat engulfed him. Enormous Bo-Peep turned and winked at him before batting away a ked and a tick with the two ends of her crook.

Mr Heckmondwike put his boot back on and stood up. Just beyond the circle of his friends was a group of advancing keds and he threw the pooser into it with all his might. It exploded in the centre of them, and the other ticks and keds fell back.

There came a distant bleat from ahead, and the Giant Lamb stood still, twisting around to focus on the Big Nuff with its terrible, odd eyes. That last pooser had briefly set fire to the oily fleece.

Mr Heckmondwike and Slake yelled, for it was the first time they had seen what damage they'd wrought upon the Giant Lamb, and they scrambled towards the Big Nuff.

"It knows!" said Slake as the head lunged at them. "It knows its fleece is infested with humans!"

"And guardian angels!" said the Gothic Princess with relish.

"You're enjoying this, aren't you?" Enormous Bo-Peep asked her.

"Helping these two cheat death? Yeah! I'm loving every moment of it! Gothy! Blood-sucking parasite slayer!"

"Take that!" cried Enormous Bo-Peep. "And that! And that! And that!"

"Blood yell!" said Slake, as the Giant Lamb arched its neck around. "If it didn't before, it looks really cross now!"

The Giant Lamb nibbled at its fleece with jaws like hydraulic pincers and the Big Nuff shivered as the fleece was undermined. Wads of coarse, white wool fell away and Enormous Bo-Peep jabbed at its eyes with her crook, but the monster merely blinked and she was blown over backwards by its great eyelashes.

Then Mr Heckmondwike was adrift, still holding grimly onto the fleece except that what he held was no longer attached to the Giant Lamb. He floated through the low cloud of the Giant Lamb's weather system, unable to make out how fast he was travelling or how far he had to fall. Other great tufts of wool were falling, and to his horror he realised that some of them were inhabited by keds and ticks. Then there was a terrible thump and he was winded for the second time that day.

He rolled off a great pile of wool and embraced a patch of grass. Smaller lumps of wool rained down around him, and he stood up in fear of meeting marauding ticks and keds only to be confronted by one rearing up in front of him. However, just as it was about to pounce there was a blast of machine gun fire and the creature disintegrated messily.

"Halt!" A desperate group of Rural Marines surrounded him. "Hands up! Come on!"

Their leader approached. He was covered in mud and his face was black.

"Wot are yew doin' 'ere?"

"Ah'm trying to kill t'monster."

"Wot? By rollin' arahnd in the bleedin' wool? Fink oim born yester-dee? Wotter yew like? Yewer Mivvering Brevren, encha?"

"Eh?"

"C'mon, yewer comin' wiv us!"

CHAPTER 84

"Mr Heckmondwike!" said Captain Keen. "This is a pleasant surprise."

"Will tha tell thine men ah am not Mithering Brethren!"

"Are you fettling well?"

"Tell 'em ah am not Mithering Brethren 'n' ah'll be nobbut graidly, tha knaws."

"Happen? Those hoggs of yours look quite fair to middling these days." Mr Heckmondwike glared at him. "Is tha tekken the piss?"

"Well done, Corporal."

"Tell 'em!"

"He's not Mithering Brethren, I can vouch for that. Dismissed."

As the soldiers filed out of Captain Keen's tent, Professor Cluttercrap joined them.

Captain Keen explained to Mr Heckmondwike that he was acting as their scientific advisor. Professor Cluttercrap squirmed a bit, but he didn't contradict him.

"Now then," went on Captain Keen. "Suppose you tell me what's been going on."

"We were attackin' t'monster."

"Who are we?"

Mr Heckmondwike paused. A full answer would not be credible. "Me and Slake." Mentioning guardian angels to someone who was rumoured to only have a banshee seemed impossibly cruel.

"What was your plan of attack?"

"Kill t'beggar."

"Hmm," said Captain Keen.

"What are your impressions of the Giant Lamb?" asked Professor Cluttercrap.

"It's covered in parasites. Its fleece is poor because it can't graze properly. And ah reckon it stays up by Nibley Edge because it can scratch its arse ont cliff top when it itches."

"Quite," said Captain Keen. "We've observed as much ourselves. We also noticed that it now has a red eye."

"Appen?"

"What did you attack it with?"

"Poosers," said Mr Heckmondwike.

"I beg your pardon?" asked Captain Keen.

"Er, poosers are disappointingly small and commercially useless potatoes," said Professor Cluttercrap in an equally perplexed tone.

"Those that grow up at Topwack Farm explode if tha throws 'em 'ard enow."

Professor Cluttercrap scribbled down some thoughts in a notebook. "More x-factor," he muttered.

"The wool seems to protect t'monster," ventured Mr Heckmondwike.

Captain Keen stiffened. "That is true. Mr Heckmondwike, I have to ask you if you have heard it bleat."

"Aye."

"Hmm. Then this may sound familiar to you. Sergeant?"

"Sir!"

The soldier played a tape machine. It was a recording of the last attack on the Giant Lamb. The pilot described how he was closing in on the monster and trying to avoid wads of wool that threatened to be snagged by the helicopter's rotor blades. Then, as they got really close, the Giant Lamb turned to look at them.

"My God! Look at those eyes!" said the pilot.

"This was before you reddened one of them," put in Captain Keen.

Then there was a terrible rumbling that sounded strangely familiar to Mr Heckmondwike, yet horribly new.

The tape-deck wriggled about on the desk as it played, and as the soldier put his hand out to steady it the tape machine self-destructed.

"Fortunately the sound reproduction is not perfect," said Professor Cluttercrap as Captain Keen extinguished the flames with a soda siphon, "otherwise we'd probably all be dead by now."

"T'fleece protects t'monster from its own bleat," said Mr Heckmondwike, "and anything inside it."

"Indeed," said Captain Keen. "How exactly did you get onto the Lamb?"

"We drove onto it, accident'ly, like."

"And how did you get awff?"

"Ah fell off on a big wad o' wool."

"And where is Slake?"

"Ah dunnaw. Ah thought thee had 'im."

Captain Keen shook his head.

Mr Heckmondwike rose from his chair. "In that case, ah'd best be off and find 'im."

"Yes, of course. I'm afraid I can't spare any men to accompany you. If you do attack the Giant Lamb again, please let us know."

CHAPTER 85

The militia flew Mr Heckmondwike to the top of Nibley Edge by helicopter, but they were too worried about wool getting ingested by their engines or snagging their rotor blades to land. So they hovered above a big wad of wool and Mr Heckmondwike jumped out. He nearly bounced back into the helicopter again but the winchman pushed him away and the pilot took the chopper upwards, creating a stronger downwash that reduced the height of Mr Heckmondwike's bouncing.

When eventually he stopped bouncing he was very ill and had to lie still for a while, but then Widdershins found him and bounced all around him as if it were on three invisible trampolines. It didn't take him long to find the truck, and he drove it west along Nibley Edge until he picked up an old drover's track that led back to Riddaw Lodge. Here he swapped the truck for Slake's V8 Mudlark and, after he'd filled it up and packed the rear end with jerry cans of Old Mr Macklefract's most volatile brew, he gunned the Mudlark towards where he thought the militia had picked him up.

Widdershins leaned out on either side of the Mudlark, its tongues streaming back like pink ribbons. He soon picked up the trail of the monster and followed it through the Forest of Riddaw. A broad section of trees had been felled, and he kept his pedal to the metal as he penetrated deeper into the darkening forest, crossing earlier incursions by the Giant Lamb that were noticeably smaller. Avoiding fallen trees was difficult, but fortunately they lay mostly in his direction of travel. The only bother they gave him was a slight tramlining effect.

However one tree tripped the Mudlark up, and it rolled end over end.

It happened so quickly Mr Heckmondwike had no time to react. One minute he was accelerating over the woodpile, the next his Mudlark was somersaulting. The worst part was the last, when he was travelling backwards and upside down, unable to see which way he was going, and then the tail came down and the nose went up. The Mudlark came crashing down on its suspension, did a little hop on rebound, as if it was a gymnast steadying herself daintily for the next exercise, and then hurled itself at the horizon as the tyres gripped, right way up and engine bellowing.

Mr Heckmondwike turned to check Widdershins, and his faithful dog was all present and correct and even seemed to want to do it again.

He began to pass pieces of orange wreckage from the Big Nuff, so he pulled up and examined them but they weren't of any significant size. He just hoped that he would find one big bit with Slake still safely inside.

Eventually, the trail headed back into the open country again and Mr Heckmondwike felt he could go even faster. Great clods of earth had been thrown up by the monster's hooves but he just used them as ramps to leap over the hollows.

He nearly missed a large orange object lying in a peaty pool. He sped past it, braked and then looped back, all four wheels churning out impressive rooster-tails of black soil. Gradually the bucking Mudlark came around, and Mr Heckmondwike pointed its flying W on the bonnet at the wreckage. Once all four wheels were facing in the same direction, the Mudlark shot forward and Mr Heckmondwike had to brake heavily. He slid to a halt beside a large lump of Nuffield that lay like a carelessly discarded piece of litter in the tracks of the monster. He leaned forward in his seat and what he saw made his heart sink.

It was the engine and transmission unit, still with the girders Slake had used to mate the two together. The girders had been bent into a gentle S-curve. All its wheels were all gone, including its steering wheel, together with the front axle that had once served Mr Floridspleen.

The roll cage was nowhere to be seen. It had come off as easily as the legs from a dead spider.

Widdershins leapt out and ran off. Mr Heckmondwike followed suit but couldn't see any clues to Slake's whereabouts. Where the roll cage had been bolted to the casting of the differential housing, the mounting points had been fractured and torn away. Where it had been welded to the girders that made up the chassis, the welds had held good but the metal around them had failed.

"Slake!" he bellowed. He shouted his name several times but then began to wonder if he really expected an answer.

He turned to look in the other direction and peered back towards the forest. Widdershins came running back and, tellingly, climbed into the back of the Mudlark and looked expectantly at the forest. He sat behind the wheel and headed off towards the forest.

Coming back that way, it was easy to see something he'd missed. He stopped the Mudlark, and Widdershins tumbled out and eagerly ran up to it. Mr Heckmondwike cautiously got down from the Mudlark and took a few steps towards it, alternately wishing it might be empty or occupied. As he approached, he began to make sense of the horribly mangled steel. Then he saw the limbs inside it.

"I kept the keds off him," the Gothic Princess said in his ear.

"Is ee awreet?"

"Well, he'll live. He's just not very talkative."

"It's not all bad then."

"He's been very lucky."

"Aye. Thanks for looking after 'im, lass."

She smiled. "Don't thank me, sir, it's just my job."

"All the same, lass …"

"You might have a word with him later, perhaps," she said as Mr Heck-mondwike knelt beside Slake. "Try and talk some sense into him. Get him to stay away from things with engines and wheels. And hide that awful tee shirt of his."

Mr Heckmondwike smiled sadly at her. "There's nay point."

"Just for me?"

He sighed. "Awreet. Ah'll dweet just for thee. But it'll do naw good, tha knaws."

"Do what you can. It should get easier as he gets older. Young men between eighteen and twenty-five are the worst, although you're not much better yourself."

"Thanks."

"Anyway, I can go now." She unfurled a pair of enormous black wings and was gone. There was just a whiff of perfume and the last of a strong breeze rushing through the trees. Then the forest was still again.

Slake was surrounded by Widdershins as it licked his face and hands. He stirred slightly.

"Slake? Can tha hear me? Slake?"

"Wha diddy wha?"

"Lie still," said Mr Heckmondwike.

"Nnngg," said Slake. "Is nice. Still is so nice. No idea how nice."

"Now don't go to sleep on me again, Slake! Just keep talking to me while I work out a way to get thee out."

"Don't wanna come out."

"Don't be a morpeth!"

"Is nice in here. Still is wonderful, I can't tell you!"

"Are you hurt anywhere?"

"All over."

"What happened?"

"Not the best person to ask. Try somebody else. Brain's been pulped. I've been rattling around in here for too long." Slake held his head in his hands.

"Listen to me, Slake. Ah reckon if ah could get a bottle jack and spring those lower tubes, ah might be able to pull thee out, awreet?"

"Okay. I'll just lie here for a bit and talk to Widdershins."

Mr Heckmondwike fetched a large bottle jack from the Mudlark, placed it under the end of one of the tubes and began to pump. The tubing was good quality stuff, but the effort that Mr Heckmondwike now had to put into forcing the tubes apart showed the strength of the blows that had bent them.

The first two attempts failed when the jack slipped along the length of the tubing, but by a careful positioning of the end of the jack the third try saw the tubes slowly spreading out. They groaned audibly and so did Slake.

Mr Heckmondwike found another piece of wreckage close by and wedged it in the gap in case the tubes tried to spring back. Then he repeated the procedure on the opposite side.

"That's it!" he panted, wiping the sweat from his eyes. "See if tha can get out now."

Slake wriggled painfully downwards. Mr Heckmondwike grabbed a boot with each hand and pulled gently. Slake's chest wedged against the concave tubes.

"I'm stuck," he said.

"Ah nivver woulda believed that thine chest would prove to be t'widest part o' thee. Breathe in!"

"Don't you mean breathe out?"

Mr Heckmondwike waited for a moment and then gave Slake's feet a tremendous pull. All of a sudden, Slake's chest collapsed and he shot out of the roll cage. Mr Heckmondwike fell over backwards and Slake landed on top of him.

They lay there for a little while, both of them unable or unwilling to move, while Widdershins administered sheepdog first aid.

Mr Heckmondwike felt worn out, but he eventually managed to push Slake's feet out of his face and gently rolled the rest of Slake over onto the grass.

"Slake?"

"Ow."

"Is tha awreet?"

"Please stop asking me that." He looked over at Mr Heckmondwike. "It's nice just lying here, isn't it?"

"We mustn't lie here too long."

"Why not?"

"Dark Time and keds."

"Right. What's the plan then?"

"Same as last time."

"What's that supposed to mean?"

"We'll plan on being spontaneous."

"Fine. Where's the Big Nuff?"

"All ower t'Wold, lad. T'monster battered it to pieces trying to scrape thee off against t'landscape."

"So the Big Nuff wasn't big enough, ha ha!"

"Nay, lad. Nowt's big enow nay more. Heck as owt, lad, this roll cage has been stoved in every which way."

"Best day's work I ever did, fitting that."

"Tha can say that agin!"

"Anyway, we caught the beast, didn't we?"

"Aye. We did at that. Can tha get up?"

"I dunno."

With Mr Heckmondwike's support, Slake found himself in an upright position.

"Okay," he whispered, sweat running off him like a waterfall, "what now?"

"To t'Mudlark, lad."

"To the Mudlark, James! And don't spare the horses! Or the sheep, come to that."

"Tha's doin' well, lad. Just a few more steps … there!"

"Why didn't you drive the Mudlark over to me?" asked Slake as he leaned against it.

Mr Heckmondwike manoeuvred him into the passenger seat and swung his feet up into the footwells. "Therapy," he said. "To boost thine confidence immediately after a trauma."

"By the spanners! Why's my Mudlark got grass on its roll cage?"

"Just a little bit of arboreal acrobatics. Ah tell ee, summat, lad. Tha builds 'em strong!"

Mr Heckmondwike strapped Slake into his seat, then took his place behind the wheel and fired up the engine.

A smile gently spread across Slake's pale, sweating features as they drove off. "Know what date it is? It's Mithering Sunday!"

"Well, ah'm mithered."

Then Slake became more serious. "We should go after the monster right now," he said.

"Why? Tha's in no fit state."

"Shouldn't we go after it now? Before it gets any bigger?"

"Not reet nah."

"It's the same principle as you making me walk to the Mudlark," said Slake.

"Oh aye?"

"If we leave it long enough to think about it, our confidence'll be blown."

"Well, let's see how tha feels after t'militia doctor's had a look at thee."

"I could murder a cheese fritter."

CHAPTER 86

Professor Cluttercrap was examining a slide under his portable microscope. Mr Heckmondwike watched him scribbling some notes as he waited for the verdict on Slake while, as usual, Widdershins lay on his feet, keeping them warm.

Outside was the sound of distant gunfire and the occasional deep bleat. Rain pattered heavily on the canvas of the tent like the impatient drumming of fingers.

Suddenly, Professor Cluttercrap jerked his head back from the microscope. Gingerly he peered into the eyepiece again. Then he began to move the slide around.

A flap in the tent opened and Captain Keen came in with the militia doctor.

"Mr Heckmondwike?" she asked him.

"Aye?"

She was young enough to be his granddaughter. "Mr Thorngumbald is badly bruised, seeing double and has ringing in his ears. He also has classic concussion symptoms and talks a good deal about lobbing poosers down lug holes."

There was a yell and a crash from Professor Cluttercrap. He threw the microscope on the floor, took off a walking boot and began hammering something with it.

"Oh not more x-factor, Professor!" exclaimed Captain Keen.

The Rural Marina doctor rolled her eyes and left.

Professor Cluttercrap peered over the tabletop with his boot in his hand. "Er, yes, I'm afraid so."

A jet flew barely overhead and crashed into a nearby mountain.

"Could you just keep it down a bit? I need to talk to Mr Heckmondwike."

"Yes, of course. I'm sorry."

"Now then, Mr Heckmondwike. I'm delighted Mr Thorngumbald is still in one piece. However, our work must continue. We are preparing for another big push."

"Oh, aye?"

"Yes. I'm going to try a new tactic."

"Appen?"

"Yes. We're going to lull the Giant Lamb into a false sense of security and then we're gonna to hit it with everything we've got."

"Well, tha's still got plenty o' stuff to hit it with," conceded Mr Heckmondwike.

"We never realised how much we'd need" replied Captain Keen.

Mr Heckmondwike's consequent thought that even this was still not enough was almost audible.

"I have to say that I'm pretty damn impressed by the way you fellows handle y'selves," said Captain Keen.

"Oh aye?"

"Abso-bloody-lutely! Goya!"

"Goya?"

"Rather! Goya! You Got Awff Yer Arse and did something about it!"

The flap behind Mr Heckmondwike opened again and Slake staggered in. "Hallo, Captain. How's the naked drinking going?"

"Reckon he's been at it already, lad!" muttered Mr Heckmondwike.

"We're looking forward to the next opportunity very much!" said Captain Keen, extending a hand.

Slake steadied himself on Professor Cluttercrap's table and looked at Captain Keen's outstretched hand. Then he took it. "I bet you are," he said, shaking it warmly, "but I still wouldn't want to be a nudist in this weather."

Captain Keen gently led him to a chair and settled him in it. "I was saying to Mr Heckmondwike and the good professor here that we are about to go in hard on the Giant Lamb."

"Rid the Wold of its menace," Slake replied with some feeling. He leant towards Mr Heckmondwike to get comfortable and hissed to him, "They've taken away my two-way!"

Mr Heckmondwike nodded inconspicuously.

"Quite," said Captain Keen. "I'm particularly impressed by the way that you and Mr Heckmondwike here attacked the monster. I think we might be able to learn something from your Mark One Eye Ball."

"Really?" the two men asked together.

"Yes. Remind me how you got on the Giant Lamb?"

"We drove onto it by mistake," said Slake.

"Well, thee did," said Mr Heckmondwike. "Ah were prevented by old Widdershins here."

The three-headed sheep dog leapt up at its name and began looking eagerly for something reasonably sized to herd.

"Oh yeah?" said Slake. "If you're so clever, why did you follow me onto it?"

"Ah just thought it were a bloody great wad o' wool."

"There's wool everywhere," said Captain Keen. "It's dangerous stuff. It clogs up everything and absorbs our missiles, shells and bullets. Every hit on the Giant Lamb releases more fragments of it. We're virtually suffocating in it!"

There was an angry bleat outside followed by a series of explosions.

"And then there's its bleat," Captain Keen went on. "It can shatter the rotor blades on our Hueycobras." He turned to Slake. "It wasn't gremlins on the Jesus bolt at all."

"Its voice box must be the size of a Mudlark," mused Mr Heckmondwike.

"It certainly knows how to apply it," admitted Captain Keen. "It can shatter armour plate and scramble the brains of my men if it puts its mind to it."

"Ah yes," said Slake. "Its mind. Captain Keen, if the voice box of the Lamb is now as large as a Mudlark then its brain must be the size of a house."

"Bigger," said Mr Heckmondwike, gloomily. "We've stood between its ears, lad, remember?"

A troubled look came over Slake's face as he did so. He gathered himself and said, "The point is, Captain Keen, we are up against an intelligent sheep?"

"It don't come much worse than that," ventured Mr Heckmondwike.

"At any rate," said Captain Keen, "I have to say that I admire the vim you displayed yesterday."

"Vim?" chorused Slake and Mr Heckmondwike together.

"Yes."

Slake looked especially confused. "Did you display any vim?" he asked Mr Heckmondwike, who looked perplexed and shook his head.

"You know," insisted Captain Keen. "Spunk."

Mr Heckmondwike and Slake became quite agitated.

"Gumption, gentlemen! Gumption! Courage!"

"Ah!" Slake leaned over to Mr Heckmondwike. "Half the time, we can't understand a bloody word he says," he whispered.

"So," said Captain Keen, "what else can you tell me about the enemy?"

"Well, it's still just a bloody great sheep really," began Mr Heckmondwike.

"Same as all the other sheeps, then?"

"Sheeps?" echoed Slake.

"Aye," carried on Mr Heckmondwike, "bar one or two notable differences."

"Size for one," put in Captain Keen.

"It's had an unnatural life for a sheep," went on Mr Heckmondwike. "Sheep," and he stressed the word, "are social animals and this has been an outcast from t'flock almost from t'beginning. It killed its mother, tha knaws, by standing on 'er, like all young lambs do when they play Ah'm-t'-king-o'-

t'castle but it squashed her. It is ma considered opinion that it's incredibly lonely because of its unique viewpoint on life."

"It's higher up for one thing," said Slake.

"Aye."

"Jolly good stuff!" enthused Captain Keen, turning to Professor Cluttercrap. "Sheep psychology. Nye Dye is one of the first things they teach us young awfficers at Sandwell."

Mr Heckmondwike and Slake gazed at him blankly.

"Know Your Enemy, Defeat Your Enemy."

"Thing is," said Mr Heckmondwike, "it's more of a natural phenomenon than an enemy."

"It doesn't seem very natural to me," said Captain Keen.

"He's got a point there," Slake told Mr Heckmondwike, earnestly. "Look at the way it uses its natural defences when we attack it. It blankets itself with impact-absorbing wool and deliberately focuses its bleat on whatever war engines you throw at it. Then it's been making fools out of me and Mr Heckmondwike for weeks. That's not a nice thing to have to live with – being outwitted by a sheep – is it Mr Heckmondwike?"

"Nay, lad."

"I have two theories about this," went on Slake. "One is that as the size of its head has increased, so the size of its brain has grown too, increasing its IQ. The other theory is that the parasites are really the masters of the situation."

"How d'you mean?" asked Captain Keen.

At this point Professor Cluttercrap joined in. "I think what Mr Thorngumbald …"

"Call me Slake, okay?"

"I think what Mr, er, Slake means is that the parasites are controlling the actions of the Giant Lamb."

"How on earth can they do that?" asked Captain Keen.

"It's not unheard of," said Professor Cluttercrap. "Some parasites are known to affect the behaviour of their host to enable the next stage of their life cycle to begin. Take for example certain thorny-headed worms, which infest woodlice. They change the behaviour of their host to ensure their predation, inducing conspicuous behaviour so that the woodlice are eaten by songbirds, in whose gizzards the next stage of the thorny-headed worms' life cycle takes place."

He looked at them and saw their disbelieving faces.

"There is also the well-known case of the worm that infests the common sandhopper, a sort of freshwater shrimp, and the worm uses two hosts – the amphipod and the duck – to complete its life cycle. This parasite forms a bright red cyst on the host and makes the sandhopper swim to the surface so that the duck sees it and eats it, allowing the life cycle of the parasite to continue."

"That's horrible!" said Captain Keen.

"I was once at a conference," Professor Cluttercrap went on, "and met a man who discovered that certain species of wasp larvae feed on the blood of their hosts, orb-weaving spiders. The spider continues its normal web-building activities until, on the night that it will finally kill its host, the larva induces the spider to build a web that is totally different from any other it has built before. Once it is finished, the wasp larva moults, kills and eats the spider, then spins the pupal cocoon inside the special canopy made by the spider."

Slake frowned. "Doesn't the spider look at what it's made and think to itself 'Whoa! Hey! That's not right!'?"

"Apparently not. So, you see, parasites really can control their hosts. Take you, Mr Heckmondwike."

"Me?"

"What makes you leave the comfort and security of your home to go and rescue a stray sheep?"

Mr Heckmondwike wriggled uncomfortably.

"I've pointed this out to him before," Slake told the professor.

"You are at the sheep's beck and call," went on Professor Cluttercrap. "They use you for food and security just like the wasp larvae use orb-weaving spiders."

"Blood yell!"

"So if we take it as read that some creatures can act out of character under the influence of a commonly occurring parasite, just think what an unnatural parasite can achieve."

"I'm not sure I want to," said Captain Keen.

"What would a sheep be like if it realised that it no longer had to be frightened of everything," Slake wondered, "and that instead everything ought to be frightened of the sheep?"

"It might not like it," said Mr Heckmondwike, still coming to terms with the idea of sheep as parasites of humans. "It might prefer to be a normal sheep."

"But it can't," said Slake. "So it would be a very unhappy sheep."

"This all assumes a degree of self-awareness that I am not convinced a sheep possesses," replied Professor Cluttercrap. "But to go back to your earlier point, Mr Slake, the orb-weaving spider doesn't stop to reconsider its actions."

"Don't all those parasites irritate their hosts?"

"Heck as like as appen as maybe they do."

"Make it a social outcast," said Slake, "and it makes quite an angry young lamb."

"Aye, a very big, very angry young lamb. But if ah follow thee reet, Professor, t'monster wouldn't knaw it was behaving outta character."

"Exactly! Or if it did, it could do nothing to stop its aberrant behaviour!"

"Are you saying we should pity the monster?" asked Captain Keen.

"You could say that it is as much a victim of its circumstances as we are," said Professor Cluttercrap.

Captain Keen didn't look like he would.

"That's the point Gloria made," murmured Slake. "The Lamb is innocent, she said. We are the ones that turned it into a monster. I reckon it just wants to be loved."

"Oh, good grief," said Captain Keen.

"Yeah! Really! Loved by its flock."

"Once it were int Woldernesse," said Mr Heckmondwike, "it had to fend for itself. It were already big enow to avoid its traditional predators, so t'problem was not one o' predation but of hunger. It had grown so big it could nay longer eat grass. It had to find an alternative. So it tries a few, even havin' a sniff at a few people lookin' at it from t'walls of Wormton, but int end it decides leaves are t'next best thing to grass. So it goes to live in Riddaw Forest. Or on it, ah spoase."

"The old debate of nature or nurture!" put in Professor Cluttercrap.

"Aye. Its nature is to be a sheep and it is naturally sheepish, but it adapts to survive."

"With a little help from its friends," said Slake. "Well, its parasites. And the Mithering Brethren. Not really friends at all, just things that manipulate it. We're the ones that made this monster. We treated it as such from the word go, and now it fulfils our expectations perfectly by simply being monstrous."

"And then there is the x-factor," said Professor Cluttercrap.

"The what?" asked Slake.

"An unknown quantity that is part of the whole equation. Mr Slake ..."

"Just call me Slake, okay?"

"The parasites should not be this big. There should be a physical limitation to their size determined by the surface area to volume ratio. This normally restricts the size of creatures that use spiracles for respiration as opposed to lungs. But this law of physics has been broken and I can't explain how."

CHAPTER 87

They adjourned soon afterwards and went outside. The sun had come out, but to the north, where Captain Keen said the Giant Lamb was currently located, it looked as if it was clouding over.

"I am awaiting news of certain new weapons that we've had under development," he told them.

"Who are all these people in white coats?" asked Slake.

"Test scientists," replied Captain Keen.

"What are they going to test?"

Captain Keen looked at them in a strange way. "Our ultimate weapon."

Slake and Mr Heckmondwike pondered this as the test scientists rushed around with clipboards and put on sinister-looking overalls.

"It's a bomb, isn't it?" Slake said at length.

Captain Keen did not answer.

The scientists were talking loudly, however, about evacuation of the vale, fallout and potassium iodate tablets.

"They sound like they're gonna use it, to me," said Mr Heckmondwike.

"They are merely preparing for a test," insisted Captain Keen.

"A test in which they hope they'll not be found wantin'," murmured the shepherd.

"Wanton or wanting?" quipped Professor Cluttercrap

"It is, as I said, the last resort," Captain Keen tried to reassure them.

"Tha means it would be the end!" said Mr Heckmondwike.

There was a commotion somewhere to the north. A blood-spattered Land Rover came careering through the assembled militia. Its crazed driver saw Captain Keen and lost control. The Land Rover hit a bump and rolled onto its side. Soldiers pulled the driver from the car. In the confusion, Captain Keen got blood all over one of his hands.

"It's horrible!" yelled the driver, struggling against his rescuers. "It's bleating at everything in its path!"

"It was a long shot but it just didn't work," said Captain Keen looking at the blood on his left hand.

"Here you are sir." A medic handed him a towel.

Somebody injected the hysterical soldier and he collapsed into a heap.

Mr Heckmondwike and Slake turned to look at Captain Keen. "What didn't work?" they asked him together.

Captain Keen had the good grace to look a little self-conscious as he cleaned his hand. "The chemical and biological weapons. We still have the last resort, though."

Slake gestured to Professor Cluttercrap. "He's not talking about that nuclear stuff is he?"

"I rather think he might be," admitted the professor.

"Sir!"

"Sergeant?"

"Picking up the sheep on radar, sir!"

"Good man."

"It's headed this way."

"Good! We're going to hit it with all we've got."

The Rural Marines' budget manager began handing out cotton wool. "You'll need this in your ears," she said.

Captain Keen began issuing unintelligible orders over the radio. "What's the GS on the monster?"

"What's a GS?" Slake whispered loudly to Mr Heckmondwike.

"General Synopsis," hissed Professor Cluttercrap.

"Who's he?" whispered Slake.

"Where are the so'n'sos?" Captain Keen demanded of someone on the radio.

Slake opened his mouth to ask a question but Professor Cluttercrap saw him and said, "Subversive Or Non Subversive Objectives. He's referring to the Mithering Brethren. We're not sure whose side they're on."

"They're not on our side," Slake assured him.

From somewhere, not so very far away, the dull crump-crump of gunfire could be heard.

"Sir! The signals breaking up!" said the sergeant.

"No matter. We should be able to eyeball the creature at any moment."

Clouds of dislodged wool were now blowing through the camp, and from the soles of their feet Mr Heckmondwike and Slake could feel a thunder that was all too familiar.

Over the horizon came the Giant Lamb. Its fleece was white as snow.

Captain Keen stood up and grabbed some of the wool as it wafted past. He handed a large tuft of it to the radar operator. "It's still affecting our radar!"

The howl of a low-flying jet announced that air cover had arrived.

"Quickly, get me contact with Crab Air," said Captain Keen.

A smaller projectile shot past them. It was heading for the Lamb, then seemed to dither. It circled and then slammed into a nearby tank.

"Pongoes calling Crab Air," Captain Keen said into the radio. "Do you read me, over?"

"Crab Air reading you lide and clear," said a crackly voice.

"Don't, repeat don't, fire any more missiles. The fur from the sheep seems to be blocking their guidance systems, do you read me? Over?"

"Rojah, Pongoes. It certainly is a hairy monster. I think I sucked a bit of its fleese into my intake. It makes the most beastly smell. I'll make another pass and use the underwing HDC. Hallo. What's that little red light for?"

A fireball sprouted silently from one of the hills behind the Giant Lamb.

"Use only the HDC," insisted Captain Keen, who had his back to the flames. "Do not use any more guided missiles. Over."

There was no reply.

"Oh dear," said the radar operator. Then the sound of the explosion hit them.

"I hope the rest of Crab Air are AOK," said Captain Keen.

A series of further explosions indicated that this was probably not the case.

"Damn," said Captain Keen. "Where's the sheep now?"

"It's run away, sir."

"Then what are my men doing?"

"Er, fighting something sir?"

"Some things by the look of it, sergeant."

Enormous sheep ticks were attacking the tanks and infantrymen. The empty ones came first because they could run faster. They were really hungry, too, and didn't seem to care if it wasn't sheep's blood they fed on. Fully fed and hideously bloated ticks waddled about behind them like corpulent gourmands looking for just one more taste of blood before embarking on the next stage of their life cycle.

The giant keds fell upon the nuclear scientists with an energy that Mr Heckmondwike found strangely heart-warming. "Look at 'em!" he said to Slake. "Reckon the Lamb's not the only thing that's increased in intelligence as well as size."

"Every parasite seems to instinctively know which is the greatest threat to its host," remarked Professor Cluttercrap. "They are targeting the scientists associated with the ultimate weapon before closing upon the regular soldiers. Do you realise what this means?"

Mr Heckmondwike and Slake shook their heads.

"The parasites are assessing the risk to their host and acting accordingly."

"Assessing risk?" said Slake.

"Precisely."

"That's summat sheep nivver do," said Mr Heckmondwike.

"That's right," agreed Slake, "that's why they need you."

"It seems the parasites have taken over the role of shepherd," said Professor Cluttercrap.

"Now hold on a minute," said Mr Heckmondwike, "ah've had enow of being compared to a bloody parasite!"

Professor Cluttercrap raised his eyebrows and pursed his lips. Then he began to laugh. "It's interesting, "he chuckled, "that only yesterday afternoon you and Slake were both epizoons."

"What?"

"Animals that live on the surface of another."

"Now, now Mr H." Slake handed him a discarded machine gun. "If you wish to fight, I suggest you squash an epizoon or two."

Mr Heckmondwike took the guns and blasted away at the oncoming parasites.

"You all right, Captain?" asked Slake.

"Yes," grimaced Captain Keen. "It's nothing really."

"Is tha wounded?"

"Not exactly. My hand's just a bit swollen, that's all."

He showed them, and they all stopped fighting. His left hand, the one that had been covered in blood, was now obviously much bigger than his right.

"Behind you!" he shouted, and they turned to fight off more parasites.

There was a terrible bleat in the distance and some tanks burst into flames. Then the Giant Lamb strode over the horizon again, still swathed in its own weather system, and walked over to the battle to look down at it.

Slake jumped up on a disabled tank and Mr Heckmondwike followed him, swatting away a giant ked. It landed on its back, waved its legs at them and slowly deflated as a pool of blood, none of it its own, slowly spread out from it.

"Doesn't look as if the militia are too worried about protecting the white coats," Slake pointed out as Mr Heckmondwike prodded another tick under the wheels of a passing tank.

"Aye! Reckon they've got enow troubles of their own."

"Git dahn!" hissed Slake as he pummelled a particularly bloated tick. Its outer skin was quite taut and it moved slowly under the weight of the blood it had eaten.

Mr Heckmondwike paused to watch and wiped his brow as he leaned on his crook.

Slake was making no progress in killing the enormous tick, which seemed to be smirking at him as it demonstrated the incompressibility of liquids to anyone who would watch or hit it.

"Look at the way the keds leave the Mithering Brethren alone!" remarked Professor Cluttercrap.

"Not now, Professor," panted Slake.

"They don't attack them at all! These creatures understand that this religious minority worships their host!"

Slake did not reply, so Mr Heckmondwike stepped over and plunged the end of his staff into Slake's tick. It was like a small dam bursting and they had to hop smartly out of the way as the crimson fluid inside swept away the outer skin and the writhing legs and mouth parts.

"What was that you were wittering about?" Slake asked the Professor.

"Look at the way the parasites don't bite the Mithering Brethren!"

"I don't know what's so special about that."

"Eh?"

"Well, would you want to bite one of 'em?"

Mr Heckmondwike pulled a face and then whacked another smaller ked high up into the air. It landed in front of a tank, which obligingly raked it with a flamethrower.

"Protect the holy host!" they heard the Mithering Brethren cry, and the Mithering Brethren fell back to regroup around the cloven hooves of the Giant Lamb.

The monster gave out a little bleat and cracks appeared in the armour-plating of the tank beneath their feet. Stunned by the sound, everyone collapsed.

Captain Keen looked grimmer than ever.

"What's tha gonna do nah?" Mr Heckmondwike shouted out to him. "Retreat?"

"Retreat? We don't know the meaning of the word." Captain Keen insisted as he fumbled with the radio with his mis-matched hands. "Signal Advance to the rear!"

"Advance to the rear!" said the sergeant.

"Advance to the rear!" echoed someone else.

He scrambled over to them and pointed with his big hand into the distance. "I need your help by going up to that farm and getting us more fuel."

"More fuel?" queried Professor Cluttercrap.

"We've hardly used any," said Slake, looking around at the stationary vehicles.

"Is this a tactic?" asked Mr Heckmondwike.

"In a manner of speaking," replied Captain Keen.

Mr Heckmondwike peered through the smoke and floating wool. "To Old Mr Macklefract?"

"That farm, there! I need you to go there now." Captain Keen thrust an army radio into Slake's arms. "But don't return until I tell you to. Understand?"

They all nodded.

"Right. Go. Now!"

They ran through the melee, grabbing jerry cans as they went, back to the V8 Mudlark, which stood outside Captain Keen's tent. Mr Heckmondwike ordered Widdershins into the back, and Professor Cluttercrap and Slake jumped into the cab before the Mudlark accelerated off the battlefield.

"We have plenty of fuel, sir," Captain Keen's sergeant quietly remarked after they'd gone.

"I know," said Captain Keen.

"And wasn't that radio the only one that can transmit but not receive?"

CHAPTER 88

Old Mr Macklefract was on the grassy sward outside the walls of Topwack Farm when they arrived, fast asleep in his bath chair, quite untroubled by the thought of parasites roaming the Wold.

"Mr Mack!" yelled Slake. "You shouldn't be out here!"

"What?" said the old man, waking with a start.

"You shouldn't be out here!"

"Who's that? Slake? Is that thee?"

"You've dropped your spectacles," said Slake. "Here … What the hell's that?"

"What? Give me ma glasses, will tha lad? Tha knaws ah can't see owt without 'em!"

"That," gulped Slake, "that thing at your feet."

Old Mr Macklefract was still fumbling with his specs. "That there? That's a stray dog. Eh, ah had to wallop it reet hard to get it to behave. It was jumping up and down all ower t'place."

"What's to do?" asked Mr Heckmondwike as he joined them.

"If there's one thing ah will not tolerate, it is disobedient sheepdogs," explained Old Mr Macklefract. At last he looped his glasses over his ears and gazed at the creature at his feet. "Oh."

"That's no dog," whispered Slake, impressed.

Old Mr Macklefract peered at the dead ked lying in a pool of blood at his feet. "What t'hell is it, then?"

Mr Heckmondwike explained what it was and what it had been trying to do. "How did tha kill it?"

"Kill it? Ah just gave it a tap or two wi' this."

"Are you trying to tell us you bludgeoned that ked to death with your ear trumpet?" Slake asked him

Mr Macklefract stared at his dented ear trumpet.

"Ee is, int ee?" said Mr Heckmondwike. "Ee doesn't knaw it but that's what ee's about."

"Blood yell," said Old Mr Macklefract.

"Perhaps they should have issued ear trumpets to the militia," Slake suggested.

"Let's get him inside," suggested Mr Heckmondwike. "And let's get us and ours inside n'all. It's dangerous out 'ere!"

They wheeled Old Mr Macklefract back into the fortifications of Topwack Farm, drove the precious Mudlark in and nearly shut the outer doors on a huge armful of jerry cans on some spindly legs. They pulled Professor Cluttercrap in roughly, making the jerry cans fly everywhere, slammed the doors and leaned against them on the inside.

"We've come here for fuel," Slake told Mr Macklefract.

"Oh aye?" Widdershins bounced around him but apparently to his approval.

"The lad's reet. T'Rural Marines are in a desperate plight. They're fighting t'monstrous Lamb, a plague of its parasites …"

"One of which you had no trouble despatching," interrupted Slake.

"And t'Mithering Brethren."

"Mithering Brethren? Ow do they fit into all this?"

"It seems they worship the Lamb," Slake explained.

Old Mr Macklefract pulled a face. "That's not reet, is it?"

"They see it as an instrument to thwart everyone," added Professor Cluttercrap.

"Who are thee?" asked Old Mr Macklefract, thrusting his ear trumpet forward, and Mr Heckmondwike introduced Professor Cluttercrap as they quickly wheeled the old man up to the house.

"T'militia are sorely pressed," he explained. "They've lost aerial cover from t'Rural Air Force. We're here on a special task."

"Oh aye?"

"Aye. They're runnin' outta fuel and as soon as we get t'all clear ont this little radio 'ere we go back and help 'em fight it out to t'finish."

They quickly filled their jerry cans and then Mrs Macklefract served up a lovely roast dinner before they settled down by the battered radio to await their instructions.

Far in the distance, they could hear the occasional crump or bleat, but the great walls of Topwack seemed as safe as ever. They still took it in turns to prowl around the perimeter, however, to check for any invading keds, ticks or religious fundamentalists.

Slake was still shaken by his experiences in the Big Nuff's roll cage, so he went to bed early, leaving Mr Heckmondwike to sit up with the Macklefracts. One by one they, too, turned in and Mr Heckmondwike knew then that he was in for a long wait.

Soon after Professor Cluttercrap relieved him at midnight, the house began to shake and something very large passed to the north, running over Old Mr Macklefract's allotment and blowing up many of his high-octane potatoes. This woke the whole household, and everyone gathered in the kitchen where Mrs Macklefract supervised the production of a midnight feast, although it felt more like a wake.

"Fritter, anyone?" Slake asked.

"What sort of fritter?" replied Mr Heckmondwike.

"Well, just fritter – we've run out of stuff to put in 'em."

"Is tha gonna sit there all night?" Old Mr Macklefract asked Mr Heckmondwike.

"Nay," sighed Mr Heckmondwike. "It's been ower twelve hours since we left 'em. Ah'm sure we oughtta 'ave heard summat before now."

"That could only have been t'Giant Lamb that woke us just now," pointed out Mrs Macklefract. "If t'militia still require our fuel they woulda followed it up 'ere."

"You know what I think?" asked Slake.

"Ah have a suspicion ah might," said Mr Heckmondwike.

"I reckon we were sent up here to save us from harm. I reckon there are no Rural Marines. Not any more. I think they've been wiped out and knew what was gonna happen."

"See if you can raise 'em ont radio," suggested Old Mr Macklefract.

Mr Heckmondwike picked up the radio, pressed the transmit button and said, "Captain Keen, do you read me? Ower?"

To nobody's surprise, there was no reply.

He tried again. "Captain Keen, do you read me? Ower?" He repeated this mantra, but between five pairs of ears – not counting those of Widdershins – and a rather dented ear trumpet they could hear nothing.

They held their meal in a relay, taking it in turns to say the same thing, but the result was always the same.

"Keep trying," said Slake as the Macklefracts went to bed for a second time that night, but Mr Heckmondwike shook his head.

"Ah reckon they're done for now, lad," he said and he got up and stretched. "Besides, t'battery's goin'."

With that he went to bed and he quickly fell into a troubled sleep in which he dreamt vividly. The Great Shepherd came to him with his fairy dogs and expressed His admiration for the way in which they had dealt with the Giant Lamb so far. He stressed the words so far, so Mr Heckmondwike asked Him how much longer his trial would last.

The Great Shepherd did not answer straight away. When He did, He said simply, "A good shepherd giveth his life for the sheep."

CHAPTER 89

Brother Guy splashed across the moor to a barn on the edge of Scar Fell
Farm. A mud-spattered Wolseley Blue Streak was parked inside, and on the
back seat was a figure, fast asleep.

"Sister Elspeth!" he said and tapped on the window.

Sister Elspeth woke up, ran her fingers through her disarranged hair
and wound the window down.

"Brother Guy!"

"Where are the others?"

"They are here, in body and mind at any rate. Look among the straw.
They tell me that thanks to the Soul Trader they have achieved fulfilment.
Now they rejoice in their new status as martyrs."

"Let me in," said Brother Guy.

Once he was safely inside, Sister Elspeth asked him how the battle had
ended.

"We successfully thwarted the militia. To be truthful, it was not so
difficult. You saw for yourself how the parasites protect the Holy Host. We
hardly had to do anything. Yet while we were attacking the militia, the Soul
Trader was stalking us! He picked off our last remaining souls in the thick of
the battle!"

"Are you and I the only ones with our souls intact?"

"So it would seem."

"What are we to do?"

"We must get the souls of these martyrs back for them."

"Yes, but how? Somehow I don't think they're going to be too happy
about that."

"Happy?" snapped Brother Guy. "What has happiness got to do with it?"

"They won't be martyrs any more. We will rob them of the fulfilment
they've sought for so long. Once they've experienced its joys, they will feel
its loss more keenly."

Brother Guy looked at Sister Elspeth suspiciously. "You seem to know
an awful lot about it."

"Of course. Think of all the successful thwartings I've been a party to."

"Are you quite sure you have never been fulfilled yourself?"

Sister Elspeth's eyes glistened in the darkness. "I rejoice in my unfulfilled state," she said.

Brother Guy swallowed hard. "Then it is just you and me. Together we must thwart the Soul Trader."

"But how?"

"That's what I wanted to talk to you about."

Sister Elspeth sighed. "We've tried everything we can think of," she said.

"There must be a way!" Brother Guy wound down the window. "Hey! You lot! You must have some ideas about how to thwart the Soul Trader, especially as you delivered your own souls into his hands."

The dispossessed ex-members of the Mithering Brethren exchanged glances.

"You know what, Brother Guy?" said Brother Eric. "You should try fulfilment some time."

"Yeah," said Sister Mandy, "why don't you offer it to Sister Elspeth!" and they all laughed.

Brother Guy did not understand the joke, but he sensed it was at his expense. He began to wind the window up again.

"Hey!" said Brother Eric, before Brother Guy had finished, "you want to know something about Hob and the Giant Lamb? Once I'd pledged my soul to him, he told me a few things. He told me that he was the one who caused the Giant Lamb."

"And you believed him?" replied Brother Guy.

"Of course! Why would he lie?"

"Why would anyone?"

"Hob doesn't lie because he doesn't need to. The Giant Lamb is nothing to do with the Almighty. It is not the Lamb of God. It's an aberration created indirectly by Hob. Remember Billy Brockhouse? It all started with him. Hob covets a very valuable soul. He can only get it by swapping it for that of a weresheep, and a weresheep can only be created by the Giant Lamb."

Brother Guy considered this for a moment.

"You've got to admit," said Sister Elspeth, "that it all fits."

"I admit nothing," said Brother Guy. "They're just jealous because you and I still have our souls!"

"But some of us still have our own souls, too!" said Brother Eric. "That's how it works! Hob may have Soul Rites to them but we've still got them so they can be enriched by the benefits of fulfilment."

"He says it does things to us," explained Sister Mandy, "makes us more desirable!" and she gave a lecherous laugh.

"Sounds almost too good to be true," murmured Sister Elspeth.

"Believe it, soul sister!" said Sister Mandy, and all the dispossessed souls gathered around the Blue Streak and began to rock it.

Brother Guy quickly wound up the window as Sister Elspeth checked all the locks on the doors, but the car was rocking so fiercely she fell on top of Brother Guy. The others all cheered and rocked the car even harder so that they rolled around on the back seat in a tangled confusion of arms and legs.

But their tormentors were weary, something they felt more keenly now that they had sensed fulfilment, and they stopped rocking the car and shuffled off to sit down in the hay.

"I tried to tell you," said Sister Elspeth, as she pushed Brother Guy off. "They're happier being martyrs."

Brother Guy reluctantly disentangled himself from her and slid over into the front seat.

"I have an idea," he said. He fired up the Blue Streak and drove off into the mist.

CHAPTER 90

The Privy Council was sitting again when Mrs Osmotherly and Gloria arrived outside the Privy Chamber. Constable Arkthwaite was doing some deep breathing exercises in the foyer and just completing counting to ten. Then he paused and began counting to ten again.

After three, Gloria asked him, "Are you all right?"

"Ten!" he yelled. "No ah am not awreet. The militia have disa-bloody-peared, the bloody Wold Service is off the air and all the bloody phone bloody lines are bloody well down between here and piggin' Bedlam! And them in there are ... are ... well, tha knaws 'em as well ah do."

"We need to know what happened out there," said Mrs Osmotherly, "although in this fog it'll be difficult to see anything."

"It'll be risky. We could end up like t'militia."

"I doubt it," said Mrs Osmotherly. "Gloria can see if any harbingers are lingering around you, Constable Arkthwaite, and we are happy to tell you that there aren't any, aren't we, Gloria? Gloria? What are you looking at me like that for?"

"Hmm? Oh, it's just that your cat has followed us in here."

They turned around and saw an old grey cat looking around the foyer a little blearily. Despite the passing of the years, his yellow eyes remained unfaded. Most of the time they had been shut. He didn't hurry his tour of inspection, preferring to conserve his energy, although he held his tail out stiffly, as if rigor mortis had already claimed it. From beyond the polished oak doors of the Privy Council Chamber came the sound of a heated debate. Apparently coming to some sort of conclusion, Indoors Food sat down and looked at Mrs Osmotherly, pointedly.

"What's he doing here?" wondered Mrs Osmotherly.

Indoors gazed at the ceiling.

"I don't know," said Gloria.

"More to the point, how did he get here?"

"Was he asleep on the back seat of your car?"

"If tha asks me," said Constable Arkthwaite, "that awd cat knaws summat."

CHAPTER 91

"So," said Mrs Osmotherly, carrying her old cat back to her car, "we muster as many vehicles as we can and form a chain into the mist, stopping only when the nearest vehicle is just about to be lost from view. Then we can find out for certain what happened to the militia."

"Eck as owt!" declared Constable Arkthwaite. "Ah knaw just t'folk who'll wanna be part of it! We'll try it from t'East Gate. Drivers can carry observers, too."

"We need to penetrate as far into the mist as we can," said Mrs Osmotherly.

"We'll keep watch from t' town walls 'n' all. And if owt happens we can allus sound our horns!" and a much happier Constable Arkthwaite jumped into his big black police Wolseley and drove off to organise the expedition.

"Of course," Mrs Osmotherly said to Gloria, "we already have a pretty good idea of what's happened out there."

She nodded. "I'll check the volunteers for harbingers as they venture outside."

"And then I'll take you with me to the head of this chain," insisted Mrs Osmotherly. "I need to know if a harbinger pops up or a banshee starts to wail."

"Oh, I'll tell you if I see one all right, Mrs Osmotherly."

"Gloria, I particularly need to know if you see one around me."

"I think most people would rather not know."

"Gloria, I don't like surprises. Especially if they're that sort."

They met again at the East Gate. Word had spread quickly across Wormton, and volunteers filled the side streets with Wolseleys, Jowetts and Armstrong-Siddeleys.

Mrs Osmotherly looked at them approvingly. "What a splendid sight!" she said to Mr Heptonstall, who was an early arrival with his wrecker truck.

"Aye."

"Of course, if anyone has any problems you can tow them back with your truck. And if we're attacked you can switch on your flashing lights and sound those great big air horns."

"Aye. Ah could."

"Now look 'ere, Mr Heptonstall," said Constable Arkthwaite, "ah don't mean to cast nasturtiums."

"Eh?"

"But we're here to do a job of work and not let ourselves get distracted by all that abandoned ordnance out there."

"Ordnance? Aye. Er, ah mean nay, Constable Arkthwaite."

"If we do this reet, we can mither about its retrieval another day."

"Aye Constable Arkthwaite. O' course."

"Do you think it's safe for us to go outside?" asked Gloria.

"More to the point," replied Mrs Osmotherly, "do you?"

Gloria looked around the Woldspeople and nodded.

First in line was Old Mr Irthlingcock in his still quite new Wolseley 18/85.

"Tha can't let him go out there!" Constable Arkthwaite whispered to Mrs Osmotherly. "Ee's far too old!"

"Gloria assures me he still has sufficient time left," the wise woman hissed back.

"There's nay need to whisper," said Mr Heptonstall, "ee's as deaf as a post."

"Ah yerd that! Pardon? Ah said, ah want to do ma bit, tha knaws, only ah need to stay close to Wormton in case I need to be excused."

"Excused?" asked Mr Heptonstall.

"Of course," snapped Mrs Irthlingcock from the passenger seat. And then she mouthed, "In case he needs to go to the bathroom," at them.

"Bathroom?" echoed Mr Heptonstall.

"It's his old trouble," explained Gloria.

"His other old trouble," mouthed his wife, forgetting her deaf husband could lip-read.

"An obsessive desire for cleanliness?" asked Mr Heptonstall, who had never been good at euphemisms.

"Mr Irthlingcock?" said Mrs Osmotherly. "Would you kindly drive off into the mist until we can't see you?"

"Ow am ah to knaw that? And stop mumblin' when tha's speakin' to me!"

"Ee's as blind as a bat and as deaf as post," said Mr Heptonstall, not without affection, for Old Mr Irthlingcock was one of his best customers, not only for new Wolseleys but also at his body repair shop.

"Well, just drive until you can't see Wormton in your rearview mirror."

"Ee might just as well stay put, then," said Mr Heptonstall, completely without malice.

"Give him a chance," said Gloria.

So Old Mr Irthlingcock fired up his Wolseley, made a good choice of gear and slowly drove off into the mist as the others watched in rapt silence from the East Gate. And, after he'd been engulfed by it completely and a few grotesquely large tufts of wool had rolled across the moor, Constable Arkthwaite said, "Reckon ah ought to go and fetch him?"

The problem was that the dark bulk of Wormton could be detected through the mist long after the tail lights of the light grey Wolseley 18/85 had disappeared. Constable Arkthwaite instructed Old Mr Irthlingcock to park within easy sight of Wormton and then drove back to the East Gate.

"Ah told 'im to flash his lights and beep 'is 'orn when ee sees the car in front disappear into the mist," he said. "Okay, Mr and Mrs Melliver, tha's next."

"This is going to take ages," said Gloria. "I wish Slake and Mr Heckmondwike were here."

"So do I, Gloria, but keep a lookout for gnomes as they leave."

CHAPTER 92

Mrs Osmotherly and Gloria alighted from their car and surveyed the moor. The cloud base was low, so low Gloria could almost touch it.

"The battlefield must be around here somewhere," said Mrs Osmotherly.

"All the vantage points are up in the cloud," Gloria observed. "The valley looks like a roomful of smoke."

Mrs Osmotherly sniffed. "There *is* a noticeable smell of burning. Come on. There's a break int the cloud over there. Let's take a look."

But Gloria didn't want to look for dead militia.

Mrs Osmotherly briskly quartered the moor with Constable Arkthwaite, working her way towards a brighter patch of green in the distance.

The foggy, misty smoke appeared to be slowly lifting. Soon the full devastation of the militia's last stand would be revealed.

Gloria perched on an upturned Land Rover. She envied Mrs Osmotherly for her detachment. She had never considered herself an agoraphobic but she missed the friendly confines of the old town. She liked the narrow protective streets and the nadgery little corners that could suddenly open up into a little courtyard or garden.

She looked back towards Wormton and saw the long line of parked cars stretching back to the unseen town. Some of the townsfolk had got out of their cars and were exploring the moors on either side. A disabled tank attracted a small group of them. Others were walking back and forth between the stationary vehicles to pass news down the line or were speaking on their twoways.

Whenever she tried Slake's number these days there was no answer.

"Come on, Gloria," she told herself, "maximise the positive. At least you can't see any harbinger gnomes out here."

She didn't voice the consequent thought that they'd already had rich pickings.

In places, the discarded wool from the Giant Lamb softened the outlines of the broken tanks and hid the remains of crashed helicopters as the mist lifted. Weather wise, the day was steadily brightening, but improved visibility only made the outlook grimmer.

A figure caught her eye not so far away, almost within hailing distance. It hopped among the blood-filled hoofprints and discarded machinery of the militia. It was very black and she didn't like the way its head was hooded. Its knees seemed to be hinged wrongly, too, and there was something vaguely disquieting about the way its coat flapped.

She looked around for Mrs Osmotherly or Constable Arkthwaite, but they had wandered off. On the road below she could still see the line of cars, but some of them had turned off their headlamps and the people must have ventured further into the moors than she could see. It was suddenly very quiet.

She peered again at the figures in the distance. They couldn't be far from where she'd last seen Mrs Osmotherly. The idea that these Bible-black figures might be Mithering Brethren, gleefully jumping around the mortal remains of the brave militia, stirred up hateful emotions within her.

Suddenly, as her emotions sharpened her senses, she realised what she was looking at. These prancing figures were not Mithering Brethren or Mrs Osmotherly or Constable Arkthwaite. They were not the familiar shapes of anyone from Wormton. They were not human at all, but carrion crows grown grotesquely huge from the potent cocktail of growth-enhancing drugs that was still contained within the blood and bodies of the Giant Lamb's parasites.

Nervously, she looked around for someone to warn, but she seemed entirely alone. Even Mr Heptonstall's truck was no longer visible, obscured by the mist or having driven off with a muffled engine.

"Think rationally, Gloria," she told herself as she felt the panic rising and her throat tightening. "Mrs Osmotherly and Constable Arkthwaite are not far away. They know the risks and certainties of life in the Wold better than anyone. All I have to do is wait here and they will find me."

Behind her, on the moors, something startled the big crows. As she span around to face it, the bonnet of a Land Rover sprang up although she'd felt no wind.

"Who's there?" she called.

Something in the wreckage moved. It looked like a combination of charred wiring harness and plastic strip that the wind had caught, but then, to her horror, it stood up against the stiff breeze and looked at her.

Gloria had to work hard to consciously re-arrange what she saw until it became credible, just as she had done with the giant crows. Eventually, she realised she must be looking at a gigantic variety of sheep parasite. Although she was worried there might be more around, she dared not to take her eyes off it. For some time it didn't move either. It just made little adjustments to its gangling legs as if getting ready to spring. They stood there, eyes locked together.

Calmly, she realised that the crows had all gone, flown away as soon as the creature had revealed itself.

A little less calmly she realised that crows that stood as tall as a man did not fear anything without reason.

She managed to lift a leaden foot and placed it gently behind the other, hoping the creature wouldn't realise what she was doing. She wondered how fast it could run. She had a vague idea that an ordinary sized sheep tick could leap on and off a passing sheep as if it were a bus, in which case she didn't rate her chances in a fifty-metre dash.

But this one seemed gorged on blood already. Maybe it wasn't hungry.

Or maybe it knew the recent feast was over and it was already on the lookout for its next meal.

She wondered what might kill it and what there was close to hand. She glanced slowly from side to side, first to make sure there weren't any more of the hideous creatures nearby and then to see if there were any weapons. There wasn't anything obvious.

Then there was a twitch of the sheep tick's front legs and suddenly Gloria was running. She heard something rattle over some metallic wreckage and dodged around a ruined tank, desperately trying to confuse it. When she looked back to see if it was following there was no sign of it.

She paused but then it came rattling over the top of the tank and leapt into the air. She screamed and ran through a gap between some abandoned trucks to weave a course through the battlefield, all the time trying desperately not to step into the red pools that stood in the wheel ruts and hoofprints.

She leapt onto a pile of disinterred coal, thrown up by one of the deeper hoofprints, and darted behind a troop carrier, only to discover it was a dead end. An upturned tank blocked the way between two more abandoned trucks. Turning around, she saw to her increasing horror that behind the wrecked troop carrier was another tick. This one was obviously fully fed. It was slothful and bloated, yet still viewed her with the interest of a gory gourmand with a very sharp set of mouth parts.

She was utterly hypnotised by its hideousness, as if she was a rabbit caught in its headlamps. The bloated tick ambled gracelessly forward with all the grace of an animated potato, but then something thudded into it. The parasite registered surprise and then the glint in its little eyes faded and it sagged to one side. Mr Heckmondwike climbed arthritically over a truck and thrust the end of his sheep crook into the sheep tick, bursting its hoard like a water balloon.

She shrieked as the other tick leapt over a truck, apparently relishing the prospect of an amazing two-for-one opportunity.

Gloria frantically looked at Mr Heckmondwike but he remained immobile. The giant sheep tick launched itself from a pile of discarded ammunition boxes, Slake popped up in front of her like a friendlier and less intimidating version of Thor, brandishing not a hammer but an enormous adjustable spanner. He looked back to grin raffishly at her, then swung the shiny adjustable spanner in a great arc towards the tick. And missed.

The tick hadn't even ducked. It just continued to accelerate towards her with a curiously desiccated alacrity.

"Tha missed, tha daft morpeth!" bellowed Mr Heckmondwike, and Slake span around and desperately slammed the spanner down next to where the tick was, but he trapped the lower segment of one of its trailing legs, which snapped off with a dry click. The giant sheep tick carried on towards her but veered off to the left slightly because, without its bamboo-like leg that Slake was now trying to pick up, it was underpowered on one side.

Gloria watched in fascination as the tick tried to adjust for its lost limb and its new status as a pentaped.

"If tha's still seeing double, close one eye!" shouted Mr Heckmondwike.

Slake swung wildly again.

"Not that one!" cried Mr Heckmondwike. "T'other un!"

The ked rolled its compound eyes and shifted itself back on course, its short, spindly legs clicking on some aluminium panelling lying on the ground.

Mr Heckmondwike clambered closer.

Slake swung again, even more wildly.

"Not me! That thing!"

Mr Heckmondwike leapt out of the way as Slake lashed out.

"Sorry!"

Just as the parasite's front legs reached up to embrace her and its mouth opened up, Slake hit the tick squarely. Up and away it flew, leaving its limbs behind it.

"Phew!" said Slake. "Got him in the end! Or was it smack in the middle?"

Gloria hurled herself at him, burrowing into his arms as if they were the walls of Wormton.

"My hero!" she cried.

"There, there," he said, a little awkwardly.

"Ee's 'ad a bit of a knock or two," explained Mr Heckmondwike.

"Well?" Slake asked Mr Heckmondwike. "*Was* it the end or the middle?"

"Middle."

Gloria noticed how unfocussed Slake's eyes were. "Are you all right?"

"I'm feeling better all the time."

She smiled at him and then kissed him hard. For some time, the only sounds were the delicate little clicks and tutts of their mouths.

When at last they parted, Slake looked even less aware than before. Mr Heckmondwike looked a little embarrassed.

But then Slake focussed on Gloria's upturned face and the light came back into his eyes. "I'm cured!" he exclaimed. "It's a miracle!"

"Come on then," said Mr Heckmondwike. "Let's get out of here!"

"We must find Mrs Osmotherly," said Gloria.

"It's awreet, she's ower there."

Not far away was a large shell crater, and as they passed it they heard voices. Looking inside they saw Widdershins showing Mrs Osmotherly and Professor Cluttercrap the body of an officer of the Rural Marines. He was just skin and bone, but it was obvious that one of his hands was as broad as his back.

Before the others could fully register what they were seeing, there was a hideous bleat from somewhere down in the valley. The Giant Lamb was approaching with the careless nonchalance of a monster that knows it doesn't have to hurry.

"Run away!" cried Slake.

"Time to get a shake on!" yelled Mr Heckmondwike. "Come on! Move!"

CHAPTER 93

Hob spotted the familiar sight of a gleaming Blue Streak parked beside the road. He pulled up, killed the ignition, parked *Nosferatu* and strode up to the driver. "Don't I know you?" he asked him.

"We've not met before," said Brother Guy, "but I've heard a lot about you."

"And I you. You're the leader of the martyrs, aren't you?"

Brother Guy bit his lip. "I am the spiritual adviser to the local cell of the Mithering Brethren."

"Same difference," said Hob. "A lot of folk have been martyred over this car, y' know."

"I do know. You granted them fulfilment and damned them for ever."

"I indulged the Virgin Mandy a little more than that. Sorry. I really must stop calling her that."

"I know what you're up to. You're behind the creation of the Giant Lamb. You want the soul of a weresheep, don't you?"

"No thanks." Hob took off his rucksack and began to rummage in it. "I've already got one, you see. Would you like to see it? It is – ah – very nice."

"You already have its soul?"

"Mm-hm."

"What about the other soul?" demanded Brother Guy, rallying quite magnificently under the circumstances. "The one you really want?"

"What other soul?"

"The one you want to swap the weresheep for."

"So. What about it?"

"What if I were to tell you that I can get it for you?"

"Oh, good grief," said Hob. "That's ridiculous. I already know who has it. He'll never give it to you, and you don't have the power to take it from him. It is also clear to me that you wish to thwart me in the mistaken belief that this will redeem my own benighted soul and so release your erstwhile comrades from their spiritual bondage."

"So," said Brother Guy, "you are a mind reader."

"Not really," replied Hob, "more of a reader of people's hearts. My card."

"There's nothing on it," said Brother Guy.

"Modesty forbids it," said Hob.

Some impulse made Brother Guy turn it over. "And no address either."

"I am never at home," explained the Soul Trader.

And Brother Guy turned over the card a second time and read out what was now printed there, where once it had been quite blank. " 'Nicholas Eldritch Hob. Soul Trader and Holder Of Soul Rites.' And somebody has scribbled here in crayon, 'Reader of people's hearts.' "

"Have they?" Hob asked, nonchalantly. "Oh yeah. Must be true then."

"Once we have redeemed your soul, Hob, then all the other souls for whom you hold Soul Rites will be redeemed as well!"

"Redeeming souls means a great deal to you, doesn't it, Brother Guy?"

Brother Guy snorted.

"Tell me. What do you do with your souls when you save them?"

"We write them down in this book."

Hob leafed through it. "Your soul savings book?"

"Yes."

"How very quaint. So how do you control these souls?"

"We don't. We simply redeem them through our good works."

"And I trade for outright possession through my, ahem, good works," said Hob and he patted the bonnet of the much modified Slakespeed and Hobtune Wolseley Blue Streak. "Would you like to see my souls?"

Before he could stop himself, Brother Guy nodded. For all his years of saving souls, he had never actually seen one. He shuffled his feet and wondered if he'd perhaps missed something.

"You want to see my souls, don't you? How many redeemers ever have, I wonder? Of course, this sort of insight into men's souls could never come for free."

"I never thought it would," replied Brother Guy, with an attempt at bravado.

"It would show such dedication to your calling," went on Hob. "You might be the first, the first ever! Think what that would do to aid you in your work! It would not be a selfish act to fulfil your own dreams of martyrdom for your cause. It would be an entirely altruistic swap in the full knowledge that by losing your own soul you would be able to see those of others. This would go beyond martyrdom. You could become a saint!"

"We were excommunicated," Brother Guy replied.

Hob smiled. "A temporary setback."

"Greater love hath no man than this," murmured Brother Guy.

"Than he lays down his soul," said Hob, "to a fiend."

He opened his sack of souls and Brother Guy peered in and saw his own soul dancing into it.

Hob shut it again.

"Sister Elspeth," he said. "Come, oh duplicitous female, and be fulfilled."

And Sister Elspeth smiled lasciviously as they withdrew into the back seat of the Wolseley Blue Streak, leaving a perplexed Brother Guy standing by the road.

CHAPTER 94

"By the ball pein hammer of St Bendix!" Slake declared as he climbed out of the Mudlark. "That was close!"

"Not as close for us as it were for them," said Mr Heckmondwike, looking back at the two wise women in Mrs Osmotherly's Wolseley Hornet.

"I never want to go through that again." Mrs Osmotherly was saying as Slake and Mr Heckmondwike drew alongside. She had barely recovered her powers of speech.

Gloria just nodded vigorously, although it might have been someone motoring across her grave.

Constable Sopp and Constable Blenk were also shattered. Slamming shut the great gates was difficult at the best of times, but with the mismatched eyes of the Giant Lamb upon them they had broken all records.

Even the normally relaxed Indoors looked a little rattled.

"Did you see the sign?" asked Gloria, trying to prise her fingers off the wood veneer dashboard.

"What sign?"

"The Bloody Great Sheep sign."

"No? We blew it up, remember?"

"It's back again!"

"Are you sure?"

"Positive!"

The Giant Lamb peered in on them from over the gatehouse, as if they inhabited a beautifully detailed model village, and a death-or-glory ked leapt off it and splattered in a half-fed red splash on the cobbles inside.

The Giant Lamb wandered idly around the town walls, peering inside. Here and there, trees grew taller than the walls and the Giant Lamb nibbled ruminatively upon their foliage, uprooting the tastiest ones and flinging root debris and masonry over the roofs of the cowering houses.

As it passed the East Gate again, its personal weather system brought a cloud over Wormton and someone shouted, "Don't let it in!" to which another voice yelled "Tha daft morpeth! Do ah look like ah'm gonna let it in?"

The Constables peered at it through the glazed arrow-slits of the guard-room in the East Gatehouse.

"What were you doing out there on the battlefield?" Slake demanded of Gloria.

"We had to see if my prediction was correct," she replied. "I saw that all the Rural Marines were surrounded by harbingers, which suggested only one thing. And it seems to be true. There are no survivors."

"I might just as well ask you the same," said Mrs Osmotherly.

"We were returnin' from Topwack Farm," explained Mr Heckmondwike.

"What were you doing there?"

"Waiting for word from the militia," replied Slake.

"Why?"

"Well, we caught the Lamb."

"Really?"

"Eck as like as 'appen as we did."

Slake laughed. "We got onto its back. Then the militia started shooting at it, and Mr Heckmondwike and I both fell off, separately and in our own ways."

"It must have been awful," said Gloria.

"Well, Mr Heckmondwike floated back to earth on an enormous tuft of wool and I eventually came away with what was left of the Big Nuff. That's a big tractor we found. We met up with the militia, and Professor Cluttercrap and were with them when they attacked the Giant Lamb." He frowned. "Or, rather, the Giant Lamb attacked us. Anyway, the Mithering Brethren were alongside the monster, fighting the militia, and there were giant keds and ticks everywhere.

"Then a strange thing happened. Captain Keen asked us to go and get some more fuel from Old Mr Macklefract over at Topwack. He said not to come back until we'd received express instructions to do so. So we hightailed it out of there, filled up loads of jerry cans and settled down to wait for his signal."

"He saved your lives," said Gloria.

"Yes."

"We must take that sign down," said Mrs Osmotherly.

"What sign?"

"The Bloody Great Sheep sign."

Slake peered at it through the gatehouse arrow-slits. "It's a bit wonky."

"We've blown it up once already."

"How likely is it that it'll step over the walls?" Slake asked Mr Heckmondwike as the sound of hoofbeats thundered outside.

"Ah'd say it were only a matter o' time," the shepherd replied as dust floated down from the ceiling.

"That's something we may not have much of," warned Professor Cluttercrap.

"Appen?"

"Yes. The logarithmically enhanced ovine biology of the monster could become unstable at any moment."

"What's he saying?" Mr Heckmondwike asked Slake.

"The Giant Lamb could go critical," explained Professor Cluttercrap.

Mr Heckmondwike shook his head, but Slake had a flash of inspiration.

"Are you failing to explain to us that this animal is likely to explode?" he asked Professor Cluttercrap.

"No," said the Professor.

"Oh, thank goodness for that."

"Rather, it would appear that I have succeeded in my attempt and that you have, er, caught my drift."

"Oh, bloody hell!"

"Explodin' sheep!" muttered Mr Heckmondwike. "That's all we need!"

Mrs Osmotherly paced up and down inside the guard house. "We never really established the link with the Soul Trader. And the professor here is convinced there's some sort of x-factor that we've missed."

"How big would you say the creature is?" Professor Cluttercrap asked Mr Heckmondwike.

Mr Heckmondwike went to another cobwebby window to consider the issue and then said, "About three hunnerd metres high by five hunnerd long."

"Any idea what it must weigh?"

Mr Heckmondwike hazarded a guess at about eleven thousand tons.

Professor Cluttercrap let this sink in for a moment. "What we are dealing with here goes beyond the realms of biology," he told them. "The Giant Lamb grew at a greatly accelerated rate. Indeed, it is still growing. In my view, that rate is sustainable only in the short term. Soon, the Giant Lamb will become unstable."

"An eleven thousand mutton-ton bomb," said Slake.

"Potentially," said Professor Cluttercrap.

"How do you work that out?" asked Slake.

"It's a similar principle to the surface area to volume ratio. The monster is fast approaching its critical mass."

"Look out!" cried Constable Blenk. "It's smoking!"

"That's just its breath," said Professor Cluttercrap. "I think."

"Ow does tha knaw it's gonna explode?" Mr Heckmondwike wanted to know.

"Well, I don't."

"So it might not."

"I think it's more likely to implode, which is possibly worse. You know. Like a red dwarf," but one look at their faces told Professor Cluttercrap that he'd lost them completely.

"Ow big a risk?"

"It's difficult to say."

"Well, try harder, lad."

"Oh, I don't know, say something of the order of one in a hundred thousand, something like that."

"Sounds quite safe to me," said Slake, brightly.

"Aye but tha's a habitual risk-taker, lad. How many times has tha met tha guardian angel?"

"Not once since I fell off the monster!"

"True enow."

"Mrs Osmotherly?" asked Gloria. "If you knew then what you know now about the road signs predicting the coming of the Giant Lamb, what would you have done?"

"Well, I would have been able to predict the arrival of the Giant Lamb. I got that completely wrong. And then I would have stopped driving around in my car."

"But because, thanks to Slake, you know that the motorscope is interactive, you could do something about it."

Mrs Osmotherly's eyes were as round as hubcaps. "Ye-es." She looked at Gloria, then at Slake. "Yes."

She noticed her cat. He sat on the doormat, willing her on.

"Yes! Yes, yes, yes, yes, yes, yes, yes! That's what I would have done. And that's what I should be doing now! Oh thank you, Gloria, thank you!" and she gave her a big hug and then the two women held hands, leaned back and danced in a circle.

The others watched unsure whether to feel happy for them or sad for them, now that they seemed to have lost their reason entirely.

"No stupid questions, just stupid answers!" laughed Mrs Osmotherly. "The motorscope is interactive!"

Gloria whooped and hummed a little bit of Disco Tex and the Sexolettes. "Do do do, do do do? D-d-d-d do, d-do! Do, do!"

"It gave warning of the Giant Lamb," said Mrs Osmotherly, "and now we can use it to get rid of it!"

"Yeah, yeah, yeah, yeah, yeah!" sang Gloria.

Then she stopped.

None of the others were joining in.

Slake pulled a face.

Mr Heckmondwike scratched his head.

Constables Sopp and Blenk gazed at the ceiling.

Professor Cluttercrap had been turned to stone and looked particularly puzzled.

"The only time we know of," Mrs Osmotherly told them very slowly, "when anyone influenced the motorscope was when the Giant Lamb was created."

"The motorscope is interactive," explained Gloria, "which means we can influence future events with it."

Wise woman and clever girl fidgeted with an excitement neither of them wished to let out prematurely.

"If we can recreate the conditions in which the Giant Lamb was called into being," said Gloria, slowly, "maybe we can reverse the process."

"Brilliant!" cried Mrs Osmotherly. "All we have to do is identify the portents and subtly re-arrange the traffic into … into …"

"Impotence? Importance?"

"We'll worry about the words later."

Indoors regarded them sadly. Clearly they'd been overworking. Sloth may be a sin, but it is just the philistine's view of meditation. He nodded respectfully at Widdershins, who nearly wagged their tails at him, and wandered outside. Everyone else followed him but they there wasn't room for them to stretch out on the back seat of Mrs Osmotherly's car, so they stood around in groups talking loudly.

"The conditions for replicating the situation will soon be ideal," exclaimed Mrs Osmotherly, "as Dark Time is approaching!"

"Erratics and Occasionals allowing," everyone added automatically.

"So, we recreate the motorscope and run the traffic movements backwards!"

"So what do we need?" asked Gloria, clapping her hands. "Wolseleys?"

"Yes," replied Mrs Osmotherly. "There were plenty of those around at the time."

"Armstrong-Siddeleys?"

"Yes"

"Jowetts?"

"Of course! Ah, you have learnt your lessons well!"

"Anything else?"

"We are looking for something a little more out of the ordinary. First of all, there was *Simurg*."

Slake grinned at her. "At your disposal, madam!"

"Then there was my 2CV."

A cloud passed over their burgeoning euphoria.

"Your souped-up 2CV?" echoed Slake.

"Yes. I'm afraid so. Unfortunately, I had it destroyed by Bessie Dooker."

"No!" said Slake. "Really?"

"I should have realised what was going on. If your lucky star fails you, you don't look up at the night sky and say, 'That'll have to go,' do you?"

Slake scratched his chin and said, "Hmm."

"It's going to be difficult to find another one," said Gloria.

"But not impossible! Slake? You don't think you could build me a replica, do you?"

"I could. When do you need it by?"

"By Dark Time."

Slake pulled another face, this time a different one. "I reckon I can do it," he said.

"Good lad. Just make me one, exactly as the same as the old one. Don't worry about the cost. Our future depends upon it."

"Put that way," said Slake, "I'm sure I can rustle another one up from somewhere."

"I also seem to recall a Dodge Demon on the Mithering road and then there was a Hillman Imp!"

"There was a Demon in Mithering advertised in *The Piston Wheel* this week," said Slake. "And I know for a fact that a very fast Imp has been for sale in Bedlam for ages."

"Good," said Mrs Osmotherly. "Just this once, the faster the Imp, the better."

"But how do we get it all together before the next Dark Time?" asked Gloria.

Slake grinned. "I've got just the thing for that!" and he jumped into his V8 Mudlark and roared off.

Pa Coppitt and Percy sauntered by on a tram, oozing curiosity. They were giving the newly restored streetcar named *Craving* a trial. and pulled up a short distance away, struggled to feign a lack of interest, and loitered just within earshot.

"Move along there," said Constable Blenk, as the Giant Lamb peered in on them again, "there's nowt to see."

The monster obeyed, but Pa Coppitt and his boy Percy did not.

"Hasn't tha got passengers to take care of?" Constable Sopp asked them, a little snappily.

"Nay, Constable Sopp," Pa Coppitt replied. "There's nay demand."

"Tha's bin creeping around town like that for weeks," said Constable Blenk. "Hasn't tha got work to do?"

"All done," Percy told him insolently.

"Ah find that very hard to believe," Constable Sopp told them.

"Aye," agreed Constable Blenk. "Appen the devil finds work for idle hands," but as they were not causing an obstruction there was nothing he could do.

Shortly afterwards, the mayoral Armstrong-Siddeley hove into view with Mr Grandlythorpe sawing away at the wheel, and Mayor Naseby stepped out of it. "Good artnoon," he said.

"Good afternoon, Your Indulgence," said Mrs Osmotherly. "What brings you here?"

Mayor Naseby glanced at the hissing tram behind him that was being polished to within an inch of its life. "Ah need to knaw what's goin' on. Where are t'militia?"

Mrs Osmotherly sighed. "There's no easy way to tell you this, Your Indulgence, but the militia has been wiped out."

"Eh? All of 'em?"

"I'm afraid so."

Mayor Naseby slowly took this in. "So this is how t'Wold ends, not with a bang but a bleat!"

But just then, the sound of a barely silenced motorbike echoed off the ancient walls of Wormton. Its tone rose and fell as it travelled across town and the sound carried before it, down the twisting streets and in all directions, so that as the sound drew nearer they couldn't tell from which street the bike would emerge. Then from the least likely direction burst a distinctive motorcycle with Slake hanging onto its wide handlebars.

He pulled up in front of the East Gate and killed the engine but kept his helmet on.

"Wow!" said Mr Heptonstall. "What's that?"

"It's a Triumph twin in a Wolseley Woldsman frame," Slake explained. "They're all the rage these days. With this thing, I can scramble over the moors to Bedlam and back. Then I can take off the front wheel, stick in the boot of the Demon or Imp and bring it back."

"What!" cried Gloria. "Now?"

"It seems like a good idea."

"What's goin' on?" asked Mayor Naseby.

"You can't just ride out there," Gloria told Slake, "elude the Giant Lamb, race over to Bedlam, dismantle your motorbike, race back in a Hillman Imp, reassemble your motorbike, evade the monster a second time, cheat death and the Soul Trader to reach Mithering, find a Dodge Demon, stuff your bike in the back of that and return here to re-create another souped-up 2CV before joining the rest of us in driving around until we get the right road conjunction to destroy the Giant Lamb finally disappears!"

"Can't I?"

"No."

"Oh." Slake did a dashing thing with his eyebrows that frankly took her breath away, and said, "It's a long shot but it might just work."

She hit him ineffectually on his chest. "You'll need a diversion to get past the monster!"

"Maybe ah could make a suggestion." Pa Coppitt had sidled up to them "If tha needs a diversion, look nay further than us." He put an arm around his son. "We've got a score to settle with that lamb, haven't we, Percy?"

"We certainly have, Dad!"

"If tha waits here, we'll go and get *Jane*, the Outlands engine."

"What?" cried Slake. "Won't it take ages to get steam up?"

"Nay, it's already up, lad!"

"D'you mean to say you've been keeping *Jane* in steam all this time?"

"Aye."

"We're so bored!" added Percy, with feeling.

"And Be Prepared is our motto!"

"Dob, dob, dob!" added Percy helpfully.

"I thought the tram's motto was *Negotium Perabulans in Tenebris*," put in Mrs Osmotherly.

Professor Cluttercrap frowned. " 'The pestilence that creepeth in darkness'? Who would choose that motto?"

Everyone wondered about this for a moment, and then Pa Coppitt said, "Well, tha can have two mottoes, can't tha?"

CHAPTER 95

Pa Coppitt and Percy readied *Jane* and the largest pair of Outland carriages, and Old Wormtonians with scores to settle against the Giant Lamb took their seats. Watches were synchronised over the two-ways and everyone settled down to wait for the monster to reappear.

It wasn't long before it obliged, trotting around the puny town walls and wearing an interested expression that was not so much that of a sheep but of a cat prowling around a bird's nest.

At Constable Arkthwaite's signal, *Jane* eased into position so that the water-powered doors in Wormton's walls opened up and, with a cheer, Pa Coppitt drove the old engine out into the Wold for the first time in ages with a determined Mrs Ollerinhulme officiating as guard again.

The Giant Lamb wandered over for a better look. It arched its neck and looked down its nose at the tram as it steamed slowly but defiantly along the line to Bedlam. The monster strolled beside *Jane* and its little train before starting to circle it, disdainfully stepping over its track. Percy piled on more coal and Pa Coppitt moved the regulator beyond the comfortable slot it usually aspired to. *Jane* took flight, as only a hundred-year-old tank engine could, and the carriages jostled each other as they rattled along the neglected, and now overgrown, track away from the comparative safety of Wormton.

Constable Arkthwaite watched their progress from the town walls and then said into his two-way, "Rubber ball!"

"It's Gum Ball, you idiot!" came Slake's voice from the other side of town, and Constable Arkthwaite heard the roar of a motorbike and the scrape of the East Gate opening.

Then he heard Mr Heptonstall tell Slake to stop. "Wait a moment, lad!" he was shouting, "What's tha going to call that machine o'thine?"

"Oh yeah!" replied Slake.

"Does it matter what it's blood yell called?" moaned Mayor Naseby.

"Of course!" exclaimed everyone else.

"To know the name of a thing gives one control over it," explained Slake. "Isn't that so, Mrs Osmotherly?"

"Of course!" she replied.

"Let me think for a moment, Mayo," said Slake.

There was an agonising silence. The monster menaced the little train even more closely.

"A Triumph-engined Greeves is called a *Grumph*," mused Slake.

"Which, by the same rule, lad," said Mr Heptonstall, "means this must be a *Wolmph*!"

"You're right! A Triumph-powered Wolseley! *Wolmph*! That's just the sound it makes when landing after a long jump, too. I did one just now at the level crossing outside the tram offices, and didn't land again until *Where the Rainbow Ends*! *Wolmph*!"

"Do that again and ah'll impound that device," threatened Mr Grandly-thorpe.

Slake grinned at him and checked his flared jeans were properly tucked into his buckled-up scrambling boots. "Trouble's goin'!" he said and he kicked *Wolmph* into life.

"Those silencers are nobbut cosmetic," Mr Grandlythorpe accused him over the din, but he would have benefited with some subtitles.

Slake mouthed "Trouble's gone!" at him, grabbed a fistful of throttle and launched himself out into the Woldernesse.

Meanwhile, Mrs Osmotherly and Gloria ran around Constables Sopp and Blenk to the Bloody Great Sheep sign that still leaned crazily outside the town walls, and fell upon it with gusto, flattening it, stamping on it, jumping up and down on it and then trying to bend it back and forth to break it, until, at length, a rather bemused Mr Heckmondwike and Mr Heptonstall dragged them and the sign within the town walls. Once the gates were slammed shut, the destruction of the Bloody Great Sheep sign carried on inside.

Meanwhile, the Giant Lamb pranced round and round the Wormton tram like some grotesque Lipizzaner dressage sheep. The thuds of its hoof-beats could easily be felt over the growing distance, and then the inevitable happened. The Wormton tram de-railed

A gasp of horror went up from the battlements as the onlookers realised what had happened, and the Giant Lamb stopped its hideous gam-bolling and peered myopically at the tram. Then it began to advance slowly.

It put one front hoof on either side of the engine and lowered its head until its nose nearly touched the carriage windows. Inside, pandemonium reigned.

Then it began to inhale purposefully.

"What's happening?" someone shouted to Constable Arkthwaite on the gate tower.

"T'monster's gonna bleat!"

CHAPTER 96

Slake rode like the wind. *Wolmph* sang *The Song of The Machine*. He gave no thought to the Giant Lamb or its parasites. He just rode.

He rode passed the turning for Diggle and rode through the shadow of Deep Doubt. He rode around the Wilber Mere and track of the Wormton Tram through the Wethermask Pass and gassed *Wolmph* across the wider moor towards Hettup and Stingey.

All along the road were crows waiting for him to crash but as he approached they just rose into the air on either side and swirled behind him as if they knew he would be returning.

At last he saw the bulk of Bedlam glittering on its plain below and he put his head down and elbows in and hugged the tank all the way down to the town.

The Bedlamites wanted to know how things were going in Wormton. He brushed aside their sympathetic comments and demanded to know where the Hillman Imp was for sale.

"Look, it's not for me but Mrs Osmotherly," he explained. "She needs the Imp for her motorscope."

"Ah," said everyone because Mrs Osmotherly and her motorscope were Wold famous in Bedlam.

"We knaw," said Mr Dobson, another of Slake's Wild Hunt cronies. "She phoned ahead on 'er two-way."

Slake followed their directions through the town to an elegant crescent of handsome houses. Their basements lay below road level with wrought-iron bridges leading up to their front doors. He went around the back of the crescent and found a substantial mews full of interesting automobiles. And there sat a dark blue Imp with a white roof.

Slake paid the sticker price and got a tank full of premium grade potane. Then he set about dismantling *Wolmph* to get it into the back of the Imp and acquainted himself with the Imp's gremlin. He explained his task and it eagerly agreed to help.

By the time he'd finished, the light was starting to go. The last thing he felt like doing was driving across the unwelcoming moors between Bedlam and home, especially with the Giant Lamb and the Horsepower Whisperer likely to cross his road.

"Ah well," he told himself, "needs must when the devil pisses on your windscreen."

At the gates of Bedlam, the Imp's exhaust sounded fantastic, and everyone grinned as he shook their hands for this could be the last time he saw them. The rough and tumble humour of the Bedlamites gave way to a terribly earnest sincerity that he found quite unnerving, worse than the anticipation of any Wild Hunt. Instead of a stomachful of butterflies, he had a sackful of very lively kittens.

The enormity of what he'd agreed to take on was beginning to dawn on him. He'd eluded the Giant Lamb once to get here, and he had a feeling it wouldn't be so easy a second time.

"I gotta get a shake on!" he declared at last and, to a rousing cheer, he blipped the throttle and shot off westwards into the gathering gloom.

CHAPTER 97

The last time he'd travelled the Bedlam road in this direction, he'd been with his friends in the Wild Hunt. Then the road had been an electric ribbon of excitement that arced across the landscape like searching lightning.

Now it was shrouded in darkness and if the crows were still waiting for him he couldn't see them, which him feel worse somehow.

The Imp sang *The Song of The Machine* and he blessed the names of all the horse-power whisperers who had driven the road to hell and come back with so many good Imp engines. Somebody had set up its suspension beautifully and he found how easy it was to balance it on the throttle through the corners. His entry and exit speeds became higher and higher and the distances between the bends tumbled as he forgot his worries and began to enjoy himself. The Imp encouraged him wickedly, and by the time he reached the Wethermask Pass he felt he was growing little tumescent tumps on his forehead just like the Giant Lamb. He comfortably fell into Wild Hunt mode, happy to be travelling without arriving and hoping that the road would last forever.

He was barely aware of Hettup Colliery as he concentrated on perfecting every gearchange, every turn exit and every minute application of throttle, brake and steering.

"The road here wraps itself around the Wilbermere," wrote Wrainwright, "like some amorous bindweed twining around a coquettish honeysuckle," and Slake's Imp skipped over the river on the ancient stone bridge and wove, as Wrainwright would have said, "a plait about the line of the Wormton Tramway."

Diggle was in darkness but the Imp ran its headlamps eagerly over the cavorting road and stone walls. The little car danced along the rising, falling, twisting, turning road and Slake glimpsed the turning to Mrs Osmotherly's house. Without the militia, the old town was no longer under a curfew, and the welcoming lights of Wormton came into view as the valley opened out and the Imp shot on to the Wormton road with its exhaust heralding his arrival.

From here it was a clear run to Wormton, and yet something obscured the lights of the old town, something big. Slake was thankful that whatever blocked out the twinkling lights was too far away for his headlamps to pick out. Then the lights of Wormton blinked out completely and he flinched.

Darkness enveloped him and although his throttle foot twitched he kept it nailed to the floor. The darkness engulfed him and then there were the lights ahead of him again. Nothing had shown up in his headlamps but through the vibrations of the Imp he felt a gigantic series of tremors. Something big and woolly was running after him.

The road flashed under the bonnet and then suddenly the East Gate flashed into view.

He never throttled back, never muted *The Song of The Machine*. He saw the planks of wood in the great doors, the massive iron hinges, the bolts that fastened them to the nearly petrified wood and the knots and the swirls of its grain. Just as he was about to start examining the doors at molecular level, they opened and the Imp buried itself in the narrow streets of Wormton. Deeper and deeper he plunged into the old town until a small thought from the back of his consciousness nervously put up its hand and asked whatever had happened to his self-preservation instinct, and Slake re-activated it as if he were at the end of a Wild Hunt. He braked heavily and Wormton gradually strobed past him more slowly until the little car pulled up just inside the West Gate.

He sat there for a while, gripping and releasing the steering wheel, moderating his breathing. Behind him the engine purred happily. On the dashboard, the gremlin gave him a thumbs-up as the special constables emerged from the gatehouse. They were very surprised to see him. Shouting a greeting to them, he turned the car around and cruised back to the East Gate. By the time he got there, he had regained his composure.

He was hugged and kissed by Gloria and slapped on the back by all the others except for Mrs Osmotherly, who smiled warmly at him.

"Any sign of the monster?" he asked nonchalantly.

"Neither fleece nor flank," replied Mr Heckmondwike.

"Where did it go after I left?"

"We dunnaw. It were poised to blast t'tram to kingdom come with one of its hellish bleats when *Jane* got in fust by popping its safety valves and put a jet of steam up its nose."

"Oh I wish I'd seen that!"

"Aye," added Mr Heptonstall, "and then we all went out into t'Wold to re-rail t'tram wi' every able-bodied man, woman and child!"

"What everyone?"

"All bar Mr Quirkmaglen, o' course. Ah spoase summan had to stay behind."

"He joined in the party afterwards though," Gloria reminded them.

"A party?" asked Slake.

"Aye, lad. We were in such high spirits after plumbing t'slough of despond."

Wolmph was carefully extricated from the back of the Imp, and Mr Heptonstall laughed when he saw the tyres. "Ah'd better fit some new ones," he said, rubbing his hands over the smooth rubber where the knobbly tread had once been

"And now we do it all again," said Slake.

Mrs Osmotherly put her hand on his shoulder. "No. Today is over and you have done enough. Sleep well tonight, Slake, for tomorrow we have much to do. We need you to race a marathon, not a sprint."

CHAPTER 98

At dawn, the West Gates were flung open and the fresh moorland air wafted into confined spaces of the besieged town.

Despite the early start, a large crowd was gathering to see Slake off, but Constables Sopp and Blenk patrolled the area just inside the gatehouse and only essential personnel were allowed near.

Mr Heptonstall had taken charge of *Wolmph*, taking it home to change its tyres and re-adjust it for faster running. Gloria had taken charge of Slake, and as he stood in the shade of the gatehouse, admiring the view of the Wold in the sunshine he felt strangely invigorated. He noticed with pleasure the blue sky and the lush green pasture, the dried mud on the edge of the road and the mountains in the distance, purple-headed with heather now that spring was here, just like the one in the hymn. He'd always thought purple was a daft colour for a mountain, but now he knew it was right.

And he also knew that his heightened sensibilities were due to his proximity to death.

"Bike's ready," said Mr Heckmondwike.

Slake turned and saw everyone looking at him expectantly. "Time to go," he said and walked back inside the town to where *Wolmph* stood.

"Did tha see owt of t'monster yest'day?" Mr Heckmondwike quietly asked.

"No," said Slake although he thought of the darkness that had engulfed the lights of Wormton.

"Even after you've brought the Demon back, we still have to create another souped-up 2CV," Mrs Osmotherly reminded him.

Mr Heptonstall had somehow got hold of the latest issue of *The Piston Wheel*. "There's none in 'ere," he said. "Ah'll try and find one. Mebbe summan in *Whose Watts* or *T'Vrooms Day Book* has one."

"Let's worry about that later," Slake told them, "and do what we can in the meantime."

He looked out of the gatehouse arch and felt a surge of reckless euphoria. He seemed never to have seen the Wold properly before. He put on his helmet and gloves and then said, "No goodbyes. I'll be back soon enough," but he still kissed Gloria.

Suddenly, Reverend Chunderclough appeared. He blessed him and said, "Jesus died so we could ride!" and Slake grinned back at him, any remaining nervousness gone for good.

"How much time have I got?" he asked Mrs Osmotherly.

"Twelve hours before Dark Time."

"Trouble's goin', trouble's gone!"

Slake kicked *Wolmph* into life, dumped the clutch and wheelied out of Wormton into the Great Wide Wold.

As he shrank again into the distance, Mrs Osmotherly whispered to Gloria, "Any harbingers?" and Gloria smiled and shook her head.

CHAPTER 99

Mrs Osmotherly's passing comments rode a wall of death around the inside of Slake's head. Only twelve hours.

Across the water meadows, he scanned the horizons for the Giant Lamb but saw nothing for miles until, well beyond the boundary of Scar Fell Farm, he espied a dark cloud – the Giant Lamb's own micro-climate. At the sound of the *Wolmph*'s exhaust, the monster raised its head over the horizon and slowly turned its head in his direction. The monster stepped daintily over the horizon, as if it were a two-dimensional prop in one of Wormton's Town's Women's Guild's productions and Slake felt himself accelerating towards it, faster than ever. He swerved and wound the *Wolmph*'s throttle all the way round to escape the gravitational pull of the Giant Lamb.

In a couple of steps it was in front of him and he felt trapped as if in its orbit. Its horns had grown and were beginning to curl, and its eyes glared at him, one a naturally sheepish yellow but burning with a hateful intelligence, the other still red from the explosive poosers he'd helped throw down its ear. Slake's sense of proximity had been distorted and his spatial perception scrambled, but he darted between the monster's thunderous hooves as it tried to stamp him out. He ran for the hills, but his progress was slower over the moors whereas the Giant Lamb could just stroll after him unimpeded.

He crouched over the *Wolmph*'s handlebars and tried every scrambling trick he knew, but he was still too close to the monster. The *Wolmph* bucked under him and he gassed the old bike up near-vertical slopes where the Giant Lamb's shadow fell cold upon him. Each time, he braced himself in case he was snorted up into its nostrils or blown away over the moors.

He crested a hill and plunged into another sunny valley. *Wolmph*'s engine hit its rev limiter. Air rushed past his ears as he plummetted. He was no longer riding, just falling. The strap of his helmet dug into his neck and his eyes watered from the cold air. Then *Wolmph* went "*Wolmph*!" and he rocketed back up into the sky again, either on rebound or up another hill, he wasn't sure which. He just gave *Wolmph* its head and tried not to think about the cold air of the descents or the hot breath on the back of his neck as he frantically climbed the hills. And so it went on, up hill and down dale, over the hills and far away.

He found the road again and, with the monster's flashing hooves on either side, laid himself down on the tank and wound the engine onwards. *Wolmph* responded with gusto and its chassis kicked and squirmed as more power than it had ever been designed to cope with surged through its wheels, but when he looked back the Giant Lamb was still right behind him. It was not so easy to outrun. When they had chased it with the Mudlarks, their speeds had been evenly matched. Now the Giant Lamb covered more ground just by standing still, and the hunter had become the hunted.

"Jesus died so we could ride!" shouted Slake.

Flashes of lightning from the Giant Lamb's pursuing weather system lit up the valley.

Slake felt a draft against his neck and glanced back to see the monster preparing for a terrible bleat.

When it came, its force nearly knocked him off his bike and *Wolmph*'s tyres left the road as it leapt forward, its Triumph engine bellowing in a chorus of *The Song of The Machine.*

Slake counted two blessings. One was the pair of earplugs he wore under his helmet. The other was the four-stroke Triumph engine beneath him. A two-stroke engine relied on gas pressure waves to run, and a bleat of that intensity would have stopped him as effectively as hitting the ignition kill switch.

But *Wolmph*'s engine roared back at the monster. Slake struggled to keep it upright as secondary pressure waves hit him. Strange frequencies and harmonies boiled the blood in his ears like an overcharged battery, and there was a warm sticky feeling inside his helmet.

The Giant Lamb bleated again just as Slake came upon a hump-backed bridge straddling the River Mither. *Wolmph* leapt into the barrage of sound and Slake crouched over the headstock to get out of the blast.

"Not you again," came a voice.

It was The Gothic Princess. She rode an ultra-modern enduro bike with upside-down forks and rising-rate rear suspension. Although her dress and hair streamed out behind her, somehow they avoided being snagged by the chain.

"Whisper horsepower, Slake," she yelled, "and ride like you've never ridden before!"

Something strange was happening. *Wolmph* did not fall to earth as quickly as before. Slake felt the pressure waves on his back and they were different. He had time to look around a third time, and there was the Giant Lamb, under its own black weather system, looking a little perplexed, for it was receding into the distance. Slake laughed and *Wolmph*'s engine roared as he realised that the monster had mis-directed its bleat just as he'd cleared the hump-backed bridge. His guardian angel had left him as quickly she'd appeared and he surfed the sound waves of the monstrous bleat as they carrying him away from the Giant Lamb faster than a simple dirt bike could ever have managed.

Slake hung on with white-hot knuckles that threatened to burn through his gloves. The air with which the monster had intended to destroy him supported him instead, and the road beneath dipped and peaked like the sound waves that carried him. Slake landed as gently as a fading sound and. *Wolmph*'s tyres chirruped on the tarmac. Slake scythed through the hills along the rolling valley towards Mithering and then stole a final rearward glance. The Giant Lamb had gone.

The sense of relief was overwhelming. His ears seemed to be on fire and as he'd flicked his head around he'd seen something red. Slake carried on riding as fast as he could, thankful that he was not required to stand his ground as the militia had been.

But any self-congratulations soon faded, as another less reassuring idea took up residence in his crowded head.

The Giant Lamb had let him get away.

Just before Mithering he pulled up by some trees. He killed *Wolmph*'s engine and turned around in his saddle to listen for the thunder of hooves and distant rumbling bleats, but he couldn't hear anything.

He unstrapped his helmet and tried to remove it, but it seemed stuck to his head. Waggling it from side to side with sticky hands, he eventually broke the seal and lifted it off. Its lining was soaked in a sinister thick red liquid that was smeared over his temples and the back of his head, matting his hair from the ears down. In places it had solidified and broke off in dark red lumps.

As he washed his bloody ears in the nearby beck, he thought the Giant Lamb must surely know he was coming back, in which case his fate was as assured as that of the militia. Gloria's assurances about his lack of harbinger gnomes seemed meaningless.

He checked his reflection in the stream to make sure his eyes weren't red as well, and tried to ensure his appearance was not too scary for the Mitheringers. Then despite Mrs Osmotherly's advice about the onset of Dark Time, he leant back in the grass and made himself comfortable among the boulders to let his hair and helmet dry.

"How am I going to get back to Wormton without being bleaten to death?" he asked the vast blue sky. "Play the part of the coward," he said before it could answer but he knew this was not for him.

If he'd learnt one thing from his career in the Wild Hunt, it was to press on regardless when everything seemed stacked against you, and while running away might offer survival it didn't include seeing Gloria again.

He sat up and, like Narcissus, looked at his reflection in the pools of the beck.

There was a sudden commotion.

He'd not noticed before but crows, jackdaws and ravens had been quietly gathering around him. Now, though, something had alarmed them. They flew off, cawing warnings to each other and Slake realised grimly that he must have smelt like road kill. Then he began to wonder with even greater revulsion what had spooked the crows but couldn't see anything.

He climbed back on his bike and fired it up and rode on.

Mithering overlooked a wide river valley and had a great ditch outside its walls. Anyone convicted of Mithering Brethren sympathies was immediately banished by the council, and exiles had camped outside it in a queer shanty town perched on the slopes of the ditch. To other distorted minds this had become a place of pilgrimage. However, as Slake approached the gates, he saw the camp was deserted. It no longer echoed to the chants of baffling mantras or belched smoke on washdays. Mithering seemed to have purged itself, just as Wormton was now trying to do.

Slake gave the name of Mr Ollerenshaw as his sponsor within Mithering, and the gatekeepers let him in without a second glance.

Mr Ollerenshaw ran a large Wolseley dealership but was no Wild Hunter any more. He rose from behind his desk in the showroom to greet Slake in a proper Woldsman's clench.

"Slake!" he exclaimed Mr Ollerenshaw. "Mrs Osmotherly said tha'd been on thine way. 'Eck as owt, lad, tha musta ridden like the wind!"

"In a manner of speaking I did. I'm chasing a daemon, a Dodge Demon, Mr Ollerenshaw. I believe you had one for sale in *The Piston Wheel*."

"Aye, we did. But it's been sold."

"Really?"

"Aye. Ah told 'er as much ont two-way."

"Mr Ollerenshaw, I need that car."

"Oh, aye?"

"Do you think the new owner would sell it on to me?"

"Nay harm in asking. He's local. Name of Staithes."

CHAPTER 100

The new owner was at home. In fact, he wasn't going anywhere.

"Ah dunnaw owt about cars," he said, "ah only bought it 'cos it were different. Ah'll nivver buy a yank tank again!"

Slake couldn't help grinning at the Demon. It stood in the street in a row of Jowetts and Wolseleys, dwarfing everything else. With its fastback outline and two clusters of no less than six tail lights, it looked like nothing else in Mithering and was painted black and yellow, nature's warning colours.

"And now the bloody thing won't start," Mr Staithes moaned, "and my wife hates it."

"Do you wanna sell it?" Slake asked him.

"Well, ah dunnaw know. It cost a fortune in petrol."

"Petrol?"

"Why yes. Shouldn't ah run it on petrol?"

"Well yes. I'm just a bit surprised you buy petrol for it."

"What else would ah run it on?"

Slake would have enlightened him about the fascinating world of home grown potane and the Campaign for Real Fuel but he didn't have the time. "Why don't you sell it to me?" he asked.

"Well ah dunnaw. Ah've not had it long."

"But it doesn't work."

"Ah knaw. And, now, so does thee."

"Mr Staithes, I appreciate your honesty. How much did you pay for it?"

"Eight, er, eighteen hundred." Mr Staithes blushed.

"Okay. Here's eighteen hundred in notes and bills of exchange. Do we have a deal?"

"Well, it seems a bit odd to me."

"Do we or don't we have a deal?"

Mr Staithes looked at the notes in Slake's hand. "Why does tha want it so badly? What's so special about this car? Maybe we should bargain a bit more. Is that you making that buzzing noise?"

Slake swiftly put Mr Heckmondwike's St Punter around his neck. "Eighteen fifty or I walk away."

Mr Staithes considered this for a while.

Slake noticed with scalp-tingling horror that a yellow and purple stripe had appeared on the western horizon. Dark Time was coming. He flashed the extra fifty under Mr Staithes' nose and when this provoked no positive effect he withdrew the money, turned his back and took two steps towards *Wolmph*.

"Okay, okay, let's settle on eighteen-fifty," said Mr Staithes and they shook on the deal.

"You could get a new Wolseley Six for that money," Slake told him, "or maybe a nice secondhand Armstrong."

While Mr Staithes happily went off to fetch the keys and logbook, Slake opened the bonnet. The car was in good condition. It just needed a service.

He tried turning it over and although the battery was sound and there was plenty of fuel, the car did not fire. He delved into the engine bay while Mr Staithes sat in the driver's seat. To Slake's relief, he found a very annoyed looking gremlin in the distributor.

"What are you doing here?" he said.

"Pardon?" said Mr Staithes.

"Nothing. Just talking to myself." Quickly, Slake began to mime to the gremlin. It was reluctant to talk at first and Slake began to wonder if, for the first time, the Mithering Brethren might have enlisted homuncular help. However, by threatening it with his spray of Holy Water, he quickly persuaded the gremlin to reverse the atrophy it had inflicted on the Demon's ignition system. Slake then explained about the forthcoming Wild Hunt experiment with the motorscope. The gremlin was fascinated and eagerly volunteered to become the car's guardian again.

"Try it now," Slake called out to Mr Staithes and the Demon burst into life.

The gremlin gave Slake the thumbs-up and disappeared into the carburettor.

Slake stood up and closed the bonnet.

"Ah hope tha hast better luck with than ah," said Mr Staithes.

"Thanks." Slake stopped grinning at his handiwork and remembered his journey home. "I hope I do, too."

CHAPTER 101

Slake didn't need to take *Wolmph*'s front wheel off to get it into the Demon's boot. He just took the tank off and tied the boot lid down.

Dark Time foregathered on the western horizon, and unless he hurried the electrical interference would soon knock his ignition out and he would be stranded in the dark at the mercy of the Giant Lamb.

Once beyond the protective walls and ditches of Mithering, the gremlin wriggled out of the dashboard and patrolled beneath the windscreen.

They drove upwards onto the moor. The Demon did not have the liveliness of the Imp but was clearly more powerful and didn't notice the steepening road. Slake doubted the weight of *Wolmph*, whose front wheel poked out from under the tied-down boot lid, made any difference either. He made a couple of exploratory prods with the accelerator, and when the tyres hooked up after spinning the Demon hurled itself at the horizon, but the narrow and twisty road that coiled up to Wormton did not lend itself to exploring the limits of adhesion.

He tried to think where the monster might intercept him. It was one of the Scar Fell Farm flock, but had spent most of its time up by the Forest of Riddaw. His favourite yet most forlorn hope was that the Wormtonians might have set up another diversion for the Giant Lamb. He wondered if he ought to stop and call them on his two-way, but felt he didn't have time. And no-one ever used the two-way in a Wild Hunt.

His spirits rose at the thought of his homecoming, and the hills looking bright and beautiful in the pale warm light preceded Dark Time. He passed the beck where he had washed his ears and drove up into the narrow passes where the River Mither foamed over impressive boulders and the road wriggled to keep out of its way. Sooner than he expected, he reached the humpbacked bridge where *Wolmph* had become airborne, and gassed the Demon so that it leapt onto the plain beyond.

This was where he had last seen the monster, but there was no sign of it, just recent gouges in the moor. The Giant Lamb, he soon found out, was behind him. The first sign that he was not alone was an uncomfortable vibration that went right through him. His faculties were blunted by it and when at last he glanced in his mirrors he was fascinated to see a blurred hoof of immense size flashing in and out of vision. Some helpful soul had stuck a small warning sticker to his door mirror that read, "Objects may be closer than they appear."

"Hold on," he said, but the gremlin had already disappeared. He mashed the throttle, and immediately regretted he hadn't familiarised himself with the Demon's power. It fishtailed wildly under acceleration on the greasy road, and he fought the wheel in a panic as the road shrank and the car swung like a pendulum from ditch to ditch. The engine bellowed *The Song of The Machine* and the tyres screamed at his incompetence, but Slake did not let off. He merely braced himself for the inevitable hoof through the roof. The big V8 shook the Demon and Slake preferred that feeling to the horrible bleat vibration. He tried to breathe deeply and focus on the road ahead. He broke off the rearview, mirror but the door mirror still showed the Giant Lamb with its lopsided yellow and red glare. It bared its teeth at him and bleated again.

The Demon shuddered then steadied itself. Slake blipped the throttle so that Demon's V8 roared back at the pursuing monster. Instead of swinging from side to side it pitched itself forward. The noise around him was intense, but the comforting sound of a V8 on song seemed to be drowning out the contra-natural bleat of the Giant Lamb.

The water meadows flashed by. Slake relaxed his grip on the wheel and began to drive like a proper skirrow. He laughed as the V8 bellowed defiance at the monster and looked around for the gremlin, but he was nowhere to be seen. Just as he had done with the *Wolmph*, he surfed the waves of sound from the Giant Lamb's bleat.

He began to wonder what else the Giant Lamb could do to stop him. "It must see where we're headed!" he shouted to the absent gremlin. "I hope there isn't some sort of trap ahead," he added, despising himself for seeking reassurance from the homunculus. "Where are you, gremlin? Y'know that sheep is unstable don't you? It could implode at any moment."

If all else failed, this then would be their fate. Slake would lead the Giant Lamb far away into the Woldernesse where he would annoy it and eventually make it so angry that it did go critical.

Wormton appeared out of the early summer haze. Its defences still stood, but if the Giant Lamb hit the right note they would come crashing down like the walls of Jericho. Slake's vision was blurring, despite the protection of the Demon's exhaust noise, and he took short cuts across the grassy sward. This lost him traction and he relived countless fearful nightmares where his wheels had bogged down and he couldn't get away. And all the time were those madly flailing hooves behind him that could crush his car and explode its half full fuel tank at any moment.

His leg was rigid and the throttle was flat out. He gripped the steering wheel too tightly, which unsettled the Demon. Onto the last straight he went, and the monster cast a shadow over him as he tried to relax. The Demon peaked out. Then the doors of Wormton were swallowing him, opening in the nick of time as if his bumper had burst them open and he shot, like the proverbial ferret down a drainpipe, into the dark coolness of the old town with the V8 popping and banging on the overrun as he slowed. Again, he took the breadth of Wormton to slow down, but this had been expected. Although the roads were clear, people leant out of their windows and waved as he passed, and as he at last reached the inside of the West Gate the special constables stood in front of the gate and cheered.

Constables Sopp and Blenk mouthed that they had heard him coming and, as his ears throbbed and his heart ached, he turned around slowly and made his way back to the West Gate.

A crowd of grinning Wormtonians swirled round his car and dragged him from it to carry him on its shoulders as if he'd just won the Mille Miglia or the Carrera Panamerica.

He saw Mr Heckmondwike and Mr Heptonstall, both grinning and waving. Even Mrs Osmotherly and Mr Grandlythorpe looked impressed, and there was Gloria, beaming her love light at him.

Mr Heckmondwike struggled through the crowd to congratulate him. "Tha did it, lad! Tha outran t'monster! Tha outwitted it!"

"How close was it?"

"Not close by any means," the good shepherd shouted back. "It were on top of thee! Ow did tha manage to cheat its bleat?"

"What?"

"Its bleat, lad! Tha should've been bleaten to a bloody pulp but tha's not!"

"Really? Maybe my zorst drowned it out."

"Aye, that Demon sounds reet grand," shouted Mr Heptonstall.

At Gloria's approach, the crowd put him down and he stared at her for a few seconds before sweeping her up into arms, kissing her and burying his face in her sweet-smelling hair.

The crowd collectively went, "Ah!" and then three cheers rang out over their heads before Mrs Osmotherly stepped forward.

"You did well today, Slake," she said. "Four times has *The Song of The Machine* been sung but we still have the greatest test to face."

There was an angry bleat from outside, and slates and plaster shivered off roofs and walls.

"Dark Time approaches and we need to re-engineer the road conjunctions at the time of the Giant Lamb's inception. And we still don't have a souped-up 2CV."

Slake disentangled himself from Gloria. "I might yet be able to help about that," he began.

"Oh, I knew you could do it," Gloria gushed at him.

"Really? Er, thanks."

To the west the sky had turned quite black, and the yellow and purple clouds swirled over Mithering.

"How much time have we got?" he asked.

"Four hours at the very outside," said Mrs Osmotherly.

"Come on," said Slake, "let's get *Wolmph* unloaded. I need to get to my workshop fast."

He strode to the back of the Dodge and stopped suddenly.

"What is it?" asked Gloria.

Slake said nothing but bent down and then pointed to the rear bumper of the Demon. There was the car's gremlin, wearing ear defenders and apparently unconscious.

CHAPTER 102

In the guardroom of the western gatehouse, Mrs Osmotherly put the finishing touches to her grand plan. Ever since Slake had departed for Bedlam, Mr Heckmondwike and Mr Heptonstall had been arranging obscure symbols under her direction on a map of the Wold.

While she considered her next move, Mr Heckmondwike went over to Gloria who was bent over an old tin of Blake's Bile Beans full of cotton wool and asked, "Ow is ee?"

"It's difficult to say. I've never cared for a gremlin before."

Mr Heckmondwike stared at the depression in the cotton wool where he assumed the gremlin lay. "Ah thought they were immortal."

"They are, but that doesn't mean they can't be sick or injured."

"Can't be much fun," remarked Mr Heckmondwike.

Gloria sighed. "Immortality's not all it's cracked up to be."

Outside, Mayor Naseby watched impotently as Constables Sopp and Blenk admitted George Ransomes and Ted Totteridge in George's old Stellite.

"Mrs Gaffathwaite tells us tha needs Wolseleys," George told them.

"Excellent!" said Mrs Osmotherly, looking up from her work. "Their car may make all the difference."

There were expressions of fascinated horror from Constables Sopp and Blenk, and then Ted entered the room with his matchbox. He gestured Mr Heckmondwike and opened the matchbox conspiratorially.

Mr Heckmondwike grimaced at the contents and went back to sit by Gloria.

"He's not still showing that shrinking pig to everyone is he?" she whispered.

"Has tha seen it?" asked Mr Heckmondwike.

"Of course not. He thinks it's too gruesome for us ladies."

"He's not far wrong."

Mrs Osmotherly turned around and Ted hid his matchbox. She pretended not to have noticed, and asked George if he would be prepared to join her and a few others in the inner ring of cars.

"Who else will be with us?"

"Old Mr Macklefract in his Jowett Short Two, Mr Heptonstall in the Imp

Slake brought back from Bedlam, and Mr Heckmondwike will drive the Demon. Slake will be in *Simurg*." She glanced at the encroaching Dark Time.

"Tha still needs thine 2CV, lass," said Mr Heptonstall, sympathetically.

Mrs Osmotherly jerked her head up. "Listen!"

From somewhere within Wormton came the sound of an engine. Everyone spilled out into the street and a green 2CV came into view.

"Good turnout," said George, looking around.

"Aye," said Ted agreed. "Lots of faces here ah dunnaw, though. Appen they're Mithering Brethren?"

Slake pulled up by Mrs Osmotherly. "There you are Mrs O. One suitably enraged 2CV."

Mrs Osmotherly was delighted. "Oh thank you, Slake," she said and flung her arms about him as girlishly as Gloria would have done.

Everyone admired the little car, even Gloria with her tin of Blake's Bile Beans.

"It's just like my old one," said Mrs Osmotherly. "Even the number is the same."

"I believe the devil is in the detail," said Slake, flushing a little.

"I prefer to believe that God is in the detail," said Reverend Chunderclough.

Mrs Osmotherly opened the driver's door and inhaled deeply. "If it smells right it is right!" she exclaimed.

An old grey cat appeared by her knees. Indoors Food stood on his hind legs with his paws on the door sill, sniffing deeply, his sides pumping like bellows. Eventually, he stood down and looked hard at Slake as if to say, "You don't fool me for a minute, sunshine."

Slake swallowed and looked away but immediately wished he hadn't.

"Hello Reynard," said a dark-haired young woman in the crowd. "You remember me, then?"

"I do," he gulped. "How, how, how, how could I ever forget?"

She turned to Mrs Osmotherly and the others. "There are strangers among you tonight."

"Strangers?" echoed Mrs Osmotherly.

A tall, distinguished man of middle years stepped before her. "Friends," he said simply.

"For all of you, one of us is familiar," said the Gothic Princess. Although youthful, to call her a girl would have been inappropriate. "Reynard Thorngumbald …"

"Please call me Slake!"

"… knows me well enough already, for I am his guardian angel."

Slowly, the other guardian angels went up to those in their care.

Mrs Osmotherly was confronted by a man who could have been an eminent doctor or a scientist, dressed in a slightly old-fashioned style. What might have been his slightly raffish son, tall, dark and athletic, strode over to a wide-eyed Gloria, and what might have been his wife appeared at the side of Mr Heptonstall.

Ted had a set of sextuplets to look after him. They could either have been saints or nuns, such were their benignly radiant expressions, and it was almost too painful to look at them, so nobody could say for certain if they had haloes or not.

Mr Heckmondwike's guardian angel emerged from the crowd, floating on her great skirts like a luxurious pink hovercraft.

But George's guardian angel was a big disappointment.

She wore a faded floral housecoat, a headscarf and slippers, and strode up to him, jabbed him in the chest with a bony finger and said, "And oil have none of dis cheatin' debt nonsense from youse, ya oidle good fur nuttin!"

"Blood yell, George!" said one of the Teds.

"Youse talkin' to me or chewin' a brick?"

"Madam, I …"

"And tat goes for the rest o'youse," she said, brandishing a terrifying combination of rolling pin and bulk tin of industrial scouring powder. "Oim Noyra O'Drenalin and don't any o' youse forget it!"

"I didn't see you on the way back here from Mithering," Slake said to his guardian angel.

"Of course not. I was helping the gremlin ameliorate the impact of the Giant Lamb's bleat. It was I who gave him his ear defenders. Hallo Gloria."

"Er, hello. Er. Great hair."

"Thanks. How is your patient?"

Immediately the gremlin regained consciousness.

"So that's how tha kept from being bleaten to death!" exclaimed Mr Heckmondwike.

"Of course," piped Enormous Bo-Peep, putting her arm through his and engulfing him in swathes of petticoat and ribbons. "And we can do the same for you with our woolverteens and pullykins, can't we, my dears?" and Mr Heckmondwike and Gloria saw all the lares and penates that a shepherd could ever wish to see. "By the way, the Great Shepherd sends His love to you all."

There was a sudden holy moment and everyone murmured their thanks.

"You're not going to dissuade us, then," Slake said to his guardian angel.

She took the adoring gremlin in her hands. "On the contrary. We are here to encourage and protect you."

"Does that mean we're going to be safe, then?" George asked her.

Noyra O'Drenalin glared at him for his impertinence. "How the divil should we know? We've never troyd to foight a giant lamb before!"

CHAPTER 103

As the baleful light of Dark Time drifted over the Vale of Wormton, a convoy of vehicles drove out of the West Gate with a green 2CV at its head.

Murders of crows, parliaments of rooks and conspiracies and unkindnesses of ravens lined the roadside and watched the cars go by with interest.

While Slake had been heroically fetching the Imp and Demon, Mr Heptonstall and Old Mr Macklefract had been hard at work in Bessie Dooker's yard, resurrecting as many old cars and trucks as they could. This included Bessie's old Wolseley 25 limousine, which she drove herself. The result was a very disreputable bunch of old vehicles, some lacking bonnets and headlamps, but all capable of influencing the motorscope. Everyone who could drive had a car apart from Mr Quirkmaglen, and even then he sent his chauffeur to join in with his Armstrong-Siddeley Special.

Mrs Osmotherly directed each car to a predetermined spot and told its driver to wait her explicit instructions. "The timing is crucial," she explained, "for the first deed was done in the shadow of Dark Time. But within the hour the static electricity will disrupt your ignition and your engines will die."

Then she drove up to a ridge overlooking the water meadows to check everything. Straightaway, she tutted and wound up her two-way.

"Mr Heckmondwike? You're supposed to be in the Demon, not the Imp!"

"Am ah?"

"Of course you are. Didn't you listen to what I said?"

"Imps? Demons? They're allus same to me."

She called up Mr Heptonstall and demanded to know what he was doing in the Demon.

"Well, ah thowt ah should be int Imp, tha knaws, but Mr Heckmondwike got there fust."

"Wait there!"

She rang Slake and told him to meet her by the Imp, then descended upon it herself.

"This is most distracting of you, Mr Heckmondwike," she scolded him.

"Aye, well, it's not every day tha gets to share a car wi' thine own guardian angel."

Suddenly, the Imp was full of pink and white. The shepherdess crook was held outside the car by a white-gloved hand.

"I think you'll both be much more comfortable in the Demon," said Mrs Osmotherly.

Slake and the Gothic Princess slithered to a halt beside them in *Simurg*. "What's up?" he asked.

"I need you take Mr Heckmondwike down to the Demon so he can swap with Mr Heptonstall."

"Nay!" said Mr Heckmondwike. ""Nay, no, nivver. Nay, no, nivver no way! Ah'm not getting in that thing and that's final!"

"Was that a yes?" asked Slake.

"Come, come," said Enormous Bo-Peep, patting Mr Heckmondwike on the arm. "Faint hearts never won fair ladies!"

"Who said owt about winning fair ladies?"

"After all the courageous things you've done, are you telling me you're afraid of a little thing like that?"

"Aye!"

"I don't believe you."

"Tha doesn't knaw what he's like!"

"Of course I know what he's like. He's an accident waiting to happen!"

"That's not a very nice thing to say," said Slake.

"It never bothered you when I told you," said the Gothic Princess, as she hopped out of *Simurg*.

Mr Heckmondwike got out of the Imp. "Ah'd rather walk," he said.

"We don't have the time," Mrs Osmotherly told him.

"This," said Enormous Bo-Peep, from the other side of the Imp, "is a man who habitually puts himself second to the safety of his flock. He has valiantly tried to destroy the Giant Lamb all by himself, and finally he rode on its back, braving hideous parasites in its fleece, and dropped explosive potatoes down its ears."

"I helped," said Slake.

"Not for nothing is there a distinction between shepherds and cowherds!" piped Enormous Bo-Peep.

"Does it really matter so much?" asked Mr Heckmondwike.

Mrs Osmotherly didn't really know, but she said yes anyway.

"I cannot believe," went on Mr Heckmondwike's guardian angel, "that a man like this can be afraid of a five-minute trip in a perfectly well engineered motor trike and ignore all assurances about his safety from those best qualified to offer them."

Mr Heckmondwike was acutely aware of the pullykins and woolverteens looking at him. The pullykins looked like overweight knitted clouds while the woolverteens resembled centaurs, except that some had the torso of a man on the body of a sheep while others had the torso of a sheep on the body of a man, with the man running about on all fours. And there were two sexes to both sorts of Woolverteen. He dreaded to think how he must appear to them.

"Is tha telling me it's safe?"

"I am your guardian angel."

"She didn't say yes," Mr Heckmondwike told Slake as he approached. "Besides, there's not enough room in this contraption for both of us."

"Oh pish!" said Enormous Bo-Peep and she blinked out of existence, only to reappear on the other side of the water meadows where she was nearly run over by Mr Heptonstall who was practising power slides in the Dodge Demon.

"Looks like she won't be coming with you after all," said Slake, "but don't let that put you off!"

Mr Heckmondwike lowered himself reluctantly into *Simurg*. "By 'eck, it's a long way down!"

"I just knew you'd change your mind. Trouble's goin! Trouble's gone!"

"Don't forget lad. Wormton needs me to drive a Demon around the legs of t'monster."

Slake didn't forget, but he took Mr Heckmondwike the long way, just as a special treat.

While everyone watched, George could be overheard talking to his own guardian angel.

"Ah expect tha must be kept very busy."

"Youse wouldn't know how much aggara vayshun it is," came the reply.

"Ah'm not keepin' thee from summan more deservin', am ah?"

Noyra O'Drenalin did not answer. She was looking out for something.

"Ah mean, hasn't tha got anyone else to be looking after?" he asked, painfully full of hope.

Noyra pointed her rolling pin at him. "Youse do the droivin' an' leave the worryin' to me, ya eejit."

There was much good-natured chaffing as Mr Heckmondwike and Mr Heptonstall exchanged vehicles. Then Slake drove Mr Heptonstall back, but as he pulled up behind the Imp he noticed something odd.

"Hey, what's that on the boot of the Imp?"

"It's somebody's old grey jersey, isn't it?" ventured Mr Heptonstall.

"Wait a moment!" said Slake. "That looks like fur!"

"Aye and that end's got a tail and this end has a nose and whiskers!"

"I never followed the fashion for the fur of dead animals," said Slake's guardian angel.

Slake watched the expanse of tousled grey fur very closely. "It's breathing," he said.

They tried to lift the old cat up, but even between them they didn't have enough hands. It was obviously an invertebrate and contained only some viscous liquid. So they left it there, having satisfied themselves that it was stuck to the engine lid by witchcraft or surface tension.

It was then that the Giant Lamb appeared from the west.

A cry of, "T'monster!" went up, and everyone blessed Mrs Osmotherly's foresight

Deep down, however, Mrs Osmotherly didn't really know what she was asking them to do. The outer ring of Wolseleys scattered as the monster charged, and the eyes of Mr Heptonstall, Mr Heckmondwike and Slake settled upon her.

She climbed into her 2CV, fired up its engine and then led them to close in on the Giant Lamb. Her guardian angel stood up behind her through the open roof and stretched out his wings to produce a shield. A row of gremlins wearing earmuffs ran along her dashboard and turned to face the Giant Lamb through the windscreen.

The Giant Lamb charged with its head down. It bleated long and hard. The sound waves thudded into them and Mrs Osmotherly's 2CV shuddered on its soft suspension and scrabbled for grip. Rain from the clouds that hung over the Giant Lamb lashed down on them. Lightning flashed. Mrs Osmotherly steered to the left, muttering "Widdershins to undo," and the other cars encircled the Giant Lamb.

The Giant Lamb was incensed, furious that its bleat, which had served it so well against the militia, seemed to be ineffective against four puny cars, and one of them no more than a motorised tricycle. It put its head down and bucked and kicked in a tantrum as if was ridden by some giant invisible cowboy in a rodeo. Foul-smelling misty breath billowed out from it, and great clods of earth began to fall around the cars scampering between its legs.

The ground shook. There was a loud "Thwack!" from Mrs Osmotherly's guardian angel, and she looked back to see a ked flying gracefully away from them. Her guardian angel behind her smiled, pulled on a mackintosh and said, in a voice like dark chocolate, "May I suggest windscreen wipers?" before batting another parasite into the underbelly of the Giant Lamb.

She switched on the wipers – only single-speed ones unfortunately – and the monster hurled another bleat at them. The cars faltered a little as it hit them, but the *The Song of The Machine* still echoed out across the valley and they kept formation.

"Spread out equidistantly!" shouted Mrs Osmotherly, in between bleats, "and keep your revs high! When we have prevailed over the Giant Lamb, make sure it doesn't topple on top of you."

The wind and rain, the roar of the engines and the life-threatening bleat of the monster drowned her out, so her guardian angel picked up her two-way, rang up her followers and held it for her so that she could speak and drive.

Everyone followed her instructions and they began to anticipate the Giant Lamb's flying hooves. The monster continued to furiously jump and kick, and circled on the spot, stirring up an even greater storm. The ground trembled and rain was shaken out of the sky. Mud from gigantic hooves flew through the air and occasionally a dislodged parasite fell to the ground.

Mrs Osmotherly and the others struggled to keep up their circling pattern. It was difficult enough to avoid the fallout from the monster and see where they were going. Slake in the open cockpit of *Simurg* was getting very muddy. His guardian angel, on the other hand, remained untouched, even by the rain. Every so often she would deflect a clod of earth from hitting her soiled driver. Around the Demon, Enormous Bo-Peep's crook was a blur as she fended off sheep ticks, and Mr Heptonstall's elegant guardian angel spread out her wings in the back seat of the Imp and created a little bubble of calm over it and the slumbering Indoors.

The Giant Lamb became desperate, as if it could read its own future in the motorscope, and struggled to break free of the contra-rotating rings of traffic. Its hooves hammered into the ground and it bleated with all its might, but the rings of Wolseleys, Jowetts and Armstrong-Siddeleys kept formation.

The monster slowed and tripped. Its persecutors hesitated, expecting it to fall, but the Giant Lamb felt a brief sense of release and suddenly gambolled away from Cost-is-lost. However, the formation of cars closed about it again, even more tightly.

"The traffic conjunctions are beginning to work!" exclaimed Mrs Osmotherly's guardian angel. "Keep the monster on firm ground!"

Quickly, she led the others into the most dangerous manoeuvre. She began a figure of eight that intersected under the Giant Lamb's belly, taking up a steady rhythm.

The Giant Lamb stared at the hypnotic pattern beneath it in horror. It bleated and bowed its head. Then it stood on its hind legs and reared up into the sky, trying to reach out over the rings of traffic that ensnared it, but the grip of the traffic was too strong, and the outer circle too far away. It crashed back down to earth to resume its bucking and prancing, and the Giant Lamb and its oppressors fell into a steady rhythm.

Round and round went the cars and the Giant Lamb kicked and reared and shook its head. Occasionally, it lost its footing and staggered, but the outer circles of traffic anticipated its collapse and moved gently outwards. Mist and cloud from its weather system swirled around it, and there were flashes of lightning. The sound of thunder rolled over that of the engines and the impact of the Giant Lamb's hooves on the rock and as the cars and bikes circulated their drivers hooted to each other if they came too close.

Mrs Osmotherly had not known what the final stage would bring, but as Dark Time grew darker it became obvious that they were missing something.

Slake called her up on his two-way. "My gremlins are getting tired."

Mrs Osmotherly's guardian angel reached down and adjusted the steering for her so that they avoided Mr Kindlysides, who was in the inner ring of Wolseleys.

"Bring on the reserves!" cried Mrs Osmotherly, and her guardian angel took off his shirt to reveal a washboard stomach. He waved it at a small group of cars at the foot of Blind Ponder, and Old Mr Macklefract swept down to relieve them in his Jowett Short Two. Behind him came Constable Arkthwaite in his Slakespeed Wolseley 6/110, Mr Gaffathwaite in Mr Heckmondwike's V8 Mudlark and George in his bodger's Stellite, complete with Noyra O'Drenalin brandishing her rolling pin and uttering blood-curdling housework cries.

The monster felt the changeover and strained even more vigorously against their efforts, but somehow the formation restrained it. It bleated in defiance and arched its back as it bucked and kicked, slowly rotating in the eye of the traffic conjunction as it searched for a weakness somewhere.

"Advance to the rear!" shouted Slake as he peeled off behind Mrs Osmotherly.

"Everyone all right?" she asked, as they pulled up on the side of Blind Ponder.

They nodded and got out of their cars to stretch their aching limbs.

"Whew! I'm glad that's over for a bit," said a mud-spattered Slake. "Life was becoming one great gambol!"

"Thee! Tha should be ashamed of thysen!" said Mr Heckmondwike. He opened the door of the Demon and four woolverteens jumped out, one of each sort.

Mr Heptonstall pulled up in the Imp. The length of grey fur on the engine cover at the back twitched its tail and awoke. It raised its head, yawned and sat up, looking around and gathering its stiff tail around its paws.

"It's working," said Mr Heptonstall as he got out.

"But it hasn't finished the monster off," muttered Mrs Osmotherly.

"Yeah, but look at it," said Slake. "It's entirely in our thrall." He spat out some earth.

They looked at the Giant Lamb. It was pogo-ing on the spot but didn't put a hoof beyond the inner circle of traffic. There was the occasional sound of a car horn from the complicated traffic conjunction around it.

"But I don't know what we can do now it is in our thrall!" complained Mrs Osmotherly. "We've recreated the conditions when the Giant Lamb was called into being and we've reversed the sequence so far, but I don't know what the final step is!"

"Never mind, lass," said Mr Heptonstall. "We're nearly there."

Gloria drove up in her Wolseley 8, accompanied by Professor Cluttercrap. "We're definitely onto something," she said eagerly.

"Er, any sign of the x-factor?" Professor Cluttercrap asked Slake.

"How should I know?" he replied.

"We need something else if we are going to destroy it!" said Mrs Osmotherly.

"Unmake it tha means?" asked Mr Heckmondwike.

"Yes."

"What would happen if tha got us to drive in reverse?"

"You wouldn't go fast enough. We've been going contrariwise, widdershins, to undo it anyway."

"Mebbe we can shoot some mint sauce at it."

"But it's not a weresheep."

"The bloody thing can't be indestructible," cried Slake, "can it?"

"No" said Mrs Osmotherly.

"Chin up, chicken," said Mr Heckmondwike.

"We're no longer alone," said her guardian angel.

Mrs Osmotherly looked around and saw a racing motorcycle cross the water meadows from the west. It was ridden in a manner that suggested the rider was neither brave nor stupid, just very, very good. It pulled up on a nearby hill and its rider took in the scene of the Giant Lamb dancing over the cars encircling its hooves.

"Oh look," said Gloria in delight. "The Wormton tram's coming to help!"

A plume of smoke drew nearer across the open moors.

"That's all we need!" groaned Mrs Osmotherly. "The Giant Lamb's got a long memory and holds a grudge against the tram. Tell Pa Coppitt to go back!"

"Mrs Osmotherly?" said Slake.

"What?"

"I don't want to sound alarmist but we're on the wrong side of Wormton for the Wormton tram."

"Then that must be the Mithering Railway."

"Coming from Wormton?"

"What else could it be?"

"I don't know, but it doesn't look like either."

A two-way squawked. "Hallo, Mrs Osmotherly."

"It's George Ransomes here."

"George! What are you doing! Don't drive and call me at the same time!"

"Ah have an urgent message from Noyra O'Drenalin," he said slowly.

Somewhere close to George there was some industrial-strength swearing and a thud from a rolling pin. Glancing back to the floor of the valley, they saw a giant ked spiralling up into the air.

There was more incoherent shouting and George said, "Ah'm to tell thee that a horseless carriage is approachin' from t'north."

Mrs Osmotherly turned to look at her two-way in disbelief. "What?

Doesn't she know I'm an autologist? A horseless carriage indeed! I have no equestrian expertise!"

Her guardian angel stood behind her and gently put his hands on her shoulders, lowering his head to hear George and Noyra more clearly.

"Nay," said George, slowly and with a greater emphasis. "It's a horseless carriage. And it's coming this way."

Mrs Osmotherly's guardian angel turned Mrs Osmotherly around to face him. "Hepsibah," he said, "Noyra is trying to tell us that there is a horse-drawn carriage approaching us, one without horses."

CHAPTER 104

"By the spanners of St Bendix!" laughed Hob as he gazed at the Giant Lamb.

Deutz's horseless carriage pulled up beside him, rocked to a standstill and then swung about again as the Foundling of Rauschenberg alighted and adjusted his waistcoat.

"I thought I heard *The Song of The Machine*," said Hob to Deutz. "And the carrion crows, well, they're always something of a giveaway!"

Between them the undulating moorland shimmered and a railway line appeared.

"Track fairies," said Hob. "What fear has Reverend Tregaskis instilled in them to make them work so fast!"

"They are nothing but a blur," remarked Caspar Deutz. He blinked in the sunlight and put on a pair of tinted pince-nez.

Down the line came an ancient locomotive that should have been scrapped long ago. On the footplate was Reverend Tregaskis. He pulled up beside them and a gang of track fairies winked into existence, flung down their pickaxes and wheelbarrows and collapsed into the muddy heather.

"So here we are," said Reverend Tregaskis, pleasantly. He turned to a cowering klinkergeist beside him. "Keep pressure up, Nutty Slack! We may need to leave in a hurry."

"Yes master!" cried the unfortunate soul, and a legion of grease bogles fell upon the brasswork while an army of wheel-tappers, wielding little hammers and oil cans, busied themselves below the footplate, checking for cracked spokes and hot wheel bearings.

Reverend Tregaskis climbed down from the footplate and they watched in fascination as the Giant Lamb strained against the motley collection of old vehicles.

"I don't suppose you've seen the motorscope in action before," said Hob.

"*Nein*," said the Foundling of Rauschenberg.

Reverend Tregaskis shook his head.

"Well, here it is. Look sharp. Someone's coming."

A 2CV barrelled up to them and a wild-eyed wise woman leapt out as other vehicles pulled up behind her.

"I know who you are!" she cried. "Get behind me, Gloria! And you, Slake! It's Old Weird Wheels himself! the Metal Guru, the Repossession Man, the Crypto-Engineer, His Malign Weirdness, the Grand Whizz-Herd and Master of the Engine Henge, the Lord High Prince of Rock'n'Roll, the Horsepower Whisperer and Soul Trader! None other than that infamous libertine and free radical, Nicholas Eldritch Hob!"

"Madam," said Hob, putting his business card back into his pocket, "I fear you have me at a disadvantage. Have we met before somewhere?"

"No, but I know full well who you are!"

Hob's hooded shades swirled as he looked at the strange vehicles that surrounded them. "Ah yes! You're the neighbourhood witch."

"Her name's Mrs Osmotherly," said Gloria, fiercely.

"I know," said Hob, impatiently, "and you are Gloria Gubbergill. Tregaskis? Deutz? These are the spell dames I was telling you about. And, seeing as we're suddenly calling each other names, you are Mr Heckmond-wike and you are Professor Cluttercrap."

"Is there anyone here you don't know?" asked Professor Cluttercrap, somewhat naïvely.

"I've met you before," Slake boasted to Hob, in case he was ignored.

Hob grinned wickedly. "Of course. I know both your titles, your Wild Hunt name and your Christian name. You are Slake, late of The Petropolis and current proprietor of the Slakespeed Tuning Emporium, as well as being one Reynard Thorngumbald of Old Wormton Town."

"What are you all doing here?" demanded Mrs Osmotherly.

"We're watching," said Hob.

"And listening," said Deutz.

"And waiting," said Reverend Tregaskis.

"And enjoying *The Song of The Machine*," finished Hob.

Slake was captivated by Reverend Tregaskis's locomotive. Gloria was staring at it, too. "It's *North Star*," he hissed at her. "It was in the Great Western railway races!"

"Who are those little men polishing it?"

"Grease bogles," he whispered.

"Mrs Osmotherly," began Hob, "I really must compliment you on your success in manipulating the motorscope."

Mrs Osmotherly hesitated, but then said, "Thank you."

"Did you begin with locomancy?"

"A long time ago."

Reverend Tregaskis raised his eyebrows at her and smiled.

Mrs Osmotherly began to feel the sin of pride creeping over her. "I still have much to learn," she said.

The grease bogles glanced at Slake and polished the brasswork extremely vigorously.

"Look at the klinkergeists!" he breathed.

The klinkergeists suddenly became nervous. They spilt ash over the grease bogles and they all became more agitated.

"And you, Slake, have done a marvellous job with this Citroën."

"Mmmm?"

"Oh yes," said Hob. "Quite marvellous. I'm so glad you followed my advice."

"What?" snapped Mrs Osmotherly.

"We were chatting in Bessie Dooker's yard only the other day," explained Hob, "and both of us decided it was wicked to scrap this little car."

"What! You mean it is my car?"

"Sorry, have I dobbed you in?" asked Hob.

"Yes!" said Slake.

Mrs Osmotherly became incandescent. "You told me you built another one!"

"No I didn't! You assumed it!"

"Semantics, semantics," sighed Deutz.

"You lied to me!"

"Well, you didn't want to hear that your car hadn't been scrapped, did you?" retorted Slake. "And if it was so bloody important, and you're so bloody clever, then why didn't you bloody well work it out for your bloody self?"

"Please!" Gloria yelled at them. "Don't start this again!"

"I paid good money to have that car scrapped!" fumed Mrs Osmotherly.

"If it's any consolation," ventured Hob, "persuading Slake, or should I say Mr Thorngumbald, to rescue your car was not exactly difficult. And you should have realised that destroying it would not have had any effect upon the fate of the Giant Lamb."

"I do now!" Mrs Osmotherly assured him.

Mr Heckmondwike put a hand upon her shoulder. "Fair dos," he said softly. "If Slake hadn't rescued it, finding or building another would have taken too much time. Getting t'Imp and t'Demon was difficult enow. Slake came up with t'goods when we needed 'em. And Mr Hob is reet."

"My dear fellow! Call me Nick!"

Mr Heckmondwike ignored him and continued to gaze at Mrs Osmotherly with such gentle intensity her guardian angel began to feel a bit of a spare part. "And tha did agree, lass, not so very long ago, that destroyin' t'2CV was akin to trying to destroy t'stars if thine stars didn't go reet for thee."

For a moment, Slake looked dangerously close to saying, "That's right!" but he didn't. He just looked like he was about to and then he seemed to think better of it. And suddenly, Gloria was very proud of him.

"What do you want?" Mrs Osmotherly asked the Soul Traders.

"Souls," they answered together.

"Whose?"

"Yours," came the reply, evidently meaning the plural.

"Why should we listen to you?"

"Because," said Reverend Tregaskis, "we know how the Giant Lamb was originally created."

Mrs Osmotherly turned to look behind her. The monster was still surrounded by her traffic conjunction but it was bucking and kicking just as energetically. "You were behind it all along, weren't you?" she said looking back at Hob.

"I feel able to admit to initiating this little enterprise."

"It was some fiendish soul trading plan, wasn't it?"

Hob nodded.

"But you'll only tell us how to destroy the monster if we sell our souls to you. That's right, isn't it?"

Hob just smiled.

Slake confronted him. "If you want a soul, take mi ..."

But Gloria had leapt between them and stifled Slake's words. "No!" she shouted. She turned to Slake's guardian angel. "Shouldn't this be your job?" she yelled at her.

The Gothic Princess blinked. "Sorry," she said, "I wasn't concentrating."

"By the lucky blue screwdriver of St Bendix!" murmured Slake. "Take my ..."

"No!" shouted Mrs Osmotherly, "take my ..."

"Nay, mine..." began Mr Heckmondwike.

But Gloria silenced him with an imperious hand and would have offered her own soul had not Slake put his hand over her mouth.

"Badness, black-hearted me!" Hob exclaimed with pleasure. "They're falling over themselves to save the Wold!"

"How many souls do you want?" Mrs Osmotherly asked him.

"How many have you got?"

At that point, Indoors Food sauntered passed. His tail and head were held up high. Those who had the sight could see that he had caught something in his mouth. Gloria had it, and from their consternation it seemed the Soul Traders had it, too. And now, for the first time, so did Mrs Osmotherly.

"What's he got?" she cried.

"It's the G-gnome!" exclaimed Reverend Tregaskis.

"What a clever cat!" said Hob, and he bent down to stroke him.

Indoors, however, walked right past everyone and sat a little way off with his back to them, watching the Giant Lamb.

"What's t' G-gnome?" hissed Mr Heckmondwike.

"He's a sort of boffin," replied Gloria.

"Can tha see him?"

"Yes. He's bald apart from great white bushes of hair on the sides of his head. He's wearing enormous spectacles and a white coat over brown trousers and what looks like a Terylene shirt with a kipper tie. In the top pocket of his white coat is a row of pens, and slung across his back, like a folk singer might wear a guitar, is a test tube."

"What a remarkable animal!" exclaimed Reverend Tregaskis.

"*Ja!*" breathed the Foundling of Rauschenberg. "His reactions must be as lightning to have caught the G-gnome."

Reverend Tregaskis did a little expressive dance and the G-gnome replied with some guttural swearing and graphic gestures.

"Remarkable! It seems that the G-gnome was about to alter this old cat's DNA when he noticed it and pounced. Does he belong to anyone?"

Indoors Food turned around to gaze at Reverend Tregaskis, with the G-gnome still swinging from his jaws.

"As much as a cat belongs to anyone, he belongs to me," said Mrs Osmotherly.

"What's his name then?" Hob asked her.

Indoors looked at him sharply.

"He's called Greymalkin," said Mrs Osmotherly, "aren't you?"

Indoors regarded them inscrutably.

"I thought so," said Hob. "Indoors? Indoors Food?"

In surprise, Indoors nearly dropped the G-gnome.

Hob produced a length of string with a screwed-up piece of paper tied to it. He flicked it out onto the ground in front of Indoors and the old cat's whiskers shot forward.

"Greymalkin?" said Mrs Osmotherly.

Deutz slowly produced a catnip mouse from his pocket.

"Grey!" Mrs Osmotherly implored. "Greymalkin? Come on Old Grey. Puss, puss, puss."

Hob wiggled the piece of string in front of the old cat but, somehow, Indoors Food managed to resist.

Deutz threw the catnip mouse at him in a finely judged and highly tantalising arc. Indoors found himself shaking his head at it, wide-eyed with whiskers bristling. His paws twitched and his bottom wiggled as if he could feel a really good pounce coming on.

It was the G-gnome that saved him. As Indoors shook his head at Deutz's flying mouse, the dangling homunculus panicked and grabbed the old cat by the whiskers to steady himself.

The spell was broken.

Indoors stood up and strolled over to the old woman who would never know his name, for all her other wisdom.

"Rats," said Hob.

"Oh bother," said Reverend Tregaskis.

"My first homunculus!" breathed Mrs Osmotherly. "And you''ve caught him for me, Old Grey!"

The Foundling of Rauschenberg put the catnip mouse back in his pocket and Hob gathered up his string.

"Well, if you'll be kind enough to hand me back the G-gnome we'll be on our way," said Reverend Tregaskis, brightly.

"What?" said Deutz, quickly. "Have you forgotten the souls of the wise women?"

Reverend Tregaskis put his arm around Deutz's shoulders and walked him away, whispering earnestly.

"What are they doing?" Mrs Osmotherly asked Hob.

"They're conferring."

"What about?"

Hob listened. "The G-gnome. And your God-given souls."

The G-gnome tried to steady himself on his captor's whiskers again, but Indoors Food unsheathed a claw and poked him sharply in the ribs, making him swing more than ever.

Deutz and Reverend Tregaskis came back.

"So," said Reverend Tregaskis, eyeing Indoors Food with respect, "if we could just have the G-gnome, we'll be on our way."

Mrs Osmotherly folded her arms. "Is he yours?"

"No," admitted Reverend Tregaskis. "We've borrowed him."

"You borrowed him," corrected Deutz, grumpily.

"Yes but you're getting the soul of the … we're all in this together," Tregaskis pointed out to him.

"From whom have you borrowed the G-gnome?" asked Mrs Osmotherly.

"That question is irrelevant," Deutz replied.

A thought occurred to Gloria. "Does this person know you've borrowed the G-gnome from them?"

"Of course!" replied Reverend Tregaskis, outraged.

"But they don't know that you've lost him."

The Soul Traders shuffled their feet awkwardly.

"Vee haffent lost him," insisted Deutz. "Vee haff found him!"

"We'd like the G-gnome back, please," said Reverend Tregaskis.

"Does the presence of the G-gnome have anything to do with the Giant Lamb?" enquired Mrs Osmotherly.

This time the foot-shuffling was accompanied by some digging in the ribs.

"I have a proposition for you," said Mrs Osmotherly, narrowing her eyes. "If you help us get rid of the Giant Lamb, you can have the G-gnome back."

There was a pause.

Then Reverend Tregaskis said, "May I consult with my colleagues a moment?"

"Of course," said Mrs Osmotherly, "but don't take too long."

The Soul Traders wandered off and began an animated debate just out of earshot.

Indoors was dribbling all over the G-gnome. Mrs Osmotherly wondered if how long it would last before being dissolved completely.

The Soul Traders were arguing. In the other direction the Giant Lamb continued its grotesque gyrations.

"With Hob on our side we have everything we need," Mrs Osmotherly whispered to Gloria.

"I don't trust them," she replied. "Our guardian angels seem to be in a trance."

The discussion between the Soul Traders had descended into a frank and forceful exchange of views.

Behind them Dark Time was gathering.

"Don't you see, Gloria? We can never do it without them!"

The exchange of views between Soul Traders was descending into an exchange of blows.

"Not only do we need Dark Time and our cars to work the motorscope, but we also need the presence of the G-gnome and Nick Hob."

Reverend Tregaskis had knocked Deutz's hat off. He was surprisingly bald for such a young man.

"I hope you're right, Mrs Osmotherly, I really do."

Hob was restraining Deutz from strangling Tregaskis.

"I just have a bad feeling about having anything to do with any of them."

Slake came up to them. "They'd better hurry up. Dark Time could knock out our ignition at any moment."

"Sssh!" said Mrs Osmotherly.

The Soul Traders were coming back.

"Try that again," Hob muttered to Reverend Tregaskis, "and you're on your own!"

"Okay," said Reverend Tregaskis, "it's a deal. Hob will ride *Nosferatu* around the Giant Lamb, won't you Hob? Hob!"

"All right!"

"I will circle it with one of my trains. That should stop it from running away."

"Good," said Mrs Osmotherly.

"And Deutz will help as well."

Deutz smouldered.

"Then, when the aberration is no more, you give us the G-gnome back. Yes?"

"Fine," said Mrs Osmotherly.

Hob spat on his palm and held out his hand. "Shake?"

"Shake," replied Mrs Osmotherly. She spat on hers and took it.

They gripped each other hard and there was a sizzling. Steam curled from their hands.

"By the spanners of St Bendix!" said Hob and Slake together.

Hob let go of her hand and turned away to Reverend Tregaskis. "I told you it wouldn't work," he hissed at him. "She *is* a Woldswoman after all."

"May I see your hand?" Gloria asked Mrs Osmotherly gently.

"Perhaps you ought to," she answered. "I'm not sure I'd care to look."

CHAPTER 105

"Trouble's goin'," said Hob as he switched on the ignition. "Trouble's gone!" and he kicked *Nosferatu*'s engine over.

The Giant Lamb turned around when it heard the sound of the big V-twin's lumpy idle and the whine of its supercharger. Its eyes grew wide, both yellow and red. It raised its nose, which had been scarred from bumping into walls, trees, cliffs and helicopters. It squared its shoulders and looked every square kilometre a devil.

Clouds hung over its head and rained on the Wolseleys that stoically kept the Giant Lamb at bay. Away from the monster, the air was warm and thick. The fine film of mud on Slake was beginning to crack off. The sky was turning black, and the Wold felt as if was being roofed over. Only a strip of light on the eastern horizon was left clear and the eldritch yellow light that slithered through it left purple shadows wherever it couldn't shine. In the east, the last natural light fell upon a fog bank, and within its swirling mist stood a solitary figure.

The Big Grey Man was watching.

"Well?" said Hob. "What are we waiting for? I'll lead, you follow."

Mrs Osmotherly nodded. "Quickly. We have even less time than before. What's more, the Giant Lamb seems to know it. When the end comes, don't get squashed by it!"

Although she spoke to the others her eyes never left Hob. The palm of her burnt hand was bandaged.

Hob smiled. He was used to not being trusted. He rolled his hand on *Nosferatu*'s throttle to signal his intent to the monster. Then he moved off, followed by Mrs Osmotherly and the others in the same order as before. Deutz climbed into his horseless carriage and it lurched into bringing up the rear.

Gloria and Professor Cluttercrap watched them file down to join the Horsepower Whisperer.

"So," said Professor Cluttercrap, happily, glancing towards Indoors and the G-gnome, "there are the x-factors!"

"Can you see the G-gnome?" asked Reverend Tregaskis.

Professor Cluttercrap nodded vigorously.

"Aren't you going to drive your train?" Gloria asked Reverend Tregaskis.

"No. I thought I'd stay here with you."

The track fairies had already built a circular track around the outermost ring of cars, and the Giant Lamb was looking very unhappy about the prospect of being circled by *North Star* and its crew of grease bogles and klinkergeists.

"I know!" said Reverend Tregaskis. He clicked his fingers and the ground shook, but not because of the hoofbeats from the Giant Lamb. It quivered in a short line beside him and a stovepipe chimney poked out of the moor. After it came an extraordinary steam engine that was obviously even older than *North Star* complete with its ghostly crew.

"I don't get the opportunity to use this one very often. It's *Catch-me-who-can* built by my countryman, Trevithick. It was designed to go round and round in circles. Track fairies! Gauntlet some standard gauge track within the broad gauge rails," and the track fairies, who had just started a tea break, put away their newspapers and became a blur of activity again

Ted Totteridge wandered up to them.

"The others want to know what's happening," he said. "Aye, has tha let tha two-way run down?"

"I'm afraid we have," said Gloria, winding hers up. "Mr Totteridge! Where are your guardian angels?"

"Ah lent them to those that can drive. Their need is greater than mine."

"I wouldn't be so sure about that," scolded Gloria, although she had done the same with hers.

Reverend Tregaskis was making a poor job of feigning indifference towards him.

"Anyway, we've, er, got some more help now, so we're going to try it again. I'd stay out of their way if I were you."

Hob stopped outside the outer circle of traffic and stood astride his bike while he unfurled a great pair of raven-black wings. He stuck two fingers into his mouth and whistled.

A highly modified Wolseley Blue Streak came into view and they could see Brother Guy at the wheel, tears of shame streaming down his face as Hob called upon him to do something helpful for the first time in his life. And there was nothing he could do to stop it.

Hob folded his wings back into the shoulders of his leather jacket and signalled to Deutz. Then he kicked *Nosferatu* into gear and descended upon the monster. Brother Guy turned in behind him and the others followed. Hob rode as if on tarmac and not the slithery surface of the water meadows. He accelerated, taking *Nosferatu* through the gears, and everyone chased after him, causing the Giant Lamb to struggle more than ever before.

They swept through the outer ring of cars, reinforced in places by mighty Wolseley tractors, as big as the Big Nuff, and closed in on the Giant Lamb. Mrs Osmotherly wound her 2CV up as her guardian angel crouched down to reduce wind resistance and spread his grey-flecked golden wings over her to protect her from the falling earth and rain.

With a supreme effort, the Giant Lamb grabbed its chance and tried to run off into the Woldernesse, but Hob was too quick for it. He gunned *Nosferatu* and rode beneath its flashing hooves to accelerate in front of it. The Giant Lamb was seized by terror as the Soul Trader appeared beneath it, and pulled up sharply. Hob put out his wings and turned on a sixpence to face the monster, which lowered its head in fear. Brother Guy joined them in the Wolseley Blue Streak. He was beating his chest and tearing his hair out, but driving brilliantly, like a man possessed.

The others caught up and the Giant Lamb began to buck and kick again, somehow drawing upon reserves of energy that had vanished when faced with Hob alone.

Hob drove straight at Mrs Osmotherly, but she held her nerve and he flashed by, diving between the front and hind legs to recreate the counter-clockwise manoeuvre she had pioneered. She threw her wheel to the left and drove around the Giant Lamb, not yet daring to go between the legs that were in another frenzy of bucking and kicking. The outer rings of cars, tractors and lorries settled back into their rhythm, and she even noticed Mayor Naseby at the wheel of the civic Armstrong-Siddeley Sapphire bumping over the muddy moor.

The Giant Lamb seemed to know the end might be near. It was dancing a hornpipe, desperately trying to make the ground beneath it impassable. Yet Hob found a way. He darted in and out of the legs of the Giant Lamb like the shuttle on a loom, and Mrs Osmotherly realised that they all needed to follow him and recreate the figure-of-eight pattern. She latched onto his taillight and grimly followed him into the tirade of hoof beats.

Immediately, she learnt not to follow him exactly. A cloven hoof stamped down in front of her, blocking her way. She braked heavily and made for a gap between the monster's back legs. The Giant Lamb tried to block her as well, but she was too quick for it, and before she knew it she had shot out from under its tail and was on a collision course with the outer ring of Wolseleys.

"Well done!" cried her guardian angel.

Slake followed them, and soon Old Mr Macklefract, Mr Heptonstall, George Ransomes and Mr Heckmondwike were looping around again under the monster within the three swirling contra-rotating rings.

Their formation became tidier and they carried on for some time but without destroying the monster.

The Giant Lamb abandoned precise blocking moves with its feet, and began a desperate frenzy of flailing hooves, kicking and bucking and rearing and shaking. It moved far quicker than a monster that size had any right to, and shook its head to avoid an invisible noose despite the futility of resistance. Yet in the face of unmaking traffic conjunctions spinning all around, it remained defiant, beating impossible rhythms with its cloven hooves.

Weary drivers began to make mistakes. Two cars crashed into a hoofprint, and Mrs Osmotherly called upon Old Mr Macklefract, Constable Arkthwaite, Mr Gaffathwaite and George Ransomes to reinforce the central road conjunctions while Slake and Hob worked to get the cars going again.

They worked side by side while the Gothic Princess kept watch.

"Just like old times," said Hob. He ran his fingers over a dented wing, and the buckled steel wriggled back into shape as if he were stroking a cat.

Slake didn't answer. He opened the bonnet, revived the stunned gremlin and checked the engine's vital fluids.

Great clods of earth from the monster's hooves came down, and rain from the Giant Lamb's weather system pelted them.

Hob held his wings over Slake as he worked on the engine. "That should make it sing its song!" said Hob.

"Try it now," Slake told Mrs Hammerhulme behind the wheel, who'd sustained a nose bleed.

"Trouble's goin!" Hob and Slake said together. "Trouble's gone!" and the engine roared into life. They punched each other on the arms and got the other car going, too.

Just before they rejoined the great unmaking traffic conjunction, Hob admired Slake's tee shirt. " 'Too fast to live, too young to die.' Y'know I could offer you a solution to that little problem," but Slake just said, "Not today thanks, mate."

And they punched each other on the arms again and went back to their vehicles.

But even with all of them going round and round under the Giant Lamb's feet, it still made no difference.

"The motorscope is still not working!" groaned Mrs Osmotherly. "We're equal to the Giant Lamb, but not strong enough to unmake it! We still need something else!"

"Courage," said her guardian angel. "The darkest hour comes before dawn!"

CHAPTER 106

From Blind Ponder, Gloria watched in despair. "It's still not working!" she told Professor Cluttercrap. "We have everything we need, including Dark Time and two Soul Traders, but it's still not enough. The Giant Lamb can keep going like this forever." She glanced at the sky. "Soon Dark Time will knock out their ignition systems."

"Hmm," said Professor Cluttercrap. "The Giant Lamb could go critical at any moment and take us all with it."

"It's such a shame," said Reverend Tregaskis. "Oh well. It's all part of life's rich tapestry."

The sky darkened perceptibly. All the cars below them had their lights on now. Even Hob used them, and on Deutz's horseless carriage a dim glow showed from its carriage lamps. Deutz had taken to leaning out of the window and holding his hat. It wasn't to see where he was going but to gaze in wonder at the Giant Lamb and all the gyrating vehicles.

Gloria looked around. The sky was nearly black. But then something flickered behind her. It was the reflection of headlamps in the radiator grille of her own Wolseley, the only car for miles around that was not involved in suppressing the Giant Lamb.

She spluttered but no words came.

Reverend Tregaskis and Professor Cluttercrap looked at her in bemusement. She pointed and began to jump up and down, but when they looked they only saw in the darkness a small, black, old-fashioned car.

"Is tha awreet lass?" Ted asked her. "Aye. Tha seems a mite vexed."

Speechless, she hugged a surprised Ted and kissed Professor Cluttercrap full on the beard.

Reverend Tregaskis looked hopeful but she ran passed him to her little old car.

Professor Cluttercrap slowly raised a hand to his lips. Strange emotions flashed through him and he thought of Professor Lillibuck in her laboratory, in her stiffly starched white coat.

CHAPTER 107

Gloria slammed the car door behind her and wiped her face. "Yuk!" she said to the gremlin watching her from behind the glass of the speedometer. "That was like kissing a cushion!"

She thumbed the starter button. "Trouble's goin'!" The engine caught and fired. "Trouble's gone! The game is awheel and I have everything to play for!"

She gassed the little old car straight down the hill, bumping over the moors with increasing speed. The Wolseley lurched from side to side and seemed in danger of falling over, but another bump always bumped it back the other way.

The needle on the speedometer prodded the gremlin and forced it to clamber round the dial. Without the aid of a seatbelt Gloria bounced around the interior like a potato in a pan of boiling water, clutching onto the wheel.

With surprise she saw that the Giant Lamb had noticed her approach. Its great mis-matched eyes lit up like pale lamps and it pricked up its flattened ears and found enough breath to give a great bleat.

She switched on her lights and without her guardian angel, who she had so generously lent to those in the outer circle, she accelerated across the smoother grassland of the valley bottom and shouted at the monster that she was coming for it.

The Giant Lamb had appeared weary, but as Gloria approached it leapt into the air and turned a somersault. When it landed the earth shook, and it gyrated wildly with all its remaining energy.

Lightning flashed and thunder shook the air as well as the earth. The ground shook from hooves that moved so fast they could not be seen and the waiting carrion crows took to the air and swirled in untidy agitated clouds, excited with the prospect of a kill at last .

The road conjunctions became ragged again. Gloria could see in the gathering gloom that the cars around its feet were surprised by the sudden energy in the monster's movements.

The little Wolseley's gremlin was hanging onto the end of the speedo-meter needle, trying to drag it past 85.

Clods of earth began to fall outside even the outer circle of cars. She couldn't see any gap, but at the moment she should have collided with them, the cars opened up and she caught a glimpse of the grinning face of her own guardian angel, riding with Miss Periwig. Then she was sucked into the chaos of the swirling Wolseleys, Jowetts and Armstrong-Siddeleys.

Brother Guy came close to crashing into her, but he howled piteously as he took evasive action.

She saw Mrs Osmotherly gazing at her in amazement. She saw Mr Heckmondwike and Enormous Bo-Peep. She saw the Foundling of Rauschenberg, who doffed his hat to her, and Hob, somehow, popped a wheelie on the mud. And she saw Slake in Simurg with the Gothic Princess giving a ked a karate chop.

The monster leapt into the air and uttered the most plaintive bleat that ever echoed around the Wold, one that was heard in Mithering and Bedlam-le-Beans. It rolled its eyes and raised its great woolly head towards heaven, imploring the Great Shepherd to rescue it. Even Dark Time flickered, and Gloria fancied she saw stars.

Lightning flashed, clouds billowed around the monster, and then it keeled over and slowly disintegrated into several thousand sheep.

CHAPTER 108

Professor Cluttercrap and Reverend Tregaskis heard a muffled pop and a sound like the tearing of a gigantic bed sheet.

"The Giant Lamb is deflating!" cried Professor Cluttercrap.

Behind them there was a yell and a squeal of delight.

Reverend Tregaskis laughed.

A very large and cheerful pig sat on top of Ted Totteridge.

"Bucephalus Epsilon of Riddaw – get off me, tha great lump!" shouted Ted, and the delighted pig rolled onto its trotters so it could look him in his face, amused that he didn't have any floppy ears over his eyes.

Ted sat upright. "Look what tha's done to ma trousers!" he said, pulling a shattered matchbox from his burst pocket.

But Reverend Tregaskis and Professor Cluttercrap were watching the end of the Giant Lamb. Its belly was unzipping like a huge pyjama case and out poured its progeny in their own fleecy jim-jams.

Mrs Osmotherly narrowly avoided hitting a sheep.

Ahead of her, Hob swerved to avoid one as well. After the Giant Lamb, they seemed comically small.

More emerged from the mist. Unlike the Giant Lamb, they showed no traffic sense whatsoever.

"Where are they all coming from?" she asked her guardian angel.

Her guardian angel stood up and replied, "The Giant Lamb."

Above them, the rain and earth had stopped falling.

"Is it giving birth to them?"

"Something like that," he replied.

The dark cloud over them was breaking up rapidly. Even as they stared at it, the sun came out before Dark Time finally closed in and bathed the upturned faces of angels and mortals alike in sunshine.

The mists parted and huge numbers of sheep tumbled away from where the Giant Lamb had been, like a disintegrating mosaic. The outline of the monster softened against the backdrop of Dark Time and collapsed. Its last great bleat still hung in the air but its note had changed. This was no longer a bleat to split armour and explode aircraft, a bleat that could kill. It was not a single bleat any more, either, but made up of many smaller bleats from many smaller mouths.

"The biomass is readjusting itself!" shouted Professor Cluttercrap.

"Look at it!" cried Ted. "Ah am lookin'! Would tha just look at it!"

"Remarkable," said Reverend Tregaskis.

"Will tha stop pushin' me?" Ted shouted at his pig.

Bucephalus Epsilon of Riddaw suddenly noticed Indoors, still with the G-gnome in his mouth. It ambled over to him and stared at the G-gnome intently.

Indoors glanced nonchalantly at the pig as if to say, "Yes?" and the pig gave the terrified G-gnome a good sniff.

There was a rustling as if a small wind was passing, and Widdershins ran past to eagerly help herd the growing masses of newly born, yet adolescent, sheep.

Headlamps groped their way through the thinning fog and sheep. The Giant Lamb's imploding weather system looked suddenly lost and very embarrassed, as if it wanted the atmosphere to swallow it whole.

The outer circle of Wolseleys slowed to a walking pace. The drivers could hardly believe their eyes at the profusion of sheep that increasingly barred their way.

Lit by the last desultory lightning flashes, Mr Heckmondwike appeared in the midst of the sheep, swinging his guardian angel around and around as if she weighed nothing at all. Then he leapt into action. He issued precise instructions to an excited Widdershins and it began to joyously sort out the bemused flock of very surprised young sheep as pullykins and woolverteens cavorted everywhere.

Slake and the Gothic Princess circulated wildly, with Simurg's horn blaring.

Mr Heptonstall did some doughnuts in the Imp and then its highly tuned engine began to cough. It went down onto three cylinders, then two, then one, and cut out completely. Mr Heptonstall got out and said to his guardian angel, "Dark Time!"

One by one, the other cars pulled up and people got out, as if standing on solid ground made them see what had happened more clearly.

The highly modified Wolseley Blue Streak came to a halt, and a dispirited figure of Brother Guy ran away from it and headed for the hills.

The stuffiness of Dark Time began to burn away the remains of the Giant Lamb's weather system as great black clouds rolled over head and disappointed crows, rooks and ravens landed in their various collective nouns and cocked their heads in amazement.

CHAPTER 109

"By the ball pein hammer of St Bendix!" exclaimed Reverend Tregaskis. "You really have done marvellously, Mrs Osmotherly."

As she pulled up by *North Star*, her engine cut out completely and the Wold fell into the total grip of Dark Time, purple turning into indigo, yellow into ochre.

Her guardian angel vaulted out of the 2CV, opened her door for her and took her hand as she alighted from it.

Mrs Osmotherly's face already hurt from grinning, and she realised that her muscles were out of practice.

Hob flicked out *Nosferatu*'s side stand and turned to look at Deutz, already dismounting from his horseless carriage. Then he, too, grinned and revved *Nosferatu*'s engine in defiance of Dark Time.

Deutz dismounted from his swaying carriage, strode up to Mrs Osmotherly, took off his hat, clicked his heels, and took her hand and kissed it. "Hammer!" he said.

Hob killed *Nosferatu*'s engine and joined them, shaking Mrs Osmotherly vigorously by the hand, this time without burning her.

"Congratulations, Mrs Osmotherly!" said Hob, warmly. "I really must compliment you on your handling of the situation."

"Why Mr Hob, I almost believe you mean it."

"Of course, I do. And call me Nick, please."

"I shall call you Hob, I think," replied Mrs Osmotherly, her smile not flickering for an instant. "Anything else is too … familiar."

He too took her hand and kissed it gently, healing her earlier wound. "As you wish, madam."

"And now I believe you have something for us," said Reverend Tregaskis.

"Ah. Yes. Greymalkin? Let's see what you've got."

She picked Indoors up and gently began to prise the G-gnome from him.

Caspar Deutz peered into the stygian darkness above them through his darkened *pince nez*. He put out an arm and a crow as tall as a man settled on it. It croaked at him like a long lost and he replied, "Waiborge?"

"Come along now, Old Grey, let go, there's a good fellow. My goodness, he's very wet. You have dribbled a lot!"

Indoors let go. He'd like to see someone else sit with the G-gnome in their mouth while everyone else drove around a Giant Dancing Lamb, and not dribble.

Mrs Osmotherly examined the G-gnome then handed it to Reverend Tregaskis.

"Good riddance to bad rubbish," she said. "I suggest you take greater care of him in future."

Reverend Tregaskis took the sodden G-gnome between his thumb and forefinger. "Have you got its box?" he asked, and Hob produced a cardboard box from his motorcycle jacket, despite it being far too big to have been fitted into one of its pockets.

"Shouldn't we punch some holes in the lid?" asked Deutz.

The giant crow was perched on his top hat and watching the G-gnome closely, who didn't appear to relish such attention.

"My dear fellow," said Reverend Tregaskis, as Hob put some fresh moss in the box, "it's the G-gnome. It doesn't breathe."

There was a brief struggle and the G-gnome was entombed with a large elastic band.

Reverend Tregaskis took the box from Hob and grinned. Then he suddenly became more earnest. "Ah, Mrs Osmotherly. There's something you should know about the G-gnome. I'm afraid there's no telling what this little rascal's been up to," and he nodded at Deutz and Waiborge the giant crow.

"Let me get this straight," said a less than delighted Mrs Osmotherly. "Are you telling me that we haven't got rid of the giant keds and ticks?"

"You probably have, but don't be so surprised if you haven't. It's all to do with the chain of causality and where the links in that chain can be broken."

"I think you'll find it's more of a helix than a chain," said Professor Cluttercrap.

"Quite," replied Reverend Tregaskis. "While the G-gnome was enjoying its freedom, it was only doing what it does naturally."

"Which isn't anything natural," explained Hob. "It can't stop interfering."

"Contravening the law of the surface area to volume ratio goes beyond interfering," pointed out Professor Cluttercrap. "And that test tube looked less than sterile to me."

"I can assure you, professor, that it was extremely fertile."

"Some of the organisms it interfered with have such long life-cycles it may be years before we know what the results might be," said Professor Cluttercrap as Waiborge sidled up to him.

"It could have interfered with anything," murmured Mrs Osmotherly, thoughtfully.

"Everything, by its past performance," put in Hob. "Everything except your cat."

"The G-gnome could have interfered with all of us!" Gloria angrily exclaimed.

"Think what that would do to a soul!" gasped Caspar Deutz.

"I already have," said Hob.

"The experience would mark it for ever!" murmured Tregaskis.

"Think of the colours!" cried Deutz.

"Imagine the blebs!" added Hob.

Mrs Osmotherly looked around for Indoors, or rather, she looked around for the cat she knew as Greymalkin. He wasn't far away. He was asleep in her 2CV. She could never call him Indoors Food. That name had been uttered by Nicholas Eldritch Hob and had taken on strange resonances. "Don't you have dominion over the G-gnome?" she asked.

"Not entirely," Reverend Tregaskis admitted.

"Does this Dora person?"

Tregaskis laughed nervously. "It's not a good idea to ask her."

"Why not?"

"It'll remind her of what happened last time," said the Foundling of Rauschenberg, gloomily.

"What do you mean, last time?"

"It escaped once before," explained Deutz. "How do you think you got the common cold?"

"And viruses," added Reverend Tregaskis.

"Dora might find out that the G-gnome escaped," said Gloria.

"I doubt very much if she's ever heard of Wormton," said Reverend Tregaskis.

There was an expanding, thoughtful silence.

Deutz fidgeted with his buttonhole. Like the rest of his attire, it was black and seemed to devour light.

Professor Cluttercrap stared at it. "That flower," he said. "W-where did you get it?"

"What? This old thing? It's just a flower, you know."

"But where did you find it?

"Oh. Around. Do you find it interesting?"

Suddenly Noyra leapt between them, brandishing her tin of scouring powder at him, her housecoat of man-made fibres bristling.

Alarmed, Waiborge flew off.

"Dontcha even tink about it!" she said. "Botany Boy!"

"But you're not even his guardian angel!" protested Deutz.

"So what!"

"She takes her work very seriously," said Gloria.

"She certainly displays considerable vim," admitted Reverend Tregaskis.

Gloria whispered to Mrs Osmotherly, "Where are the other guardian angels? Like yours and mine?"

"Mmyes," she said, narrowing her eyes. "I don't trust these three shady characters."

The Soul Traders shrugged.

"I don't suppose," began Mrs Osmotherly, "you could arrange for the G-gnome's mischief to be put right."

"Perhaps," said Hob.

"But only if one of us offered you their soul."

"We would need some sort of incentive," admitted Reverend Tregaskis.

Hob took a sharp intake of breath and began to kick the tyres on Mrs Osmotherly's 2CV, disturbing Indoors Food. "It would have to be a really good soul," he said. "Or souls."

Deutz was also looking at Ted Totteridge, trying to count his guardian angels on his fingers. "Ja. We would want several quite exceptional souls."

"Each!"

Ted saw them looking his way, and turned behind him to see what they were looking at.

"No!" snapped Mrs Osmotherly. "There's been too much soul trading already!"

Hob, Tregaskis and Deutz looked at each other. Reverend Tregaskis shrugged his shoulders.

"Speaking of soul trading, Deutz," said Hob, "Do you have what I need?"

"If you have what I want."

The Soul Traders turned their backs to the others. Hob opened his rucksack and showed Deutz something inside. "I got it just before it was shorn of its proclivities."

"Ja, the proclivity towards life."

Hob beamed with delight and held up an extraordinary handkerchief to the light. "Fortunato!" he murmured.

Beside him, the Foundling of Rauschenberg held up what appeared to be a similarly sized piece of fleece. "Never mind the quality or lack of colour – feel the thickness!"

"What's going on?" demanded Mrs Osmotherly.

"Oh, they're just attending to some business," replied Reverend Tregaskis.

"What sort of business?"

"How badly do you want to know?"

"Not as badly as you would like me to."

"Ah well." Reverend Tregaskis sighed. "It was not an entirely fruitless journey," and he carried the G-gnome in its box, back to his hissing *North Star*.

The grease bogles and klinkergeists parted respectfully, and he climbed onto the footplate to check the gauges and water levels.

Hob appeared beside Mrs Osmotherly. "Rest assured," he told her, "that I have what I came for. We will leave the Wold in peace."

Mrs Osmotherly glared at him, but there was nothing she could do.

Deutz put his carpetbag in his coach and climbed in after it.

"Perhaps I should mention," said Hob, "that there is a lot of ordnance lying around here. Some of it is nuclear. The militia were contemplating using it on the Giant Lamb."

"We don't want that sort of thing left around here," said Mrs Osmotherly, rather imperiously.

To her surprise, Hob agreed. "Just how much do you know about Dark Time?" he asked her.

"I know when it is about to happen."

"But do you know what it is?"

Now it was Mrs Osmotherly's turn to fidget.

"Shall I tell you?"

"You'll not have my soul!"

Hob laughed. So did Caspar Deutz in his carriage and Reverend Tregaskis on the footplate of *North Star*. At his lead, all his grease bogles joined in.

Desperately, she looked around for her guardian angel, but there was no sign of any of them except for Noyra, who was guarding everyone else.

Hob stopped laughing.

His rucksack wriggled violently.

"I admire a woman with spirit. But you can't stop yourself being curious. It's a man-made phenomenon."

"But it's been happening for centuries!"

"I didn't say it was a recent one. If you don't believe me you can ask Old Thunderpants …"

"Old Thunderpants?"

"You know. Big chap with a beard and eyebrows. Moves in mysterious way. In fact, I think He's over there."

He pointed at the vague outline of the Big Grey Man, who started and quickly faded back into the mist. The pullykins and woolverteens scampered after him.

"The Great Shepherd?" asked Mrs Osmotherly.

"If you like. Perhaps you should ask Him. Oh, He's gone. I'll give you another clue. Its origins are nuclear. Hence my warnings about the nuclear weapons the militia brought with them."

"But Dark Time has been going on for ages!"

"You can choose not to believe me," said Hob, "but be careful with the nuclear stuff anyway. You wouldn't want to end up with two Dark Times now, would you?"

"And yet you defy it, Hob," said Mrs Osmotherly.

"Call it a perk of soul trading. And we defy it still because it annoys the heaven out of Old Thunderpants!"

"Why have you told me this?"

"To make you curious, of course. Believe me or not, I admire you. There are few mortals who can best a Soul Trader, but you, Mrs Osmotherly, have managed to best three of us. I salute you."

"And I salute you!" added Reverend Tregaskis.

"And I!" added Deutz.

"It is time to leave," said Hob. He turned towards *North Star*. "Cheerio, Your Irreverence. I wish you dry rails, a good head of steam and dutiful lares and penates."

"Farewell, Hob. And you, Deutz. You're not such a bad old stick. Good fuel, free running and bad women, the pair of you! Until we meet again, good hunting."

Reverend Tregaskis blew the whistle, and track fairies tumbled off his train and scampered round to the front of *North Star*. They winked out of existence and as the track stretched into the moor, *North Star* and *Catch-me-who-can* moved off, whistling goodbye. The Wormtonians found themselves responding to some ancient instinct and waved the old trains off. Behind them the track melted into the ground until there was no sign there had ever been a gauntled section of standard and broad gauge railway on that part of the moor.

"Goodbye, Deutz, old chap," said Hob, warmly shaking the hand of the Foundling of Rauschenberg.

"*Auf wiedergeisten*, Hob. See you in some ancient necropolis somewhere," and Caspar Deutz closed the door to his horseless carriage and it lurched off silently into the gloom of Dark Time.

Hob strode over to *Nosferatu*. "Dark Time will end soon." He glanced down to the valley where Mr Heckmondwike and all the other shepherds were sorting out young sheep. He pulled on his helmet. "Until our paths cross again, Mrs Osmotherly."

"I saw you coming at the start of all this," she replied. "If you ever darken the Wold again, I'll see you coming again."

Hob grinned. "Let's see, shall we? Until the next time! Trouble's goin'! Trouble's gone!" and he kicked *Nosferatu* into life and rode off into the darkness.

A movement caught Mrs Osmotherly's eye, and the guardian angels of Gloria and Slake emerged from behind Constable Arkthwaite's Wolseley, holding hands. When they realised people were looking, they quickly dropped their hands and went to their respective charges.

The other guardian angels nonchalantly returned. Mrs Osmotherly looked at her guardian angel and then at that of Mr Heptonstall. It was obvious that they made a very fine pair, but she couldn't help feel a pang of disappointment.

Then Mr Heptonstall's guardian angel caught her eye. She nodded towards Mrs Osmotherly's guardian angel and mouthed, "He's my brother," at her.

Mr Heptonstall's guardian angel smiled again and nodded back towards the valley. In the lightening gloom, she saw the unmistakable outline of Mr Heckmondwike, working his vast new flock. When she turned around, her guardian angel had vanished. Mr Heptonstall's guardian angel noticed her looking around, and gestured towards Constable Arkthwaite's Wolseley. Mrs Osmotherly's guardian angel was just disappearing behind it with Enormous Bo-Peep.

Mrs Osmotherly blushed, both for herself and her guardian angel's choice of paramour.

She marched down to the valley floor. Mr Floridspleen was arguing about something with Mayor Naseby across the bonnet of the civic Armstrong-Siddeley. Mrs Skellmersmell was handing out sandwiches from the back of her 6/110 estate car and Slake, Mr Heptonstall, George Ransomes and Old Mr Macklefract were tucking into them and talking as if they'd just been riding in the Wild Hunt.

Mr Heckmondwike strode the Wold like its emperor, whistling to his dogs and directing the other shepherds.

"All's well wi' t'Wold," he said, as Mrs Osmotherly strode up to him. Then, noticing her odd expression, he asked, "Is tha awreet? Tha looks a trifle flushed."

"No, I'm all right," Mrs Osmotherly reassured him. "Really."

"Tha did a remarkable thing today, lass," he told her.

"We all did."

"But we couldn't have done it without thee," and he held her tenderly and kissed her.

Mrs Osmotherly took his hand and pulled him gently yet urgently behind a Mudlark.

"I suppose tha'll be off now," George said to Noyra O'Drenalin.

"Oi, we will at that!"

"Fine use our own guardian angels were when we needed them!" snorted Gloria.

"Ah don't be blamin' dem, Miss Gloria," said Noyra. "Dey moight be guardian angels but some toymes dey don't all have der soight dey oughta!"

"Our work is done here," said Mrs Osmotherly's guardian angel, and winked out of sight.

The other guardian angels said goodbye and suddenly were not there.

Slake strode up to Gloria and put his hands around her middle.

"I knew you'd be all right," she said.

Slake raised his eyebrows in mocking surprise.

"Yes. I knew you'd be fine. All around the militia, I could see the harbingers of their doom but I never saw any around you."

"Ah," said Slake. "Aha!"

"Sometimes my gift is a curse."

He stroked her hair. "There, there." Then he said, "D'you see any around me now?"

Gloria looked. "No."

Slake licked his lips. "That must be a great comfort."

"I can't tell you."

"Attractive, almost."

Gloria smiled and wriggled as tightly into his arms and ribs as she could. And Slake, cheater of death and survivor of the Giant Lamb, the Wild Hunt and the Soul Trader, swelled a little as she said, "No harbingers. Guaranteed!"

CHAPTER 111

For days afterwards, Mr Heckmondwike and all the other shepherds worked the vast new flock. The sheep hadn't known life as lambs and occasionally sought to challenge Widdershins as it herded them. This rebellious spirit didn't last long, however, and the three-headed sheepdog revelled in its re-gained authority as the sheep adapted to a life as one among hundreds. Mr Heckmondwike could see some unfathomable light fading in their eyes. When he had time to consider it, he assumed it was a vague memory of a terrible solitude and being something greater than the sum of the flock.

Gloria found him one day, effortlessly skewering a giant sheep tick on an adapted shepherd's crook.

"There can't be many parasites left now," she observed after the usual niceties.

"Mebbe not," he replied, carefully wiping the blood off his crook with a mild acid. "Ah wanna prevent 'em from breeding."

Gloria shuddered at that possibility. "The reason I came out here," she said, "is to invite you to a little celebration at *Where the Rainbow Ends*."

"Oh aye?"

"We haven't really seen anything of each other since we destroyed the Giant Lamb."

Mr Heckmondwike gazed at a distant flock. "We didn't destroy it. We converted t'monster back into what it should've bin to start wi'."

"Will you join us?"

"Aye. Thanks. Ah'd be delighted."

So the following evening, Mr Heckmondwike put on his best suit and flat hat and drove his magnificent Wolseley tractor into town.

That spring there was a plague of giant butterflies which fluttered surprisingly noisily across the Wold to settle on the western walls of Wormton and bask in the evening sun. They produced a giant mosaic that could be seen for miles. It often caught the eye of Mr Heckmondwike when he looked up during his remaining battles with the giant keds, and close up it was even more spectacular.

Mrs Osmotherly saw them too, from the windows of Diggle, and she wondered idly if the future could be predicted from their flight patterns.

Slake and Gloria had admired them as well, venturing out of Wormton to picnic on sweetmeats during the sunny evenings. The butterflies captivated Gloria, but while Slake agreed they looked very nice he said there had been terrible problems from giant moths and maybugs when the Wild Hunt had hit Bedlam recently.

The natural twilight of night was foregathering and an eveningale was singing in the market square as Gloria and Slake wandered arm in arm from the cottage hospital.

"Just don't say we're on a double date," said Gloria when she told Slake. "It embarrasses Mrs Osmotherly and Mr Heckmondwike."

Technically, she was overdressed. On their own, court shoes were considered pretentious in Wormton and when wearing them with an expensive evening gown and jewellery, Gloria looked seriously out of place. Slake felt he was accompanied by a very glamorous guardian angel and he could not take his eyes off her.

The Wormton tram was bustling about, still dealing with the backlog of traffic. Despite the lateness of the hour, all the tramway's locomotives were in steam, and the staff nearby were shouting, "Shacons to go!" to each other. Outside The Golden Fleece a poster announced the first livestock market since Wormton's isolation had begun, and "No Vacancies" signs were spattering the frontages of guest houses once again.

Gloria steered the increasingly puppy-like Slake around another lamp-post. It felt good to be admired, but whatever Slake did, he seemed to do it wholeheartedly. She gazed back at him. He had wonderful hair if he used a good quality shampoo, and she was looking forward to running her fingers through it later.

At *Where the Rainbow Ends*, two special parking places had been reserved and as they turned the corner a two-tone grey Wolseley Hornet turned into one of them.

"Hallo you two!" said Mrs Osmotherly as she alighted.

"Oh you look fantastic!" enthused Gloria. "Doesn't she, Slake?"

"Hmm? Oh, yes. Yes indeed."

"Is it true that you've regained your seat on the Privy Council?"

Mrs Osmotherly pulled a face. "Yes. I've got to listen to all that fatuous hot air again. But I am their wise woman and I suppose it is my duty."

There was the sound of a big, barely silenced, diesel and Mr Heckmondwike arrived on his tractor.

"Mr Heckmondwike!" exclaimed Mrs Osmotherly. "What a magnificent tractor!"

"Oh, aye, it's, er, not too shabby."

Slake winked at her. He'd been coaching her what to say.

"Does tha like the roll bar, lad? Isn't that the lucky one off the Big Nuff?"

"Aye. We'll use up all the bits from it by and by."

They filed inside, nodding to Daisymaid and Mr Kindlysides who were sat at a table for two, and Mrs Skellmersmell met them and guided them to their table. She handed them individually tailored menus to which they all chorused, "My favourite!" Mrs Skellmersmell said, "It's all ont house, toneet!" and after some good-natured arguing, her four guests put their money together to tip the waitresses.

"What would everyone like to drink?" asked Mrs Skellmersmell. "Mrs Osmotherly?"

"A bottle of Mithering Green Ale, please."

"The same again for me, please," said Gloria.

"And for you, Mr Heckmondwike?"

"Ah'll have a pint of jellied ale, please."

"One lump or two?"

"As many as tha can get in a pint glass, lass."

"And you, young Mr Thorngumbald?"

"Slake!" hissed Gloria. "She's talking to you!"

"Hmm? Oh! Ah, I think I'll have some Old Sawe's Irascible Anorak if you please, Mrs Skellmersmell."

"Seen this?" said Gloria as Mrs Skellmersmell left them. She held up a magazine.

Mr Heckmondwike and Slake peered at it in bewilderment.

"Why that's Mrs Osmotherly, isn't it?" said Slake.

"That's right," Gloria told them. "She's made the cover of *Witch* magazine. It's a good picture of Greymalkin, too, don't you think?"

There was a bleary grey cat on her lap.

"Aye, well he's awake," admitted Mr Heckmondwike.

"What's it say?" asked Slake.

"Oh just that she's the Wold's most eminent autologist."

"Does it mention the Giant Lamb?"

"No," Mrs Osmotherly said quickly. "We don't want to publicise that."

"You're right there," agreed Slake. "To the casual observer, none of that ever happened. You'd have to know where to look to find evidence for it."

"Or read the motorscope very well."

When their drinks arrived, Gloria was fascinated by Mr Heckmondwike's jellied ale.

"It's a Wold speciality," he explained. "It's a combination of ale 'n' gravy, or the jelly in a pork pie, a sort of meat stout. Wrainwright mentions it in 'is book, but nay very favourably. It's summat of an acquired taste, but very filling."

A very curvaceous young waitress brought out their first course, a selection of mutton baps and some lamb-and-mint flavoured crisps.

"Nice buns, Clytemnestra," Slake told her.

"Oh thank you," she replied. "Please – help yourselves."

Gloria felt almost relieved that Slake was reverting to type again. It was nice to be admired occasionally but not all the time. "So," she said, "what does the future hold for me, Mrs Osmotherly?"

"A Wolseley is moving into the garage of your house. All is well in the Wold."

"Apart from the rump of the Mithering Brethren. When shall we ever be rid of them?"

"And the plague of giant parasites."

"Their numbers are dwindling fast," Mr Heckmondwike assured them.

"And I've repossessed Mr Brother's Blue Streak," added Slake.

"I hear you have an assistant, Mr Heckmondwike," said Mrs Osmotherly.

"Aye. He's an orphan from Mithering – a foundling – who heard that the Great Shepherd was around Wormton."

"And he thinks the Great Shepherd is Mr Heckmondwike," said Slake with a smirk.

"Is this true?" asked Gloria.

"Ah dunnaw what ee thinks," said Mr Heckmondwike, "ee can think what ee likes! He's a bit serious-minded but useful against keds."

"What are you having, Mr Heckmondwike?" Gloria asked him.

"Ah have heard they do a very good shepherd's pie."

"Shepherd's pie?" exclaimed Slake. "But that's cannibalism!"

"Slake." Mrs Osmotherly leant forward to deliver her loud whisper so that the other customers of *Where the Rainbow Ends* might notice. "This is *Where the Rainbow Ends*. If you don't behave you will be asked to leave and we shall continue this celebratory slap-up binge without you."

Slake was very well behaved for the next ten minutes until Clytemnestra returned to check if their meals were satisfactory.

"I must confess," he told her. "I just can't get enough of your buns."

Clytemnestra smiled, delighted at the compliment.

Some old ladies nearby nodded approval at his remarks.

"What do you say, Mr Heckmondwike?" he said as Clytemnestra wiggled away.

"Eh? Oh. Aye. Very nice."

Gloria glared at him.

Clytemnestra was chatting to Mrs Skellmersmell at the counter. Another waitress arrived carrying two large teapots.

"Good gracious!" exclaimed Slake. "What an enormous pair you've got there!"

Suddenly, his guardian angel appeared. "Hallo again," she said.

Slake looked very dismayed. "What are you doing here?" he asked.

"Only my job," replied the Gothic Princess, smiling sadly.

Mrs Skellmersmell was approaching rapidly for a woman of her build.

"Slake," said the Gothic Princess, "I think it would be wise of you to leave now," and Slake, for once, did as he was told, hotly pursued by Mrs Skellmersmell with what she called her serving wand.

They ran out of the tearooms and into the street, where what should they bump into but a large rucksack, underneath which was Professor Clutter-crap. Mrs Skellmersmell suddenly felt awkward brandishing her serving wand in front of a man of science so she hid it behind her back, made the appropriate pleasantries and discreetly returned to *Where the Rainbow Ends*.

The others watched Slake chatting to the professor in the street, framed in the windows with a stained-glass rainbow over their heads, until Gloria said, "Let's join them."

The night was freshening and Mrs Osmotherly pulled her shawl around her shoulders as they left *Where the Rainbow Ends*. They passed a taxi rank and an old man in a Wolseley 16/60 hailed them.

"Ow do, Mr Melliver," said Mr Heckmondwike.

"Eh up! Fettlin' well thysens?"

"Aye, nobbut graidly, tha knaws."

"Appen? Those hoggs o'thine look reet fair to middlin' these days."

Mr Heckmondwike's craggy features broke into a broad grin. Even a Woldsman can only hide his pride for so long. "Aye. Heck as likely as appen as mebbe tha's reet. Not too scabby, e'en tho it's me that says so as shouldn't."

"How are your wormuts doing, Mr Melliver?" asked Mrs Osmotherly.

"Heck as owt, Mrs Osmotherly! Heck as owt!" and he gave her a bouquet of them from an improvised vase on the dashboard of his taxi. "Nivver knawn a year like it for 'em."

"Did you find what you were looking for?" Slake was asking Professor Cluttercrap.

He shook his head sadly. "I saw it in the buttonhole of the Foundling of Rauschenburg, but it doesn't seem to grow anywhere around here."

"How badly do you want a Black Orchid?" Slake asked him with a wry grin.

"Badly," replied Professor Cluttercrap, "but not that badly."

"I expect your colleagues will be fascinated to hear all about your adventures in Wormton," Gloria said to him brightly.

Professor Cluttercrap shook his head even more sadly. "I'm afraid if I even breathed a suggestion of what has happened here my professional reputation would be in ruins."

"But they should know what growth hormones and the motorscope can achieve!"

"They won't want to know that the law of surface area to volume ratio has been violated! They would have to revise their most basic assumptions about the physical universe. No, I shan't mention it once I'm home."

The tram behind them whistled. Pa Coppitt and Percy were waiting for them.

"So this is goodbye," said Gloria.

"Yes, I suppose it is," said Professor Cluttercrap.

She held out her hand.

Professor Cluttercrap took her hand and shook it and then shook Slake's as well.

"Have a safe journey," said Slake.

"Thank you."

"Oh!" said Gloria and she flung her arms around the skinny man of science and hugged him fiercely. "Take good care of yourself, Jeremy" she insisted.

"Still no harbingers tonight?" Slake asked her.

Gloria smiled. "No. None on either of you."

"Wait a moment!" said Slake. He ran over to Mr Melliver's taxi and spoke to him. The old man nodded eagerly and gave him something.

"There!" said Slake when he re-joined them. "Wormuts are no substitute for a Black Orchid, but it's what we've got and Mr Melliver says you're welcome to them, Botany Boy!"

Professor Cluttercrap stared at his wormut in delight. It was a black one.

"What did you say this was?"

"It's a wormut."

"Odd," said the professor, absent-mindedly polishing his spectacles on his beard. "Wrainwright never mentions wormuts."

"Jeremy?"

"Ah."

His guardian angel held up her indemnity form. "You're coming home."

"It feels as if I am at home already," he said, glancing at her and his precious wormut.

"Then I can tear this up," and she did so. "Thank you for looking after him."

As the tram pulled away slowly they all shouted "Goodbye everybody!" and they stood waving until the tram shrouded itself in smoke and turned the corner.

They went back to their table and ate their food, gradually descending into that warm comradely glow that creeps up on those who have faced danger together and survived to tell the tale. None of them wanted that evening to end, but eventually, after interminable cups of coffee, Mrs Skellmersmell had to ask them to leave so she could go home, too.

"Does tha really like ma tractor?" Mr Heckmondwike asked Mrs Osmotherly as they left *Where the Rainbow Ends*.

"Of course I do," she said as if it was the most natural thing in the

Wold.

Mr Heckmondwike grinned.

"Back to work tomorrow," sighed Gloria.

"You should be self-employed," said Slake, "not live to work."

"I suppose you'll be building more cars for the Wild Hunt."

"Aye!" said Slake.

Mr Heckmondwike beamed. "Eh, lad! Tha said aye instead of yes!" He stopped and gave Slake a Woldsman's handshake. "Welcome back, lad!"

"Mr Heckmondwike? It's been surreal! Now take Mrs Osmotherly home."

Mr Heckmondwike wedged Mrs Osmotherly debonairly between the mudguard of his tractor and its power-take-off shafts and started it up.

"Goodbye!" they all shouted and he revved the engine so that the Wolseley jumped up a little on its front tyres. Then off they went, doing at least thirty miles an hour in high gear.

"I wonder what their immediate future holds," mused Gloria.

"Same as ours?" suggested Slake.

Gloria said, "I saw some cherry bums flying round them."

Slake laughed.

They walked back to Simurg at that point but Slake was becoming increasingly thoughtful. When they reached his trike, he paused. "Before I drive you back to your place," and they giggled slightly at the prospect, "there's one thing I really must do."

"Oh," said Gloria. "Don't be too long."

"I won't. I just have to go back to Frogheat."

They jumped into Simurg and drove there quickly. Slake hurried into the house and picked up a brand new pair of pyjamas he'd been saving before returning through some of his cluttered workshops. It was by the big cupboard of special tools that he stopped, and even though he was in darkness he looked out of the dusty window to check on Gloria.

She was still seated in Simurg, gazing at the moon, which was a full one, running her fingers through her hair.

Then he opened the tool cupboard and said to the hundreds of very belligerent gremlins inside, "Plashed on their fireworks, didn't we? All right you lot, you can let them go now."

The gremlins stood at their ease and many ugly harbinger gnomes floated out into the night air, cursing vehemently now that their moment had passed, taking their wheelbarrows and fishing rods with them.

EPILOGUE

As the directors of BiggaBeast filed out of the boardroom after the presentation on modifying the gullibility gene, Billy Brockhouse caught sight of
something odd in the corridor. He wondered if someone was playing a prank
on him. If they were, it would be the end of their career.

They seemed not to notice the horse-drawn carriage as they passed it.
It didn't have any horses in its shafts, for they were folded back over the
empty driver's seat.

He summoned his secretary. Miss Prism was the sort of secretary who
might grace the pages of a men's magazine, a self-made woman to match
Billy's self-made man. Clever to begin with, she had developed her intellect
even more by the careful use of exotic smart drugs, and upon attaining her
desired IQ had rephased her metabolism and reconstituted her physique so
that her naturally pear-shaped figure became an hourglass one.

"Who's making the next presentation?" he asked her.

"Presentation, Mr Brockhouse?" queried Miss Prism, taking off her
pussycat glasses in a gesture that was worth an extra fifty thousand alone.
"There are no more presentations."

Three ravens regarded Billy solemnly from the coach.

"Then what's that doing there?"

Miss Prism turned around. "Where?"

"Someone is going to pay for this," he said as anger rose inside him.
"Somebody's taking the piss."

If Miss Prism thought a little ridicule might benefit him, she didn't say
so. She pouted her recently inflated lips. Unkind souls suggested that she didn't
use the stairs any more but kissed her way up the outside of the skyscraper.

"They may have slipped me some Dupe Drops," ranted Billy, "but
they'll need to give me a bigger dose than this!"

Miss Prism remained unmoved. She walked over to him, looked at the
readouts on his jacket and held his wrist to check his pulse. Then she tutted,
pulled out a pill box and said, "Open." She popped a pill into Billy's mouth
and said, "You know you shouldn't get yourself in a state."

Billy swallowed his tension pill. He felt better straightaway, before it
had a chance to take effect. "I can still detect bullshit, y'know," he said. He

looked hard at Miss Prism. "You really can't see it, can you?"

"What?"

He pointed. "That."

Miss Prism looked back at him warily. "I'm afraid I must get on with my work on the clumsy gene," she said, and turned on her heel and left.

Billy approached the horseless carriage. Somewhere, a disquieting memory was fumbling at a bell rope. The three ravens rolled their eyes at him.

"*Guten abend*, Billy."

He wheeled around and there, at the head of the table, sat a curiously dressed man in a tall hat and prodigious mutton chop whiskers.

"Who are you?" demanded Billy.

"My name is Deutz. Caspar Deutz." His accent was foreign.

"What the devil are you doing here?"

Deutz smiled. "When abusive language loses its impact, how predictably do non-believers return to blasphemy."

"Do you know who I am?" cried out Billy in his rage.

"You are Billy Brockhouse, CEO of BiggaBeast and president of the Brockhouse Group of Companies, a man with a reputation for bringing home the bacon, even if it has been created in a petri dish and never seen a pig."

"I'm calling security!" Billy marched up to the table, grabbed his executive phone and began to punch in a number.

All Deutz did to halt his finger-jabbing was to say, "I have come for your soul, Billy."

Billy paused.

"You can feel it is not your own, now. Can't you?"

Billy nodded. "You aren't bullshitting me."

"Your situation is quite hopeless, you know."

"Okay," said Billy after a deep breath. "Do you have a card or something?"

The Foundling of Rauschenberg smiled. "*Ja* but I have no need. I believe you know an associate of mine by the name of Hob."

Billy shivered as somebody pulled a wheelie over his grave. His soul felt looser on him than ever.

"Ah, I see that you do. You and he had a little agreement."

"That's nothing to do with you."

"Oh but it is, Billy. You see, I swapped soul rites with him."

"How many souls did you have to give him?"

Deutz frowned. "Just the one. He gave me many others, amongst which was yours."

Billy sagged at his own insignificance.

"I got a skateboard as well," added Deutz, brightly, pulling it out of his carpetbag.

"I want to give my daemonstration skills back."

Deutz performed an ollie. "Of course you do but it's too late." He began a dignified circuit of the boardroom.

"Please, Mr Deutz, can't I appeal to your better nature?"

Deutz looked surprised and nearly lost his balance.

"Just this once, can't you show some mercy?"

"That would be a new experience for me," admitted Deutz, beginning another lap.

"A novelty for you," agreed Billy. "Couldn't you, just this once, let someone keep their soul to enjoy their fulfilment?"

"Well, I suppose I could," said the Foundling of Rauschenberg slowly.

Billy beamed at him.

"But not today."

Billy sagged.

"Honestly, Billy. Thirty years to the day since you trod in a cowpat and met Hob, your sense of bullshit has not improved. You must forgive me, but I am a Soul Trader. Consideration has passed from the promissor to the promissee, and the promissor has granted his soul rites to a third party. Me. And my little ruse just then has created the most magnificent bleb in your soul. It is almost like a jewel," and Deutz, who had been picking up speed as he spoke, whizzed behind his stagecoach, ducked under it and leapt the length of the boardroom table to land in a dead stop on his skateboard.

The ravens cawed their approval.

For somebody from the 1830s who had been kept in a tiny cell for the first sixteen years of his life he was remarkably good.

"Ja, your soul is mine," said the Foundling of Rauschenberg, taking Billy's soul, "but the rest of you is yours to use as you see fit."

"Have I died?"

"Not yet. But your soul has passed on this evening." Deutz picked up Billy's executive fountain pen, and on the executive toys and hi-tech desk furniture tapped out the same riff that Hob had played on Billy's phials many years before. "You know, Billy? In different ways, we both deal in supernature." He held up Billy's soul to the light to admire it. "Supernaturally," he said and then turning it, he added, "Perhaps hypernaturally."

The door to Deutz's coach opened and a two-metre-tall crow squeezed out from it. The ravens looked on respectfully as it hopped onto the table and gazed down at Billy with its beady eyes.

Billy shrank back. "No!" he cried, but the Foundling of Rauschenberg was concerned only with his new soul.

"Ubernaturally?" wondered Deutz. "Ja. Übernatürlich. That suits," and he didn't even look up as the crow skewered the rest of Billy with its beak and began to wrench off strips of flesh.

A drop of blood landed on Billy's soul.

Deutz looked up.

"Hey, Waiborge!"

Waiborge the giant crow paused from tearing at Billy's broken body.

"You've got his blood on his soul." He turned back to Billy's soul and said, "Not bad. Ja?"

Billy's soul shivered.

"*Ach, mach dir nichts draus.* Never mind, Billy." Caspar Deutz picked up his skateboard and climbed onto the boardroom table, which began to buckle and turn up at the edges. "You know vot they say? Heaven is a half tube."

Also by Bob Blackman

THE HORSEPOWER WHISPERER

FAST AND FURIOUS MEETS CARRY ON SCREAMING

Ever felt your spirits are being sapped? Are the colours being rinsed out of life's rich tapestry? Is your soul being destroyed? Ever thought it might be deliberate?

Nick Hob is the Horsepower Whisperer.

He talks the torque and races in the Wild Hunt.

With a few well chosen words, he inspires engines to great feats of speed, power and endurance. And he will share this power with you if you will trade with him your soul.

But after answering a Save Our Souls message from a doomed airliner, he can barely believe his Extra Sentiency Perception. He's been short changed. Something in Post Unification Euphobia encourages severe soul erosion.

Can Hob offer salvation?

Or is he just another destroyer?

PART ONE OF THE SOUL TRADER TRILOGY

www.anarchadia.co.uk

In preparation by Bob Blackman

THE GREY ONES

GEORGE ORWELL'S 1984 MEETS THE HITCH–HIKER'S GUIDE TO THE GALAXY

Monsieur Cadvare and Nenuphar find themselves in Anarchadia, without the dubious protection of Nick Hob, the Horsepower Whisperer, only to discover that the Grey Ones have got there first.

The Soul of All Souls, Kevin Mullins, is hiding from the soul traders. They don't know what he would sell his soul for. Come to that, neither does he.

Therese Darlmat is frantically trying to stabilise the paraverses but the Peacock Angel is in Lanson and the Grey Ones have a proposal for him they know he can't resist.

Then there is the farewell gig to end all farewell gigs. They've re-formed although they'll never reform. They've been away for 65 million years but now they're back – The Monsters, the greatest rock band the world has ever seen.

With Hob entombed in a giant communion wafer, hope is fading fast as the forces of bland are set to stop the Wild Hunt for ever.

PART TWO OF THE SOUL TRADER TRILOGY

www.anarchadia.co.uk

In preparation by Bob Blackman

THE SINGING SANDS

A BIT LIKE THE DA VINCI CODE BUT WITH MORE BEACHES AND HORSEPOWER

Roy Shaddocks goes to Wheal Rammoth as a favour to Carbines, an engine sourcerer to rival Nick Hob.

He soon settles into the newly formed design team and adapts to life in Bendisporth, racing in the Wild Hunt on his Suzuki X7 and getting to know the posh girls from the nice enclave.

But gradually his curiosity about the fate of earlier engineers in the area grows, especially as the first one of all was the Great Smith himself, the legendary St Bendix.

St Bendix lived some 1,500 years before and established a radical theological college until it was swallowed by the sands for its "quickedness" and now nobody really knows where it was.

But Roy discovers there's still a link between going fast and the teachings of St Bendix.

And when that's the case, Nick Hob – the Horsepower Whisperer and Soul Trader – can never be far away.

www.anarchadia.co.uk

In preparation by Bob Blackman

THE WILD HUNT

SPINAL TAP AND THE GUMBALL RALLY ROLLED INTO ONE

The Forces of Bland have double-crossed the Forces of Evil. They've been artfully manipulating the oldest struggle for thousands of years and now there's nothing to stop them destroying our very souls for ever.

With the Forces of Good driven underground and the Forces of Evil undergoing the worst sort of purgatory and muzak imaginable, hope seems an impossible luxury.

But isn't that Monsieur Cadvare driving one of Hob's souped up automobiles? And isn't that Nenuphar with him – the animal charming vegetarian?

If they can spring Hob and the other saints and sinners from purgatory, enlist the help of The Monsters (the ultimate rock band), rev up the Horsepower Wars again, stop Kevin Mullins losing his soul and get good and evil to co-operate with each other for a change, then a solution might present itself.

Pretty big if.

PART THREE OF THE SOUL TRADER TRILOGY

Printed in the United Kingdom by
Lightning Source UK Ltd., Milton Keynes
142624UK00001B/51/P